Simple Choices

Nancy Mehl

BARBOUR
PUBLISHING

For more information about Nancy Mehl, please access the author's
website at the following Internet address: www.nancymehl.com

Cover image: © Chris Reeve/Trevillion Images

Published by Barbour Publishing, Inc., P.O. Box 719,
Uhrichsville, OH 44683.

*Our mission is to publish and distribute inspirational products
offering exceptional value and biblical encouragement to the masses.*

Member of the
Evangelical Christian
Publishers Association

Printed in the United States of America.

Acknowledgments

For this last visit to Harmony, I want to thank the people who made this journey so special.

As always, to Judith Unruh, Alexanderwohl Church Historian in Goessel, Kansas: You kept me on track throughout the series. I can't thank you enough.

To Sarah Beck, owner of Beck's Farm in Wichita: Thanks for all your help. The Harmony Series was made better because of you.

To Deputy Sheriff Pat Taylor the real one: Thank you for always being available to help me with research, and thank you for allowing me to use your name. I hope I didn't besmirch it too much. LOL!

My thanks to Doctor Andy (Andrea McCarty) for being the world's best doctor and for helping me with all my medical questions! You're the greatest!

Thank you to Marjorie Vawter, my wonderful editor. Your hard work is always appreciated.

Thank you to Alene Ward, owner of DesignsbyAlene.com, who is one of those "divine connections" God puts in our lives. Thank you for creating "Sweetie's Christmas Quilt." One for our contest and another one for me! I will treasure it for the rest of my life. I look forward to the future and more adventures together!

To Penny and Gus Dorado: Thank you for always being ready to help in any way you could. You're both very precious to me.

To my agent, Janet Benrey: Thanks for your help along the way. You will always have a special place in my heart.

As always, my thanks to the folks at Barbour: Becky, Mary, Shalyn, Ashley, and Laura. You gave me a chance, and I will always appreciate that.

To the Mennonite people and their rich heritage: I hope you feel I've represented you well.

Special thanks to my wonderful husband, Norman. I'm so thrilled that we're working together now. There's no one else I'd rather share my journey with. I love you.

To my son, Danny, who has always encouraged me: I am still amazed that God has allowed me to be your mother. You are one of the most incredible people I've ever known. I'm so blessed.

And finally, to the One who has set my feet in a broad place: Without You, I have nothing. With You, I have everything. Without You, I am nothing. With You, I can soar like an eagle, move mountains, and become more than I ever dreamed I could be. I love You so much. My most fervent prayer is that when people read my books, they will see You.

DEDICATION

To Fred Mehl, my wonderful father-in-law, who battled the great darkness that is Alzheimer's. You were never diminished in the eyes of those who loved you. We always saw the real man you were, a man of strength, love, character, and incredible creativity. I've tried to represent your struggle through the character of Papa Joe. I pray I've succeeded. We all still miss you.

ONE

You will get packed right now because. . .because . . .I said so!" Yikes! I almost turned my head to see if my mother had crept up behind me. *Because I said so?* Isn't that what parents say when they can't think of anything else?

"You are *not* my mother, you know," Hannah said defiantly.

Like I wasn't very well aware of that. I shook my head, trying to come up with something that sounded wise. I could use some of Sweetie's good old homespun smarts right now. She'd know what to do. Several of her past pearls of wisdom flitted through my head, but none of them seemed to fit this situation. There was something about pigs flying, but that didn't seem appropriate either. Feeling defeated, I slumped down into a nearby chair. "Listen Hannah, you know how hard it was to talk your parents into letting you come to Wichita for six weeks and take art classes. I fought for you. I promised to take care of you and not let you get into trouble. But. . .but just look at you!"

The beautiful young woman who stood in front

of me certainly didn't resemble the chaste, quiet Mennonite teenager I'd brought to Wichita six weeks earlier. Her simple clothing had been replaced with jeans and a sleeveless T-shirt that stated TODAY WILL BE THE BEST DAY EVER! I had the distinct feeling this would not prove true.

"Robin gave me these clothes so I wouldn't feel like such a freak, and I like them," she responded. Her bottom lip stuck out in a definite pout.

A twinkle of silver caught my eye. "She gave you that bracelet, too?"

Hannah raised her wrist. "It's a friendship bracelet."

The bracelet was made with silver and colored beads, and a silver heart dangled from it.

"It says 'Love, Friend, and Forever.'" She pointed to engraved inserts evenly spaced between the beads. "It means Robin and I are forever friends. But you want to send me back to Harmony where I don't have any real friends at all!"

I sighed so forcefully, it was a wonder the girl stayed on her feet. "That's ridiculous. You have all kinds of friends in Harmony. I actually thought I was one of them."

No response. Just more pouting.

"Listen," I said forcefully, "I want you to put on the clothes your parents sent with you. I'm responsible to them, and I can't take you back to Harmony looking like this." I stared closely at her. "Is—is that mascara? And are you wearing lipstick?"

"Everyone wears it." Her bottom lip stayed in the pout position.

I pulled myself up from my chair, fighting the urge to say *If everyone jumped off a cliff, would you jump off, too?* Boy, I really *was* turning into my mother. "We're leaving this afternoon, and that's all there is to it. Allison is returning from her vacation in the morning, and she wants her apartment back. We are going home to Harmony!" The note of hysteria in my voice seemed to startle Hannah, and she took a step back. Had I scored a point? Maybe becoming slightly unhinged would get the results I so desperately needed. I was trying to come up with something really over the edge when Hannah's bottom lip began to quiver and tears filled her eyes.

"I—I love it here," she said, her voice breaking. "And Mr. Monahan said I could live with him and his family and attend a high school that has special art classes. He practically guaranteed me an art scholarship to college."

My anger began to melt. Hannah wasn't really fighting against me—she was fighting for her dream. Unfortunately, I couldn't help her. "Look, Hannah, I understand. I really do. But this is not the way to go about it. We need to go home and talk to your parents. I'll explain the opportunity Jim's offered you. If it's meant to be, then it will happen." I frowned as my eyes traveled up and down her body. "But you need to get rid of those clothes and clean off your face. If you go back looking like that, they'll never agree to let you leave Harmony. Or even your room for that matter."

She stared down at her sandals. "They won't let

me live here," she said, her voice so soft I could barely hear her. "We both know that."

I didn't respond, but I was fairly certain she was right. However, sharing that thought at this moment might trigger another bout of resistance that I didn't have time to deal with. "Your parents love your paintings," I said, trying to sound reassuring. "They know you have real talent. You can't be completely sure they'll say no. But even if they do, you're only a year away from graduating and turning eighteen. Remember that Jim said if you couldn't go to high school here, he'd still try to get you into a good art school or college. Your grades are excellent, and you have a good shot at being accepted." I walked over and put my hands on her shoulders. "Hannah, you have to go home. Your parents love you, and you love them. You can't stay here without their permission. If you put up a fight now, you'll lose Jim's support as well as mine—and you'll hurt your mother and father. I know you don't really want to do that." I put my hand under the teenager's chin and pulled her face up so she had to look at me. "You know I'm right."

Tears spilled from her china-blue eyes. "I—I know. It's just. . ."

"You're afraid if you leave, you'll never find a way to come back?"

She nodded, and her face crumbled. "It's so wonderful here, Gracie," she blubbered. "Wichita is exciting and full of so many opportunities. If I get stuck in Harmony, I'll never be anything!"

I raised one eyebrow at her, wondering if she'd

forgotten that I'd chosen Harmony over Wichita. I'd found the love of my life, and my freelance work as a graphic artist was going very well. "If your parents won't let you come back and finish high school in Wichita, in a year you'll be free to determine your own future." I let go of her chin and shook my finger at her. "But if you want me to talk to them about Jim's offer, you'll clean your face, change your clothes, and get packed. If you don't, I won't raise a finger to help you when we get home. And I mean that."

The young girl's eyes grew wide as she weighed her options, but both of us knew she had no real choice. She turned slowly and headed toward the guest bedroom. While she packed, I set about writing Allison a quick note, thanking her for the use of her apartment. As I wrote, I couldn't help but compare myself to Hannah. Here she was fighting hard to stay away from Harmony while I was fighting just as hard to get back. Odd how two people can see the same thing in totally different ways. I loved the small Mennonite town with its friendly residents and old-fashioned flavor. Yet Hannah regarded Harmony as her prison.

I folded the note and put it under the glass candy dish on Allison's fireplace mantel, aware that she'd see it since she never actually put candy in the dish. She only used it to hold her car keys. I stared at my reflection in the mirror over the mantel. Although I still looked the same—reddish-brown hair and green eyes—the apprehension in my face was obvious. Quickly looking away, I sat back down in the chair next to my already-packed suitcases.

I felt like a traitor. I'd never suspected our visit to Wichita would turn out like this. If I had, I never would have pushed Emily and Abel Mueller to let Hannah come. They'd resisted my old art teacher's offer to enroll their talented daughter in his six-week summer art course. Their concern for Hannah had made them reluctant to let her go. But I'd finally convinced them to trust me, and now their worst fears had been realized. Hannah's view of the world outside Harmony had changed her. How would I be able to explain it? I chewed my lip and worried for a while. Finally, I picked up the phone and called Sam, hoping he could make me feel better. No answer. Great. He and Sweetie were probably out in the orchard picking apples and peaches.

Sam and his aunt worked hard on their fruit farm. Correction. Soon to be *our* fruit farm. My wedding to Sam was now only two weeks away. Thankfully, my absence hadn't caused any major problems since we'd planned a small ceremony, and Sweetie had taken over all the preparations. It was Saturday and my parents would be arriving on Monday—along with my grandfather.

I'd been surprised when my mother called to tell me Papa Joe was coming. My grandfather's Alzheimer's was originally considered to be advanced, but recently he'd seemed to rally. Doctors said his lack of speech and other symptoms may have had more to do with depression than the disease. When new medication began to help lift the hopelessness he felt after losing my grandmother and moving into the nursing home, he began to talk again. Although Alzheimer's still continued its evil and devastating march against him, according to my parents, there were times when he almost seemed like the man he used to be.

Now Joe wanted to see Harmony once more before he died, and my parents felt he should have the chance before he slipped into the darkness of the disease for good. I looked forward to seeing him even though the last time we'd been together, the man I'd known had seemed so far away. I had some fear that this visit wouldn't be any different. Seeing him as just a shell of the robust man he'd once been broke my heart.

With the conflict between Hannah and me finally behind us, I felt more relaxed than I had in days. I'd almost drifted off to sleep when Hannah called my name. I opened my eyes to see the girl I'd brought to Wichita. Her pastel pink dress and plain brown shoes replaced the contemporary clothing her friend Robin had given her, and her long blond hair had been pulled into a bun and tucked under her white prayer covering. I rose from my chair and looked closely at her face. No sign of makeup.

"Thank you, Hannah. I know this is hard for you, but..." I reached out to touch her, but she jerked away from me.

"Don't tell me you know how I feel, because you don't. Maybe you like hiding out in Harmony, but I don't intend to spend the rest of my life buried there."

I felt a rush of indignation. Somehow I'd turned into Hannah's enemy even though I'd gone out of my way to give her this opportunity. It didn't seem fair. I grabbed my bags. "Let's get going," I said sharply. "We're already leaving later than I'd planned."

Without a word, Hannah picked up the soft cloth valise her mother had sent with her, and we walked out of the apartment. On the way to the car, all I could do was wonder what would happen when we reached Harmony. An uneasy sense of dread filled me—and it stayed with me all the way home.

TWO

"I was kinda afraid somethin' like this would happen," Sweetie said, handing me a tall, cold glass of her home-brewed iced tea. "That girl ain't never seen nothin' outside Harmony and a few small towns around here."

She joined Sam and me as we sat in white rocking chairs on the huge wraparound porch of their beautiful red Victorian house. Even though it was July, a cool breeze helped to push the hot, humid air away. It felt good to be home, but I couldn't get the situation with Hannah out of my mind. "Abel told me that sometimes they drive to Topeka to eat dinner," I said. "I assumed since she'd seen a larger city, she wouldn't be overwhelmed by Wichita."

"Pshaw," Sweetie spat out. "That Chinese restaurant they go to is right on the edge of town. Hannah ain't never been all the way inside Topeka."

"Man, good thing I didn't take her to Kansas City or St. Louis. She would have really gone off the deep end."

Sam reached over and took my hand. "It's not your fault, Grace. You were trying to help her. You couldn't possibly have anticipated her reaction. Quit beating yourself up."

I threaded my fingers through his and squeezed lightly. "I'm glad you feel that way, but I have to wonder how Emily and Abel are going to react."

"They're not stupid people," Sweetie said. "And they love you. Besides, they're not gonna give Hannah permission to live in Wichita with some guy they don't even know. It ain't never gonna happen. After that child figgers it out, she'll settle down."

"I hope you're right."

"Truth is, the Muellers oughta be thankin' their lucky stars. Those girls that went missin' in Topeka still ain't been found—alive or dead. At least Abel and Emily know where their daughter is."

Sweetie was referring to the disappearance of two young women who'd vanished about a month apart before I left for Wichita. At first, it was assumed they'd taken off on their own. But investigators now suspected they'd been abducted.

"I don't think anyone in Harmony really took much notice," I said. "You know Harmony. No one believes something like that could happen here."

"Seems strange after two murders that occurred right on their own turf," Sam said.

I shrugged. "One took place over thirty years ago, and the other was committed by an outsider. I'm not saying folks in Harmony aren't wary of strangers, but most of them truly believe God has blessed this place with special protection."

"And so He has," Sweetie said. She sat up in her chair and stared at me. Her ever-present bun had fallen to the side of her head, making me think of Princess Leia in *Star Wars*. Of course, Sweetie would need another bun on the other side, hair coloring to cover her gray, and a lot of plastic surgery to come close to looking like Carrie Fisher. She yanked at the T-shirt under her cutoff overalls, trying to adjust it so it wouldn't tug so tightly at her neck. "Anyways," she croaked loudly, "we need to stop talkin' 'bout all this bad stuff and start thinkin' 'bout your weddin'. I got almost everything ready, but I need to go over it with you. There's a few decisions left that you gotta make."

I sighed, let go of Sam's hand, and settled back comfortably in my rocking chair. "Let's talk about it later, okay? I'm really tired, and I need to go home and unpack. Besides, I'm sure Snickle is ready to get home, too."

As if on cue, a plaintive *meow* came from around the corner. Snickle, my cat, and Buddy, Sam's dog, trotted up to us. Snickle greeted me by rubbing up against my leg while Buddy jumped up in my lap, almost spilling my tea. Snickle and Buddy had become great friends, and I had to wonder if Snickle really would be happier at our house. Staying with Sweetie and Sam while I was in Wichita may have changed his perspective as to what home really looked like. I wasn't too concerned though. After the wedding, we'd be living here anyway, so I guess in the long run, being with me for two weeks wouldn't ruin him. As if reading my mind, Sweetie piped up.

"Are you gonna drag that poor cat back to your place again? Why don't you just leave him be? He loves it here, and you're over every day anyway. Wouldn't that be easier on you both?"

Sweetie, who had sworn up and down that she hated cats, was crazy about Snickle. And he was nuts about her, too. Frankly, he spent more time hanging around her than he did me. Persnickety feline.

"You're probably right," I said, stroking Buddy. "If you don't mind, I think I will leave him here. With my parents and my grandfather coming, it might be best."

Snickle ran over to Sweetie and nuzzled her leg as if thanking her for allowing him to stay with his good doggy pal. Sweetie chuckled and bent down to stroke the calico cat that had become her friend. "You know, we tried keepin' him inside since he ain't got no claws to defend himself with, but he kept slippin' out. Funny thing is, Buddy keeps him in line. If Snickle starts to wander too far, Buddy barks and barks. Then he starts rounding this silly cat up and pushin' him home. I ain't never seen nothin' like it before." Snickle jumped up in Sweetie's lap, turned around once, and lay down. He didn't even look my way.

"Guess I know where I stand," I said with a smile.

"If it makes any difference, *I* like you," Sam said laughing.

"That's good, 'cause in a couple of weeks, you won't be able to get rid of me."

"You decided what to do with your house yet?" Sweetie asked.

"No. I can't sell it; it's been in the family too long." My father and his brother had been raised in that house. And Benjamin, my uncle, had left it to me when he passed away. I'd thought about renting it out, but that didn't feel right either. "Guess I'll let it sit until God gives me some direction."

"Good idea," Sweetie said. "Ain't smart to get ahead of the Lord. You'll know what to do when the time comes."

We sat quietly sipping tea until the sun began to set behind us. Rosy fingers of light reached out and touched the wispy clouds that floated over our heads. There was something about the skies over Harmony at sunrise and sunset. Stroked with God's paintbrush, they were a sight to behold. As I sat there with Sam and Sweetie, for the first time since driving Hannah home, serenity began to overtake my concern for her.

Our trip hadn't been pleasant. The silence between us was nothing like the relaxed atmosphere I enjoyed now. Although I'd counseled her to wait a few days to tell her parents about Jim's offer, I had no idea if she'd followed my advice. For all I knew, the Mueller household was in an uproar now, and I could be at the center of it. Abel, Emily, and I had been through a lot together. I prayed we could weather this storm as well.

Reluctantly, I lifted Buddy, kissed him on the head, and put him down. Then I stood to my feet. "Guess I'd better get home. I dumped my luggage inside the door before I came over. If I don't unpack and wash my dirty laundry, I may have to pull my winter clothes out of storage. And it's way too hot to wear anything heavy."

"Good thing I finally got your electrical problems solved while you were gone," Sam said. "Now you can actually turn on your lights and run your washer at the same time."

I grinned. "Much more convenient than washing

my clothes in the dark. Thank you."

He stood up and took me in his arms. "I'm tired of saying good-bye to you," he whispered. "I can hardly wait for the day when all I have to say is good night."

I sighed and leaned into him. "Me, too." We stayed that way until we heard Sweetie clear her throat.

"I ain't in the way on my own front porch, I hope," she said with a throaty chuckle.

"Actually, you are," Sam said, finally letting me go. "But what can we do? We're used to you."

Sweetie's gruff laughter carried through the deepening shadows, almost drowning out the song of the cicadas as they serenaded the encroachment of night.

Moving into Sweetie's house after the wedding might seem strange to people who didn't know us, but it was as natural to me as breathing. Sweetie was family, and living with my husband and his aunt felt completely right. I couldn't help but think back to the first time I met Sweetie. Rough, nosy, and caustic, she seemed unpleasant—someone to avoid. Now she was almost a second mother to me. I'd learned an important lesson from Sam's aunt. Judging anyone too quickly is a big mistake. People have many layers, and if you want to really know someone, you've got to invest some time and patience. Beneath Sweetie's harsh exterior, I discovered a strong, brave, and humble woman who'd turned out to be a role model for me. Her difficult life had toughened her, but it hadn't broken her spirit or her ability to love. My respect for her only grew as I got to know her better.

"I'll walk you to your car," Sam said, grabbing my hand.

I waved good-bye to Sweetie and ran my hand over Snickle's back. Buddy followed us down the steps.

"Pick me up for church in the morning?" I said, as I leaned against my car.

"Sure," Sam said. "How 'bout lunch at Mary's afterward?"

Even though Harmony's only restaurant retained Mary Whittenbauer's name, Mary had departed our small town months ago. Her secret dealings with a shady real estate agent who'd wanted to build a resort and casino near Harmony had been exposed, along with her involvement in a grisly murder. After testifying against the agent and being granted immunity, Mary left the state. No one knew where she was now. Her former cook, Hector Ramirez, currently ran the restaurant, along with his wife, Carmen.

"Sounds good," I said, "but after we eat I need to go home and get things prepared for my family's visit."

"Need help?"

I grinned. "I'm not blind, you know. Even though I wasn't home long, it was obvious little elves had been cleaning the house and stocking my fridge."

Sam held his hands up. "I am guilty only by association. Sweetie knew you wouldn't have much time to shop and dragged me to the store in Council Grove. And you know I don't clean, but I do follow my aunt's orders. She even forced me to move furniture so she could sweep under it. I really doubt you'll find much to do tomorrow."

I leaned over and kissed him. "Good thing I don't have privacy issues, huh?"

He chuckled. "You've got that right. It will only get worse when you move in here."

I laid my head on his chest. "I love this place—and you. And believe it or not, I'm just crazy about Sweetie. You know, if you ever want me to cook for you, I need to get back to those lessons Sarah and I started with Sweetie before I left."

"I think Sarah's passed you by. She never missed a lesson while you were gone. In fact, she's already graduated to frying chicken and baking apple cobbler." He rubbed his stomach. "I got to be the guinea pig. Tough job."

"Poor baby. I feel for you."

He sighed dramatically. "I know. It's a burden I must bear with bravery."

I laughed at the silly look on his face. "Can you forget food for a moment? Let's get back to Sarah. How's she doing?"

"I don't know." He shrugged. "I'm a guy. We're not very good at figuring out how women feel."

I reached up and brushed a lock of sandy-blond hair from his eyes. "You're one of the most sensitive, insightful people I've ever known. Even if you are male."

"Thanks, I think." His expression turned serious. "To be honest with you, I think Sarah's in a lot of pain. She and John have kept their word and stayed away from each other. But there's this deep sadness in their eyes." He stared at me for several seconds before continuing. "You know, if I ever lost you, I believe I'd look exactly the same way."

I kissed him softly. "You won't ever lose me, you know. In a few days, I'll be yours forever."

He wrapped his tanned, muscled arms around me. "I thought you already were mine forever."

We kissed again, and then I pushed him gently away. "If you keep that up, I'll never get home."

"Fine by me."

"Now I know it's time to go." I got into my bright-yellow Volkswagen Bug and started the engine. Sam motioned to me to roll down my window.

"I thought you were going to sell this car while you were in Wichita," he said frowning.

"I tried, but I couldn't find anything else I wanted to buy."

"In all of Wichita there wasn't one other car you liked? I find that hard to swallow."

"Well, you can believe what you want. If I have to get rid of my slug bug, I want a car with personality."

Sam pointed to his ancient truck, held together more by rust than metal. "You mean like that?"

"Definitely not the kind of personality I'm going for. No decent hillbilly would be caught dead driving that poor thing. Thanks anyway."

"Are you calling me an indecent hillbilly?"

I shrugged. "If the truck fits. . ."

"You just don't appreciate the kind of character brought about by use and age," he sniffed, trying to look offended.

I nodded. "You must be right 'cause I think that sorry excuse for transportation should be put out of its misery."

"Women just don't understand a man and his truck."

"Thank God for that."

He gave me his most pitiful look, which made me giggle. "And here I broke down and bought something new just to make you happy. You haven't said one word about it."

I gazed at the big, beautiful red truck parked in the circular driveway. His decaying, beaten-up model had been pulled up next to the barn as if it had been relegated to second place. "I apologize. I truly applaud you, but why keep the old one?"

"Because contrary to the theory that male members of society have no real feelings, I'm emotionally attached to it."

I gave him a big smile. "Well, you're emotionally attached to me, too. But if you ever test-drive a newer model, you'll end up in worse condition than that aged rattletrap."

He stuck his head into my window and kissed me soundly. "You have nothing to worry about. I'd rather stick with my old, comfortable model. The new versions with all the bells and whistles scare me."

I slapped his arm. "I'm not sure what that means, but I'm pretty sure I don't like it."

He stood up and pointed toward the road. "Go home. I'll see you in the morning."

"If you're lucky." I put the car into gear and started down the driveway.

"I love you, Grace," Sam hollered as I headed toward Faith Road.

"I love you, too!" I yelled back.

Getting to my house from Sam's didn't take long. We live a little less than a mile from each other. As

I drove, my mind drifted back to our conversation about Sarah Ketterling and John Keystone. They were certainly star-crossed lovers, separated by differences in their faiths. Although I understood the reasons they chose to deny their feelings, my heart ached for them.

I pulled into the driveway of my cute yellow house. When I'd left, my grandmother's purple irises were in full bloom. But now, in the heat of summer, only green stalks remained. Knowing that I'd missed so much of their flowering beauty made me sad. Mama's irises were a special love we'd shared. "Irises represent faith, hope, and wisdom, Gracie," she'd tell me as she worked in the garden at her home in Nebraska. "They remind me of God's faithfulness. Through faith and hope we inherit His promises, and through His Word and His wonderful Holy Spirit, He gives us wisdom we could never gain from human knowledge. These purple irises also signify royalty. Someday our heavenly Father will put crowns on our heads because we are children of the King."

I could still hear her as she talked about her beloved flowers and the God she loved more than anything else. Even though she'd been happy in Fairbury, I knew she missed her irises in Harmony. How I wished she could have come back before she died to see them still growing. They were a reminder to me of her faith in God and her love for me. I felt blessed to tend them for her all these years later.

Thankfully, under the illumination of the yard light, I could see that the marigolds Sam had planted by the front porch were thriving. At least I would be able to enjoy them for a while. I was grateful for the light so I could find my way to my front porch. In the country, where there are no streetlights, on cloudy nights it can get so dark it's actually impossible to see your hand in front of your face.

I got out of the car and hurried inside. My suitcases still sat inside the door where I'd dropped them. I dragged the biggest one toward the kitchen, opened it up, and removed a plastic bag full of dirty clothes. A visit to the basement and a few minutes later, the washer was churning away. I'd put the wet clothes in the dryer tomorrow morning. Right now I needed a good night's sleep. I couldn't help but smile at the wringer washer Mama Essie had used to wash her clothes, sitting in the corner of the basement. When I first arrived in Harmony, it was all I had. Thankfully, when I was a child, Mama had taught me how to use the old-style washer. Even after leaving Harmony and her Old Order ways, she'd preferred the wringer washer to the "newfangled" machines.

As I trudged up the stairs, I was surprised to hear someone knocking on my door. I glanced at my watch as I hurried to find out who would visit this late. A little after nine o'clock. Normal in Wichita but really unusual in Harmony where the sidewalks are rolled up around seven.

I pulled the door open and found Pastor Abel Mueller standing on my porch, his face beet red. Before I could say anything, he blurted out, "Gracie Temple, why in heaven's name are you trying to destroy my family?"

THREE

Abel was halfway through his second cup of cold cider before his color began to return to normal. I grasped my hands to keep them from shaking. I'd never seen the gentle Mennonite minister so upset. And he'd certainly never been this angry with me before. It hurt me deeply to think I was the cause of his distress.

"So you do understand," I said for the third time. "I had no idea until the lessons were almost over that Hannah felt like this. By then it was too late."

Abel set his cup down on the table next to the couch. "I'm trying, Gracie," he said. He shook his shaggy head, and his beard quivered. "But Emily is devastated. She and Hannah have always been so close. Now it's like we don't even know our own daughter."

I stared down at the floor. "I'm so sorry, Abel. I wish now I'd never taken her to Wichita. I was just trying to help."

"Somewhere inside I know that, Gracie. But right now my father's heart is breaking. Hannah has never been this rebellious toward us. Before I left to come over here, I had to send her to her room for yelling at her mother. She insists we let her live with that art teacher and go to school in Wichita. But we can't do that. It's our job to raise our daughter—not anyone else's. Besides, if this is how she acts after being in the big city for six weeks, what would happen to her if she lived there during an entire school year?"

"I don't know," I said, raising my head to meet his eyes. "To be honest, I planned to encourage you to let her go."

Abel started to sputter, but I held my hand up to stop him. "Let me finish. Jim really could do wonderful things for her. I'm confident she could get into a good art school or college—probably with a full scholarship. But with the way she's responded to being away from home, I can't recommend it now."

"Well, thank goodness," Abel said. "Maybe knowing that you've changed your mind will help to convince Hannah it's the wrong move. As far as college, she will have to make her own decision after she graduates high school. Most folks in our church believe a young woman should get married and settle down after school is over. And that's liberal compared to the old beliefs that eighth grade was far enough for any young person—especially the girls."

He took a deep breath and let it out slowly. "But things change, and I have come to believe that I must allow her to choose her own way in life even if it isn't the one I want for her. God isn't asking us to follow His path because we have to. He desires His children to pursue His will because we want to." His eyes sought mine. "But in this situation, I must wonder if I should have been stricter. Two of our elders came to me before Hannah left. They both felt I was making a mistake, and I dismissed their concerns. But now. . ."

He rubbed the back of his neck as if trying to relieve stress or pain. "When you first came to Harmony, you challenged me about our beliefs. Perhaps now you see why we live a separated life. Hannah leaves our church and our town for a few weeks, and she brings back the rebellion and disrespect rampant in the world outside our borders."

"I understand what you're saying, Abel. But there are many, many good Christian people living in big cities who still keep Christ as the center of their lives. I love Harmony, too, but this place isn't a panacea against evil. The people who live here have chosen to live a certain kind of life, and that's fine. But Hannah made a choice, too—one that none of us saw coming. The problem isn't Wichita. . ." I hesitated to complete my sentence, so Abel finished it for me.

"It's Hannah," he said, his words slow and methodical. He clasped his hands together. "But still, if she hadn't left our protection. . ."

"The problem would still be in her heart. There is something she longs for, Abel. Something she hasn't found here."

His face flushed and his jaw tightened. "Her art. One of the elders also cautioned me about this—this talent of hers. He said Hannah's interests could lead to vanity and self-involvement. I didn't pay any attention to him. It seemed silly and old-fashioned. Maybe I've been foolish. . ."

"But Abel, if that were true, why would God give her such a wonderful gift? That doesn't make any sense."

"But why would He give her something she can't handle? Something that would lead her away from Him and her family?"

I reached over and covered his hand with mine. "That hasn't happened. Hannah is acting out a bit, that's all. I think you're blowing this out of proportion."

"I don't know," he said hesitantly. "Maybe. I know some children rebel during their teenage years. I've certainly counseled many families in crisis. I just never thought Hannah would—"

"Be a teenager?" I smiled at him. "I think the best thing we can do is to let her work this out in her own mind. It could all blow over in a week or two. Hannah loves you and Emily. And Harmony is the only home she's ever known."

He nodded and patted my hand before pulling his away. "I believe it's wise to put the subject of her future on hold for now. We've told Hannah we expect her to adjust her behavior. As you say, perhaps she will settle down now that she's home. If God has a different plan for her life from what Emily and I would choose, we won't stand in His way. But right now, it's Hannah's heart that concerns me most."

Although I firmly believe God has a plan for everyone's life, I'm also aware that He doesn't force our steps. We all have the right and ability to pick a different direction—the one that isn't God's will for us. I prayed that wouldn't happen to Hannah.

I'd thought about mentioning Hannah's wardrobe malfunction in Wichita, but I just couldn't bring myself to do it. What would it help? The knowledge that she'd rejected her simple clothing for jeans and a T-shirt wouldn't give Abel and Emily additional peace of mind. They had enough to deal with now.

"What about our painting lessons?" I asked.

Abel stood up, his wide-brimmed straw hat in his hand. "Let's wait on that for now, Gracie. But please understand that Emily and I still love you. Just because we hit a bump in the road doesn't mean our buggy has completely turned over."

"I understand, and I promise to watch out for any future bumps. This one just snuck up on me."

He ambled toward my front door. "I know. When Hannah settles down, we'll consider restarting her lessons. I'm sure she'll be eager to continue."

"All right." When Abel closed the door behind him, I covered my face with my hands, trying to compose the emotions that raged through me. I prayed this situation would turn around, but frankly, not seeing Hannah for a while might be good for both of us. I'd said everything I could to encourage her to be patient. I was out of advice and although I would never admit it to Abel or Emily, I understood her desires. I'd felt the same way once. The big city had drawn me—as had the yearning for what I thought success entailed. But coming to Harmony had changed me. I'd found real peace and contentment here, something I'd never experienced in Wichita.

"Help Hannah find her way, God," I prayed quietly. "Show her the path You have for her, even if it isn't the same one someone else might choose for her."

I headed to the kitchen and made a cup of hot chocolate. The July heat hadn't chased away this nightly habit. Fixing cocoa from scratch takes longer than pouring a premade package of mix into a cup of hot water, but I really enjoy the taste of real cocoa powder, sugar, and milk, heated and topped off with whipped cream. I carried my cup upstairs to the bedroom and changed clothes. Then I turned on the small window air conditioner and the old, thirteen-inch television that sits on my dresser, wiggling the rabbit ears around until I got a halfway decent picture.

Television in my house is not without its complications. Sam and Sweetie have satellite TV, so when I want to watch something special, I go over there. Here, I just take whatever I can pick up through the tower Sam erected outside my house. At least I'm able to make out the news and a few programs I like. The many hours I used to spend in front of my set in Wichita has been reduced to only a few shows here and there. TV lost a lot of its pull on me after moving to Harmony. I chuckled to myself. Must be the Mennonite influence. The ten o'clock news was just coming on, so I set my cup of cocoa on the table next to my bed, got in, and wiggled under the covers.

"Police are investigating the disappearance of a young college student in Emporia," the grim-faced announcer said. "Melissa Dunham went missing after a night out with friends. Miss Dunham never returned to her apartment last night, according to her roommate. Police are treating the situation as suspicious. If you know anything about the whereabouts of Melissa Dunham, please notify the authorities." A picture of a young, fresh-faced woman with long blond hair and blue eyes filled my fuzzy TV screen. The girl looked remarkably like Hannah. "Police are still searching for two other young women who are still missing from Topeka. A local spokesperson declined to comment as to whether these cases might be linked to this most recent disappearance." Two more pictures popped up on the screen. Both girls had long blond hair, and at least one had blue eyes. I couldn't tell the color of the other girl's eyes from the photo. They both reminded me of Hannah as well. A strange sense of disquiet filled me, and it took much longer than usual to fall asleep. When I finally did, I kept seeing the missing girls' faces in my dreams, superimposed over the face of the young Mennonite girl I'd grown to love.

Four

It was a little after twelve thirty when church let out the next morning. It felt wonderful to be back among my friends at Harmony Church. Ruth Wickham hugged me so tightly I almost couldn't breathe, and Wynonna Jensen, the pastor's wife, squealed when she saw me. Pastor Jensen's sermon brought such peace to my troubled soul. He talked about how important it is to forgive ourselves as well as others. That it actually helps to show our faith in God's forgiveness. Many people, he said, say they believe God has forgiven them for their mistakes, but they continue to condemn themselves.

"If you truly believe in God's promise to be faithful in forgiving your sin," he said, "you would never throw that act of love and grace back in God's face by continuing to punish yourself. Do you think your faults are stronger than Jesus' sacrifice for you? True humility is believing God's Word and not trying to create a false sense of righteousness based on your own behavior."

His words led me to remind myself that taking Hannah to Wichita, and being away from Sam,

Sweetie, and my friends, was a sacrifice done out of kindness. I hadn't purposely set out to cause a problem in Hannah's family. And besides, in the end, her reaction was her responsibility, not mine. I asked God to forgive me for beating myself up about it and submitted myself to His unending grace. I felt lighter and less troubled when we stepped out into the sunshine after church was dismissed.

"Let's get to Mary's before they're out of chicken," Sam said, gently pulling me away from the entrance.

Hector serves fried chicken family-style on Sundays, and the town turns out in droves to get their fair share. Thankfully, Abel usually preaches longer than Pastor Jensen so the members of Harmony Church get to their chicken dinners before the members of Bethel Mennonite. Harmony residents love to tease Abel about it. He always laughs and says, "I believe the good Lord cares more about your soul than your stomach." But the truth was, most of the Bethel folks went home to eat after church anyway, so it didn't really matter that much.

Sam left the truck parked in front of the church, and we walked hand in hand down the wooden sidewalk to the restaurant. Younger Harmony residents know many of the older folks like to eat out on Sunday, so they purposely park farther away, leaving plenty of spaces close to Mary's front door. We walked past the small stores that lined Main Street. Cora's Simple Clothing Shoppe, Harmony Hardware, Ruth's Crafts and Creations, and Menlo's Bakery were just a few of the small, homespun businesses along the way. All closed on Sunday, thank you very much. Sunday is the Lord's Day in Harmony, and no one would think of being open—except for the restaurant. Somehow hungry residents didn't seem to notice the inconsistency. But since Hector and his family always attended Mass during the week at the Catholic church in Sunrise, no one questioned the contradiction too closely. Harmony residents love to gather together at Mary's. It's akin to family dinner at Grandma's even though Hector certainly didn't look like anyone's grandmother.

I couldn't help but feel sad when I saw the large sign that says MARY'S KITCHEN still hanging on the two-story brick building that houses the popular eatery. I secretly hoped one day Hector would rename the establishment and remove the name of the previous owner. I had nothing against Mary, but seeing her name every time we came to town brought back painful memories.

We entered the bustling eatery with its old-fashioned diner feel. Blue walls filled with old photographs, wooden floors that squeak when you walk on them, booths with checkered tablecloths, and tables with yellow laminate tops. Every tabletop held red and yellow plastic containers for ketchup and mustard. The place was filling up quickly, but we managed to find a table. We had to wait awhile for service. Two women I didn't know were taking orders. A couple of Hannah's friends, Leah and Jessie, worked during the week, but being Conservative Mennonites, they never work on Sundays. Leah had been brought up in a stable, godly family. Unfortunately, Jessie's life had been a hard one so far. Her father, Rand McAllister, was abusive to her and her mother. His death last year was a tragedy—of sorts.

As awful as it sounds, since his funeral, his family seemed to blossom. Jessie actually smiled once in a while now. A rather unattractive girl when I'd first met her, she'd changed once her father's tyrannical rule ceased. A glow of happiness that brought life to her features replaced her usual sullen expression. The sallow-faced young woman now had color in her cheeks and a sparkle in her eyes. And she'd lost quite a bit of weight. Of course, working at the restaurant probably helped.

I have real respect for people who serve food to the public. I'm not sure I'd be able to last through an entire day on my feet, running orders back and forth. In Harmony, though, if one of Hector's waitresses runs behind, it's not the least bit unusual to see a patron jump up, go back to the kitchen, and fetch their own food or get their own drink. In fact, most of the time, they'll even check with other customers to see if they need anything. Life in Harmony is a lot different from what I was used to in Wichita. Frankly, after being gone for a while, it takes a few days to adjust to the way things work here.

One of the women taking orders shuffled up to the table. "What would you folks like to drink?" She didn't bother to ask about food since chicken was the only thing on the menu today. Sam and I both ordered coffee with cream.

After she walked away, Sam crooked his head slightly to the right. "Something you don't know. Not long after you left, Bill Eberly started dating."

I looked toward the area Sam indicated. Bill Eberly sat alone in a booth against the wall. I caught his eye and waved to him. He smiled and returned the gesture. Bill Eberly is one of my favorite people—a kind man whose wife died several years ago. Sam's statement surprised me though, because I'd been told Bill was a one-woman man who would probably never marry again.

"Who?" I asked, turning my attention back to Sam.

His right eyebrow arched in amusement. "Guess. Go ahead, you won't believe it."

"I'm not going to guess. Either tell me or don't. Doesn't matter to me."

"Okay, never mind."

I reached across the table and lightly slapped his arm. "Okay, okay. Um, he's dating Ida. Is that it?"

"Well, if you're not going to be serious. . ."

My friend Ida Turnbauer is over eighty years old and an Old Order Mennonite. Sam was right. I wasn't being serious. "Would you just tell me? You know I hate guessing games."

"All right, but you sure take the fun out of stuff."

I guess the look on my face caused him some concern because he finally blurted out, "Thelma McAllister. He's dating Thelma, and it looks pretty serious."

"Thelma McAllister?" I gasped. "Jessie's mother? Rand's wife?"

"Well, she's not actually his wife now, you know. She would be his widow. But yes, *that* Thelma McAllister—like there are two of them living in Harmony."

At first, I could barely believe it, but as I considered the idea, it began to make sense. Thelma was a good woman who'd been beaten down by years of abuse by Rand. Just as Jessie had changed after Rand's death, Thelma had also come out of her shell. Well, maybe *shell* wasn't the right word. Perhaps cocoon described it better. When Rand was alive, she always carried herself like someone who'd given up on life—and on herself. Before I left for Wichita, though, I'd caught a glimpse of her one day in the restaurant, and I hadn't recognized her at first. She had a totally different countenance. Even her personality had transformed. She'd begun to open up and talk to people. In fact, she seemed to enjoy social interaction. And she was funny. I could see someone like Bill being drawn to her.

"Wait a minute," I said. "Thelma and Jessie aren't supposed to date anyone outside of their faith. Bill isn't Mennonite."

Sam paused while the waitress brought our coffee. When she walked away, he smiled triumphantly. "That's changed, too." Seeing my frown, he chuckled. "Do you think you have to be born into a Mennonite home to join the church? Well, you don't. Bill's been taking some instruction from Abel. When he's finished, he'll officially become a member. He and Thelma are already going to church together."

"Wow. Sounds like they're pretty serious."

Sam nodded. "I think they are. You should see them together. I've never seen Thelma so happy, and Bill reminds me of the man he used to be when Edith was alive."

I poured cream into my cup and stirred it. "How's Jessie taking their relationship?"

He shrugged. "I don't know. She doesn't act thrilled about it. I think she needs some time to get close to Bill, though. After the way Rand treated her, she will probably be a little hesitant about accepting him right off the bat."

I started to respond, but our waitress came over with a large tray full of food and began to fill our table. I thanked her, and she asked if we wanted anything else. I looked at the huge plate of fried chicken, the bowl of mashed potatoes and gravy, green beans, a basket of homemade rolls, and chuckled. "I can't think of one more thing we could possibly need."

She smiled and walked away. "Who is that woman?" I asked Sam.

"She's Carmen's sister, Connie. And the other woman is Connie's daughter."

"They don't live here, do they?"

"No. They both live in Council Grove. They just started coming to the restaurant on Sundays to help out. Carmen was running herself ragged without Leah and Jessie."

"That's nice of them."

Sam nodded in agreement. "Let's pray. I'm starved."

I felt certain Sweetie had cooked her usual Sunday morning pancakes and sausage and that Sam had partaken liberally, but I didn't tease him. He worked hard, and his lean, muscled body was a testament to the fact that he needed fuel to get all the necessary chores done on his large fruit farm. He prayed, thanking God for the day and for the food on the table. Then we dug in. I glanced around the restaurant and noticed several other people praying over their food. I hadn't witnessed much public praying in Wichita, but it was par for the course in Harmony.

As always, the chicken was crisp and buttery tasting, the whipped potatoes and gravy thick and creamy, and the green beans with bacon and onions were delicious. I took several bites while I built up the courage to ask Sam the question I'd wanted to ask ever since I got home.

"So did you spend any time with Pat while I was gone?" I said finally. Immediately I felt an emotional door slam shut.

The smile slipped from Sam's face. "You know we're very busy in the orchards right now."

"You're not so busy you couldn't have found a couple of hours to spend with your father."

Sam took a sip of coffee then put his cup down with a thud. "Look, Grace. You just got back. We'll talk about it at some point but not today, okay?"

"You said that before I left. There never seems to be a right time to discuss Pat."

"He abandoned me and my mother."

"For crying out loud, Sam. He didn't even know your mother was pregnant. How is that abandoning her?"

He brushed away a lock of hair that had fallen over one eye. "Well, he certainly didn't check to find out, did he? He took advantage of her, and then he was gone."

We'd been over this more than once. Sam seemed to judge his father by his own standards. "I get it, but as I've said before, neither one of them were living for God." I knew this was difficult for him and tried to keep my tone as gentle as possible. Truth was, his attitude frustrated me. "Even so, I don't believe your father would have left had he known your mom was expecting." I reached across the table and took Sam's hand. "It was your mother's responsibility to tell him, but she didn't. And remember, when she contacted him a couple of years ago, he immediately set out to find you. He even gave up an important job he loved to become sheriff of a rural county where most of the time the biggest crime he faces is chicken stealing."

Sam pulled his hand back, and a frown creased his handsome face. "Right. Except he waited for over a year to tell me who he was. And actually, he didn't even tell me. You figured it out."

Sam scooped another big helping of mashed potatoes onto his plate, a signal that our conversation had ended.

I couldn't help but sigh with frustration. Sheriff Pat Taylor became my friend last year during a particularly trying time. In fact, he'd saved my life. Through a series of incidents, I'd discovered he was Sam's real father. Since then, Pat had done everything possible to forge a relationship with his son. But Sam's resistance had stalled their connection and when they were together, the tension was palpable. Before I picked up my fork, I let out another deep sigh.

Sam stopped eating and scowled at me. "For goodness' sake, Grace. If you keep that up, you'll hyperventilate. We'll sit down sometime this week and have a long discussion about Pat if it will keep you conscious. Okay?"

I waved my fork at him. "Very clever. You know my folks will be here, and you're counting on my being too busy to talk to you." I jabbed my fork at him like a pointer. "It won't work. I'll definitely find the time. You've got to figure this out before the wedding. Your father should be sitting on your side of the church. He's family, you know."

For the first time since we'd begun this uncomfortable conversation, Sam grinned. "Oh sure. And I suppose you're planning to sit him down right next to Sweetie?"

Touché. If Sam's acceptance of his father was minimal, Sweetie's was almost nonexistent. Although Sam's aunt had come a long way in her spiritual walk since I'd known her, the subject of Pat Taylor was "sorer than a boil on a pig's behind," as she would say. I'd even dragged both of them to a meeting with our pastor, Marcus Jensen. He'd done a great job of explaining forgiveness and how we had no right to withhold it from anyone after God had sacrificed so much to forgive us. For a while, I thought he had them. But when we walked out of his office, the Goodriches were right back where they started. It confused me some since they were both such kind, forgiving people in every other area. This was simply one stronghold they protected with ferocity. Meanwhile, Pat just kept trying. If he ever decided to give up and move on, I wouldn't blame him. But instead he'd dug his heels in, determined to ride it out. In truth, he was as stubborn as his son, although in my eyes, he was in the right while Sam stood with both cowboy boots planted squarely in the wrong.

Out of the corner of my eye, I saw someone walk up to our table. I turned to find Bill Eberly smiling at me. "Glad to see you back, Gracie."

"Thanks, Bill," I said, returning his smile. "It's good to be back."

Bill is a nice-looking man with an easygoing manner. His brown hair is sprinkled with gray, and his dark-green eyes almost always twinkle with humor. His road hadn't been an easy one since the death of his wife, Edith. Not long after her passing, his two grown children moved away, leaving him alone and grieving.

"So how did Hannah enjoy her art classes?" he asked.

"She did very well. The instructor thinks she's quite talented." I congratulated myself on sidestepping the Hannah-fought-tooth-and-nail-not-to-return-to-Harmony issue. But my mouthy fiancé wasn't quite as clever.

"Yeah, she didn't want to come back," he offered. "Grace had to practically drag her home."

I shot Sam a look that made his eyes widen. Men.

They have no clue when it comes to discretion.

"Wow," Bill said. "This certainly isn't a good time for young women to be where they shouldn't be. Have you two heard that another girl is missing? This one from Emporia?"

"I caught something about it on the news last night," I said.

Bill looked around and then stepped closer, lowering his voice. "I have a nephew who works for a newspaper in Topeka. He says the police think all three girls might have been kidnapped by the same man. They're trying to keep that away from the media, though, so they don't spook the guy. You know, in case the women are still alive. If the kidnapper thinks the authorities are closing in on him, the police are afraid he might harm them." He shook his head. "We need to pray for those poor girls and their families."

"But why do they think the cases are connected?" I asked. "I mean, maybe these girls took off on their own."

Bill shrugged. "My nephew has a friend on the police department." He lowered his voice again. I had to strain to hear him. "Please don't repeat this. My nephew's friend told him it was off the record, but in one of the situations in Topeka, someone saw the girl being picked up in a red truck. And in Emporia, there were truck tracks on the dirt road where that young woman disappeared."

"What about the other girl in Topeka?" Sam said.

"She was out walking and never came home," Bill said. "No one reported seeing her get into a truck, but all the girls look so similar."

"That's not much to go on," Sam said, frowning. "Lots of people in rural areas have trucks. Someone sees one red truck, and there are tracks from a truck at a second location?" He shook his head. "Doesn't make sense. Why would the police think these situations are connected based on flimsy evidence like that?"

"I'm not sure. Maybe they have something else that links the missing girls together." He grunted. "My nephew isn't the best source of sound information. He could be blowing his friend's comments out of proportion."

I frowned at Sam. "All the girls have long blond hair and blue eyes. Like Hannah." I could hear the alarm in my voice, and Sam noticed it, too.

"Hannah's not out running around by herself," he said reassuringly. "And she'd never get into a stranger's vehicle. Never. Besides, I'll bet none of the girls dressed like Hannah, did they, Bill?"

He shook his head and smiled at me. "No, these were modern girls, Gracie. Not Mennonite." He patted my shoulder. "I'm sorry. I didn't mean to alarm you. I shouldn't have said anything. I'm sorry."

"It's not your fault," I said. "Hannah's been on my mind, and some of her recent actions have me concerned. You're both right. This has nothing to do with her."

Sam grunted. "A red truck, huh? I have a red truck. You do, too, don't you, Bill?"

He nodded. "Yep, and so do a lot of other folks around here. Oh, I just remembered. The truck had an odd bumper sticker. The witness didn't get a real good look at it, but I guess she told the police something about it that they found helpful." He shrugged. "My nephew didn't go into any other details."

Sam pointed toward the front window of the restaurant. "I see four red trucks parked out there right now, and I can guarantee you that at least three of them have bumper stickers. The police are going to need a lot more than that to find this guy—if there really is someone out there abducting young women."

Bill nodded. "You're right about that." He straightened up and grinned at us. "Well, I better get going. I'm having dinner at Thelma's tonight before church. I need to take a nap and sleep off Hector's fried chicken before I tackle Thelma's yummy pot roast." He chuckled. "It's a hard life, but I'm doing the best I can."

Sam and I laughed, even though our previous discussion left me feeling decidedly uneasy. After Bill walked away, I finished my meal while Sam talked, but I couldn't concentrate on the discussion. Ida had taught me to listen when something disrupts my inner sense of peace. And I felt as if my peace was busy jumping up and down, frantically waving its arms.

FIVE

After lunch, Sam took me home. I spent the rest of the day trying to get ready for the arrival of my parents and Papa Joe. The situation with Hannah made it difficult for me to concentrate. I couldn't help but wonder what was going on at the Muellers'. I stopped and prayed once again that God would bring peace to them. Somehow I managed to get everything done I'd planned to do. The room my dad grew up in sat ready for my mother and father, and I'd cleaned out my room for Papa Joe since it had been his bedroom when he and Mama Essie lived in the house. I'd temporarily moved into Uncle Benjamin's room. When I surveyed the space I'd prepared for my family, I felt certain everyone would be comfortable. The rooms were clean, the furniture polished, and each bed was covered with one of the beautiful quilts I'd retrieved from trunks in the basement. Most of the furniture pieces had belonged to the room's original owner. Temple furniture was certainly made to last. I loved knowing that my family would be able to enjoy many of the furnishings they grew up with.

I finished much earlier than I'd anticipated thanks

to Sam and Sweetie's efforts before I got home. There was plenty of food in the house and the main rooms had been cleaned so perfectly there was almost nothing left to do. I decided to run over and see Ida. Since she only lives half a mile from me, I chose to walk. I hadn't gone very far when I realized I'd made a mistake. The July sun beat down relentlessly on my uncovered head, and I remembered that Ida doesn't have air-conditioning. Even though I considered turning around more than once, in the end I kept going. If someone Ida's age could handle the heat, surely I could.

As I entered her yard, the front door swung open. "Ach, my Gracie! I have been hoping you would come to see me."

I hurried up the steps and flung my arms around her. "I missed you so much."

"Not as much as I missed you, my dear child," the old woman said, her voice breaking. "Please come inside. I can hardly wait to hear all about your trip." Her blue eyes, faded with age, shone with tears.

When I stepped inside Ida's simple home, I was pleasantly surprised. Although the interior of the house was warm, it wasn't as bad as I'd expected. The shades were drawn, keeping the room cooler, and a slight breeze from outside flowed through the space with vigor. Ida noticed my interest.

"My house was designed to circulate the air," she said with a smile. "The windows and doors in the front and back are situated in a way that brings the wind from outside through my main rooms." She chuckled.

"However, it is still very warm."

"I've visited you when it was hot outside, but I never noticed that your house was designed differently from anyone else's."

"I believe you were not aware of the heat because you were comfortable here. But today you are thinking about the heat, so for the first time you see the difference. Is this not the answer?"

I nodded. "I think you're exactly right."

"Your house is designed in the same way," she said. "If you will open the windows in your living room and the windows near your back door, you will find that the air will move through your home just like mine."

"Maybe I'll try that in the fall, but on days like this, I'm afraid any cool air in my house will have to come from my air-conditioning. I guess I'm a wimp."

Ida laughed. "You are certainly not a wimp in my book. Now you sit here while I get something cold to relieve you."

Ida's refrigerator runs on propane. It seems odd that while propane gas burns under the appliance, the inside stays cool. I watched the elderly woman toddle off toward her kitchen. In deference to the hot summer temperatures, she'd shed her usual apron. The sleeves on her dress had been shortened, and the large collar she usually wore had been removed. But her dress was dark blue, not a good color in the heat, and her ever-present black prayer covering sat atop her head, covering her steel-gray hair, which had been pulled into a tight bun. I'd learned from my friend Sarah that in Harmony, married or widowed women wore black prayer coverings while single women, like her, wore white. Good way to let the gentlemen folk know you're available, I guess.

I wiped the sweat trickling down my face and rubbed my hands on my jeans. Shorts would have been more comfortable, but not wanting to offend Ida, I'd opted for jeans and a T-shirt. It's true that Ida's house was cooler than it could have been, but I was still second-guessing my clothing choice when Ida came back into the room carrying a large glass of lemonade. As I took it from her, I realized she wasn't sweating. It was obvious I was more sensitive to the high temperatures than she was. Maybe some people adjust to this kind of heat when they're not used to air-conditioning. Obviously, I would never be one of them. All I could think about was going home and sitting in front of the air conditioner until my face froze.

"Now, Gracie," she said, as she sat down again, "before we talk about anything else, you must tell me about Hannah. How did she do in Wichita? Was your art teacher able to help her?"

I took a big gulp of lemonade before answering her. "It—it didn't go well, Ida," I said. "Hannah loved Wichita. In fact, she wanted to stay there. My teacher offered to let her live with him and go to a local magnet school that specializes in art classes." I put the lemonade down and sighed. "The truth is, I had to force her to come home."

Ida was quiet for a moment. With anyone else, I would have expected a stern "I told you so," but that wasn't Ida's style. "My, my," she said softly. "And how do her parents feel about this?"

"What do you think? They're very disappointed. And not just in Hannah. They're upset with me, too. Obviously, taking her to Wichita was a mistake. A big mistake."

"*Ach, liebling.* I am not sure you are right about this."

I raised my eyebrows at her. "How can you say that? Hannah's angry and taking out her frustration on her parents. She's being a—a pill!"

Ida smiled. "Please understand that I am not saying Hannah's actions are correct. God says in His Holy Word that children should respect and obey their parents. She is clearly in the wrong. But is it not better that the Muellers find out how Hannah feels now when they can still have an influence over her? Would it have been better for Hannah to have moved away from those who love her and then had this reaction?" Ida shook her head. "No. I am a firm believer in God's promise that all things work together for our good for those of us who love Him and are called according to His purpose. Hannah loves God, Gracie. She will find the right way, and God will use this experience to teach her something very valuable."

"I hope you're right, Ida. I really do."

"I am certain God's Word is truer than the circumstances that surround us." She peered into my face. "And I am also sure that it is time for you to forgive yourself. You have done nothing wrong.

Hannah is responsible for her own choices. What you did for Hannah you did because you care for her. That was the intent of your heart. You must remember this. You gave up six weeks of your own life to help someone else."

"Pastor Jensen preached about forgiveness this morning, and I know my heart was in the right place. I just wish I'd listened to you and the Muellers. You both warned me taking Hannah to Wichita might turn out badly."

The elderly woman laughed lightly. "And do I look like God to you? My dear sweet Gracie, people have opinions about things. Sometimes they believe they know what is right, but God is the only One who really knows the truth. You must not always take my advice to heart. You had to make a decision, and you chose the path you thought was right. We all make choices we wish we could take back. But I think our Father does not like it when we feel condemnation for our mistakes. He paid the ultimate price so there would be no separation between Him and the ones He loves. Why do we want to turn our back on His gift of forgiveness and righteousness?" She smiled. "Long ago I became convinced that true humility is believing what God says instead of following what we feel or think. So when God tells me that there is now no condemnation for those who are in Christ Jesus, I humbly choose to believe Him—even if I don't feel worthy of His acceptance." She shrugged her thin shoulders. "Only one of these things is true. Either there is no condemnation—or there is. I must choose.

And I choose His truth over mine."

"That's exactly what Pastor Jensen said. God must be trying to tell me something." I reached over and hugged her. "Thanks, Ida."

"Just remember that God loves you, child. Every minute of every day, and that will never, ever change." She sighed. "And when you try to do something right, but it looks as if you were wrong, some people will misunderstand. I have certainly experienced this myself. That is why we must not seek to please people—but to please God. Trying to keep people happy with us is impossible and will always cause us unnecessary pain and confusion."

"I love Abel and Emily so much; it hurts that they blame me."

"Ach, no," Ida said with a wave of her hand. "I am certain they do not really blame you. These are godly people who know it is not your fault. They are just worried about their little girl. You must not take their words seriously right now."

"I'll try not to," I said, praying she was right. Abel and Emily were like family, and the idea of losing their friendship troubled me deeply.

"We must pray right now," Ida said, grasping both my hands. "We must pray for Hannah."

We closed our eyes and Ida began to pray. She thanked God for loving Hannah and giving her wisdom. She also prayed for peace in the Muellers' home. As she spoke, faith rose up inside me, and by the time she'd finished, I knew God had heard her prayer. I felt a wave of calm assurance wash through me.

When Ida let go of my hands, I picked up the

glass of lemonade she'd brought me. I was suddenly so thirsty I could barely stand it. "This is delicious," I said after taking a long drink.

"*Ja,* my mother taught me to make lemonade," Ida said. "I will tell you the secret." She leaned over as if someone were listening, ready to steal her recipe, and sell it the masses. "It is honey." She straightened up, a look of pride on her face. "My mother used honey and I use honey."

I took another drink. It really was delicious. "It's wonderful. Where do you get the honey?"

"I used to buy it from Abigail Bradley. Unfortunately, I am on my very last jar. She sold her hives several months ago due to her poor health. She could no longer keep her honey business going." Ida frowned. "I do not believe you have met Abigail. She is a very private person. She does not leave her house anymore and has not done so for quite some time. Her neighbor gets her groceries when they buy their own, and they check on her when they can. However, in other areas she will not allow people to assist her. The house she lives in needs repair, but all offers to help her have been rejected. I assume it is her pride that compels her."

Abigail Bradley. I'd heard the name before but where? Suddenly I remembered. "Sarah mentioned her once. She seemed uncomfortable talking about her though. I believe Sarah actually called her 'strange.'"

Ida sighed and shook her head. "I understand how Sarah feels. Abigail is. . .unusual. But she has had a very hard and confusing life. Abigail is the only child of very strict parents. As a young woman, she spent many years in rebellion against them and their beliefs. Then she married a man named Bradley. During her marriage she chased after some very different kinds of religions. I believe her husband also had some odd beliefs. Now what was it..." Ida strained to recapture a fading memory. Finally she shrugged. "Oh my. I am not sure, but it was something unusual. If I remember right, spaceships were involved somehow." She gave me a small smile. "It was the seventies. A very strange time in the world. There were many curious beliefs circulating back then." Ida giggled at the look on my face. "You think I am so separated from the world, I do not know about the seventies?"

I grinned. "Nothing you know surprises me anymore, Ida. But I have to ask. Without TV or newspapers, where did you get your information?"

She chuckled. "Well, I like to visit with my friends at the restaurant, and they talk about many things." She held a hand up to her cheek. "In fact, I have heard conversations in that place that would have turned my hair gray if it had not already happened!"

Her expression made me laugh. "Why Ida. You're blushing."

"You see," she said, shaking her finger at me. "I am not quite as sheltered as you believed."

I'd lived in Harmony long enough to know that whatever Ida had overheard would be considered incredibly tame by most standards. But to her it was probably scandalous. "So tell me more about Abigail," I said, draining the last of my drink.

The old woman stood to her feet. "I will do so but first, more lemonade."

After she disappeared into her kitchen, I gazed around the sparse but comfortable living room. I knew Ida missed her husband, but she had adapted without complaining and feeling sorry for herself. In fact, I couldn't remember her ever voicing one word of self-pity. She was a remarkable woman, and when I compared myself to her, I definitely came up short.

"Here we go," she said, as she came back with two glasses in her hands. "I had a lemonade earlier, but I have decided to splurge and help myself to a second one." She shook her head. "Sometimes I think the honey stimulates me too much, but today I will not be concerned about that." She handed me my glass and sat down again. After taking a sip, she placed her drink on the table next to her. "Now where was I? Oh yes. Abigail. After her husband 'went off the deep end,' as she put it, she left him and traveled, trying to *find herself*, whatever that means." Ida's forehead wrinkled in confusion. "I have no idea why a person would need to find herself. We are with ourselves all the time, ja?"

I grinned. "Ja."

"Anyway, after running around the country for many years and becoming ill, she was taken in by a Mennonite couple who cared for her. Although they were not Old Order, their mother was. Abigail latched on to her like a puppy following its mama, I guess, although I am certain Abigail would express it differently. She told me the mother was her *mentor*. So, she adopted the Old Order ways." She held her hands up in a gesture of surrender. "That is the whole story. To be honest with you, I feel she became Mennonite not because she believed in our ways but because our lifestyle reminded her of the parents she left behind. And perhaps she was also looking for a place to hide." Ida frowned. "I do not want to escape from the world. I choose to keep my life free from distractions that may separate me from my precious Savior. However, I fear Abigail has a completely different reason for her choices."

"But how did she end up in Harmony?" I suddenly realized I was no longer feeling hot. Hopefully it was because of Ida's interesting story and not the first stage of heatstroke.

"Actually, the family she lived with brought her here during a visit to a relative who owned the house where Abigail now resides. When the family member died, Abigail bought the house and moved to Harmony with her son. Until then, the boy had been living with his father, but he died, leaving the child without a home. So Abigail brought him here, and he lived with her until he left for college. He moved away not long after your parents left Harmony. Abigail has stayed alone in that house ever since." She rubbed her hands together like she was cold. "In truth, I was glad to see her son leave. He was such an unhappy boy. Abigail brought him up very harshly, with many rules and restrictions. Several people tried to help, to tell her she was hurting him. He became extremely withdrawn and would act out sometimes in town with the other boys. Unfortunately, after Abigail became frustrated with his behavior, she eventually kept him home almost all the time." She rubbed her chin. "I remember that he had a girlfriend once. He was very much in love with her. A beautiful girl as I remember with hair the color of wheat and startling blue eyes. What was her name?" Ida stared into space for a moment. "Melanie, I think. Melanie Pemberton. But Abigail's interference broke them up. The girl's family moved away not long after that, and I never saw C.J. smile again. It was so sad. I was glad to hear he was going to college." She sighed. "Higher education was discouraged back then in our group, but I believed C.J. needed to get away before Abigail broke his spirit."

"Did Abigail know my uncle Benjamin?"

Ida nodded. "Oh yes. In fact, I believe Abigail had some interest in him as a husband. Benjamin did not return her feelings, but he was close to the boy until he left Harmony." She smoothed out her skirt with her age-spotted hands. "Your grandfather did not like the boy, though. When they were young, he forbade your father and your uncle from spending time with him outside of school. I have no idea why, but Joe felt C.J. was a bad influence. I disagreed with him at the time because I felt C.J. needed good examples in his young life. Joe would have none of it." She sighed. "Joe could have been such a help to the boy. To this day I do not understand why he could not extend a hand of friendship. Joe wouldn't talk about it. So you see why I was happy when C.J. went away. I hope he has turned out right. He has been in my prayers for quite some time."

"When was the last time you saw Abigail?"

"It has been a while," Ida acknowledged. "Our small group used to take turns meeting in each other's homes, but then she refused to leave her house. We started gathering together at her place, but now our numbers have dwindled, and there are no more home churches. Most of us have chosen to attend Bethel, including the Ketterlings and the Voglers. That just leaves the Beckenbauer brothers and Abigail. The brothers have both been too ill to attend church, so Abigail has been alone. I have invited her several times to Bethel, but she has declined my invitations. She believes the church is too liberal." She smiled sadly. "I have tried to talk to her about this, but it has been to no avail. I am not certain her standards are the only reason for her refusal. I think she is now too afraid to leave her home. The last time I saw her was in May when I hitched up Zebediah and rode over to see her."

"Are you worried about her?"

"Well, as I said, her neighbors were checking on her and buying her groceries, but with the wheat harvest going on, I am sure they do not have the time to keep a close watch on her. I must admit that I am concerned." She jabbed at her right leg with her finger. "This leg of mine has been so stiff and sore the last few months, and the trip to Abigail's takes quite a while. But that is no excuse. I will ride over to see her after I visit with your parents and grandfather tomorrow." She clapped her hands together.

"I am so excited. Do you know what time they will arrive?"

"Sweetie is hosting a big dinner tomorrow night to welcome them. One reason I came over was to invite you. Either Sam or I will pick you up around six if that's okay."

"Oh ja. I would love to go. But you do not need to worry yourself about me. I will hitch up Zeb and carry myself."

"I thought perhaps Zeb would rather stay in his shed since it's so hot. Wouldn't that be better for him?" The horse was as old and decrepit as its owner. I dreaded the day something happened to him. Ida treated him like a dear, beloved friend.

"Well, you may be right," she acknowledged. "If it would not be too much trouble. . ."

I stood up, leaned over, and kissed her cheek. "It would most definitely not be too much trouble. Now I must get home. I need to get to bed early so I'll be bright and cheerful when my family arrives."

Ida also stood to her feet. "Ach, I hope I will be able to sleep tonight due to my exhilaration. Do you believe your grandfather will remember me?"

Ida knew my grandfather was battling Alzheimer's. "I'm not sure, but it's his short-term memory that seems to be the most affected. I think it's very possible he will know exactly who you are."

"I hope so," she said, a tinge of sadness in her voice. "How awful for him to be trapped in a mind that does not work the way it should. It is so heartbreaking, ja?"

"Yes it is." I gave her a quick hug. "I'll see you tomorrow."

"See you tomorrow, *liebling*. And remember, we have prayed for Hannah and God has listened. I expect everything to turn out right. You must do so, too, ja?"

I nodded. "Thanks, Ida. I always feel better after speaking to you."

"That means more to me than you know, my dearest Gracie," she said softly.

I'd already opened the front door when a thought struck me. "Ida, what if I go by and check on Abigail sometime in the next few days. Would that help?"

"Oh Gracie, I do not know. She does not know you, although I did tell her about you." She considered my question for several seconds. Finally she said, "Perhaps if you tell her who you are and that I sent you, she will receive you." She looked at me hopefully. "It would be wonderful if you could make certain she is well. And it would save Zeb and me from that long ride."

"Even if she refuses to see me, at least we'll know she's okay," I said. "Let me get my folks settled in, and then I'll drive over there. Don't worry about her, okay?"

"Ja, ja. Thank you, Gracie. You are such a blessing to me." Her face crinkled up in an angelic smile.

"And you are a blessing to me." I waved good-bye and closed the screen door behind me.

After I got home, I spent the rest of the evening adding a few last touches to the house. On the way back from Ida's, I'd picked some of the wildflowers that grew near the large lake behind my property.

I placed the flowers in vases and scattered them throughout the house, making certain the upstairs bedrooms had the loveliest arrangements.

Although I climbed into bed early, I had trouble falling asleep. I kept thinking about seeing my family again. It had been a while since I'd been to Nebraska, and it was the first time they'd been to Harmony in thirty years. Their departure had been under negative circumstances, and I couldn't help but wonder if they'd see the differences now. The tyrannical bishop who once ruled the town with an iron fist had been gone a long time. Abel Mueller's compassionate leadership helped to change Harmony's complexion—along with the commitment of its citizens to keep the peace they worked so hard to protect. I felt sure my parents would be pleased to find their hometown's current condition.

Finally, a little after eleven o'clock I fell asleep. It seemed like only minutes later when I awoke to the sound of pounding coming from downstairs. I struggled to sit up and focus my eyes so I could see the numbers on the clock that sat on the dresser across the room. Five thirty? The insistent knocking continued. Dressed only in a pair of boxers and a T-shirt, I grabbed a robe out of the closet and hurried down the stairs, trying to pat my hair into place. I flipped on the front porch light and swung the door open to find Abel and Emily standing there. The looks on their faces sucked the breath out of my lungs.

"She's gone, Gracie," Emily said, tears running down her face. "Hannah's missing!"

SIX

By seven thirty, my little kitchen was full to overflowing with people. Sweetie and Sam drove over after my frantic phone call. I'd called Pat Taylor, and as he tried to sort out the situation with Abel and Emily, Sweetie glared at him while Sam stayed busy trying to ignore him.

"So you checked on Hannah around five o'clock this morning?" Pat said. "Isn't that a little early?"

Emily shook her head. Her large brown eyes reflected her fear. Her prayer covering sat crookedly on her head, and stray brown hairs touched with silver peeked out from underneath it due to a hastily pulled-together bun. "I wake up early every morning. It's my quiet time with the Lord." She stared at the bleary-eyed law enforcement officer who clearly hadn't expected to be rushed out of bed at sunrise. Her eyes spilled over with tears. "I—I just felt as if something wasn't right. When I opened the door to her room, I could see that her bed was empty."

Pat frowned. "Was the bed messy? Had it been slept in?"

Emily hesitated for a moment. "No. As a matter

of fact, it was made up. I hadn't thought about it. What does that mean?"

He didn't answer. Instead his eyes darted around the room, studying each of us carefully. I felt like a bug under a microscope. Everyone but Sweetie met his gaze. "Anything unusual happen lately? Any reason this young woman has to be upset or angry?"

I quickly filled him in on Hannah's desire to stay in Wichita. "But that couldn't possibly have anything to do with this," I said. "For one thing, Hannah adores her parents and would never just leave without a word. She knows how much it would hurt them. And anyway, she has nowhere to go. Jim Monahan, the art teacher in Wichita, would never allow her to stay with him without her parents' permission."

"I'm gonna need his contact information," Pat growled. He put his notepad on the table and scowled at us. "Any other place she might go?"

"Not that I can think of. Well, maybe my friend Allison's since that's where we stayed. But she doesn't even know Allison. There's really no reason she'd head there."

"Give me the number anyway," he said, sighing. "You people really don't think a girl who didn't want to come home would run off if she's forced back? Have any of you actually thought this out?"

"Of course they have," Sam retorted. "Abel and Emily know their daughter, and they're frightened. Maybe you should pay attention to what they're trying to tell you."

Pat locked eyes with his son. "I'm paying

attention," he said, his tone a little softer, "but Hannah hasn't been abducted. She's run away." He turned his gaze to Abel and Emily. "You said there was no sign of forced entry. Her bed was made. Did you happen to check to see if any of her clothes are missing?"

"Of course not," Abel snapped. "Our minds were a little occupied. Checking out her wardrobe wasn't our first concern."

"Look Pat," I interjected. "Even if she ran away of her own accord, you still need to find her. She could get into trouble."

"I agree, and I have every intention of looking for her," he said. "A girl who's lived the kind of sheltered life she has shouldn't be out there on her own." He stopped and studied Abel and Emily for a moment. "She would be on her own, right? Is there a boyfriend in the picture?"

"Hannah hasn't run off with a boy," I said.

"There's no boyfriend," Abel agreed.

"Well, actually. . ." Emily said, looking at her husband.

Abel's eyebrows knit together as he stared back at his wife. "What are you saying? There's a boy in her life? Why don't I know anything about this?"

Emily lifted the skirt of the apron she wore over her dress and wiped her eyes. "The boy isn't actually in her life, but Hannah told me last week she has a crush on Jonathan Vogler. I doubt he even knows it."

Pat picked up his notebook again and scribbled in it. "Won't hurt to check it out."

"What do you intend to do, Sheriff?" Abel asked,

skepticism written clearly on his face.

"I intend to look for your daughter. I'd like to come by your place and inspect her bedroom, if you don't mind. Any clues I can find as to her frame of mind might help me to locate her."

Abel stood to his feet and held his wife's arm as she rose from her chair. "That would be fine. We'll meet you there."

"Don't straighten up," Pat said, his tone serious. "In fact, don't touch anything. Just wait for me."

"Yes, we understand. You have our address?"

"I do. You go on. I'll be right behind you."

"Abel—Emily," I said. "If you need anything. . ."

"I think you've done quite enough," Emily said angrily. "I'd appreciate it if you'd just stay away from us for a while." She turned and fled out my front door.

Abel waited until he heard the door slam. "I'm sorry, Gracie," he said gently. "Emily's nerves are on edge." He gave me a smile that didn't reach his eyes. "Please be patient with us." He quickly followed his wife out of my house.

I put my head in my hands. Emily's words played over and over in my mind. I could feel tears on my fingers, but I didn't care. The loudest voice in my head at that moment was the one that criticized me. Was this really my fault? Sweetie's voice cut through my thoughts.

"That's just ridiculous," she sputtered. "Gracie, don't you pay her no nevermind. You ain't done nothin' wrong. You was tryin' to help that girl. Don't you let them bad words get into your head, you hear me?"

I nodded but didn't say anything. Sweetie's sentiments echoed Ida's and Pastor Jensen's, but I still felt responsible.

After a long silence, Pat said, "Guess I better get going."

"Wait a minute," I choked out. I picked up a napkin on the table and wiped my eyes. "I didn't want to say anything in front of Abel and Emily, but what about those other girls who have gone missing? Hannah looks just like them."

Pat looked at me like my brain had just jumped out of my head and run out of the room.

"An unhappy girl running away has nothing to do with that," he said. "Besides, no one's sure those cases are even related."

Without telling him who said it, I recounted Bill's information. As I talked, Pat's eyebrows kept rising higher and higher. When I finished he glared at me. "And just who told you all this?"

"I—I can't tell you. It was said to us in confidence."

Sam let out a long breath. "Which actually means you're not supposed to share it with anyone."

I waved my hand dismissively at him. "This is important, Sam. Hannah's life could be at stake. I'm not going to risk her safety just to keep a secret."

"Except that it may not be correct. Word-of-mouth information isn't very reliable."

"I don't care," I said sharply. I ignored Sam and focused my attention on Pat. "Look, I have a bad feeling about this. I realize it looks like Hannah's run away. But things are different in Mennonite families.

There's a bond that is too strong to be broken. Hannah would never just leave. She wouldn't. . ." Suddenly, something Hannah said before we left Wichita flashed through my mind. *"Maybe you like hiding out in Harmony, but I don't intend to spend the rest of my life buried there."* I gulped and stared at Pat with wide eyes.

"What?" he asked.

"N–nothing. It's just. . ."

"You might as well tell us, Grace," Sam said matter-of-factly. "Honesty is always the best policy."

I rolled my eyes at him. "And a stitch in time saves nine, but overused clichés aren't helpful right now."

"Quit stalling," he said. "You just remembered something. Did Hannah threaten to run away?"

"No. I mean. . .maybe." I stared back at the three pairs of eyes fastened on me. "Look," I said with a sigh, "she said something in the heat of the moment about not wanting to live in Harmony. But she wasn't referring to *now*. I'm sure she meant after she graduates."

Sweetie grunted. "I don't think you know what she meant." She shook her head. "Time was Mennie kids wasn't allowed to go past the eighth grade. Now they're finishin' high school and goin' off to college. Seems to me this girl is pushin' the line. She should be grateful she's got folks who support her as much as they do."

I felt my face flush. "I hardly think you're an expert on child rearing. In fact, none of you have a clue about what a real family should be. You can't even solve your own problems. I doubt seriously you can figure out anyone else's."

As soon as the words left my mouth I knew they were wrong. Sam's face flushed, and Sweetie's expression turned almost toxic.

Pat cleared his throat and stood up. "Look Gracie, I'm going to look for Hannah, and I'll post a missing person's report. But that's all I can do unless I find some compelling evidence that makes me believe something else is going on here besides a simple case of a girl who's left home because she didn't get her way." He picked his hat up from the table. "If you find anything that might send me in a different direction, you let me know. I'm going over to the Muellers' to look around. I'll keep you updated. Good-bye."

His last word was directed at everyone in the room, not just me. But I was the only one who responded. Sam and Sweetie's attitude toward Pat wasn't going to help us find Hannah. I waited until I heard the front door close. "I am so tired of this," I said pointedly to them both. "Can't you two forget your anger for a while? Hannah should come first now." I stood up and faced them, my hands on my hips. "You both sit in church every Sunday and hear about the goodness and forgiveness of God. But when it comes to practicing it, you're pretty pitiful."

Sweetie rose to her feet. "I'm headin' home. I got work to do." She pointed her finger at me. "I know the Word says I gotta forgive that man, and I'm tryin'. But it's not gonna happen overnight. When I do it, it's gotta be from my heart. And my heart just ain't in it yet." She frowned at me. "Besides, maybe you need to quit bein' Holy Ghost junior. Sam and I will deal with things in our own way—and in our own time." She dropped her hand to her side and stomped out of my kitchen.

I stood there with my mouth open. "I—I do not think I'm Holy Ghost junior," I stammered. "Why in the world. . ."

Sam came over and put his arms around me, covering my mouth with his before I could get another word out. Finally he took his lips from mine. "Listen," he said gently, "you're very passionate about the people you love, and I adore that in you. But sometimes you need to leave things alone and let people work situations out on their own. You've told me and Sweetie your opinion about Pat more times than I can count. Now hush and let us deal with it in our own way. Your comment about none of us having a clue about what family means was not only unkind, it was untrue. Sweetie and I understand family better than most people. That might be why we're so careful to protect it. Until Pat proves himself, we have no intention of opening ourselves up to a relationship that might end up being destructive."

I gently pushed him away. "I just want you to be happy. He's your father. . ."

"Grace," he retorted, "I know who he is. So does Sweetie. You don't need to constantly remind us."

I slumped back down in my chair. Sam went to the coffeemaker, picked up the pot, and carried it over to the table. After taking care of refills, he sat down, too. "I love you," he said with a smile. "And I respect you. But that's a two-way street."

His comment stirred up my indignation all over again. "I do respect you, Sam. How can you say something like that?"

"I can say it because sometimes you treat me like a child, and I'm not your child. I'm going to be your husband. It's okay to try to help me, but it's not okay to try to straighten me out all the time. Since I found out who Pat really is, you've tried to get your point across by shaming me, encouraging me, tricking me. . ."

"Hey, wait a minute! I've never tried to trick you."

Sam gave me a lopsided grin. "Oh really. What about that goofy story you read to me the other day from the Topeka paper? About the man who had a fight with his brother?"

"You mean the one where he finally decides to visit his brother and finds out that he's been dead inside his house for a year?"

Sam nodded.

"I wasn't sharing that story because of you and Pat. I read it to you because it was just. . .creepy."

His right eyebrow disappeared under his bangs, but he didn't say anything. He didn't have to.

"Okay, okay," I said heatedly. "I get it. I really do. No more comments about Pat. But I really do think. . ."

"Grace," Sam warned.

"I said *okay*." I took a sip of coffee. "Let's change the subject. I'm really worried about Hannah, Sam. Something's just not right. I really don't think she'd run away without a word."

He stared at the table for a few moments. "You know what? I tend to agree with you. Pat doesn't know Harmony the way we do. I realize Hannah saw something in Wichita that excited her, but to throw away everything she's believed in her entire life and leave this place and her parents behind? It's very hard to accept."

I sighed with relief. "Thank God someone believes me. But what can we do?"

"I don't know. Let's wait until Pat goes over to the Muellers' house. Maybe he'll find something helpful that will point him in the right direction. In the meantime, what was the name of that boy Hannah likes?"

"Jonathan Vogler."

"Aren't they that Old Order family that lives right outside of town?"

I nodded. "Ida said they just recently started going to Bethel. I've seen them, but I don't know them at all."

"I think I'll check up on him," Sam said. "See if he knows anything."

"Great. Can I come with you?"

"Well, I don't mean right this minute, Grace. But I will try to find out what I can as soon as possible. Besides, don't you need to hang around here and wait for your parents?"

I put my hand on the side of my face. "Yikes! My parents. I almost forgot." As realization dawned, a feeling of dread filled me. "Oh Sam, I promised my mom and dad that Harmony had changed. They think they're coming to a wonderful, peaceful town. Instead they're coming to a place full of anger—and most of it's directed at me."

"Grace, Harmony is *not* full of anger. For crying out loud, just because Emily's blaming you for the way Hannah's acting, it doesn't mean five hundred people are in some kind of uncontrolled frenzy."

His frustration made me realize I'd blown the situation out of proportion. "You're right. I'm just so anxious for this homecoming to go well. You know my parents wanted us to have the wedding in Fairbury. They were both reluctant to come back to Harmony. They only agreed because of me. If they get here and everything is messed up. . . Well, it just can't happen, that's all." I blinked back tears that threatened to spill down my cheeks again.

Sam reached over and put his hand under my chin. "We need to pray for Hannah, and we need to pray over your parents' trip. Then you need to trust God and stop worrying, okay?"

I nodded. Sam removed his hand from my face and took my hands in his. We prayed for several minutes. When we finished, I felt better.

"Why do I keep forgetting that God doesn't want me to worry or fret about anything?" I smiled at Sam. "I'm so thankful I have you to get on my case when I start trying to do God's job for Him."

Sam stood to his feet and pulled me up with him. "Keeping you straightened out is my cross to bear, I guess."

I laughed. "Poor boy. Do you think you can

handle it?"

He put his arms around me. "I'm a pretty determined fellow, willing to spend the rest of our lives finding out."

His warm breath on the back of my neck made me shiver, and I playfully pushed him away. "I need to clean up the kitchen and get ready for my folks. My dad said he'd call me before they left, and I haven't heard a word. I'm guessing he forgot. I have no idea when they'll show up."

"I've got some apple picking to do. I could come back when I'm done and wait with you."

"Oh that would be wonderful. That way I can introduce you to my folks when they arrive. And I wouldn't have to sit here by myself."

"Sounds good." Sam started to walk out of the kitchen, but at the doorway he stopped. Then he turned and frowned at me. "Do I have your word that you won't spend your time worrying about Hannah?"

I held my right hand up as if swearing an oath. "I promise."

I followed him out to the front porch and waved good-bye as he drove away. The rising sun spread its colors across the awakening sky with blues, pinks, and oranges. I stared out across the green farmland and lush trees that made up Harmony. But my mind was filled with thoughts other than the beauty of the countryside. Where could Hannah be? Was she safe? I tried to keep my promise and cast my care on the Lord, but uneasiness filled my heart. Of one thing I was certain: no matter what Pat Taylor said, I would do everything in my power to find the young Mennonite girl and bring her home.

SEVEN

Sam made it back to my place by two. A little after three o'clock I heard a car door slam outside and rushed to the front door. I flung it open in time to see my father get out of his car. When he saw me, he smiled widely and said, "Hi, Snicklefritz!"

I ran down the steps and flung myself into his open arms. Even the use of a nickname I hated couldn't take away my joy at seeing him. There's something about fathers and their daughters. I can't explain it, but every time I see my dad I instantly feel safe.

"Don't lean on him," my mother exclaimed loudly. "His leg is still giving him problems."

I let go of him. "I thought your leg would be completely healed by now."

"It's getting stronger every day," he said. He scowled at my mother. "You hush, Bev. You're making me sound like an old man. I'm fine."

"Phooey," she retorted. She reached into the car and pulled out a black cane. "He still has pain. The break hasn't healed just right, and the doctor told him to take it easy."

She came around the car and handed the cane to

my dad who took it reluctantly. "Well, bum leg or not, I'm still glad to see you."

"Me, too, Dad."

As I hugged my mother, I could smell her perfume. Chantilly. The only scent she ever wore. "I've missed you so much," I whispered to her.

"Not as much as I've missed you."

I looked toward Sam who had come down the stairs and stood watching us. I ran over and grabbed his arm, pulling him toward my parents. "Dad and Mom, this is Sam."

My father stepped forward and stuck out his hand. "Sam, I'm happy to finally meet you. I'm sorry it took us so long to get together. First I couldn't travel, and then Gracie spent all those weeks in Wichita. I regret that. I don't like meeting my son-in-law-to-be only two weeks before he marries my daughter."

I looked closely at Dad. There was an edge to his voice I recognized. He's a very civilized man, but I can always tell when he's upset. Sam obviously noticed, too, because his smile tightened.

"I'm sorry about that, too, sir," he said. "I would have come to Nebraska to meet you, but it seemed like every time I could find the time to leave the farm, Grace was in Wichita. I hope we'll have some quality time together before the wedding."

"I hope so, too." My father's serious tone matched his expression. An uncomfortable silence was interrupted by my mother's cheery voice.

"Well, I'm certainly grateful we're getting together now." She shot my father a quick look of disapproval.

"We would have come to visit before now, but Daniel's leg and his attitude toward Harmony prevented it."

My father started to protest, but my mother hushed him. "Now Daniel, why don't we let Sam help us with our bags? You need to stretch that leg out, and it wouldn't hurt you and Papa to take a nap before dinner."

In the excitement I'd almost forgotten about Papa Joe. My father opened the car door to the backseat and held out his arm.

" 'Bout time," my grandfather said as he climbed out of the car. "Thought you were gonna leave me in there all day."

"Papa Joe," I cried. "I'm so glad to see you!"

Although he was frailer and his hair was much thinner, his smile reminded me of the grandfather I remembered. I was thrilled to see the old familiar twinkle in his eyes. I rushed over to hug him. He felt thin beneath his Windbreaker.

"I'm glad to see you, too," he said.

"It's Gracie, Dad," my father said loudly.

I let him go and looked into his face. Didn't he know me?

"I'm aware that it's Gracie, Daniel," he responded brusquely. "I haven't completely lost my mind."

My father shot me a quick look. He was obviously concerned, and I felt the same way. The last time I'd seen Papa Joe, I couldn't get him to talk to me at all. He'd just stared at me as if he'd never seen me before. I'm no expert on Alzheimer's, but I'd read that people can suddenly seem to snap out of it, and then without warning, retreat behind that black curtain again. Could that be what worried my father?

"Let's get you inside," I said, taking his hand. "I'll bet you'd like to rest a bit before dinner."

He took his hand from mine and wrapped it around my arm for more support. "I am a little tired," he confessed. "It was a long drive." He suddenly stopped and stared at the house. "Oh my," he whispered. I looked into his face and saw tears well up in his eyes.

"What is it, Papa?"

"I wondered if I'd ever get to see this place again." His eyes scanned the house and the yard. He pointed to the flower bed surrounded by bricks in the middle of the front yard. "Essie's irises," he said, choking up. He swung his gaze back to me. "Thank you for keeping this place, my darling Gracie. Thank you for letting me come home."

I hugged him, too emotional to speak. But in my heart I thanked God for guiding me to my decision to stay in Harmony so I could be a part of this moment. What if I'd sold the house the way I'd originally planned?

I saw my father wiping his eyes. My mother grabbed his arm and helped him up the steps and into the house. Papa, Sam, and I followed behind them. Thankfully, except for a few changes, I'd kept the inside as close to the way I'd found it as possible. Papa Joe stopped at the large cherry secretary and ran his hands over it.

"This is where I work, Papa." I opened the rolled top to show him my keyboard that pulled out on a sliding shelf. I also opened the cabinet doors so he could see my flat-panel monitor. Sam had removed one of the shelves so it would fit inside. He'd also added the sliding shelf. I loved the old secretary and was happy I could use it as a work space without compromising the integrity of the design. I'd purchased a padded antique chair that matched the secretary as if it had been made for it. My CPU was tucked away between the side of the secretary and the wall so it wasn't noticeable.

"It's beautiful, Gracie," Papa said, his voice so soft I could barely hear him. Then he made his way over to the rocking chair my uncle had crafted. He stared at it a few moments before lowering himself into it. "Benjamin made this, didn't he?"

"Yes, Papa. In fact, Harmony is full of his rocking chairs, birdhouses, and bird feeders."

He smiled. "I taught him how to build those things. We used to work on them together. I'm glad he kept at it. He was very clever with his hands."

"Papa, why don't you stay there while Sam and I carry our luggage upstairs?" my dad said.

"I've got some cider in the refrigerator," I said. "I'll get everyone a glass while you're doing that."

"Sounds great." My father looked at Sam. "Maybe you'll help me get the bags from the car? Then we can get them into the appropriate rooms."

"Daniel Temple, you are not carrying suitcases up the stairs," my mother said sharply. "The doctor told you to rest that leg. Sam looks quite capable of getting our luggage by himself."

"Of course. I'd be happy to," Sam said with a smile.

My father grunted. "I guess working on a farm means he should be capable of manual labor." He glared at my mother. "I'll go out and show him what to bring in if that's acceptable to you."

"Of course it is. And maybe you can work on your attitude while you're out there."

My dad didn't say another word, just headed toward the front door. My rather confused fiancé followed behind him, casting a worried glance my way. All I could do was shrug.

In several phone conversations about my upcoming marriage, I hadn't caught a hint of animosity. His rude comment about Sam was out of character for my usually well-mannered father. I waited until the door closed behind them.

"What gives?" I asked my mother who stood near the kitchen door with her arms crossed. "Is Dad upset about the wedding for some reason?"

She shook her head. "I have no idea what's going on. He was fine until we started getting close to Harmony. Then suddenly he began complaining about not having time to get to know Sam before you get married." She sighed. "I think it's coming back here again. Bad memories. Then there's the pressure of watching Papa deal with this awful disease. Give your father a little slack. He's under a lot of pressure. I'm sure he'll snap out of it."

"I hope so. All I need is one more person who's upset with me."

My mother's eyebrows shot up. "Who's upset? Is something wrong?"

I put my hands up in a gesture of surrender. "Let's talk about it later, okay? I'm really happy you're here, and I'd rather spend the day catching up. I'll fill you in on all the Harmony drama tomorrow."

She hesitated. "Well. . .all right. But you know I don't like secrets."

I chuckled. "Yes, I'm very aware of that, but this has nothing to do with secrets."

I'd started toward the kitchen when Papa Joe spoke up. "Hey, Gracie. What do you get from a pampered cow?"

I grinned at him. "I don't know, Papa. What do you get from a pampered cow?"

A big smile creased his face. "Spoiled milk."

I laughed, although to be honest, I felt like crying. I never thought I'd hear my grandfather tell another one of his awful jokes again. It filled my heart with joy. Unfortunately, that feeling was short-lived, for his next comment reminded me of the cruelty of Alzheimer's.

His face lost its jovial look, and he stared at me through narrowed eyes. "Now Gracie, whatever you do, don't forget your grandmother's wedding present. She'll be upset if you do."

I opened my mouth, but no words came out. Papa looked quizzically at me, as if my reaction confused him. Suddenly my mother spoke up.

"Gracie won't forget, Papa. Thanks for reminding us."

A look of peace settled over his face, and he leaned back in the rocking chair as if her words had allayed his concerns.

"Let's get that cider, Gracie," Mom said quietly. "I'm sure Papa would love some."

A few minutes later, we all sat in the living room sipping the fresh cider Sweetie had left in my refrigerator. Sam had carried all the suitcases up the stairs under my father's direction. Dad seemed more relaxed when they came downstairs.

"This is delicious," Dad said. He smiled at me. "Thanks for putting Mom and me in my old room. I can't believe how good it looks." He shook his head. "It's almost as if I just walked out the door of this house yesterday. Almost everything is the same."

"Except for the lights and air-conditioning," my mother said laughing. "That's one thing about Harmony I don't miss. Surely everyone has electricity by now, don't they, Gracie?"

"Just about. There are a few holdouts. Ida Turnbauer doesn't, but she has a phone. And there are a few families outside of town that still live without the modern conveniences."

"I can hardly wait to see Ida," Dad said. "She was so good to me and Benjamin growing up. A truly kind lady. Your grandmother was very close to her."

I nodded. "She's become a very good friend."

"She's a good friend to everyone in town," Sam added. "I would say she's probably the most loved and respected woman in Harmony."

My dad smiled. "I'm glad to hear that. It means a lot to me to know that she's happy." He looked at Sam. "I can hardly believe your aunt is Myrtle Goodrich. She was the most beautiful woman in Harmony when

I was a boy. And as stubborn and hardworking as they come. When her father had his accident, everyone pitched in to help her." He chuckled. "And believe me, it wasn't an easy task. She had her own way of doing things and was bound and determined not to be seen as needy. We almost had to convince her she was doing us a favor by letting us help with her farm. I'm glad she was able to sell it and buy her new place. I got a glimpse of it on the way here. Incredible. Doesn't look anything like it did when we left Harmony. I can't wait to get a closer look."

"You'll get your chance at dinner tonight," I said, relieved that his mood had finally lightened.

"I look forward to it." He put his glass down and stood up. "I think I'd like to lie down for a bit before supper. And I think you wanted a quick nap, didn't you, Papa?"

Everyone looked at my grandfather who just stared into the distance, as if no one else were in the room.

"Papa?" I said. "Are you ready for a nap?"

"Never mind, Gracie," my father said. "We'll all go upstairs together." He grabbed his cane and leaning on it, walked over to where my grandfather sat. He helped him to his feet. "Come on, Papa. I'll take you upstairs."

"Daniel, let me do that," Mom said. "Your leg. . ."

"I can take care of it, Bev," my father snapped. "I'm not completely useless."

My mother frowned at him, but she didn't say anything.

Papa Joe looked at his son as if he'd never seen him before, but my father ignored the lost expression on his face and led him to the stairs like an adult would lead a little child, speaking to him in soft tones and encouraging him to keep going. No one in the room said a word until we heard the door to Papa's room close.

"You told me he was a lot better," I said to my mother.

She sighed. "He is. A few weeks ago he suddenly began to have moments of clarity. Then he started talking again. As we told you on the phone, he's on a new medication. Papa was severely depressed after Mama died. When the doctor started treating him for his depression, Papa got better. His emotional condition could have caused a lot of the symptoms we saw." She smiled sadly. "I can't explain why he suddenly has the ability to relate to his surroundings, but it's important to remember that he still has Alzheimer's. That hasn't changed. Several people from our Alzheimer's support group told us their loved one went through a period of improvement toward the end. I have no idea if the change we're seeing is the medicine. . .or something else." She hesitated. "This may sound silly to you two, but I almost wonder if it isn't a gift from God—a brief reprieve before he dies." She smiled sadly at me. "Besides the Alzheimer's, he has serious heart problems. This may sound awful, but I hope he dies from his heart condition before the Alzheimer's robs the last vestiges of his personality."

"I understand," I said. "But I still pray for healing. I believe with all my heart that it isn't God's will for Papa Joe to suffer."

Mom smiled. "I believe that, too, Gracie. But to be honest, I don't think Papa wants to be healed. He misses Mama a great deal. I think more than anything else in this world he wants to be with her." Her brow wrinkled in thought. "Strange though, how he rallied because of this trip. It was so important to him. He said it's because he wants to see Harmony again, but I get the feeling there's another reason as well. Something he doesn't seem willing to share with us."

"Maybe he wanted to see me," I said.

Mom patted my hand. "I'm sure that's true." She smiled. "Here I am trying to figure out what someone with Alzheimer's is thinking. I don't really have a clue why this trip meant so much to him, but he was absolutely determined to come. And you know Papa when he makes up his mind about something."

I laughed. "Yes, he's like a mad dog with a bone. You might as well just give in and forget it. I hope he gets whatever he wants from this visit. I'm certainly thrilled to see him." I sighed. "Boy, I hate Alzheimer's."

"No more than your father and I do," my mother assured me. "And please understand that we still pray for healing, too. We know nothing is impossible with God." She choked up. "When his mind seems to clear, every time I hope it's a sign. . ."

I got up and went over to her, wrapping my arms around her neck. "Papa is so fortunate to have you in his life. You've always loved him like he was your own father."

"Your other grandparents live so far away, and we don't see them very often. Papa and Mama were always near us after they left Harmony. They really have been like my very own parents all these years."

"I know."

I sat back down and drank my cider while Sam and my mother talked about the fruit farm. My mother is a great conversationalist. I think it's because she's really interested in people. Sam had just started sharing about the new pumpkin patch he and Sweetie just planted when my dad came back into the room.

"Papa's lying down now," he said. "He'll be confused sometimes. The best way to handle it is to just go along with him."

"We learned in our support group that some people try to straighten out loved ones who have the disease when they get confused," Mom said. "But it only frightens them." She leaned her cheek on her hand. "One day I pretended to be Essie an entire afternoon. It made him very happy."

"That makes sense," I said, but truthfully, none of this made sense at all. I couldn't comprehend why a man like Papa Joe, who had lived his life as a good, decent Christian man, should have to face something this awful at the end of his life. Where was the justice in it?

My mother rose to her feet. "Well, I don't know about anyone else, but I think I'll join Daniel for that nap. This has been a tiring day."

"I'd better get going," Sam said. He stood up and

smiled at my parents. "I'm looking forward to this evening. I know Sweetie and Ida can hardly wait."

"We're looking forward to it, too, Sam," Mom said. "I believe Gracie said we should be there at six, is that right?"

"We'll eat at six, but you can come early if you'd like, and I can show you the orchards."

"We'll have plenty of time to see your farm while we're here," my father said. "Six is soon enough. Bev and I need to get some rest this afternoon."

There was that tone again. I shot him a look, but he ignored me.

"Sure, that's fine," Sam said. "Whatever's best for you."

He turned to leave, and I followed him. "Let me walk you out," I said. Once we were on the front porch, I closed the door behind us. "I'm sorry, Sam. My dad is usually so easy to get along with. It's just stress. Coming back to Harmony, worrying about Papa Joe. And of course his leg. . ."

Sam grabbed my hand and pulled me down the stairs. Then he wrapped his arms around me. "I understand, Grace. Really. Don't worry about it. Tonight he'll get to see some old friends, eat some good food, and have the chance to relax a little. We'll be fine. Stop worrying."

I leaned against him. "I wish we were already married. Maybe we should have eloped."

He put his hand under my chin, raised my face to his, and gazed into my eyes. His own eyes always reminded me of the gray clouds that paint Kansas skies before a storm. "I disagree. You see, I'm waiting for that moment."

"What moment?"

He smiled. "That moment when you walk down the aisle. When everyone sees the incredibly beautiful woman who has decided to become my wife. I want to promise before God that I will love you for as long as I live. And I want to put my ring on your finger so the whole world knows you're mine." He shook his head. "No eloping for us. I intend to experience every moment of our wedding and keep it in my heart for the rest of my life."

"Okay," I whispered. "Let's do this right." I ran my hand down his cheek. "I love you so much, Sam. I can hardly wait to be your wife. Every day seems like an eternity."

"But it's not," he said, kissing the top of my head. "Eternity starts the moment we each say 'I do.'" I felt his body stiffen. He let me go and took a step back, his gaze locked on something over my shoulder.

I turned to see what he was looking at. My father stared out the window at us.

"Oh great," Sam said softly. "Now he thinks I'm pawing his daughter."

"Don't be silly. He isn't thinking any such thing." I grabbed his hand and walked with him to his truck. "I'll see you at six."

He opened the truck door and climbed into the cab. "I love you, Grace," he said as he started the engine.

"I know."

While I watched him back out of my driveway and

turn onto Faith Road, I thought about how blessed I was to have found someone like Sam Goodrich. Then I turned to go into the house. Once inside I found that my father had abandoned his spot by the window, and everyone had already gone upstairs.

After pouring myself another glass of Sweetie's delicious cider, I went back out on the porch and sat down in my uncle's rocking chair. I certainly shared Sam's feelings about our wedding, but Hannah's disappearance left me wondering if the ceremony would really happen on time. How could we celebrate our new life unless Hannah was home? And if she'd actually been abducted, what would the outcome be? If it was terrible, Harmony would be in mourning, and a wedding would be inappropriate. I hadn't shared my concerns with Sam because there were no decisions to be made yet. The guilt I'd been fighting against returned to haunt me as I considered the harsh truth that kept invading my thoughts. If I'd listened to Abel and Emily in the first place, Hannah would never have gone to Wichita. And she might not be missing now. If something awful happened to her, I would never be able to forgive myself. And Harmony, as loving as it was, would not forgive me either.

I finished my cider, put the glass on the floor next to me, and prayed.

EIGHT

We got to Sam's a little late. My parents and Papa Joe got out of the car at Ida's and spent several minutes in the old woman's house hugging and reminiscing. I was a little worried since Sweetie doesn't do well when people arrive late for dinner. But surprisingly, when we pulled up to the house, she came out on the porch with a huge smile on her face. Her overalls were gone, replaced by her Sunday church clothes. She looked very nice. I was touched to know that seeing my family was so important to her. Sam came out on the porch behind her.

"Oh my goodness," Sweetie said as we got out of the car. "Daniel and Beverly. I'm so glad to see you again. It's been such a long time." She hurried down the stairs and grabbed my mother's hand. "Why Bevie, you're just as pretty as you was the last time I seen you. I woulda knowed you anywhere."

"Oh Myrtle," my mother said, "I think you're stretching the truth a bit, but please keep it up." They both laughed and hugged each other.

Then Sweetie turned her attention to my father. "If it ain't Daniel Temple," she said, her voice breaking slightly. "Still as handsome as the day you left." She looked over at me and smiled. "Your father is one of the best people it was ever my pleasure to know. Even as a boy, every last soul in Harmony knowed they could rely on Daniel and Benjamin Temple. They was young men to look up to." Then she spotted Papa Joe who waited a few feet behind my father. She blinked back tears. "And here's the reason why. Joe. I can hardly believe it."

"Why if it isn't little Myrtle Goodrich," Papa Joe said with a smile. "Still as beautiful as I remember."

I figured it wouldn't be appropriate to point out that Papa's memory wasn't what it used to be. I'd seen pictures of Sweetie as a young woman, and if I hadn't known better, I would never have made the connection. Years of working outside in the sun had damaged her once-flawless skin and aged her beyond her years. But Sweetie beamed like someone who had just been given a million dollars. Sam came over and put his arm around me. He looked pleased to see our families together.

"Why Joe, you always was the kindest man I ever met." Sweetie walked over and gave Papa a hug. "I remember you used to love green bean soup with ham. Essie cooked up some for my father, and she gave me the recipe. I made it for dinner hopin' you'd enjoy it."

Papa chuckled. "Schaubel Zup! Oh my goodness, Myrtle. I haven't had Schaubel Zup since I lost Essie. I can hardly wait to taste it again."

"And I got friendship bread warmin' in the oven. I hope it's as good as Essie's, but I wouldn't bet my farm on it."

Papa smiled at me. "Your grandmother made the best friendship bread in Harmony."

"I thought Mama didn't make bread." The story I'd been told was that because her parents had put such an emphasis on bread making when she was young, Mama refused to do it after she got married.

"You're right about that," Papa said. "But friendship bread isn't like regular bread. It's more like dessert." He laughed. "Just you wait. You're in for a real treat."

"Well let's get outta this hot sun and cool off inside," Sweetie said, taking Papa's arm. "The food's ready and the company's here. Can't ask for nothin' better than that."

I noticed my dad watching Papa and Sweetie climb the stairs together.

"Papa seems like his old self today," I said to him in a low voice. "You'd never know there was anything wrong."

Dad nodded. "He's been swinging back and forth like this for the past month or so. He seems confused and upset, and then suddenly he's Papa again." My father put his arm around my shoulders. "Don't get too excited, Gracie. We've been through this before. In an instant everything can change."

"I know, but this is nice. I really never thought I'd get more time with him. Whatever's going on, I'm grateful."

He was silent as we went into the house. I saw my mom take his hand. I couldn't imagine what my dad was feeling. Watching his father suffer through this insidious disease had to be incredibly hard on him. Hopefully Papa would be alert for the rest of the day.

"Come on in and sit down," Sweetie called out as we came down the hall. "We're eating in the dining room tonight."

Usually when I come over for supper we eat in the kitchen. Sweetie's beautiful dining room is reserved for special occasions. The walls are a lovely shade of deep red with white wainscoting almost halfway up. Crown molding accents the ceiling, which supports a large, intricate brass chandelier with small bulbs that flicker like candles. The long windows along one wall let in the light, and cream-colored valances with red flowers sit atop each one. Over the large white-marble fireplace, a gorgeous painting portraying the outside of the house gives the room a unique feeling of history. The dark mahogany furniture could easily overpower the room with its size and design, but instead it fits perfectly. It's certainly hard to believe that the rough-edged and sometimes unkempt Sweetie Goodrich lives in this house. But anyone who judges her by her physical appearance or her misuse of the English language will miss seeing her for who she really is. There is depth, intelligence, and beauty in the heart of this rugged woman. The dining room table was covered with her fine linen tablecloth and matching napkins. And her good china, an incredible blue-and-red-designed pattern called Bird of Paradise, sat waiting for dinner. I had no idea how much it was worth, but I knew it was expensive and very collectible.

"Your home is beautiful," my mother said. "I have to admit I was a little nervous about seeing this house again. When we left Harmony, Bishop Angstadt lived here, and my visits were never pleasant." She gazed around the room. "But there's not a trace of him left, Myrtle. You even painted the outside red. It changes the entire look of the place."

Sweetie grunted. "That was surely my intention. Ain't no hint of that man here no more."

"Beverly is right," Ida said, adjusting her long black skirt under her as she sat down. "This is the most attractive home I have ever seen."

"Why, you've been here before, Ida," Sweetie said. "Many times."

The old woman smiled. "Yes, and every time I come, I think the same thing."

I knew Ida meant every word she said. Even though she lived a much simpler life than Sweetie, there was no judgment, no condemnation toward others who didn't choose her lifestyle. Ida had taught me many things, but one of the most important was the grace God has toward His children. That even though some of us may choose different paths in our lives, our roads all still lead home—to Him.

Sweetie excused herself and left the room. When she returned a few minutes later, she carried a large china soup tureen in her hands. Sam jumped up and helped her place it in the center of the table. She took off the lid and the wonderful aroma I'd caught when we'd come in, filled the room. "Schaubel Zup," she proclaimed with a smile. "Sam, why don't you help me bring in the rest of the food?"

He followed his aunt to the kitchen. They returned with homemade rolls, Sweetie's wonderful, creamy coleslaw, and peach marmalade made from the peaches they grow on the farm.

"Joe, I wonder if you'd ask the blessing," Sweetie said when she sat down.

I cast a quick glance at my father, wondering if Papa Joe was capable of handling the task Sweetie had just given him. When he was younger, he could "pray the devil back to hell" as Sweetie would say. But could he do it now?

"I'd be happy to, Myrtle." Papa reached out and took my hand and my father's hand. I reached for Sam. Feeling his strong fingers cover mine gave me a sense of security.

"Dear Lord," Papa prayed, "we thank You for family and dear friends. We thank You for this wonderful food and ask that You bless the hands that prepared it. May God, who supplies seed to the sower and bread for food, supply and multiply our seed for sowing and increase the harvest of our righteousness. Amen."

Everyone around the table echoed Papa's "Amen." I opened my eyes to see my father's mouth quiver with emotion. He probably hadn't heard Papa pray for a very long time. I picked up the pitcher of iced tea sitting next to me, filled my glass, and gave the pitcher to Sam who got up to make sure everyone who wanted iced tea was served.

"If you'll pass me your bowls," Sweetie said, "I'll

fill 'em up with soup." While we did as she'd requested, my mother started asking Ida about the changes in Harmony since they'd left.

"Oh my, Beverly," Ida said, shaking her head. "So much has changed. Since Bishop Angstadt died, we have become a new town." She put her hand on her chest. "Please understand that I am not his judge. What I say is only what I have seen since his passing. Perhaps we were not as understanding of Bishop Angstadt as we should have been. I do not know, and I do not presume to know his heart. There is one Judge who will decide at the end of time what our deeds deserve. I am content to let Him determine those things. But I can certainly tell you that when the bishop was gone, it was as if our little town emerged from the shadows." She paused as Sweetie spooned soup into her bowl, thanking her when she finished. "Many of the women, including me, gathered together and prayed for Harmony—that it would deserve the name it had been given from that moment on. We asked God to bless our town with peace. And He has." She picked up her soup spoon and paused. "I hope you will see us with new eyes. Surely there are also good memories from your life here."

My mother laughed lightly. "I have wonderful memories of Harmony, Ida. You certainly are one of them." She leaned her head against my father's shoulder. "And, of course, I found true love in this town. It gave me my husband and my child, as well as the best mother- and father-in-law any woman could have. And now Gracie is here, and she loves

it. She has found her soul mate here just as I did."
She nodded. "Yes, there are many good memories—
and more to be made, I'm sure. Besides, it was never
Harmony that was the problem. It was the bishop."

"There were others in the church who should
have stood up to him and didn't," Dad said, frowning.

"I wonder if you mean me," Ida said. Her eyes
searched my father's face.

"Oh my goodness no, Ida," he said quickly. "You
were always so supportive of us. I can never thank you
enough for your constant love and encouragement.
And Herman." Dad shook his head. "What a good
man he was. I miss him." Herman Turnbauer had
been Papa's best friend. They worked in the fields
together and lived like brothers. My father smiled.
"Herman always had a story for Benjamin and me.
Stories from the Bible. He really made the Bible
come alive. I still remember learning about Joseph. A
man who wouldn't turn his back on God or feel sorry
for himself, no matter what happened to him."

Papa Joe chuckled. "When times were hard,
Herman would call me by my given name, Joseph,
just to remind me that we couldn't give up, and that
circumstances never change God's plan." He smiled at
Ida. "I still hear him sometimes. 'Joseph, don't give up.
Stand up straight. God has deliverance in His mighty
hand!'"

Ida gave a soft cry and put her napkin to her face.
When she lowered it, there were tears in her eyes. "Oh
Joe. Sometimes I swear I hear him whisper to me in
the dark before I go to sleep. I miss him so."

"I know, Ida, I know. There are moments when I'm sure Essie is sitting right beside me. Or she comes up behind me and puts her hand on my shoulder." Papa stared down at the table the smile gone from his face.

"Goodness gracious," Sweetie said, loudly. "You all are gonna turn this celebration into a sobfest if you don't stop it." She sniffed and dabbed at her eyes with the bottom of her apron. "Now, let's get to eatin' this good food before it gets cold."

"Sounds good, Myrtle," Papa Joe said, pasting a smile on his face with effort. "I'm so hungry I could eat a horse." He winked at me. "Gracie, do you know what made the pony cough?"

"No, Papa. What made the pony cough?"

Papa looked around the table as if he was getting ready to tell the funniest joke ever written. "Because he was a little horse," he said chuckling.

Everyone laughed. "Oh Joe," Ida said, her eyes twinkling with laughter. "I must admit that I have missed your jokes. Essie and I used to giggle together every time you told a new one."

Papa pointed a finger at her. "You told me you laughed because they were so bad. I remember that."

I snorted. "Well, don't worry. They're just as bad as they used to be."

Papa's smiled widely. "I take that as a compliment."

"You should," Sweetie said with a smile. " 'Cause that's about the only one you're gonna get for a joke like that."

After another round of laughter, we began eating

Sweetie's soup. I had no idea if she'd ever made this dish before, but I'd certainly never had it in all the times I'd eaten dinner at her house. Big chunks of ham, fresh green beans, carrots, and potatoes floated in a creamy broth. I filled my spoon and brought it to my mouth. An explosion of flavor greeted me. The ham was tender and the vegetables perfect. And the broth combined creaminess and spice at the same time. It was absolutely delicious.

Papa Joe took his first taste. "Goodness," he said dreamily. "It's wonderful." He smiled at Sweetie. "You've outdone yourself, Essie. You really have."

His words caused my stomach to clench. My father's face fell, and an uncomfortable silence filled the room. But Sweetie didn't miss a beat.

"Why thank you, Joe," she said, her tone upbeat. "I'm so happy you like it."

"I do," he said, holding up another spoonful. "Now Daniel, you and Beverly eat your soup. We won't wait for Benjamin. He knows better than to show up late for supper." He shook his head. "I can't count the number of times I've told that boy to be home before your mama puts food on the table. He may find himself missing his meal tonight. I just might send him to his room hungry." He turned toward Ida. "And where's Herman tonight, Ida? I know he doesn't like to miss Essie's cooking."

Ida nodded. "You are right about that, Joe. He would have loved to be here, but unfortunately he could not get away."

Papa patted her arm. "He's such a hardworking

man. Why don't we send some soup home with you? You can heat it up for him later."

"Thank you, Joe. I would appreciate that."

Papa looked over at me. "Now who is this young lady again? I'm sorry. I just don't seem to remember your name."

"That's okay, Papa," my mother said. "I may have forgotten to introduce you. This is Gracie. She's a friend of mine."

I opened my mouth to respond, but I just couldn't. Sadness overwhelmed me, and I sat there, trying desperately to hold back a flood of tears. How could he go from the Papa I knew so well to this confused man? Mumbling out a lame excuse about needing to check on something, I fled the room. A few moments later, my dad opened the door to the screened-in back porch where'd I'd escaped to cry.

"I–I'm sorry, Daddy," I said tearfully when he sat down next to me on the white wicker love seat. "I tried, I really did. I just couldn't. . .couldn't. . ."

"Pretend?" My father stroked my hair. "It's okay, Snicklefritz. I know exactly how you feel. I've had to walk away many times myself."

"How could God let this happen?" I asked, wiping my face on my arm. My father reached into his pants pocket and pulled out a handkerchief. Outside of Harmony, he's one of the few men I know who still carries one.

"Oh Gracie. God doesn't *let* it happen. Disease and illness were never His plan, but sin and destruction came into the world. Again, not His plan and certainly not His will." He smiled at me. "Believe me, God hates what's happening to Papa even more than we do. I think we always need to remember that there is no sickness or destruction in heaven. That knowledge should help us to know who God really is, and what He really wants for His children." He shrugged. "And remember people get healed all the time. I've seen people wonderfully delivered from disease. Of course I've also known some who weren't."

"Why doesn't everyone get healed, Dad?"

He sighed. "I don't know, honey. It could be for a variety of reasons. We aren't going to understand everything in this life, but I do know one thing."

"What's that?" I sniffed, blowing my nose into his hankie.

"That whether we're delivered from our circumstances or we have to walk them out, God is with us every step of the way. His love never changes, and it never fails. He'll always find a way to bring us through every trial of life if we trust Him."

"Seeing Papa Joe like this makes me feel so sad." I leaned against my father's shoulder.

"It makes me sad, too." He put his arm around me. "But you know what? Most of the time, Papa's very happy. When he's with us and when he's not. The times he drifts away he almost always goes to happy places where my mother is still alive and where his life was good."

"What about the other times?"

"Well, when he quit talking we thought he'd left us forever. When we'd go to visit he'd just stare at us—

as if he had no idea who we were. He's verbal now, and we're grateful. But there have been a few times when he's gotten terribly upset. It's as if he's trapped between reality and the disease. I'm sure it's horribly confusing to him, and he lashes out."

"He's not violent, is he?"

My father was quiet for a moment, and then he hugged me tight. "A couple of times he's been rather physical."

"That's not Papa at all."

He kissed the top of my head. "No, it's not. I think the darkness begins to come over him, and he simply tries to fight his way out. It has nothing to do with anyone around him. The first time it happened, I took it personally. But I've learned to let him get it out of his system. When he calms down he's fine."

"So what will happen to Papa now?"

"I don't know. When he stopped talking we assumed the end was near. But now that he's communicating again, we're not sure what to expect next. My guess is that at some point he'll fall silent once more."

"W—will Papa die here?"

My dad sat up straight and gazed directly into my eyes. "No, Gracie. If he gets too bad before we leave for home, Mom and I will get him transferred to a hospital or nursing home nearby. After the wedding, we'll take him back to Nebraska."

"Okay." I wiped my face once again and handed the handkerchief to my dad.

He smiled. "You keep it."

I couldn't help but laugh. "Okay. I'll wash it and then give it back to you."

"I would appreciate that very much. Now let's get back in there before Papa sends me to my room. I didn't like it when I was a kid, and I doubt I'd like it any better now."

I giggled. "I think I'd enjoy seeing that. Payback for all the times you did it to me."

He grunted. "Yes, I'm sure you would. Hopefully I can spare myself the humiliation." He grabbed my hand and pulled me up. "Now get going, young lady. And no more tears in front of Papa, okay?"

"I'll try."

My dad and I went back to the dining room together. Mom grabbed my hand as I walked past. "You okay?" she whispered.

I nodded. Papa Joe was busy eating his soup, smacking his lips with delight. I sat down next to Sam who reached over and gave me a quick hug. It seemed that my grandfather hadn't noticed my unexplained exit. I breathed a sigh of relief.

"Sweetie was telling us about the girl who's missing, Gracie," my mother said. "Isn't Hannah the one you took to Wichita?"

I nodded. "Yes. We're not sure if she just ran away or if something else happened."

"Oh honey. I'm sorry. You must be very worried. I know you care a great deal about her."

"She's very special to me. Everyone's concerned." I launched into the story of Hannah's reaction to Wichita and how she seemed to change.

"I hope you're not blaming yourself," my dad said. "It's certainly not your fault. Take it from two people who know what it's like to want a different kind of life."

I glanced over at Ida who smiled at me. "I did at first. But a dear friend straightened me out." I pointed my soup spoon at my father. "This situation isn't the same as yours, Dad. You and Mom wanted to get married, and Bishop Angstadt wouldn't allow it—ever. But Hannah knows she can go to art school in a year. I can't believe she'd leave her parents and her home just because she's impatient."

"You could be right," he said. "But when Mom and I lived here, there were other people our age who left for the same reasons you said Hannah gave. It happens."

"Well maybe." I turned his comment over in my mind. Was I wrong? Had Hannah really run away because she saw a future beyond Harmony? As hard as I tried, I just couldn't believe it. I started to say that when the doorbell rang.

"Now who in tarnation can that be?" Sweetie murmured. "Botherin' people when they're tryin' to eat." She got up and went to the door, mumbling all the way. Most people in Harmony knew better than to bother Sweetie at suppertime. I felt sorry for whoever was waiting on the other side of her front door. We heard voices and then footsteps in the hallway. Pat Taylor came in, his hat in his hands.

"Pat needs to talk to you, Gracie," Sweetie said. Her sour expression made it clear she wasn't happy about her impromptu visitor.

I started to stand up, but Sam grabbed me and pulled me back into my seat. "Is this about Hannah?" he asked.

Pat nodded, and I gasped.

"Why don't you tell all of us, Pat," Sam said. "If something has happened. . ."

"It's not bad news," he said quickly. "We still haven't found her." He gazed around the table. "I don't want to interrupt your dinner."

"A little late for that," Sweetie grumbled.

Pat nervously rotated his hat with his fingers. "Maybe I should come back some other time."

"Nonsense," my dad said. He stood up and pointed to an empty chair at the end of the table. "We've all heard about Hannah's disappearance. Why don't you have a seat and tell us what's going on? I know we're all very interested."

"Yes, Pat. Please sit down," I said. "Are you hungry?"

He looked at Sam who didn't offer any kind of encouragement, but he slid into the chair next to my dad anyway. "Uh, no. That's okay. I just wanted to bring you up to date. I should have called first, but I was in the area. I tried your place first, but when I found out you weren't home, I thought I'd check to see if you were over here."

"I'm glad you did, Pat," I said.

My father stuck out his hand. "I'm Daniel Temple, Sheriff. I'm Gracie's father. And this is my wife, Beverly, and my father, Joe."

"I'm happy to meet you," Mom said.

My grandfather didn't say anything, but he nodded at Pat.

"Daniel Temple," Pat said. "Your brother was Benjamin?"

"Yes, that's right," Dad said. "Did you know him?"

Pat shook his head. "No, not really. I only met him a couple of times. I hadn't been sheriff for that long before he died. He seemed like a very nice man."

I glanced over at Papa. A few minutes ago he'd thought Benjamin was still alive. How would he react to Pat's statement? Thankfully, he didn't appear to have heard it. Instead he seemed to be focused on buttering his roll.

"Thank you," my father said. "So what is this news you've brought about Hannah?"

Pat scooted up closer to the table. "The girl who disappeared from Emporia has been found. She ran off with her boyfriend. And although neither one of the girls from Topeka have been located yet, the police are pretty sure they know who abducted one of them. An ex-boyfriend threatened her the day before she went missing, and he hasn't shown up for work since the day she disappeared. The police are confident he's got her. They just don't know if they'll find her alive."

"How awful," my mother said. "I can't imagine what her parents are going through."

"About the same thing Abel and Emily are, I imagine," I said. "So only one girl is left who could have been abducted by a stranger?"

"Yes. The girl who got into the red truck is

the only remaining mystery." He shrugged. We'll probably find out it's another case of someone running off with a boy her family doesn't approve of." He looked at me. "I wanted you to know about this so you'd quit worrying about Hannah being abducted."

"I appreciate that, but I still have a hard time believing she took off because she's mad at her parents," I said.

Pat grunted. "Maybe this will change your mind. Some snooping around uncovered a little more going on between this Vogler boy and the Mueller girl."

"What do you mean?" I asked.

"Seems that before Hannah left for Wichita, they'd been meeting pretty regularly behind their parents' backs."

"That doesn't sound like Hannah," Sam said. Hannah was special to him. He'd encouraged her in her art and even made frames for her pictures.

"Well, Jonathan Vogler came clean when I questioned him. They think they're in love but didn't want their parents to know. Afraid they wouldn't approve. One more reason for her to be unhappy at home."

"Hannah couldn't have loved him very much if she wanted to stay in Wichita," I said.

Pat shrugged. "I have no idea. Maybe he planned to meet her there."

"So you're absolutely convinced she ran away?" I was starting to wonder if he was right.

He nodded slowly, but an odd look flickered across his face.

"What?" I asked. "Is there something else?"

"It's probably nothing, but. . ."

"Tell me," I said, pressing him.

"The Muellers can't figure out what Hannah was wearing when she left. All of her dresses seem to be in her closet. At first I doubted they could remember every article of clothing their daughter owns, but I guess Mrs. Mueller makes all her daughter's clothes so. . ." His eyebrows knit together with concern. "Gracie, are you okay?"

I'd felt the blood drain from my face so it wasn't hard to imagine how shocked I looked. "I—I—I mean. . ."

"Grace, what's wrong?" Sam peered into my eyes.

I gulped and took a big breath. "Hannah's clothes. She—she got some jeans and a T-shirt from a girl she met in Wichita. I don't know why I didn't realize. . . I mean, she must have taken them with her when we left town."

"You mean she could have been wearing these new clothes when she left her house?" Pat sighed and pulled a notebook out of his pocket. "You should have told me this from the beginning. I put out an all-points bulletin based on my assumption she was wearing something more. . ."

"Mennonite?" my dad said.

Pat nodded at him. "Exactly. I figured she wouldn't be hard to find dressed like that. But if she blends in. . ."

"She could have slipped right past anyone who was looking for her," I said. "I'm so sorry, Pat. I just didn't realize how important it would be. I thought about telling her parents about the clothes, but they're already so upset with me. . ."

"Upset with you?" my dad said. "Why would they be upset with you? You're not responsible for their daughter's actions."

I recognized the irritation in my father's tone. Papa tiger defending his cub. Mix in a tendency to mistrust anyone with spiritual authority in Harmony. "Dad, the Muellers didn't want Hannah to go with me to Wichita. I talked them into it. Everything they worried about happened. Hannah changed in Wichita."

"I don't care," he said sharply. "It's their job to raise their daughter the right way. If she goes off the deep end the first time she gets away from them, they only have themselves to blame."

Oh dear. This wasn't going well. I grabbed Sam's hand under the table as a signal for help.

"They're just worried about Hannah, sir," he said, taking the hint. "They love Grace. I'm sure it's just the pressure they're under."

Sam's reassurance seemed to mollify my dad somewhat. "Well, I suppose that makes sense. I just don't want anyone trying to make my little girl feel guilty about something that's not her fault."

"Thanks, Daddy. I'm fine." Ida's words of encouragement had really helped me, even though I still wished I'd listened to Abel and Emily when they'd originally expressed their concerns. At the time, I'd been more focused on Hannah's art than on her heart. If only I could have that moment to do over. A quick look at Ida made me realize I was going in the wrong direction. . .again. I smiled at her and tried to push regret out of my thoughts. I needed to concentrate on Hannah—not myself.

"Describe these clothes," Pat said. "I'll correct the APB and get this information out as soon as possible."

I gave him a detailed description of Hannah's outfit. Good thing I'd looked at it so closely. "Oh, she probably had her hair down, and she might have been wearing makeup. Not a lot, but some."

He wrote everything down and then closed his notebook. "Unfortunately, if she was hitchhiking, she would have blended in with anyone else out there on the highway."

"Do children still hitchhike?" my mother asked. "I don't see many girls asking for rides anymore. Too dangerous."

Pat nodded. "You're right, they don't. But is Hannah aware of that? She's lived such a sheltered life I have no idea if she knows how to protect herself from danger."

"But that just proves my point," I insisted. "That she could be in real trouble."

"I understand that, Gracie," Pat said. "But it doesn't change the fact that she's listed as a runaway, and as far as we know right now, that's exactly what happened. Finding out that she put these clothes on of her own volition before leaving home makes it even clearer that she had a plan. And it wasn't to stay in Harmony. I figure she's on her way to Wichita. I've talked to your art teacher and your friend Allison.

Neither one of them have seen her. Is there anyone else she might contact?"

I thought for a moment. "Her friend, Robin. The one who gave her the clothes. And you might check with Jim again. It's possible she made friends with someone else in her class that I'm not aware of."

He flipped his notebook open again. "Do you have Robin's contact information?"

I shook my head. "But Jim would."

"Okay, I'll call this Monahan guy again." He stopped writing and looked up at me. "Have you talked to him since you got back?"

"No, I tried to call them before we came over tonight but they were both out. I left messages to contact me if they hear from Hannah."

This time after he closed his notebook he put it back in his pocket. "I guess that's all I need now." He stood up. "Again, sorry to interrupt your family dinner. I'll be on my way."

"Are you sure you won't eat with us?" my dad asked. "There's plenty, and this soup is out of this world."

Pat's eyes darted toward Sam. "No, but thanks anyway. . ."

Sam stood to his feet. "Of course you'll stay. Sit down. I'll get you a bowl from the kitchen."

"Sam!" Sweetie hissed.

He ignored her while Pat gazed at him with his eyebrows arched in surprise. "I should have introduced Sheriff Taylor when he first got here," Sam said. "This is my father."

"Your father?" my dad said. "Why, I had no idea . . . Gracie, I thought you told me Sam's father wasn't around."

"Daniel, hush," my mother said in a loud whisper. "I'm happy to meet you again, Pat," she said smiling. "Now you *must* sit down and share dinner with us."

"Yes, sit down, Pat," Sam said. "Please."

Pat lowered himself slowly back into his chair. "Thank you. This looks really good."

"Oh for cryin' out loud," Sweetie said. "Sit down, Sam. I'll get the bowl." She stood up and stalked out of the room.

"Sam and Pat just recently reunited," I explained to my mother and father, hoping my brief explanation would satisfy them for a while. I could see the questions in their expressions. I prayed they'd hold them until I could get them alone and fill in the details.

"Well that's wonderful," Dad said jovially. "I'm so glad this happened before the wedding. Now we can all celebrate together."

Grateful Sweetie was in the kitchen during this little announcement, I picked up my spoon and went back to work on my soup. It was a little cold, but I could almost swear it tasted even better now.

"Pat, we're planning to go into town tomorrow," Dad continued. "My wife and I haven't seen Harmony for a long time. Maybe you could join us for lunch?" He looked over at me. "What time did you plan for us to eat?"

I broke open a roll and reached for the butter. "I don't really care. Whatever works for everyone else. I intend to drive over to Abigail Bradley's place in the morning, but that shouldn't take long. I'll be home in plenty of time for lunch."

"Then how about meeting us at eleven thirty at the restaurant in town?" Dad said, smiling at Pat.

"I'll do my best," Pat said, "but I'll have to check in to the office first. Why don't you folks go ahead, and I'll try to meet you there."

As Sweetie came into the room with another soup bowl in her hands, my father said, "So I guess you were very involved with uncovering the body of Jacob Glick on our property last year, Pat?"

Before Pat had a chance to respond, Papa Joe jumped to his feet, flinging his arms around wildly, his eyes wide with alarm. His hand hit Sweetie who was nearby, and the china soup bowl in her hands flew across the room and shattered against the fireplace.

"You've got to stay away from him, Beverly," he shouted, staring at me. "I've seen the devil in his eyes! Please! You've got to stay away!"

NINE

The air-conditioner in my car had a hard time working against temperatures that promised to hit one hundred degrees by the afternoon. Even though it was only ten in the morning, the air outside was already stifling. As I drove down dirt roads to Abigail's house, the terrible scene from last night's dinner played over and over in my mind. It had taken quite some time to calm Papa Joe down.

No one had suspected that Jacob Glick's name would evoke such powerful emotion. Obviously Papa's long-term memory was still working. He remembered Glick and had been aware of his proclivities toward young women and girls. Last night he'd been reminded of his concern for my mother when she was young and had thought she was still in danger. After my grandfather calmed down, my dad took him back to my house to rest. Papa stayed confused until my parents finally got him to bed. He'd kept shouting something about evil and that he had to protect us.

"This may have been a mistake," my father had said when he came downstairs. "I expected some confusion, even extreme disorientation from time to time. But I had no idea Papa would come unglued like this. Gracie, I'm sorry if Papa embarrassed you in front of your fiancé and his family. Maybe Mom and I should take him back to the nursing home. We could be back within the week and still have plenty of time to help you get ready for the wedding."

"I don't want him to go, Dad. This might be the last chance I have to spend time with him. We'll all just be more careful and try not to say anything that will upset him."

After some cajoling, my father finally agreed to give it more time. In the light of a new day, I wasn't certain I'd made the right decision, but I knew having Papa here on the day I married Sam was extremely important to me.

At breakfast, Papa seemed to have no memory of his outburst the night before. In fact, he was relaxed and happy. The only glitch came when he tried to ask for pancake syrup but couldn't remember what it was called.

I spotted the road Abigail lived on and turned down it. A couple of miles later, I saw a large white house looming ahead. As I got closer, I could see it was badly in need of paint and upkeep. A screen door on the side of the house hung by its bottom hinges, and an old, rusted tractor sat in the yard. Various items littered the yard including pieces of farm equipment and discarded furniture. Sitting back from the house was an ancient barn and off to its side was a large shed that looked deserted.

I turned into the dirt driveway, being careful to

avoid several rusted tools and pieces of lumber lying on the ground. The house appeared to be abandoned. Could Ida's friend have moved without telling anyone? I stopped my car, got out, and made my way to the rickety front porch, passing a large tree that looked as dead as everything else on the property. The boards on the decrepit porch squeaked and groaned with each step I took. I found myself watching my feet and praying the rotting wood wouldn't splinter under me. When I finally reached the entrance, I knocked on a screen door that was so loose it jiggled each time I rapped my knuckles against it. After trying several times to roust someone, I decided to make my escape before the entire structure buckled and crashed down around me.

"Can I help you?"

I was already spooked enough by the ghostly look of the disintegrating property, but hearing a man's voice from behind me caused me to emit a high-pitched shriek that should have toppled the house without any further assistance. I swung around to find a shirtless man about my father's age standing at the foot of the steps. His reddish-blond hair almost glowed in the sunlight. He was well built and muscular, but his fair skin was turning red from exposure to the elements.

"I'm sorry. I was looking for Abigail Bradley. A friend of hers sent me to check on her...to make sure she's okay."

He came up to the steps and held out his hand. "I think you'd better get off that porch before you go right through the boards. I haven't had a chance to fix it yet."

I took his arm and held on while carefully making my way back to solid ground. When I got to the bottom, he let go of me but stuck his hand out again. "I'm C.J., Abigail's son."

When I shook his hand, I noticed his firm grip. "Oh, I had no idea you were here. Ida Turnbauer told me about you. I understand you live out of state somewhere?"

He let go of my hand and smiled. "Yes, I live in California, but Mom had an accident and broke her leg. One of her neighbors called, so I took some time off work to care for her while she recovers." He motioned toward the house. "I had no idea this place was in such bad shape. I'm trying to fix it up before I leave."

"How long has it been since you've been back to Harmony?"

He sighed. "Too long, obviously. Mom is very independent and always told me she was fine in her letters." He shook his head. "I should have checked on her sooner. I feel bad about it."

"Well, it's great you're here now." I gazed at the house. "Looks like you've got your work cut out for you."

C.J. chuckled. "That's the truth. Two different families who live nearby have already offered to help." He pointed to a pile of lumber lying next to the house. "One of them brought this by, along with a case of nails, and the other has offered me some white paint when I'm ready for it."

I laughed. "That's Harmony. Don't be surprised if a truckload of people show up to help with the work. No one is an island here." I put my hand up to shield my eyes from the sun and stared at the house again. "In fact, I'm surprised people haven't been by before now to help your mother get the house in shape."

"Oh, they tried, but Mom shooed them off. Like I said, she's pretty independent."

The dilapidated screen door suddenly opened. An old woman dressed in black and in a wheelchair appeared in the doorway. She wore a black prayer covering over her gray hair. "C.J., who is that you're talking to?" she asked in a thin, reedy voice.

"Hello, Mrs. Bradley," I called out. "I'm Gracie Temple, Daniel Temple's daughter. Ida Turnbauer asked me to check on you."

"Daniel Temple," she hollered, her tone rising. "Benjamin's brother?"

"Yes ma'am."

C.J. put his foot on the bottom step. "Mama," he said sternly, "don't come out on the porch. It won't support you and that wheelchair."

"But I want to talk to this girl," she whined.

"I told you it's not safe."

Abigail moved her wheelchair back and angrily slammed the door shut. C.J. looked embarrassed. "If you have time to visit, you can use the back door. Until I support the porch and replace the rotten boards, she can't come out here."

"I totally understand." I looked at my watch. "I

don't have much time right now, but maybe I could come back some other time for a visit?"

He smiled. "Mom would love that. Give me a few days to make some improvements, then come by anytime. I'd tell you to call, but my cell phone doesn't seem to work very well out here, and Mom doesn't have a phone." He sighed. "Or air-conditioning. I'm not used to this heat."

"You should come into town. The restaurant has great food, and it's nice and cool."

"Sounds wonderful. I'll do it." He stuck his hand out once again. "I'm glad to meet you, Gracie, and I hope to see you again soon."

I shook his hand and smiled at him. "Same here."

As I headed to my car, I looked back to see Abigail sitting at the front window, watching me. I waved to her, but she just closed the curtain. Ida's description of Abigail Bradley was right on the button. She was definitely strange, but at least Ida could stop worrying about her now.

The temperature had continued to climb, and the interior of my car felt like an oven. I rolled down the windows, but all I managed to do was let in more hot air. As I headed back onto the dirt road that led to Abigail's house, I had no choice but to roll the windows up again. Driving on unpaved roads meant dust—and lots of it. The air conditioner blew hot air at first, but after driving a few minutes, a little cool air started to eke out of the vents.

I couldn't help but think about C.J. and his attempts to fix his mother's house. Noble sentiments, but in this heat, not such a good idea. When I got home, I'd tell Sam about it, and see if he could find some people to help. Unfortunately, Sam and Sweetie were picking fruit right now and had very little extra time. What few hours Sam could find were being spent with me and my family.

I'd just started to turn onto Faith Road and head for home when something shiny in the road caught the rays of the sun. The light hit my windshield, and the reflection was so bright it made it hard to see for a moment. I pulled over and got out, wondering what it could possibly be. It took me a minute to find it, but when I did, the discovery took my breath away. Lying in the dirt by the side of the road was a silver bracelet with colored beads. A silver heart hung from a chain, and the three inserts were engraved with *Love*, *Friend*, and *Forever*.

Hannah's bracelet.

TEN

Sam put the phone down and shook his head. "Pat's been called out on another case, Gracie. It will be a while before he can get here. He can't make it to lunch today and asked that we explain the situation to your parents. He also said to remind you that he's got the whole county to take care of and can't keep running to Harmony for every little thing."

"Every little thing!" I snapped. "Finding Hannah's bracelet proves something's wrong, Sam. We've got to find her. She's in real trouble!"

We sat at the table in his kitchen. Sweetie was out in the orchard working alone. My frantic cries had brought Sam inside to find out what was going on.

He ran his hand through his sun-bleached hair and sighed with frustration. "Explain to me why you're so convinced this means something. So Hannah dropped her bracelet. In my book, it proves she really did take off on her own. She changed into her new outfit, walked out to the road, and probably found a ride. Her bracelet fell off by accident."

I started to say something, but he held up his hand and shushed me.

"Before you go off on a tangent, I totally understand that she shouldn't be out there by herself.

There are dangerous people who would be more than willing to pick her up for all the wrong reasons. But at least we know she wasn't abducted like the girl in Topeka. Hannah left under her own power."

"You're missing the entire point!" I held up the bracelet for him to see. "Don't you notice anything odd?"

Sam stared at the silver jewelry in my hand. Finally he shook his head. "No, Grace. It looks like a bracelet. Nothing more."

I flung it down on the table. "Would you like to explain to me just how it fell off when the clasp is still fastened?"

"Obviously it slid off her wrist."

I picked the bracelet up and held it out to him. "Hannah's tiny, I grant you. But this bracelet is too small to slide off anyone's wrist—even hers." I unclasped the catch, put the bracelet on my own wrist, and snapped it shut again. I grasped it with my other hand, showing him there wasn't any wiggle room at all. "I'm not big either, and even though my wrists may be a little wider than Hannah's, there's not that much difference. Look at this. Can you see that there's no earthly way this bracelet could have fallen off accidentally?"

He stared at my wrist with a dubious expression. He even reached over and pulled at the bracelet to see just how tight it fit. After a brief silence, he let out a deep breath. "Okay. I see your point. So how did it come off?"

I snapped the clasp open and took the bracelet off, putting it on the table in front of us. "Hannah purposely removed it and dropped it on the ground." My voice quivered with emotion. "She left it behind so we'd know she needed help, Sam. It's the only thing that makes sense."

I watched his expression as he turned this information over in his mind. "What if she just didn't want to wear it for some reason? Maybe it was uncomfortable. Or maybe she decided she didn't like it."

"No," I said emphatically. "She loved that bracelet because Robin gave it to her. And I saw it on her wrist. It fit perfectly."

"Maybe she had it in her pocket, and it fell out accidentally."

I shook my head. "Those jeans are tight, and the pockets are more for looks than for function. *If* she could have gotten the bracelet inside one of them, there's no way it could have just fallen out."

His frown only deepened as he considered the possibilities. "Are you certain this is Hannah's bracelet? Maybe it belongs to someone else in Harmony."

"Oh sure," I said with a snort. "Lots of conservative Mennonite girls wear bracelets like this. The odds are astronomical that anyone else in Harmony would have a bracelet sold at an upscale shop in Wichita. Give me a break."

"Okay," he said finally, "I see what you mean. It's probably Hannah's bracelet. She wouldn't have just tossed it away because she didn't want it anymore; it couldn't have fallen off her wrist or out of her pocket. She probably took it off on purpose. But why close the clasp again? Why not just drop the open bracelet on the ground?"

"Because then it would look like it actually had slipped off," I said, trying to keep the impatience I felt out of my voice. "She was trying to leave a clue behind that would let us know she needs help."

"You think she'd have the presence of mind to think that through?"

"Yes, I do," I responded quickly. "Hannah is extremely intelligent. With the time she had available, this was the only thing she could come up with."

"But who would know about this bracelet?" he asked. "You're the only one. How could she know you'd find it?"

"This is Harmony. People don't steal from each other here. Whoever found it would take it to town and show it around, hoping to find the owner. Of course it would eventually get around to me."

He raised an eyebrow. "And you think Hannah thought all that out in what was probably a matter of seconds?"

I shook my head. "No. I think she only had a short amount of time, and the bracelet was the only thing at her disposal. Hannah played a Hail Mary—and it worked. That's all that matters."

"I guess. . ."

"Look, Sam. You have to admit this bears looking into."

His gray eyes peered into mine. "Okay. Yeah, I guess so. But if you start insisting that Hannah really has been abducted, and she shows up at her boyfriend's, you're going to have a lot of explaining to do. This is a very serious conclusion to reach—that Hannah really was taken against her will."

I scowled at him. "You think? I've been trying to get someone to listen to me since she first went missing."

"Yeah, but that's because you thought some guy

123

had been abducting young women from around here. Now we know that at least two of those women weren't kidnapped."

I rubbed my temples to try to relieve the beginnings of a tension headache. "Oh, do we? We actually only know that one wasn't abducted. The police *think* the other girl in Topeka was taken by her ex-boyfriend. But until they find her with him, they don't actually know for sure, do they?"

"I guess that's true." He was quiet for a moment while he pondered my argument. "Oh by the way," he said finally, "I decided not to bug Jonathan Vogler or his family. Sounds like Pat's already checked out his story. I don't want to scare the Voglers or make them feel responsible for what's happened."

I shrugged. "That's fine. I doubt there's much more he can tell us at this point. I'd rather have you help me convince Pat that he needs to take finding Hannah's bracelet seriously."

He grunted. "We'd better leave that to you. When it comes to getting Pat to do something, you seem to have more influence than I do." His gaze swung to the clock on the kitchen wall. "We're supposed to meet at Mary's at eleven thirty, right?"

I nodded and looked at my watch. "Shoot. It's already a few minutes after eleven. I've got to get home and round everyone up. I also need to call Ida and tell her Abigail's okay." I started toward the kitchen doorway but stopped and turned back. "I know you think I have some kind of magic influence over Pat, but it's not true. He listens to you. Will you please call him one more time? Explain to him that the bracelet is important new evidence."

Once again Sam's eyebrows disappeared under his long bangs. "New evidence? Can I put it another way? You know how he hates it when you act all Nancy Drew."

"Put it however you want. Please, just convince him to talk to me, okay?"

Sam smirked and gave me a snappy salute. "Yes, Miss Marple. I am ever your loyal Mr. Stringer."

"I shouldn't have introduced you to those Miss Marple movies," I retorted. "You've been throwing Miss Marple in my face ever since."

"You do remind me of her in many ways," he said with a grin. "But I am grateful you don't actually look like Margaret Rutherford."

"That would make two of us." I waved good-bye, hurried out of his house, and headed back to my own. When I got there I called Ida to let her know Abigail had broken her leg but that her son was staying with her. She was upset to find out about her friend's accident. Probably feeling guilty that she hadn't checked on her sooner. Although last night I'd asked her to go with us, today she'd turned me down because of all the walking we planned to do. I checked with her once more.

"Ach, thank you, Gracie, but this leg of mine would only slow you down. I believe I will stay in today and rest. All the excitement from last night wore me out. But thank you for wanting me."

After the phone call, I cleaned up a bit. Then we all piled into my dad's Crown Vic since my Bug would have been a tight fit, and we drove into town. We ran a little late because my parents had an argument about Dad's cane. At first he refused to take it even though my mother insisted. Probably a pride thing. Eventually he gave in and tossed it in the car under protest.

On the way to town I told my parents about finding Hannah's bracelet. They agreed with me that the discovery was troubling. "We'll keep Hannah in our prayers," my mother said. "God is an expert at leading the lost home."

When we pulled up in front of the restaurant, Sam's truck was already there. As we got out of the car, I noticed my mother's tears.

"Mom, are you okay? Is something wrong?"

She closed the car door and reached into her purse, pulling out a tissue. "Oh Gracie," she said, dabbing at her eyes, "it's been thirty years since I've been in this town. In all that time, I never allowed myself to miss Harmony. But now that I'm here. . ." She stood next to the car and gazed around at the shops and the people, a good number of them wearing the simple clothing worn by many of the Mennonite townspeople. Next to us sat a buggy and a horse, tied up to a post. "I can hardly believe it, but it looks almost the same. I mean, the names of some of the shops are different, and there wasn't any restaurant back then, but the buildings all look just like they used to. And the wooden sidewalks. . ." She blew her nose into her tissue. "And the people. I'd almost forgotten the beauty of long skirts and prayer coverings. It's been so long. . ."

"Oh for crying out loud, Beverly," my father grumbled. "It's just a town." But I noticed that as he helped Papa Joe from the car, his eyes swept the scene around him. Although he refused to meet my gaze, the emotion on his face was obvious.

We finally made it inside the restaurant, although it took some time due to my dad's leg and Papa's slow gait. Sweetie and Sam already had a table and waved us over. As we sat down and greeted each other, Sweetie watched Papa Joe carefully, probably concerned after the scene last night. Thankfully, Papa seemed to be fine this morning, although he was rather quiet.

I spotted Jessie heading our way. She smiled when she saw me. "Hey, I heard you were back," she said as she came up to the table. I introduced her to everyone. She put her hand on my shoulder. "Everyone's heard about Hannah. Anything new?"

"Not that I know of. Sheriff Taylor put out an APB, but so far she hasn't been found."

"Well, kids run away. It happens all the time." She shook her head. "I did it once myself, but when I found out there was no place to go, I came home. Hannah will show up before long. I'm sure she's okay."

Knowing about Jessie's abusive father, I would have been surprised if she hadn't tried to leave home. "I hope you're right," I said. "We're praying for a good outcome."

"Everyone is, Gracie," she said seriously. "I've seen this town pray together before. Incredible things happen." She turned her attention to the other people at the table. "If you folks will tell me what you want to drink, I'll get it while you look over the menu."

Everyone gave her their drink order, and she shared Hector's daily specials, which were fried catfish nuggets and chicken and noodles. I watched as she walked away, still amazed by the difference in her since her father died. Jessie would be all right, as would her daughter, Trinity. I was sure of it.

"So what's good here?" my dad asked.

"Everything is top-notch," Sweetie said. "I consider myself pretty good in the kitchen, but Hector gives me a run for my money." She glanced at the menu, although it wasn't necessary. Everyone in Harmony had already memorized the available dishes. When you only have one restaurant, it's not hard. "I like the steaks. Hector uses a steak rub that makes 'em tender and delicious. And his fried chicken is somethin' to write home about."

"And Dad, he makes really good fried liver and onions," I said.

Although my mom hates liver, my dad and I love it. Really good liver, fried, with crispy edges and tender in the middle, can't be beat when surrounded by a pile of onions browned in the same grease. My mother just sighed, and Sam looked at me with a puzzled expression.

"I didn't know you like liver. I don't remember you ever ordering it."

"I've got news for you, big boy. There *are* a few things I do without you sometimes. Eating liver and onions is one of them."

"Well, it's a fine time to learn that your fiancée likes liver a week and a half before the wedding. Seems the husband-to-be is always the last to know."

"Very funny."

"Okay you two," Dad said, laughing. "Let's knock it off about the liver. I want to concentrate on the menu."

"And I want to concentrate on the wedding," Mom said. "Sweetie, now that I'm here, I'm ready to help you."

"That's great, Bevie. Why don't you come to the house for a while after we're done in town, and we'll go over everything. I could surely use the help."

Now that was a surprise. Sweetie actually allowing someone else to be a part of her plans. Sweetie was a lone wolf who usually didn't like anyone near her projects. Of course, planning a wedding takes more work than cooking a meal or decorating a room—both endeavors I'd been shooed away from in the past. But Mom was the bride's mother, and she had every right to be involved in the wedding plans. Apparently even Sweetie recognized this.

We chatted until Jessie came back with our drinks. I kept an eye on the entrance, hoping Pat would show up. A few minutes later, we ordered. Dad and I went for the liver. Mom ordered the catfish nuggets and Sweetie asked for fried chicken. Sam's order was no surprise. He ordered a rib-eye steak. Sam's nuts about steak. It's his very favorite food. Papa Joe settled on the chicken and noodles. Mama used to make great chicken and noodles. I hoped Hector's recipe would hold up next to Mama's.

Sweetie and my father started a conversation about people and events from years ago—before I was born. As they talked, my attention was divided between watching for Pat and listening to Dad talk about his childhood in Harmony. I figured he could tell I wasn't giving him my full attention, but he seemed to have his own distraction to deal with. I caught him frowning at Sam more than once. His reaction to Sam when they first met troubled me. Something wasn't right, but I had no idea what it was. Certainly, it would have been better if they'd met before now, but the reasons were pretty clear. I couldn't believe Dad would hold something against Sam that wasn't his fault. My father had always been a fair man. In dealing with him, it was always best to confront the situation head-on. Next chance I got, I'd ask him directly to explain his odd response toward Sam. With Hannah's situation, Papa Joe, and the wedding looming, I didn't need one more weird situation to deal with.

In a small town where everyone knows each other, my parents and Papa Joe drew attention. Several people came up and spoke to them. Ruth was taking a break from her store, and I was happy to introduce her and tell my parents that she donated flowers every month to put on Benjamin's grave. Joe Loudermilk from the hardware store stopped by the table. Although Joe moved to Harmony after my grandparents left, his dad had known Papa. I couldn't tell if Papa really remembered Joe's father, but he acted like he did, and they had a nice but short visit. The Scheidler brothers from the local farm implements store came over, too, and I introduced them.

By the time our food arrived, my parents had met almost every single person in the restaurant. Even Hector came out to greet them and Papa. Before he left, he told them their lunch was on him—a kind of welcome back to Harmony gift. Once our plates had been delivered, we were left alone to eat. Harmony folk were nothing if not well mannered. Dad said a quick prayer over our food, and we all dug in.

"Oh Daniel," my mother said softly, "this catfish

is wonderful. I've forgotten what fresh catfish tastes like."

My dad laughed. "We've had fresh catfish since we left Harmony, Bev."

She shrugged. "Well, maybe so, but it didn't taste like this."

"How's your liver, Dad?" I asked.

He grinned. "It's the best I've had in years. You know your mother never makes it. I always have to sneak some when she's not around."

"Sneak it?" Mom said, raising her quiet voice a bit. "Are you sneaking it now, Daniel? My goodness. You make me sound like an old nag who doesn't want her husband to enjoy his favorite foods."

My dad winked at me. "I'm sorry, dear. I didn't mean to make you sound that way. When we get home, you can make lots and lots of liver and onions for me. I look forward to it."

My mother's look of disgust made me giggle. She pointed her fork at my dad. "You're making me look silly," she said, trying hard not to laugh.

He blew her a kiss. "Again, I apologize. It's just so easy."

Sweetie chuckled. "You two act just the same as you used to. I remember you teasing each other when you was kids. Some things never change."

"I agree," Papa said smiling. "Beverly is just as sweet and beautiful as she was back then. I've never seen any woman keep her looks the way you have, Bev. Except Essie. She was the most beautiful woman I ever saw—right up to the day she died."

"Yes, she was, Papa," my mother said, tears filling

her eyes. "She certainly was."

"Sam," my father said, "we didn't get a chance to look around your farm yesterday. When we get back, I'd love to have a tour."

Sam, who had just stuck a big piece of steak into his mouth, nodded, chewed quickly, and swallowed. "I'd be happy to take you around, sir. You, too, Mrs. Temple."

My mother smiled. "I think you can start calling us Daniel and Beverly, Sam. We're going to be family."

"Thank you, Beverly," he said. "I'd like that."

I just started to say something about joining them on the tour, when I noticed everyone's attention drawn toward the front door of the restaurant. I looked over to see a woman dressed in a black two-piece suit come into the room. Wearing black in July, unless you were Old Order Mennonite, was unusual in this heat. Actually, anyone wearing business apparel in this town stuck out like a sore thumb.

Jessie was at a table near the door, talking to the Scheidler brothers. I saw her walk over to where the woman stood, looking around the restaurant. They spoke briefly, and then the woman left. I wondered what she'd wanted, but I had to wait until Jessie came back to check on our drinks before I could ask her.

"She was looking for Abel," Jessie said. "She's already been to their house. I suggested she go over to church. I think I saw his car there when I came in."

"Did she say why she wanted to talk to him?" I asked.

Jessie shook her head. "No, but she seemed pretty serious. I hope it's nothing bad about Hannah."

My stomach turned over as I looked toward the

front window of the restaurant. I could see the woman standing next to her car, writing something down on a pad of paper. "Excuse me," I said to everyone at the table. "I'll be right back." I hurried out the door and down the steps, reaching the woman's car just as she was getting in.

"I'm sorry to bother you," I said. "But I was told you're looking for Abel Mueller. Does this have anything to do with his daughter, Hannah? I don't mean to be nosy, but I'm a friend of the family, and I've been so concerned. . ."

The woman squinted at me, her eyebrows knit together in a frown. "I'm sorry, but I'm not able to share anything about the Muellers with you. You'll have to ask them for information. Right now, I'm just trying to locate them."

I glanced over at the church. Sure enough, Abel's dark-blue car was parked next to the side entrance. "Well that's his car." I pointed toward it. "You should try the side door because he may not hear you if you knock on the front door."

She put her hand up to shield her eyes and stared toward the church. "What in the world is wrong with that automobile?" she asked. "It looks like someone has painted the bumpers black."

"That's right. It's a Mennonite thing. Some people believe keeping their car as plain as possible will help to curb envy." I shrugged. "Abel only did it because he didn't want to offend people in his congregation who hold with the practice."

"That's the silliest thing I ever heard," she snapped, each word said with emphasis. "What is wrong with these people?" She turned to look at me with suspicion. "Do you paint your bumpers, too?"

"No, I'm not Mennonite. But Abel..."

"How well do you know the Muellers?" she said, interrupting me. "What can you tell me about them?"

Her rude attitude was beginning to bug me. "Actually, you'll have to talk to them yourself," I said sharply. "I don't know you, and I have no idea why you're here. If you'll excuse me." I'd turned on my heel to leave when she called out to me.

"What's your name?"

I whirled around. "I'm Gracie Temple. And you are?" I knew my tone now matched hers, but I didn't care.

"You can call me Mrs. Murphy."

"Then you can call me Miss Temple." With that, I stomped off toward the restaurant, irritated and angry. When I got to the table, Sam grabbed my arm.

"Who is that?" he asked.

"I have no idea. She wouldn't tell me. But I don't think she's up to any good, and she's headed to the church. Should I call Abel and warn him?"

"You don't even know what she wants. Why do you assume she's out to hurt Abel?" he said.

"Them business-suited types is always up to no good," Sweetie interjected, waving a piece of chicken around to highlight her pronouncement. "I'd call if I was you."

My dad shook his head. "What do you intend to say? Watch out, Abel, a woman in a business suit is coming your way? Doesn't that sound a little silly?"

"I—I guess so," I said slowly. I still felt alarm bells going off inside me, but rather than jump in the middle of Abel's business, I elected to keep my nose where it belonged—for now.

Halfway through lunch, Pastor Jensen came into the restaurant, and I introduced him to my family. Since he was performing the wedding ceremony, they were especially glad to meet him. He sat with us for a few minutes while he and my parents went over details for the rehearsal. Jessie came back to refill our drinks and overheard them talking.

"Who's making the food for the reception?" she asked.

"I plan to," Sweetie said. "The Menlos are making the wedding cake."

Jessie frowned. "How many people are you expecting?"

"It's a small wedding," I said. "Only about twenty people."

Jessie laughed and winked at Sweetie. "So you're planning to start a war in Harmony, are you?"

"What do you mean?" I asked, alarmed.

"Well, I kinda tried to tell you. . ." Sweetie said.

"This is Harmony, Gracie," Sam said, grinning. "The whole town will just assume they're invited. You're going to have some hurt feelings if you try to keep them out."

"But you never said anything. . ."

Sam shook his head. "I started to, and so did Sweetie. But then you left for Wichita, and we never got another chance."

"I've lived here all my life," Jessie said. "They're telling you the truth. I'd expect at least a hundred people. Maybe more."

"A lot of folks feel they know you, Gracie," Pastor Jensen said. "With finding Jacob Glick's body on your property and catching his killer, you're already famous in Harmony. A real celebrity. And Sam knows lots of people through his fruit farm." He smiled reassuringly. "It's your wedding—yours and Sam's. If you only want twenty guests, we'll find a way to do it. But I can't promise you that people won't be offended."

I glanced at Papa. The last time someone brought up Jacob Glick's name, his reaction was severe. But he seemed to be staring at some of the old pictures on the wall and didn't appear to be listening to us. I'm sure he recognized many of the people and places. Thankfully, the one picture with Glick in it had been removed.

Relieved that we weren't going to experience another outburst, I shrugged at Sam. "What do you think?"

"I think we should let everyone who wants to attend do so. Besides, we'll get more gifts that way, won't we?"

I slapped him lightly on the arm. "It's not about the gifts."

"I'm more than willing to do whatever I need to do," Sweetie said. "But I'm not sure I'm up to cookin' for over a hundred people."

"That's why I brought it up," Jessie said. "Hector would love to prepare the food for your reception. If Sweetie would allow him to help, together they could do a great job."

"What do you think, Sweetie?" I asked, preparing myself for an explosion. Again, she surprised me.

"I think that would be great," she said with enthusiasm. "Tell Hector I'll come back by this afternoon when it's slow and go over the details with him." She swung her attention to my mother. "You can come with me, Bev, if that's okay. We can work on it together."

Mom happily agreed to her proposal, and I was left to wonder what had happened to the real Sweetie. It was like watching *Invasion of the Body Snatchers* played out right in front of me. She had definitely changed since our first meeting. God was busy moving out the negative personality traits and keeping the good ones. Thankfully Sweetie was still Sweetie, and there wasn't anyone else like her.

With my reception plans on the way to completion, and the size of my wedding blown up at least five times, everyone seemed happy. Jessie went back to the kitchen to inform Hector, and Sweetie and Mom put their heads together to decide what kind of food should be served. I kept waiting for them to ask my opinion, but I seemed to be a side note at this point. Fine with me. I couldn't care less what people ate as long as they were happy.

I glanced over at Papa to see how he was holding up. He'd started off pretty good, but now he seemed distant again. As if he were somewhere else. His silence concerned me. Dad tried to engage him several times, but Papa just nodded, seemingly focused on his food. I'd begun to wonder if we needed to take Papa home when the front door of the restaurant swung open and C.J. Bradley walked in. I was glad to see him, but I'd hoped it was Pat. I waved him over.

"I see you took my advice," I said when he reached our table.

"You were right," he said, taking off his cap. "It feels great in here." His sunburned face made it clear the cap was a new addition. One he should have added quite some time ago. "I needed a break and your suggestion was too good to pass up."

I introduced C.J. to everyone at the table. "I remember you both," he said to my parents. "But just barely. You left town not long after I arrived."

My father shook his head. "I'm sorry. It's been a long time, and my memory's not what it used to be."

"Well, I remember you," my mother said. "You were friends with Melanie Pemberton when I knew you."

C.J. nodded. "Yes, that's right. Melanie and I planned to be married, but she moved away."

"I don't suppose you've kept track of her down through the years."

C.J. grinned. "As a matter of fact, we recently connected again. Believe it or not, after I finish getting Mom back on track, we intend to take up where we left off all those years ago."

My mother clapped her hands together. "Oh how wonderful. I'm so thrilled to hear that, C.J. Please tell Melanie I said hello."

"I certainly will do that."

My father frowned as he looked at C.J. "I sure apologize for not recalling you. It seems I should."

I remembered Ida telling me that Papa wouldn't allow my father and Benjamin to play with C.J. when they were boys. Obviously this was why Dad couldn't clearly place him. This was one situation where Papa's memory lapse was a blessing. It would be embarrassing if he said something rude to C.J. I glanced at Papa, but there was no recognition on his face when he looked at C.J.

"It's all right," C.J. said. "I'm sure Beverly only

remembers me because she was friends with Melanie. After your parents moved away, I got to know your brother, Benjamin. He was very kind to me." He smiled. "He showed me how to make birdhouses and we put several rocking chairs together before I went to college. I was so sorry to hear he passed away. I wish I'd gotten the chance to see him again." He turned his attention to Papa Joe. "It's certainly good to see you again, Mr. Temple. It's been a long time. How are you, sir?"

He stuck out his hand, and Papa took it, but his expression was blank.

"I'm fine, thank you," he said. "Nice to meet you."

C.J. looked a little surprised as he released Papa's hand. Next time we were alone, I'd have to explain Papa's condition.

"So you haven't been back to Harmony since you left for college, C.J.?" my mother asked. "That's a long time, isn't it?"

"Oh no. I've been back to see Mama several times. I just hardly ever make it into town. My mother prefers to stay on her own property." He ran his hand through his short reddish hair. "Honestly, I think she may be slightly agoraphobic. Of course she swears she's fine and just wants to be left alone."

"How long are you staying?" my father asked.

"I'm not sure. I don't see how I can go until Mama's back on her feet and the house is in better shape."

"This is a busy time for our wheat farmers," Sam said. "They're working hard to bring in their harvests, but I'm sure I can round up a few men to come out and help you."

C.J. smiled. "Thanks, I really appreciate it, but to be honest, right now I'm just assessing the problems and taking care of the emergency fixes. Let's wait until I have a better idea of how to proceed." He sighed. "Besides, my mother doesn't take to visitors very well. I'd have to get her permission, and I'm not sure she'll give it."

"Well, why don't you let me know after you get a better idea of what needs to be done. And if she'll agree to it, we can help you get your repairs done a little faster."

"I appreciate that more than I can say," C.J. said. "I may have been gone from Harmony for quite some time, but I certainly remember the way neighbors helped neighbors here. You don't find that in California."

"Harmony is different, that's for sure," Sweetie said. "I've been here a long time myself. Sure don't remember seein' you and your mama together. Sorry. I guess we just didn't run in the same circles."

"Oh Miss Goodrich. I'm sure you don't remember me, but I couldn't possibly forget you. All the boys in Harmony knew who the prettiest gal in town was."

Sweetie blushed. "That was a long time ago."

"I guess so, but I recognized you right away."

I fought a grin. C.J. was nothing if not diplomatic. He certainly didn't tell Sweetie she hadn't changed, yet his words made her happy. Good for him.

"I bet you was one of them rowdy boys who used to watch me whenever I came to town," Sweetie said. She narrowed her eyes and stared at him a minute. "In fact, I think you was the boy who used to whistle at me sometimes, ain't you?" Her face lit up with recognition. "Tarnation, your hair was bright red back then, weren't it?"

C.J. broke out laughing. "Oh no, my sins have come back to haunt me. You're right. That certainly was me."

Everyone at the table joined in the laughter except Papa Joe. He smiled and looked around the table, but I could tell he was lost. It was like we'd all gotten in our car to take a trip and left him standing on the curb watching us go.

"Them was some happy times back then," Sweetie said, chuckling. "You boys was always gettin' in trouble, though, as I remember."

C.J. nodded. "The pastor of the church wasn't too happy with us most of the time. But there was another man. . .what was his name?" His face wrinkled as he tried to pull up the memory. "Ugly man. I think he was the church custodian. Anyway, I swear that man hated us with a passion. I always got the feeling he was sweet on you, Miss Goodrich."

"Call me Sweetie," she said. "My friends do. And you're talking about Jacob Glick."

C.J. snapped his fingers. "That's it. Jacob Glick." He shook his head. "Hope he's not hanging around here somewhere. That's one man I'd rather not ever run into again."

"I guess your mama didn't tell you," Sweetie said. "Glick died about thirty years ago now, so you don't have to worry about him no more."

I waited for Sweetie to say something more about Glick, but thankfully she didn't. Good. I didn't want to see Papa upset again, and besides, I was tired of thinking about Glick. Better to let sleeping dogs lie.

I cringed inwardly. Another Sweetie-ism. Yikes. I certainly didn't mind emulating her in many ways, but there were some aspects of Sweetie's personality that should remain with her alone.

Just then Jessie returned to our table. "How about some dessert, folks? Hector just took some peach cobbler out of the oven."

I'd been convinced I didn't want dessert, but Hector's peach cobbler was something no one could resist. Sam, Sweetie, and I nodded in unison.

"Think I'll pass," Mom said. "I'm full."

"Bring her a small piece, Jessie," I said. I held up my hand when my mother started to protest. "Trust me, Mom. If you don't want it, I'll take it home. You really don't want to pass up Hector's hot peach cobbler."

"That's good enough for me," my father said, smiling. "Bring Papa and me some, too." He looked up at C.J. "Why don't you join us? The cobbler's on me."

"Oh thank you," he said. "But I've bothered you folks long enough." He patted his pocket. "I brought my trusty notepad with me, and I plan to do some scribbling in it until I have some kind of work-able repair schedule. But thank you for asking. Maybe some other time?"

My dad nodded. "Definitely. We'll be here for another week and a half. Let's get together soon."

"Thank you, Daniel." He put his cap back on his head. "So nice to talk to all of you. Hope you have a wonderful afternoon."

We all echoed his sentiments. C.J. found a table near the door and sat down. Sure enough, he brought out his pad and pen and began to write.

"Nice fellow," Dad said. "Good to run into people who lived here when we did."

Sweetie snorted. "He does seem like a nice fella now, but he was a little terror when he was a kid."

"Now Sweetie," Sam said. "Most boys are a handful when they're young."

"Well, you weren't," she said, one eyebrow raised higher than the other. "And Daniel and Benjamin weren't neither."

"But I'm exceptional," Sam said grinning. "I was raised by the most beautiful and wonderful woman who ever walked the streets of Harmony."

"Now wait a minute," Dad said. "I think I married the most beautiful and wonderful woman who ever walked the streets of Harmony."

"You two are both incorrigible," my mother said. "Hush up."

My father's expression turned from amused to alarmed. I followed his gaze and realized that Papa Joe was drawing a steak knife across his palm. A line of blood began to form.

"Papa!" Dad exclaimed. "Stop that." He reached out and grabbed the knife from his other hand. "What do you think you're doing?"

"Evil, evil, evil, evil. . ." Papa stared at his hand while repeating the word over and over.

ELEVEN

My mother jumped up and wrapped her napkin around Papa's hand, her face lined with worry. "Gracie, didn't you say Harmony has a doctor now? The cut isn't very deep, but I think we need to have someone look at it."

Jessie set a large tray filled with bowls of cobbler and ice cream on our table. "Here you go, folks," she said as she began to pass them out.

I stood up. "Jessie, will you take the ice cream off mine and Papa's and keep our cobbler warm? We've got to go across the street for a few minutes."

Dad started to protest, but I stopped him. "You guys eat your cobbler. The doctor's office is just across the street. I'll take Papa over there and have John take a look at him. When we're done I'll bring him right back."

"But Gracie. . ." Mom said.

"No *but Gracie*s," I retorted. "Dad needs to rest his leg. Besides, Papa's my grandfather, and I can take care of this. We'll be back as soon as John's done." I took Papa's arm. "Come on, Papa. We're going across the street, okay?"

"Sure, Gracie," he said with a smile. "That sounds fine."

Dad started to object again, but my mom put her hand on his arm. "Let her do it, Daniel. She's very capable, and Papa is safe with her."

My father sighed. "All right. Thanks, Gracie. But if you need us. . ."

"I know just where you are. Besides, now you can grill Sam without me around. I'm sure you'll enjoy that."

Sam's face fell. "Maybe I should come with you. . ."

"Nothin' doin'," Sweetie said. "You stay here and take your medicine." She winked at me. "If it gets too intense, I'll come runnin' for you, Gracie."

"It's a'deal." I led Papa to the door of the restaurant and we stepped outside to the sidewalk. I held tight to him as we went down the stairs. When we got to the bottom, he grabbed my arm with his other hand.

"Gracie, you've got to protect yourself. He's evil. He's so evil."

"Papa, who are you talking about? Jacob Glick?"

That veil of confusion dropped over his face again. "Yes. . .yes. . .Jacob Glick. He's evil. Don't let him hurt you. You've got to protect yourself."

I squeezed his arm. "Papa, Jacob Glick is dead. He's been dead almost thirty years. He can't hurt me—or anyone."

He shook his head vigorously. "He's evil. Evil, evil, evil. I caught him. I caught him."

"Caught him doing what?"

Papa stared at me like he didn't know me.

"Papa, you caught him doing what?"

My grandfather shook his head and patted my hand. "We need to get home, Essie," he said. "The boys will be wanting dinner. Hope the buggy's nearby."

"Oh Papa." I couldn't keep the sadness out of my voice.

"It's okay, Essie. We'll make it in plenty of time."

Ken and Alene Ward, a young farm couple who lived about a mile down the road from Ida, had come out of the restaurant and were standing behind us. I wasn't sure just how much of our conversation they'd overheard, but as I began to pull Papa away, I felt a hand on my shoulder.

"We're going through the same thing with my father," Alene said softly. "We'll be praying for you."

"Th—thank you," I said, trying to keep myself from bawling. I finally convinced Papa to come with me, and we made our way across the street to what used to be Keystone Meats. Now the sign read, JOHN KEYSTONE, M.D. Our small town had gained a doctor, but thankfully we hadn't lost our meat store. Rufus Ludwig, a newcomer to Harmony, opened up a new shop in a nearby abandoned building. Rufus was a genial man whose past was rather mysterious. He would only say that he'd moved to Harmony from Illinois and was someone who needed to start over. Most folks in Harmony respected his privacy, although there were a few busybodies like Esther Crenshaw who had decided he was an ex-con. Regardless, Esther bought her meat from Rufus along with everyone else. Ludwig's Meat was a blessing for the restaurant as well as our residents. Although it's not the only source of beef available since we have two local townspeople who raise cattle and sell fresh meat from their farms, it's a lot easier to run to Ludwig's when you need something for dinner.

Papa and I walked into John's office and found four members of the Breyer family waiting. The Breyers are a very large family who live on the edge of town. Cecil Breyer works at a grain elevator near Emporia. His job is considered the most dangerous in Kansas. Every year, people die from accidents at grain elevators. But Cecil's love for his eight children keeps him going back since the pay and benefits are so good. For some reason, at least one of Cecil's kids seems to always be sick. Good health insurance was vital to the family.

"Why hello there, Gracie," Abbie Breyer said when she saw me. "Doc's with Moses now. Shouldn't take more than a couple more minutes."

Before I could respond, the door to the back room swung open and John came out with little Moses. John smiled when he saw me.

"Abbie," he said, patting the small boy on the top of his head, "Moses has the flu. I gave him a shot. All you can do now is make sure he rests and give him lots of liquids." John pointed at Moses. "And by liquids I mean water or juice. Not pop."

"Ah Doc," Moses moaned. He pushed the bangs of his long brown hair out of his face. "Pop makes me feel better."

John chuckled. "Well, it doesn't make your body

feel better." He smiled at Abbie. "Water and juice, Abbie, okay?"

She nodded. "What should he eat, Doc? I tried to get some soup down him, but he wouldn't have none of it."

"I hate soup," Moses said glumly. "It tastes like throw up."

"Moses!" Abbie said, her face reddening while the other two children with her giggled with childish delight. "I'm sorry, Doc. Sometimes the things he says. . ."

John laughed and shook his head. Then he knelt down in front of the small boy. "Okay, Moses. Just what kind of food doesn't taste like throw up?"

Moses' face brightened immediately. "Ice cream," he said with a dreamy smile. "Ice cream doesn't taste like throw up."

John stood up. "Abbie, you still make your own ice cream, don't you?"

She nodded. "Don't like all the chemicals in the store-bought stuff. I've been making these children ice cream their whole lives."

"Then I prescribe ice cream," John said, trying to look serious. "Feed him ice cream three times a day until he's hungry for something else."

Moses' eyes got big as he stared up at John who towered over him. "You are the very best doctor in the whole world," he said, his voice full of awe.

"Well thank you, Moses. That's not what you said when I gave you the shot, though."

Moses thought this over. "Well," he said slowly, "people change."

Abbie turned her face away so Moses wouldn't see her laugh. She covered her mouth and tried to make it sound as if she had to cough. A few moments later, after composing herself, she turned back toward her son. "Okay, Moses. Tell Doctor Keystone good-bye, and let's get going. Gracie needs to see him now."

John frowned at me. "Are you okay, Gracie?" Then he saw the white linen napkin wrapped around Papa's hand. "Oh, looks like you cut yourself," he said to Papa.

"John, this is my grandfather, Joe Temple."

"How do you do, Mr. Temple?"

Papa didn't respond, he just stared at John as if he was trying to place him. But since Papa had never met John before, it was an exercise in futility.

John smiled at Papa anyway and pointed toward the back room. "Go on in, and we'll take a look."

John said his good-byes to Moses, his mother, and his brother and sister. Then he followed Papa and me into his exam room. I gazed around, impressed by the change. It had gone from a place that stored meat to an exam room that was clean and nicely stocked with medical equipment.

"Almost looks like you know what you're doing," I quipped.

"Almost," John said with a grin. He led Papa over to a chair. "Let's take a look at that hand."

Papa's gaze was locked on John's face, his eyes wide, his hand clenched tightly around the cloth napkin. I started to explain where we were and why we were here but suddenly I remembered that John looked quite a bit like his father, Jacob Glick. Except Glick's face was twisted in a way that displayed the evil in his soul, while the same features in his son turned out quite differently. John's aquiline nose accented his good looks. Glick's nose had just added to his long, horsey face. John's dark hair and eyes echoed his father's, but where Glick's overgrown black eyebrows had made him seem to be permanently scowling, John's eyebrows fit his features. And the dimple in John's chin was manly and attractive whereas his father's had given his face a misshapen appearance. But did Papa see the difference, or did he think he was looking into the eyes of Jacob Glick? Would he have another episode? The possibility frightened me.

I touched John's shoulder. "Can I talk to you just a moment? It's really important."

I explained to Papa that I had to speak to the doctor for just a few minutes and asked him to stay where he was. He nodded, but his eyes were still glued to John.

John looked at me strangely but agreed to come with me. We stepped into a supply room next to the exam area. I quickly explained Papa's condition and his reaction to John's father's name.

"So you're afraid he'll think I'm my father?" he asked.

"Maybe. You don't look like him really, but your coloring is the same. And the shape of your face. I just wanted to warn you. . ."

"Okay, I understand. I'll do my best to treat him, but we should probably get back in there. I don't think we should leave a confused man alone for very long."

"One other thing," I said slowly. "He—he cut himself on purpose. We were eating lunch at Mary's, and when I looked over at him, he was slicing his palm with his knife."

"I hate to say this, but you need to keep a close eye on your grandfather. Keep him away from objects that could injure him. Don't let him near a hot stove or even hot water without watching him. I've seen some really awful accidents."

"Have you treated many people with Alzheimer's?"

"A few, although I'm certainly not an expert. My best advice is to try to keep him as calm and relaxed as possible. If he's confused, don't try to 'snap him out of it.' Too many people do that in my opinion, and it only makes it worse."

"That's the same thing my parents said."

He smiled. "Good, then they're on the right track. Now let's get back in there. I'd hate for your grandfather to get any more disoriented. . .or bleed to death in my exam room. It would be such a bad way to start out my new practice."

I chuckled. "The cut's not *that* deep, but we thought it would be good if you'd take a look anyway." I reached out and grabbed his arm before he had a chance to leave. Then I peeked around the corner and checked on Papa. He sat docilely in his chair, staring off into space. "Before you go," I said quietly, "how are things going between. . . Well, you know, with you and. . ."

"Sarah?"

"Yes, Sarah. I've been gone six weeks, you know. Has anything changed?"

He shook his head. "I realize you've been gone six weeks because it's been that long since anyone stuck their nose in my business."

I felt my face flush. "Well, it's not like I don't know about you two."

John reached out and put his hand on my shoulder. "Yes, I know. You've been right in the middle of it, haven't you?" He sighed, removed his hand, and ran it through his thick black hair. "We've kept our promises, if that's what you mean. But it hasn't been easy. Seeing her walk past me—not talking to her. It takes something out of me each time it happens."

"And Sarah?"

He shrugged. "She doesn't seem to see me at all. If we're in the same room, she acts like I'm not there. Her father came in last week, and she waited outside."

"I'm sorry, John. I'd hoped things would be easier by now."

His dark eyes peered into mine. "I don't think they'll ever be easier, Gracie. My love for her hasn't diminished one bit. If anything, it's stronger now than it was before." He stuck his hands in his pockets. "But there's nothing that can be done. She won't walk away from what she believes, and I can't believe in God just because she does. If I tried to pretend, she'd know. And I'd know. We'd be living a lie, and I can't allow that to happen."

"I understand." I admired John for his ethics, realizing that some people might not be quite so honest.

"Well, let's see what we've got." He pushed the door open and we went back into the exam room. Papa still sat in his chair. He was quiet but smiled when we came in.

"Mr. Temple, I'm Doctor Keystone. I understand you cut your hand?"

Papa held out the hand covered with the napkin. "I believe I did, Doctor," he said. "I have no idea how it happened. Just clumsy, I guess."

John pulled up a stool and positioned himself right in front of Papa. He gently removed the cloth and inspected the cut, which had stopped bleeding. "It's not too bad. I think we can just clean and bandage it. Stitches aren't necessary."

"That's good, Doctor," Papa said. "Thank you."

Papa appeared to have moved past his initial response to John. I breathed a sigh of relief. While John rounded up the antiseptic and bandages, I glanced at the certificates on his wall. "So the medical profession allowed you back, huh? How many hoops did you have to jump through?"

"Not too many. I had to get licensed in Kansas, and because I'd been out of the loop for three years, I had to take some brush-up courses. But all in all, it wasn't too painful."

"Well, the town is certainly thrilled. How do the more conservative Mennonite residents respond to you?"

John sat down again and began to clean Papa's palm with disinfectant and a large cotton ball. "Great. They have no problem with me at all. I think a long time ago some Old Order Mennonites may have gotten their medical services through their local area oversight committee. But as far as I know, that doesn't really happen anymore."

"So everything's smooth sailing?"

He turned around and grinned at me. "I didn't say that. I'm still not used to having my bill paid in food."

I laughed. "What kind of food?"

He turned his attention back to Papa who smiled up at me. "Anything you can think of. Baked goods, meat, corn. . . Last week, one woman tried to give me a beautiful quilt her mother made. I turned her down. I couldn't take something that meant so much to her."

"Gracie," Papa said, frowning, "have you found your grandmother's wedding present yet? She'll be very upset if I don't make sure you get it."

I shot John a quick look. "No, Papa. I haven't found it. But let's not worry about it right now, okay? We need to get your hand taken care of. Then we'll find Mama's gift. Okay?"

Papa nodded slowly. "Okay, Gracie. But I can't have Essie upset with me."

I patted his shoulder. "I know. I know. We'll look for it when we get home."

"Okay. Well, am I gonna keep my hand, Doc?"

"I think you will, Mr. Temple." John finished wrapping gauze around Papa's hand and secured it with tape. "Gracie, I'm sending some bandages home with you. Just keep the cut covered and clean. Change the bandages once a day. In a few days it should be fine."

"We will," I said. "Are you ready, Papa?"

"Yes, I believe I am." He frowned and rubbed his stomach. "Are we late for dinner? I'm getting hungry."

I smiled at him. "We had to leave lunch because you cut your hand. Let's get back to the restaurant, okay?"

"Why yes. That sounds good." He held out his other hand to John. "Thank you very much, Doctor. What do I owe you?"

John shook Papa's hand. "Nothing, Mr. Temple. All I did was clean out your cut and put a bandage on it. I have no intention of charging you for something so trivial."

Papa studied John for a moment. "Well, it isn't trivial to me, son. And I think you can call me Joe now."

John smiled. "Thanks, Joe. I appreciate it."

Papa continued to stare at John for a while. His forehead was wrinkled in thought, and I was almost certain it was because of John's resemblance to his father. I took his arm, attempting to get him out of the office before he made the connection. "Come on, Papa. Let's let Doctor Keystone go back to work. We need to get to the restaurant before someone decides to toss out your peach cobbler."

Papa's eyes widened. "Can't let that happen. Let's get moving, Gracie girl."

I laughed and waved good-bye to John. When we stepped out onto the sidewalk, the heat was invasive. As folks in Kansas say, "It's not the heat, it's the humidity." Today it was both. I led Papa across the street and into Mary's. My father got up when he saw us and then came over to take Papa's arm and help him to the table.

"I hope Jessie kept Papa's cobbler warm," I said. "He's still hungry."

"It's waiting for him in the kitchen," Dad said. "Along with yours."

Papa smiled at his son. "Good for you, Daniel. Waste not, want not."

Dad smiled. "I know, Papa. You taught us that very well."

I was just about to sit down when I heard someone call out my name. Pat had just walked in the front door, and he waved me over. I excused myself and hurried over to meet him.

"It's about time," I said. "Where have you been?"

"I've been a little busy. Didn't you get my message?"

"Yes, but I really need to talk to you. It's important."

He glanced quickly around the room. "I need to speak to you, too. Can we go outside for a moment?"

His grim expression caused a shiver to run down my spine. I gazed back at the table where Jessie had just put my cobbler on the table again. After catching my father's eye, I held up my finger as a way to let him know I was going outside and would be back soon. "Okay, let's go," I said to Pat.

I followed him out the door and down the steps. He finally stopped next to one of the wooden rails where residents who rode horses or drove buggies into town tied them up. He leaned against it and stared at me, his arms crossed. "Look, I know how you're going to react to this, but I want you to try to keep your cool."

A prickling sensation spread across my scalp. "Is—is it Hannah?" I croaked out.

"No, we still haven't found Hannah, but the police have found the girl who went missing from Topeka. The one they believed was abducted by her boyfriend. She wasn't with him at all. Thankfully, she's fine. Just took off on her own for a while."

"That's wonderful news."

"We also found the other girl. The one who got into that red truck."

I breathed a sigh of relief. Maybe there wasn't some kind of crazed serial killer running around Kansas after all. "Okay, and what's her story?"

"She was in the middle of a cornfield about ten miles from here." He hesitated a moment, his eyes locked on mine. "She's dead, Gracie. She was murdered."

TWELVE

I guessed I swayed a little because Pat reached out and grabbed me by the shoulders. "Come over here and sit down," he ordered. I lowered myself to the edge of the wooden sidewalk behind us. Truth was, I did feel a little dizzy.

"You say she was murdered? How—how do you know that? Could she have died accidentally?"

He sat down next to me. "No, Gracie. She'd been strangled, and there was evidence she'd been bound for several days before she was killed."

"Do they have any idea who did it?"

Pat took off his hat and ran his hand over his closely cropped hair. "There are some things about this killing that match several others across the country over the last several years. The FBI thinks it might be the same man. He's never been in Kansas before, but he may be here now."

My eyes filled with tears that trickled down my face. My previous relief over the absence of a serial killer in the area evaporated. "But—but that means Hannah. . ."

"That means absolutely nothing as far as Hannah

is concerned," he said gruffly. "I still think Hannah ran away. It's just a coincidence that it occurred at the same time. Believe me, I've seen this happen before. There can be a couple of similar circumstances in cases that cause concern during a situation like this. But it doesn't mean they're connected."

I started to ask him how he could possibly know this seeing he was just a sheriff over a small county in Kansas, but then I remembered that he used to work in an area that probably gave him a lot of experience dealing with awful crimes. "But Pat, this is a serial killer!" I cried. "Hannah looks just like the girl in Topeka. How can you possibly tell yourself that these disappearances aren't related? The truth is that Hannah may have been abducted by the same man!"

He stared at the hat he held in his hands. "If the girl in Topeka *was* killed by this guy, and that hasn't been confirmed yet, he doesn't stick to blonds. Remember that the other two girls are okay. It's just a coincidence they all had blond hair like Hannah. There's no real link between the murdered girl and Hannah."

"But I have proof she was taken against her will."

He frowned at me. "And what would that be?" The impatience in his voice made it clear he was beginning to get frustrated.

"I found her bracelet on the road out of town."

He shook his head and sighed. "And how does this tell me she was taken against her will?"

I slowly explained the entire thing—about how the bracelet couldn't have slipped off her wrist. And how it had to be a message from Hannah that she was in trouble. Throughout my entire diatribe, his stoic expression didn't change. Surely I was getting through to him, but I couldn't tell. Finally I stopped talking and waited for his reaction.

"Look, I've already turned over the information about Hannah to the Kansas Bureau of Investigation so they can determine whether or not Hannah's case could be related to the others. Finding a bracelet that may or may not have been owned by Hannah isn't going to change anything."

"But it's proof. . ."

"No, it isn't proof," Pat said, his tone sharp. "It's just a bracelet. The KBI isn't going to find this *evidence* compelling."

"Well, maybe they would if they ever hear about it." I wiped my face with the back of my hand.

Pat took out his handkerchief and started to hand it to me.

"No thanks. I think I'm through. For now anyway."

He stuck the piece of cloth back into his pocket. "Look Gracie, I'm not going to lie to you. The KBI has no interest in Hannah's disappearance. There are certain signs they look for. Hannah's case doesn't have any of them."

"Like what?" I demanded.

He sighed. "I'm not going to tell you what they are. Why don't you just let the people who are experienced in this sort of thing do their job? You need to concentrate on your wedding."

"I know about the red truck—and the weird bumper sticker."

His eyes widened. "And how did you hear about that?"

"I can't tell you."

He glared at me like I'd just committed a felony. "Okay. Did anyone see Hannah picked up by someone in a red pickup with a 'weird' bumper sticker?"

"Well no, but. . ."

"But nothing," he said. "There is no evidence whatsoever that ties Hannah to the guy they're looking for."

I could feel my temper rise. "What kind of evidence, Pat? What do you need to believe she's been kidnapped?"

"Something a lot more solid than your feelings and a lost bracelet."

I shook my head. "It's all I have." I looked into his eyes. "How about going the extra mile because we're family? Does that mean anything to you?"

"That's not fair."

"I don't care. Nothing will make me give up on Hannah. Nothing."

Pat sighed. "Gracie, I'm not giving up on Hannah. That's ridiculous. But my years of work in law enforcement tell me this girl ran away. I can't just ignore that."

"I'm not asking you to," I said emphatically. "All I want you to do is open up your mind to the possibility that something else *could* have happened to her. Share what you know with me. Let me in, Pat."

He scowled at me. "You'd make a great interrogator, you know that? I swear, if you breathe a word of this to anyone else. . ."

I held up my hands in mock surrender. "I won't. I promise."

Pat scanned the area around us, looking to see if anyone else was in earshot. When he seemed satisfied, he leaned in closer. "It would be nice to find the truck. No one is completely sure what the bumper sticker says, but there's a bear on it."

"A bear? So the killer is a hunter?"

"Or he loves the zoo," Pat said sarcastically. "I have no idea why there's a bear on his bumper sticker."

"Okay, but at least that helps. Is there anything else?"

Pat blew his breath out slowly. "Well, there's the way that he kills his victims, but you don't need to hear about that."

I didn't argue. He was right. I didn't want those kinds of images in my head.

Pat put his hat back on his head and stuck his finger in my face. "If you tell anyone else what I just told you, I'll find something to charge you with and lock you up until the day of your wedding." He shook his finger several times for emphasis. "And I mean that."

I pushed his hand down. "So is that it? A bear on a bumper sticker? You put me through all that for something so insignificant? How are we going to find Hannah with nothing more to go on than that?"

Pat shrugged. "Believe it or not, I've had cases with even less. At least it's a start."

"So the FBI is investigating every man with a red truck?"

"No, of course not. But they are tracking the ones with violent criminal records who have attacked women." He sighed and shook his head. "The problem is that his truck's been mentioned in the media. Chances are he'll dump it."

"That means authorities wouldn't have anything to tie him to the murders."

"That's not true. They have solid DNA evidence."

"Oh great," I said, unable to keep the sarcasm out of my tone. "Don't they actually have to find a suspect before they can test for DNA?"

Pat rubbed his eyes, and I realized for the first time how tired he looked. "I know. It's not much, but right now it's all we've got." He pointed at me again. "You stay out of this, understand? If you think you have any more *evidence*, you come to me and me only. All the KBI needs is some little red-haired girl sticking her nose where it doesn't belong."

"Seems to me they need all the help they can get," I retorted. "We have no idea how much time Hannah has left."

"I've told you from the beginning that Hannah isn't part of this," Pat said in a low voice.

"But the bracelet. It just doesn't make sense."

"Look, could you trust me just a little? Hannah ran away. She'll find out she can't make it on her own and come home. Just concentrate on your upcoming nuptials. Really."

"But what about this murder? Abel and Emily will panic when they find out about it."

"I'm going over to talk to the Muellers right now.

163

I think they need to hear about it from me before anyone else. Please keep it to yourself for now."

I shook my head. "This will terrify them."

He grunted. "I'll assure them that we still believe Hannah's situation isn't related." He frowned. "Besides, I thought you Christian types weren't supposed to be afraid of anything because you believe God takes care of you."

"That's true. But sometimes it takes time on our knees and our willingness to fight the good fight of faith to get us through the stormy parts of life. Christians aren't perfect, you know."

"Yeah, I know," he said wryly. "You're just forgiven. I've heard it all before." He stood to his feet and helped me to mine. "You okay now?"

"Yes. But why did you come to me about the murder before the Muellers?"

"I tried to talk to them first, but they're meeting with someone from Child Protective Services."

My mouth dropped open. "Mrs. Murphy? Is that who she is?"

"You know her?"

I explained my encounter with the woman outside the restaurant.

Pat nodded. "Yep, that sounds like her. I've had run-ins with her before. She's good at her job, but she certainly isn't the easiest woman to deal with."

"But why would she be bothering Abel and Emily?"

Pat put his hat back on his head and pulled the brim down to shield his eyes from the sun. "Someone phoned in a complaint. Said the Muellers' lifestyle forced the girl to flee from her home."

"What?" I sputtered. "That's ridiculous. The Muellers are wonderful parents."

"Well, someone in Harmony doesn't seem to agree with you." He held his hand up to stop any further protests. "Look Gracie, give Mrs. Murphy a chance. She's actually pretty fair-minded."

"She could use some better people skills," I muttered. I turned and stared over at the church. Abel and Emily's car was still there along with another car that most probably belonged to the infamous Mrs. Murphy. "I'll bet it was that nasty-minded Esther Crenshaw who called in. She's got her nose in everyone's business, and she's always ranting on and on about how wrong the Mennonites are about everything."

Pat grunted. "I thought Christians weren't supposed to judge others."

I snorted. "Unfortunately, some of us don't seem to have gotten the message." I looked at him carefully. "That's the second time you've made a snide remark about Christians. Christianity isn't based on what Christians do, you know. Every time I hear that old excuse I recognize it for what it is. A cop-out. It's not hard to figure out that we're called to follow Christ, not each other."

Pat's eyes narrowed. "What do you mean it's a cop-out? A lot of people out there aren't interested in your religion because you people say one thing and do another."

"Hey, it's not called Gracieanity, you know. Christ alone is our example. We're trying to become as much like Him as we can, but it's a process. None of us will reach perfection in this life." I stuck my finger into his chest. "And you're smart enough to know that. That's why I said your excuse is a cop-out." I grinned at him. "The good news is that Jesus will even take someone as ornery as you."

Pat tried to glare at me, but his mouth quivered and he ended up laughing. "You're something else, Gracie Temple. If anyone could get me to darken the door of a church, it would be you." His voice softened. "But don't count on it, okay?"

I shrugged. "I'll keep praying for you anyway."

"You do that."

I gave him a quick smile before changing the subject. "Pat, I'd like to check on Abel and Emily after that woman is finished. I need to make sure they're all right."

"Not until I'm done," Pat said sternly. "You wait until I'm gone to pounce on them."

I started to protest his use of the word *pounce* when we both turned our heads at the sound of a car door slamming. The dark sedan parked next to Abel's car took off slowly from the church. It pulled into the street and started coming our way. I saw Mrs. Murphy behind the wheel. She stared at me as she drove past.

"That's my cue," Pat said. "You get back inside with your family. And remember what I said. Keep your mouth shut until after I leave the church." He glared at me. "Do you understand me? Not a word."

"Trust me, I don't intend to mention anything about the murder to my family. It's gruesome and depressing, and I don't like being the bearer of bad news."

"Good." He patted me on the shoulder and took off toward his cruiser. I watched as he drove away and whispered a prayer for the Muellers and Hannah. After Pat got out of the car and went into the church, I hurried back into the restaurant. Of course, by the time I got back to the table, everyone was getting ready to leave. A small foam box sat where my plate had once been. My cobbler. At least I could take it home and eat it later. Dad went up front to pay for our meal, but Carmen, Hector's wife, shook her head when he tried to hand her the payment. Obviously Hector had informed her that our lunch was to be a gift. My father put his money back in his billfold, and he and Carmen talked for a few minutes. I waited until they were finished for a chance to say hello to Carmen. She hugged me and told me how happy she was that my family had come to visit. Since she and Hector had taken over the restaurant, Carmen had become one of my favorite people. After thanking her profusely for their generosity, I started to walk out of the restaurant. Before I reached the front door, I heard Jessie call my name. I turned to see her coming my way.

"Gracie, can I ask you a quick question?" she said, her voice low.

"Sure. What is it?"

She took my arm and led me a few feet away. I

167

motioned to my parents to go on. My father nodded and started herding everyone out the door.

"I'm really sorry to bother you while you're with your family," she said.

"It's okay," I assured her. "Is something wrong?"

She crooked her head just a little. "That man over there. What's his name?"

I let my eyes follow the direction of her slight gesture. "Oh, that's C.J. Bradley, Abigail Bradley's son." I noticed the troubled look on her face. "Why?"

"Well, it's odd. When I first waited on him, everything seemed fine. In fact, we were having a nice conversation. And then I mentioned Trinity."

"I don't understand."

She shrugged. "Me either. When I brought up her name, he asked about my husband. When I told him I wasn't married, he got real quiet. Now he's. . .I don't know. Cold. Like I've offended him. Any idea why?"

I remembered what Ida had told me about C.J.'s mother. "I think he might have been brought up under rather strict religious rules, Jessie. He may have been a little shocked that Trinity was born. . .you know. . ."

"Out of wedlock?" she finished for me. She sighed. "This town has been so supportive of me and my daughter I guess I'm not used to getting that judgmental attitude. I know God has forgiven me, and that's what matters most."

"C.J. seems like a nice man. Just forget it and move on. I'm sure he'll come around. Sometimes we have automatic reactions to situations before we think them through. I'll bet that's what happened."

"I hope you're right. Having to wait on someone who dislikes me isn't much fun, but I'll do it if I have to."

"Do you want me to talk to him?"

She shook her head. "No, but thanks. I'm sure you're right. He'll probably get over it." She gave me a quick hug. "Thanks for letting me talk about it."

"Anytime, Jessie. You know that."

I watched as she walked away, and then I looked over at C.J. He was busy writing in his notebook and didn't notice me. He didn't seem like the kind of person who would be put off by Jessie's situation, but I didn't really know him. Besides, it could be Jessie's imagination. Maybe if it happened again, I'd speak to C.J., but right now, I had other things to deal with.

I jogged out the door to catch up with my family. Today wasn't going to be very enjoyable with a murder filling my thoughts. My concern for Hannah had grown every second since she'd gone missing. Finding her bracelet had convinced me she was in trouble but knowing the girl from Topeka had been murdered made me feel even more strongly that she was in danger. After we finished our tour of Harmony, I intended to pull Sam aside and persuade him it was time we took Hannah's disappearance and recovery into our own hands. I didn't want to upset Pat, but I was beginning to wonder if someone should contact the media about the missing Mennonite girl. People should be looking for her. And if she really *had* run away, which I doubted, maybe she would see the report and contact her parents. The more I thought about it, the more sense it made.

While everyone else waited, I ran into Ruth's and picked out some flowers. Then we all drove to the cemetery where my Uncle Benjamin was buried. I worried about Papa's reaction. Would he remember about Benjamin? As we got out of the car, I pulled my father aside.

"Dad, I'm concerned about Papa. Maybe I should stay with him in the car. What if he doesn't remember that Benjamin is dead?"

My father gazed out across the cemetery. "Papa deserves to see his son's grave. I won't take that away from him. If he seems too disoriented, I'll distract him, lead him away. But I have to give him this chance."

I wasn't convinced it was the best decision for Papa, but it wasn't my business to argue with my dad. Benjamin was his brother and Papa his father. It was his call. We walked past the monuments until we found Benjamin's grave. Although I hadn't been there since before I left for Wichita, a bunch of wildflowers had been placed in the cement vase at the base of the engraved stone. Who had put them there?

"Sweetie and Ida tended to the grave while you were gone," Sam whispered in my ear, answering my question.

I nodded, unable to speak. What precious friends I had, and how grateful I felt for them at that moment.

" ' 'Tis Grace that brought me safe thus far and Grace will lead me home,'" my mother read on the headstone. She turned tear-filled eyes to me. "And Grace did bring him the peace he couldn't find on this earth," she said. "I'm so proud of you."

I shook my head. "I only proved what I already knew in my heart: that Dad couldn't possibly take another person's life. I only wish Uncle Benjamin had found the truth before he died." I reached out and took my father's hand. "His love for you and his desire to protect you kept him from having the kind of relationship two brothers should have had."

My father wiped tears from his cheeks. "You know what, Gracie? The older I get, the less it matters what happens in this life. I know my brother and I will have eternity together. And that's what I cling to." He looked around at our assembled group. "And that goes for all of you. Even if we have to say good-bye for a while in this life, we are assured that it won't be for long." He squeezed my hand. "I'm so grateful to God for His wonderful promise."

Papa knelt down on Benjamin's grave. "I'm grateful, too, son," he said brokenly. "I can hardly wait to give Benjamin a hug. I know Essie is with him now and that they're waiting for the rest of us." He looked up at us. "You know, I'm fully aware that I have one foot in heaven and one foot on the earth. Soon I'll set both of my feet on that side, and Essie, Benjamin, and I will be there to greet you when you arrive. That will be a great day, won't it?"

My father bent down and helped Papa up. Then he wrapped his arms around him. "Yes, Papa," he whispered. "That will truly be a great day."

We stayed at Benjamin's grave for a little while, and then we walked through the rest of the cemetery.

Mom and Dad pointed out the graves of people they'd known. Several times they linked their arms together and wept at the names of people they'd loved. Sweetie knew most of the names and was able to bring my parents up to date on past history—marriages, children, and how people had died. She had some great stories about Harmony residents that I'd never heard before. By the time we finished, I felt even more tied to Harmony. As if I'd been raised here, just like my parents.

One grave was missing though. John had allowed Abel to perform a small memorial service for his father, more for John's comfort than to memorialize Jacob Glick. Then Jacob's ashes had been scattered somewhere private. John had never shared the location and as far as I knew, no one ever asked. Although he wouldn't have faced opposition had he wanted to bury Jacob in the Harmony cemetery, John refused. His concerns weren't for himself but for those his father had harmed.

We drove back into town to visit the shops. Mom and Dad knew several people including the Menlos who owned Menlo's Bakery. Papa's memory seemed clear as a bell while they talked about old times. They all reminisced for quite a while, and Mr. Menlo insisted they try some of his baklava. By the time we left, we had an apple spice cake, a bag full of Mrs. Menlo's fudgy brownies, and a box of the best baklava I've ever tasted. We stopped back by Ruth's Crafts and Creations, and my father was able to see some of Benjamin's beautiful birdhouses and feeders. Most of them had been purchased by townspeople, but there were three houses and two feeders left. Dad ran his hand over them slowly. He'd seen the ones I had at the house, but these were brand new, not faded by time and weather like mine.

Ruth came from behind the counter and stood next to my father. "When you get ready to leave town, you come on by here," she said softly. "I'll have these packed up for you."

He nodded. "Thank you. If you'll just make up a bill, I'll pay you when my wife decides what else she wants." He winked at Ruth. "I'm glad my car has a big trunk. Looks like she's buying out your inventory."

Ruth shook her head. "You don't understand, Daniel. I'm giving them to you."

My dad started to argue with her, but she grabbed his arm. "Now hush. This is what Benjamin would have wanted, I'm sure of it. I don't want to hear another word about it."

My father, who prides himself on his self-control, paused only a second before wrapping his arms around the stout shop owner. I turned away and concentrated on some hand-painted plates mounted to the wall. I'd cried so many times lately, I was afraid of drying out my insides. We spent quite awhile in Ruth's and by the time we left, my father's words had proven true. My mother's stack of new acquisitions was impressive. I'd shown them some of Hannah's paintings, and they'd agreed that she was incredibly talented. As I stood in front of the colorful pictures, I couldn't help but wonder if she'd ever paint again.

Papa spent most of his time gazing at a display of beautiful quilts, mumbling to himself. When I went to fetch him so we could leave, he grabbed my hand.

"Now Gracie, have you found Essie's wedding present yet? She's gonna scold us both if you don't find it. It's really, really important."

"I'll find it, Papa. We've still got plenty of time."

This seemed to satisfy him, and he followed me out of the shop, first stopping to receive a hug from Ruth. She'd been a young woman when Papa knew her and her parents, and she clearly remembered him, even bringing up times they'd spent together. Even though he pretended to recall the events she mentioned, it was obvious he had no idea who she was. Ruth's sad expression as she watched Papa leave made my heart ache.

We spent some time in Cora's Simple Clothing Shoppe talking to Amos and Cora Crandall. Although they hadn't lived in Harmony when my parents and Papa were here, it turned out Amos's parents had. They shared several stories passed down to them and we discovered that Amos's father and Papa used to go fishing together. Their conversation sparked some animation in Papa's face. Thankfully he remembered Norman Crandall and could even tell us a couple of big "fish stories" that made everyone laugh.

My mother grew nostalgic over some of the garments sold at the store and ended up buying two lovely pastel dresses. I had little faith that she would actually ever wear them, but since I had several similar dresses in my own closet, I certainly wasn't the person to protest her choice.

We made the rounds of quite a few other places in town, including Joe Loudermilk's hardware store and the Scheidler brothers' farm implements store. My mother loved Nature's Bounty, a shop that sells dairy products, fresh fruits, and vegetables. The store used to be owned by Joyce Bechtold, a woman who had been in love with my uncle. Even though I believe he loved her, too, he'd never reached out to Joyce. Instead, he'd remained trapped, trying to protect a family secret that didn't need protecting. After he died, Joyce left town, brokenhearted. Now the shop was run by Florence Avery, wife of a dairy farmer who supplied most of the milk, eggs, and cream. Flo was a very nice woman, and my parents purchased assorted fruits and vegetables that Sam and I toted back to the car. Their stash was growing. Hopefully we'd be able to get the trunk closed after loading everything that waited at Ruth's.

The last visit on our route was to Ketterling's Candles and Notions. I could hardly wait to see Sarah and her father, Gabe. My mother pulled me aside before we reached the front door.

"This is Sarah? The girl you told me about?" she asked quietly.

I nodded. "Yes, she's the one who's in love with Dr. Keystone."

I'd told my mother all about Gabe and Sarah and how that although we were now dear friends, my first introduction to Gabe was pretty bumpy. A man hurt by the devastation of losing his beloved wife to an outsider, he'd withdrawn into a world he thought he could control. Unfortunately he'd dragged Sarah into it, too. Thanks to the efforts of a loving community, Gabe had finally come out of his shell and joined the human race—to an extent. His complete commitment to his faith kept certain boundaries strong, including not allowing his daughter to become involved with an unbeliever like John Keystone.

"Their story is so similar to ours. I feel such compassion for them," Mom said.

"Except that you and Dad were both believers. John isn't. I can't fault Gabe for not wanting his Christian daughter to marry someone who doesn't know God."

"Does Sarah feel the same way?"

Dad, Sam, and Papa were busy looking over farm equipment through the Scheidler brothers' window so we sat down on one of the many benches along the boardwalk.

"Yes, she believes that she shouldn't be unequally yoked," I said. "But she's also very protective of her father. I told you that his wife, Sarah's mother, ran off with another man. Gabe's carried that hurt for a long, long time." I wiped the sweat off my forehead with the back of my hand. It seemed much hotter now than when we'd started our tour. "Sarah believes if she left her father, it could destroy him. She loves him too much to risk it."

My mother sighed and stared off into the distance. "But that's not her job, Gracie. We need to find our fulfillment from our relationship with God, not from other people. Her father needs to let her go so she can experience the life God has called her to live."

"I know, Mom. I tried to tell her, but she doesn't want to hear it. If I say anything else about it, I could ruin our friendship."

The men had finished their survey of farm machinery, so Mom and I got up and followed them to the candle shop. As we entered, Gabe looked up from something he was working on behind the counter.

"Gracie!" he said, his face breaking out into a big smile. "I heard you were back."

He held out his arms and embraced me in a big hug, something he never used to do. I was still adjusting to the changes, although I loved seeing the difference in his personality. Then he approached my father. "You must be Daniel," he said, holding out his hand. "I knew your brother. In fact, we were friends. I'm so happy to meet you."

Dad seemed somewhat taken aback by Gabe's Old Order attire and customary beard. I was sure it brought back memories from his youth. Gabe and Sarah were one of the few Old Order families left in Harmony. But ever the trouper, Dad quickly regained his composure and took Gabe's hand.

"Good to meet you, too, Gabe. I've certainly heard a lot about you—and your daughter."

I quickly made the rest of the introductions. When I got to Papa, Gabe nodded. "My family and I moved here shortly before you and your wife left

Nancy Mehl

Harmony," he said to Papa. "I'm sure you don't recall me, but I certainly remember you. You were very highly thought of in this community. I'm honored to see you again."

Papa took his hand and smiled, but the blank look was back. He stared at Gabe's clothing and beard and frowned. I wondered if he was also remembering the past. But whatever his thoughts, he kept them to himself.

"I still remember coming here when Levi Hoffman ran this store," Dad said. "We bought candles and lanterns for our home. Levi was a good friend of our family."

Gabe nodded. "He was a good friend to many people here. What happened to him was sad. I hope someday he'll return to Harmony. People in this town still pray for that day."

"Yes," Dad said. "We pray for that, too."

Just then the curtain that separates the main shop from the rooms in the back parted and Sarah entered the room.

"Gracie!" she said, laughing. "I've been waiting for you."

I ran over to the beautiful young woman in the dark dress and apron, her raven-colored hair tucked under her prayer covering, and hugged her tightly. I was startled to feel her bony frame under my grasp. She looked even thinner than she had before I left.

"I've missed you so much," I said, feeling somewhat emotional. Sarah was my very best friend in Harmony. An Old Order Mennonite and a very modern girl from the big city. Strange combination, but somehow it worked.

She finally let me go and stepped back to smile at me. "I've been keeping up my cooking lessons with Sweetie. I think I've passed you by, you know. Will you be ready to begin again soon?"

"I think we can work in one more lesson before the wedding. Can I call and let you know when? I really need the rest of this week to go over wedding plans and spend some time with my family."

Sarah looked at her father. "That would be wonderful as long as Papa will let me take off some time from the shop."

Gabe's eyes crinkled with amusement. "Saying no would only hurt me in the long run. I'm the one benefiting from your lessons." He patted his stomach, which was flat as a board. "I may have to go on a diet if this keeps up, but it's worth it. Sarah is becoming quite the cook." His face lost its jovial look for a moment. "Can't figure out why I keep gaining weight and she seems to be losing it though. Doesn't make sense."

"You do look thinner, Sarah," I said. "Are you feeling all right?"

She blushed slightly and looked down toward the floor. "I think I've been working too hard and forgetting to eat. But I promised Papa I'd do better, and I will." She swung her gaze up to me. "Now, no more talk of how much I weigh. I want to hear all about Wichita."

Gabe leaned back against the counter behind

him. "Of course, we've heard about Hannah. The whole town is abuzz. What's really going on, Gracie? Did she run away?"

I hesitated before answering, torn between keeping folks in Harmony from becoming frightened by the idea of a killer who might target their daughters and an overwhelming desire to warn these people I loved so much. Not certain if Pat was finished talking to the Muellers, I decided not to share everything quite yet. "We honestly don't know, Gabe. Sheriff Taylor thinks she's a runaway. A few other people aren't so certain." I sighed. "I just wish she'd show up. I can't help but blame myself some for this situation. If I hadn't taken her to Wichita. . ."

"Don't be silly, Gracie," Gabe said. "Even though Sarah and I believe in a separated life, we don't believe that alone will keep us unspotted from the world. People have free will. They have the right to make decisions. Good ones or bad ones. Hannah Mueller has godly parents who taught her right from wrong. Her reaction to what she saw in Wichita was her own." He shook his head. "It's unlikely she would have lived all her life here anyway." He motioned toward my father. "In the old days, young people were expected to stay in their hometowns. Schooling past the eighth grade was not only discouraged, but in many families it was forbidden. Do you remember?"

Dad nodded. "My brother and I were allowed to finish high school and my parents knew we intended to go to college. But my mother and father were rebels in their day." He smiled at Papa who returned his smile. "But yes, that's the way it was."

"Today, children are allowed to go to college even in the more conservative communities," Gabe said. "I believe the Muellers would have allowed Hannah to leave if she had that desire, so she would have seen life outside our little town eventually. It was something inside her, Gracie, that sparked a fire. It wasn't you." He shook his head and his eyebrows drew together in a frown. "Sometimes I wonder, though, if the old ways aren't better. I worry about the world and its effect on young people." He smiled at my father. "Of course I've changed my mind about many things since your daughter came into my life. I'm sure I'm not through learning, but I thank God all the time for her friendship. I know I'm better for it."

I felt my face get hot. "Th–thanks Gabe," I stuttered, surprised by his kind comments.

"I know Hannah will come back, Gracie," Sarah said reassuringly. "And then she might not want to leave Harmony again. Some people do, and some don't. Papa and I have seen folks take off, thinking they can't find happiness here. But after being out in the world for a while, they realize how special this town is and they come home."

I nodded. "Funny how different we all are. Here I left the big city for Harmony, and Hannah wants to leave Harmony for the big city. I love this place and can't imagine my life anywhere else."

Out of the corner of my eye I saw my parents exchange looks. I knew they felt differently. They couldn't get out of Harmony fast enough, but I was learning that we all have a path to follow. One that God has prepared for us. Reasoning has nothing to do with finding the place you belong. He is the only One who knows the way—and my way was in this town. And with this man. I grabbed Sam's hand.

"Well, we'd love to look around your shop," my dad said, changing the subject. "Gracie has been going on and on about some stationery you make, Sarah. And we must have some Honeysuckle Grace candles. Gabe, I understand you created these candles as a tribute to my daughter?"

Gabe smiled. "Yes, I did. They're over here."

Dad followed Gabe to a large shelf full of candles while Sarah led my mother over to a display table with sets of stationery she'd designed through a procedure called woodblock printing, a craft not practiced much anymore. Blocks of wood are carved with special knives, creating grooves in the wood. One design can actually be made up of several different blocks using various colors. Once the design is carved into the block, paint is rolled over it. The paint fills the grooves and then the paper is placed on top of the wood. A rubber roller is moved back and forth lightly until the pattern emerges. It takes real skill. Too much paint can cause unsightly blobs and an uneven design. Also, rolling unevenly can ruin a pattern. I'd destroyed many sheets of expensive paper before finally gaining some skill. Even still, not everything I did turned out right. Complex designs and colors mean that more blocks are carved, loaded with paint, and the paper that has already been rolled is rolled again. If done right, the second, third, and sometimes fourth blocks will deepen the design and add interesting details. Making a mistake with the last block was frustrating to say the least. The entire procedure would have to be started again. With Sarah's help I'd created a few patterns of my own, but I wasn't anywhere close to her level of expertise.

I took Papa's hand and led him over to a small bench in the corner of the room. We sat next to each other and watched as Mom and Dad looked over all the wonderful items for sale in the shop. Papa took a deep breath, enjoying all the incredible aromas in the room. There's nothing like a candle shop to excite the senses.

Papa pulled on my arm. "Gracie, who is that man?" he whispered. "I don't know him."

"No, I'm sure you don't, Papa," I said. I quickly explained that Gabe had moved to Harmony not long before he and Mama left. "You probably didn't get the chance to meet him and his daughter."

Papa shook his head. "I understand that, but something is wrong," he said slowly. "I know this place. But not this man."

"Oh Papa, I'm sorry. I should have explained. You're thinking of Levi Hoffman who used to run this shop. But he—he moved away." No sense in telling him that Levi was in prison. Papa didn't need to know that.

His expression brightened some. "Yes. Yes, that's it. I used to come here when Levi ran this store." He patted my knee. "Thank you, Gracie. I was confused for a moment."

"That's okay, Papa. I understand."

We sat there quietly, but Papa seemed much more relaxed. As she had in several other shops, my mother bought everything she could get her hands on. Funny thing, usually my mother was a very frugal person. I'd never seen her spend money like this.

Finally we left the candle shop, picked up Mom's purchases from Ruth, and headed home. My dad, who'd wanted to tour Sam's farm this afternoon, asked for a rain check. I could tell his leg was bothering him. Besides, both my parents looked really tired. Sweetie offered to meet with Hector by herself and get some different ideas for the reception. My mother gratefully accepted. Being outside in the heat all afternoon had drained everyone's energy. I was grateful we'd have an afternoon to rest. Running around in Sam's orchards didn't sound very appealing to me either. When we got to the house, Dad took Sam aside for a few minutes while Mom and Papa went inside the house. I waited until they finished talking, then I walked Sam to his truck to say good-bye. I'd asked him and Sweetie over to my place that night for dinner, but they'd declined.

"You need some time with just your parents," Sam had said. "We'll get together tomorrow."

Instead of getting into his truck, he paused with his hand on the door handle. "Your father just told me he wants some time to visit with me tomorrow while Sweetie and your mom talk about the wedding. I guess we'll walk around the farm for a while." His handsome features twisted with concern. "I'm not sure he approves of me, Gracie."

"Don't be silly. He just wants to get to know you better. I'm sure he likes you."

"Well, I hope so. But sometimes I catch him looking at me. . .I don't know. Strangely."

I laughed. "I look at you strangely all the time, and I like you."

"Very funny." He ran his hand through his long blond hair. "Well, I guess I'll find out tomorrow how he really feels."

I leaned into his chest. "Don't worry. If he forbids me to marry you, we'll change our names, run off to a foreign country, and start a new life."

I felt him heave with laughter. "And what will our new names be?"

I stared up at him. "Hmmm. Let's see. How about Grace Marple and Sam Stringer? No one will ever suspect it's us."

"Okay. But which one will you be?"

I pushed myself away from him. "I can be Sam and you can be Grace. That should really confuse people."

"That would confuse me, too. Maybe we should just stay here and work it out."

I raised my hands in a gesture of surrender. "Okay, but I'm offering you a life of excitement and intrigue."

He leaned down and kissed my nose. "Trust me. Being with you gives me all the excitement and intrigue I can handle."

"Good. That's my goal."

I kissed him good-bye and sent him on his way. When I got inside, Papa had gone upstairs for a nap, and my mother was busy unloading all her purchases. I glanced over at my dad who watched her with a worried expression. He'd obviously found her uncharacteristic buying spree troublesome. After unwrapping everything, she suddenly announced she was tired.

"I'll put all this stuff away later," she said, yawning. "But for now, a nice nap would help get my energy levels back up to normal. The heat really takes it out of me."

"You go on, honey," Dad said. "I intend to rest my leg a bit. Think I'll stay down here and find a way to prop it up for a while."

"How's it feeling, Dad?" I asked. "I noticed you left your cane in the car when we had lunch, but you took it when we walked around town."

He nodded. "It's a bother, but thankfully, my leg's feeling stronger every day." He raised his hand before my mother had a chance to say anything. "I know, Bev. I'm supposed to use my cane all the time. At least I used it most of the day. That should certainly make you happy, so no nagging, okay?"

Mom pointed her finger at him. "This has nothing to do with making *me* happy. We'll all be happy if you'll just be responsible and take care of yourself. And any nagging you get will be well deserved."

"I know, I know. Now get to bed, young lady. We need to be on high alert tonight. Gracie's cooking."

She smiled at me. "I know whatever you make

will be wonderful, Gracie. I have utmost confidence in you."

My father gave a dramatic shudder. "I can't forget the last meal she cooked for us. It almost turned out to be our actual last meal. I swelled up like a fat balloon."

"Oh Dad," I retorted, "you know that wasn't my fault. The recipe in the paper was a misprint."

My parents both laughed.

"Most cooks would realize that a cup of salt for eight servings of beef stew is too much," my mother said.

"Well I know that *now*. But you can't fault a gal for trying."

"Maybe we should look over the recipe for tonight," Dad said. "You know, for our own protection."

"I'll have you know that Sweetie taught me how to prepare tonight's main course. I've made it twice already, and no one has died."

"That's just the kind of recommendation I like before I eat," my father mumbled. "Here, try this. No one has died."

My mother shook her head and waved a hand at us. "I've had enough of you two comics. I'm going to bed. See you later."

She climbed the stairs, leaving my father and me alone. "How about something to drink?" I asked him.

"Sounds crazy since it's so hot outside, but I'd love a cup of coffee with cream. How about you?"

My father and I shared a love of coffee. One thing I missed in Harmony—Starbucks. An iced caramel macchiato would taste great right about now. But coffee with plain cream was growing on me. "Sure, I'll put a pot on."

Dad followed me into the kitchen and sat down at the table. "This place brings back so many memories," he said quietly. "Mama fixing breakfast in this kitchen. All of us crowded around the table. Papa praying. Then we'd talk about what was going on in our lives." He stared out the kitchen window. "I think families are missing out on something important nowadays. Gathering together around the supper table. Really listening to each other. We're becoming a generation that tunes each other out, I'm afraid."

I filled my metal coffeepot with coffee and water and set it on the stove to percolate. Dad frowned at me. "You have electricity now. Why don't you have a coffeemaker?"

I turned on the gas burner under the pot. "Oh, I have one, but I like the taste of coffee in a regular pot, and I don't have a lot of counter space in here. Do you mind?"

He shook his head. "Not at all. I like coffee made the old-fashioned way. Has a deeper, richer taste."

I came over and sat down at the table. "Sam tells me you want to talk to him tomorrow. Mind if I ask what that's about?"

He just shrugged but didn't answer me.

"Look Dad. Anyone who spends time around Sam can see what a wonderful man he is. But I've noticed . . .I don't know. You've spoken to him rather harshly a few times. And I've caught you looking at him in a weird way. I mean, you *do* like him, don't you?"

My father let out his breath slowly. "Yes, I like

him, Gracie. It's just that in all the time you two have known each other, it's hard to believe you couldn't find a few days to come to Nebraska and introduce Sam to your mother and me. After all, we are your parents." He leaned back in his chair and crossed his arms. "It's not like I don't know what it's like to be young and in love. But I truly don't believe I'd have left Harmony with your mother unless Mama and Papa knew my bride-to-be and approved of her. I've never been given the chance to approve or disapprove of Sam. What if Mom and I didn't like him? Would it make any difference?"

I thought about his question for a moment. "Well, I'm certain beyond a shadow of a doubt that Sam and I are meant to be together. What you're actually asking me is if you and Mom wanted me to disobey God's will for my life, would I do it? I guess the answer to that question is no."

He was quiet for a little while, and his gaze drifted back toward the window. Finally, he sighed. "I understand, Gracie, and it sounds right. Maybe some of those old ways are still inside me, but I would have felt better about this marriage if you and Sam had made more of an effort to visit us before becoming engaged. And I really would have liked it if Sam had asked us for your hand."

I snorted. "Asked you for my hand?" I searched my father's face but couldn't see any sign that he wasn't serious. "Wow, Dad. Does anyone do that anymore?"

He frowned at me. "Yes, Grace Marie, they do. Milton Olshaker's son-in-law went to him first before he asked their daughter, Debbie, to marry him."

I raised an eyebrow. "Who in the world is Milton Olshaker?"

"You know the Olshakers? From church?"

"Oh wait a minute. I *do* remember them." I grinned at him. "Debbie Olshaker? I imagine Milton and his wife were thankful *anyone* wanted to marry Debbie."

"Grace Marie," my father gasped. "That's unkind. Besides, Debbie looks better now. She got her braces off and has started plucking her eyebrows. . ." Although he tried to fight it, he burst out laughing. I joined in. "Okay, okay. Bad example," he said, wiping his eyes. "But the point is. . ."

"The point is, my dear old dad," I said softly, "you feel left out. I'm sorry. I really do understand. What can Sam and I do to make it up to you?"

He reached over and grabbed my hand. "Nothing," he said. "You're right. I guess I feel like I'm losing my little girl." He let go of my hand and pointed his finger in my face. "And please don't tell me I'm gaining a son. I'm not quite ready for that yet."

"But you will be, Dad," I said gently. "When you get to know Sam the way I do you'll be proud to call him your son. Besides, Sam could really use a father figure in his life."

"But he has a father, although I must admit they don't seem very close."

I told my father the story of Sam and Pat, getting up in the middle of my story to turn down the burner and pour our coffee. I got the cream out of the refrigerator and put it on the table. Then I finished explaining the confusing relationship the best I could.

"Oh my," Dad said when I was done. "I had no idea." He shook his head. "I feel sorry for them both, but Sam needs to forgive his father and find a way to build a relationship."

"That's what I keep telling him, but he's still trying to work through some issues."

Dad nodded. "People have to deal with their feelings. They just fester inside if you don't." He smiled. "If Sam is the man you say he is, he'll find a way."

"I'm counting on it. I was so encouraged last night when he insisted that Pat join us for dinner. That was a real step in the right direction."

"I'm not so sure his aunt felt the same way."

"Sweetie's having a hard time. She blames Pat for leaving her sister."

"So what really happened to Sam's mother? You said she contacted Pat and told him where Sam was."

"That was a few years ago. After she wrote to Pat she moved from the town where she'd been living. Left no forwarding address. Pat's looked everywhere for her, and he has lots of ways to track people. More than a regular person would have at their disposal. But he hasn't been successful in finding her. She said in her letter that she was really sick and wanted to tell Pat the truth before she died. Pat's even checked through death records, but he hasn't found anything."

"Has Sam talked to Pat about his mother?"

I shook my head. "No, and he doesn't like to talk

about her with anyone. I've learned not to bring up the subject."

"Sounds like he's carrying some unresolved problems into your marriage."

I shrugged. "Maybe. But look at the mother- and father-in-law I'm giving him. I figure we're even."

Dad wrinkled his nose at me. "Ha, ha." He sipped his coffee. "Mmmm. Very good. Why is it everything tastes better in the country?"

"I have no idea, but I know exactly what you mean."

My dad stared into his cup for a moment. "One other question about Sam, then I'll leave it alone."

I raised my eyebrows at him. "And that would be?"

"Why does he always call you Grace? I've never heard him call you Gracie. Not once."

"Sam believes God's grace brought me into his life. Calling me Grace is meaningful to him. A way of letting God know he's grateful for His gift."

My father sighed dramatically. "Well, if that isn't the corniest thing I've ever heard."

"Dad!"

We both burst out laughing, and my father almost spilled his coffee.

"Oh my," he said when we settled down a bit. "I couldn't pass that up. You set me up so perfectly."

"Glad I could assist your attempt at humor," I said grinning.

"Actually, I really appreciate that he sees you that way. Your mother and I named you Grace for a reason. After doctors said we might never have children, we prayed that God would do what medical science couldn't. And a couple of months later, you were conceived. That's why we named you Grace. Sam's got it right."

"Oh Dad."

"I love you, Grace Marie," he said, his voice full of emotion. "I want you to be confident of that every moment of your life."

"I am, Dad. I really am."

My father picked up his cup. "I noticed you talked to Pat for quite awhile outside the restaurant today. Is everything all right?"

"No. No, it's not." I told him about the police finding the body of the girl in Topeka.

"That's terrible. Does Pat think the cases are related?"

"No, he doesn't. He still thinks Hannah ran away."

My thoughts turned back to my conversation with Pat, and my attention drifted away until Dad said, "Gracie, you're twirling your hair again."

I let go of the strand of hair wrapped around my finger. "Sorry. I just don't know what to think. I mean, according to Pat, Hannah's situation doesn't match the profile of the other cases."

"Other *cases*. What do you mean?"

"I guess there are some similarities between this murder and several others. The police think the killing in Topeka is the work of a serial killer."

My father frowned. "I just can't believe something like that could touch Harmony."

"Why? There have been two murders in Harmony.

Living simply doesn't keep evil away, Dad. It takes more than that."

"I know, I know. It's just. . ."

I smiled. "Evil doesn't belong here?"

He chuckled. "Yes, I guess that's what I mean. There's something different about Harmony. Something. . ."

"Yes, I know. Something special. That's why I moved here. You seemed so upset when I made that decision, I figured you'd never understand."

My father ran a finger around the rim of his cup. "Oh, I understand, Gracie. You know, when your mom and I left Harmony, it was one of the hardest things I've ever done. I've been so angry. . ."

"Because of the way you were treated?"

He stopped and stared past me, out the window again. I couldn't blame him, it's a beautiful sight. Deep-green grasses sprinkled with colorful wildflowers and lush trees that line a crystal-clear lake. After pausing for several seconds, he shook his head. "You know, I thought that's why I had such negative feelings toward this place. But now I don't know. I'm starting to wonder if I was more upset about what was happening to Harmony than how your mother and I were being treated. Funny I didn't see that until we came ho. . .back."

"You started to say 'home.' Wow, Dad. After all these years and all the negative things you've said about this place, you still see it as home?"

He was quiet as he stared at his coffee cup for a while. "Isn't it silly? Yes, I guess I do. My bitterness toward some of the people here made me forget all the wonderful things about this place." He rubbed his hand across his face. "Funny how we do that to ourselves. A couple of unpleasant memories can drive out all the good ones if we let them."

I started to agree with him when a shout from the living room stopped our conversation cold. We both jumped up and hurried out of the kitchen just in time to see Papa standing at the top of the stairs, his eyes wild and his hair messed up.

"I can't find it!" he yelled. "I can't find it anywhere! Essie will be so upset. . ."

Before either one of us could rush to his side, Papa stepped out as if he were standing on a solid floor. We watched in horror as he tumbled down the stairs.

THIRTEEN

Thanks again for coming over here," I said to John. "I know it's an inconvenience."

He put his stethoscope back into his medical bag. "Like I said, it's no problem. My only other patient was Franklin Marshall. Lancing the boil on his foot can wait a bit."

"The life of a doctor is really glamorous," I said, grinning.

John smiled. "No kidding."

"So my father will be all right?" Dad asked.

"He's fine," John said. "He'll probably be a little sore. Just make him rest for a couple of days. If he complains of any unusual pain, let me know, but I can't find any broken bones."

"What a stupid thing to do," Papa said, adjusting the quilt I'd tucked around him as he lay on the couch. "I can't imagine what I was thinking."

Papa had no memory of even getting out of bed, and he had no explanation what it was he'd been attempting so hard to find. Ever since he'd arrived, he'd been trying to find something—a wedding present from Mama. My father believed it was something lodged in his memory from long ago and triggered by all the talk of my upcoming wedding.

"Don't worry about it, Papa," I said, putting my hand on his shoulder. "Must have been a bad dream. I'm just glad you're okay."

Papa mumbled something unintelligible, and his eyes closed.

"I gave him something for the pain," John said. "He'll be a little sleepy." He held out a bottle to me. "You might give him one of these every four to six hours for a day or two. Then just if he complains of pain."

"Will they make him more confused?" my mother asked.

"Maybe a little, but he'll be comfortable and relaxed. Alzheimer's patients can get agitated quickly. You shouldn't have any more outbursts for a while."

"I shouldn't have brought him to Harmony," Dad said slowly.

John shook his head. "Look Daniel, it's not my job to tell you what you should or shouldn't do. But do you think your father would be happier in a nursing home or here with his family? Yes, there will be some confusion. Some problems. But he really wants to be in Harmony. I guarantee you he's more at peace here than he would be back in Nebraska." He slapped my dad lightly on the back. "You can do this. Someday when he's gone, you'll be glad you made the effort. Regrets are poisonous. Trust me. I had to learn that the hard way. Living with them is tougher than enduring the problems you're having now. As long as you keep him safe—make sure he doesn't hurt himself or wander off—he'll be fine."

"Someone will have to stay down here with him if he can't be upstairs," Mom said. "What if he gets up in the middle of the night and tries to go outside or something?"

I chuckled. "Mom, this is Harmony. Even if that happened, he'd have to walk twenty miles to the highway. There's nothing out here that can harm him."

"Still. . ." she said, her face twisted with worry.

"I'll put my sleeping bag in the living room and camp out on the floor. It's no problem."

"You don't need to do that, Snicklefritz," my father said. "I'll do it."

I snorted. "Oh sure. You lying on the floor with your bum leg. Mom and I will end up with two patients."

My father started to respond, but I held up my hand. "Just give it up. I don't mind a bit. In fact, it will give me more time with Papa before you all go home. I'd really like that."

My mother grabbed my father's arm. "Quit fighting your daughter, Daniel," she scolded. "You don't have to be the one to do everything. Let us help sometimes."

"Very good advice," John said. "Gracie, call me if you need anything. I think I'd better head back to the office. A boil awaits."

I laughed and walked with him to the door. Before he left, he gave me a hug. "You'll be fine," he whispered in my ear. "You're the strongest person I know."

I stood staring at the front door after he closed it. John Keystone was so different from the cold, angry man I'd first met. I suspected his love for Sarah was the main reason. Love can certainly change people.

"Nice man," my father said. He came up and put his arm around me. "You certainly have made a home for yourself here. I wish. . ." His voice trailed off. I started to ask him what he was going to say when my mother interrupted.

"My goodness, it's almost five o'clock. Do you need help with dinner?" she asked.

"No. You two relax awhile. I'll get busy."

"And just what are we supposed to do?" my father grumbled. "No TV, except for that sad little set in your room."

I put my hands on my hips. "Well, for crying out loud. What did you do for entertainment when you lived in Harmony?"

My father got a mischievous look on his face. "I used to sneak out into the woods with your mother and neck."

"Daniel Christopher Temple!" my mother exclaimed. "I was a proper Mennonite girl. I never, ever necked!"

I burst out laughing. "Why, Mom. I'm shocked. Here you made me think you never even kissed Dad until you were married."

"Oh you two," she said, her face red, "I never said anything like that."

I started to fire back a smart-alecky answer when someone knocked on the door. "John must have forgotten something." I quickly swung the door open and was surprised to find the infamous Mrs. Murphy standing on my front porch. I was so shocked I couldn't think of anything to say.

"I'm sorry to bother you," she said frowning. "I'd like to talk to you for a few minutes if you don't mind."

Mrs. Murphy's dark hair, pulled back in a tight bun, gave her an almost oriental look. The severe hairstyle seemed to match her uptight personality.

"I—I don't know," I said hesitantly. "If you're trying to find dirt on Abel and Emily Mueller, you've come to the wrong place."

She sighed and her stern features softened a little. "Well, that's just it. I've talked to the Muellers, and I've spoken to several other people in town. I'm not getting any information that makes me think Hannah Mueller ran away because she was being abused. I still don't understand the rigid rules these people live by, but I don't find any reason Hannah should be removed from her home once she's found."

"Well that's a relief. But what is it you want from me?"

She glanced at her watch. "I wonder if I could buy you dinner in town? I'd like to talk to you a bit so I can wrap this case up."

I just stared at her, not knowing what to say. I needed to fix supper for my family, yet I was willing to do anything I could to send this woman packing. Maybe getting her to ease up on Abel and Emily would help to make up for the trouble I'd caused them.

"You go ahead, Gracie," my mother said from behind me. I turned to find her standing a few feet away, listening to our conversation. "I can cook for us tonight. You fix supper another night."

"Okay," I said slowly. I looked at Mrs. Murphy.

"Can I meet you at Mary's in about twenty minutes?"

"That would be fine." She turned, went down the stairs, and headed out to her car without saying good-bye. Her brusque manner was certainly intact even if her suspicions about Abel and Emily had abated some.

I closed the door and turned to look at Mom. "I don't trust her. What if this is some kind of trap? What if she tries to make me say something awful about the Muellers and then uses it against them?"

"Do you actually know anything awful about them?" my father asked as he watched the exchange between my mother and me from the rocking chair.

"Well. . .no."

"Then I think you're safe."

My mother grabbed my hand. "Now show me what you were going to make for supper. I may not fix it quite the way you planned to, but I'll try not to poison anyone."

"You're a great cook," I said with a smile. "I think the chances of doing bodily harm to this family is much more likely with me standing over the stove."

"Wow," Dad said. "I think I'm grateful to Mrs. Murphy for showing up when she did."

My mother giggled. "Come on." We walked hand in hand to the kitchen where I showed her the ingredients I'd put together for Sweetie's famous meat loaf recipe.

"No problem," she said. "And I'll make sure there's something left in case you and your grandfather decide you want to make a meat loaf sandwich in the middle of the night."

I'd actually forgotten about our late-night forages into the refrigerator when I was young. Mama and Papa would come to visit, and Papa would wake me up after everyone had gone to bed. He'd make us meat loaf sandwiches, and we'd watch TV together until we were both too sleepy to stay up any longer. Papa and meat loaf sandwiches. The best sleeping pill in the world.

I went to the bathroom and freshened up a bit. Then I decided to change my blouse since I'd sweated much more than was ladylike that afternoon. It only took a few minutes to run upstairs, pick out a clean blouse, throw the sweaty one in the laundry hamper, and hurry back down to the living room. I checked on Papa who was still fast asleep, then said good-bye to my parents.

When I got to the restaurant, I discovered that Mrs. Murphy had already gotten us a booth in the corner. I assumed she wanted as much privacy as possible. I tried to quell the nervousness I felt. This was my chance to help the Muellers. I prayed God would give me the right words and keep me from saying anything stupid.

"I hope this booth is okay," Mrs. Murphy said as I approached.

"It's fine." I scooted in across from her. "I'm still not sure what you want from me, though. The Muellers are wonderful parents. If you think I'm going to disagree with the other positive things you've heard about them, you're mistaken."

She shook her head and started to say something when Leah, another one of Hannah's friends, came up to the table. A beautiful, delicate girl with deep-chestnut hair, she'd caught the attention of most of Harmony's young men. But Leah was very devout and not easily impressed by anything except a heart committed to God. I admired her. She's definitely the kind of young woman a mother would like to see her son marry.

"Can I get you something to drink?" she asked.

Mrs. Murphy and I both ordered iced tea.

"Do you need a few minutes to decide what you want?"

"Well, I think it might be nice if I had a chance to look at the menu before I give you my order," the social worker snapped.

To her credit, Leah didn't respond. She walked over to where the menus were kept and grabbed a couple, handing them to us. "I'll be back in a few minutes," she said softly. I could see the hurt in her eyes.

"People here aren't rude to each other," I said when Leah walked away. "Most of us have memorized the menu and don't need to see it."

Mrs. Murphy shook her head. "I'm sorry. Guess I'm used to things working a little differently. I can be impatient." She gazed around the room. There were a couple of Conservative Mennonite families eating supper together, dressed in plain clothing, the women and girls with prayer coverings over their buns or braids. Other patrons wore overalls or jeans and T-shirts, having just come in from harvesting. The room was filled with the aroma of sweat and grain dust mixed with the great smells emanating from Hector's kitchen. "I just don't get this place. This is the first time I've ever been in a town that was so. . .so. . ."

"Peaceful?" I interjected helpfully.

She glared at me. "I was going to say *backward*."

"I'm sorry, maybe I misunderstood you. I thought you said you were forming a positive opinion about this town—and the Muellers. Am I mistaken?"

She sucked in a deep breath and let it out slowly. "You're right. Sorry again. I spend so much time interviewing the world's worst parents, when I find good ones, I'm still suspicious."

I raised my eyebrows with interest. "So you're admitting Abel and Emily are good parents?"

Leah came up to the table with our drinks. She put them down and then hesitated.

"Sorry, Leah," I said. "Give us a couple more minutes. I don't think Mrs. Murphy has looked at her menu yet."

She nodded and started to walk away.

"Wait a minute," the social worker said. "I–I'm sorry I was rude. It's been a bad day, but I shouldn't have taken it out on you. Forgive me."

Leah gave her a beatific smile. "I already did that, ma'am. Please don't worry about it. I'll be back in a bit." She left to tend to another table.

"Now see? That's just what I mean," Mrs. Murphy said, exasperation showing in her expression. "What's up with that? The people here aren't. . .aren't *human*!"

I couldn't stop my mouth from dropping open. "Surely you've met Christians before. It's not like we live on another planet."

She grunted, picked up her tea, and took a long drink. Then she set it down with a thump. "Oh yes, I've met *Christians* before." She said the word in the same way someone might say *cockroaches* or *poisonous snakes.*

"I take it you weren't impressed."

She unfolded the napkin wrapped around her silverware and put it neatly on her lap. "Look, let's not get into some kind of religious debate. I didn't ask you here for that."

"Fine. You said you wanted to talk about the Muellers. Just what do you want to know, Mrs. Murphy?"

"First of all, you can call me Susan if you wish."

There was a little voice inside me that wanted to tell her she could continue to call me Miss Temple, but I quashed it. "I'm Gracie. So what is it you want to know. . .Susan?"

She took another sip of her iced tea, and I noticed her hand trembled slightly. What was that about? I spotted Leah watching us from across the room. "Why don't we decide what we want to eat before we talk? That way Leah won't have to wait for us."

Susan reached up to pat her hair. As if a stray hair had a chance of escaping that tight bun. Her hair almost looked sprayed on. "It's hardly our job to make our waitress comfortable. She can wait until we're ready to order."

I could almost feel my blood start to boil. Her earlier show of humility hadn't lasted long. "Look here, Susan. . ." I drew out her name with emphasis. "Maybe you treat people that way in Topeka. .

.or wherever you're from. But we don't do that in Harmony. Either you decide right now what you want for supper, or I'm out of here."

She actually bit her lip to keep from saying whatever was on her mind. Then she flung open her menu and perused it quickly. I waited a few moments then waved at Leah to come over. She walked up, flipped open her notepad, and waited.

"I'd like a fruit salad and a slice of banana bread," I said with a smile.

Leah wrote down my order. "And for you, ma'am?" she asked Susan.

Susan's look of disgust as she stared at the menu couldn't have been any more obvious. "I don't know. I suppose I'll try the fried chicken dinner."

Leah explained the sides, and Susan picked mashed potatoes, green beans, and salad. As Leah walked away, Susan leaned over and said in a loud whisper that Leah could hear, "Surely even a cook in a greasy spoon like this can figure out how to fry chicken."

Leah didn't turn around, but I knew she'd caught the mean comment. I'd had enough. As Sweetie would say, "This ole dog ain't gonna hunt no more."

"Listen, *Mrs. Murphy*," I said harshly. "I gave up dinner with my family to come here because I care about the Muellers. But I don't intend to spend another minute with you. You think this is a hick town? There isn't anyone living here who doesn't have more class in their little finger than you do in your whole body. At least in Harmony we have manners. We know how to act. You obviously don't." I slid out of the booth and stood up. "I'll wait in the kitchen and take my dinner with me. You can sit here by yourself. That way you'll get to spend time with your very favorite person in the whole world. My guess is it won't be a new experience for you."

I started to storm out, but Susan stood up and grabbed my arm. "Please," she said, desperation in her voice. "Please don't go. I'm sorry. If you'll just let me explain. . ."

I had no intention of falling for that again, but as I tried to wrestle my arm out of her strong grip, I heard a voice that seemed to come from inside me. It was so loud, I looked around to see if someone nearby had actually said it. I clearly heard, *"Don't go."* That was it. Two words. *Don't go.* I took my other hand and pried her fingers off my arm. Then I sat back down.

"Okay," I said in a low voice. "But this is it, lady. I mean it. Knock it off."

I was shocked to see tears streaming down her face, and I started to feel like a heel. *Wait just a minute*, I told myself sternly. *She's the one who was nasty and hateful. Why am I chastising myself?*

"I—I just found out today that my husband is seeing another woman," Susan said between sobs. "Someone from our church. Can you believe that? Someone I thought was my friend."

Rats. Now I was going to feel sorry for her. Not fair. Not fair at all. "I'm sorry, Susan. I really am." That not only explained her attitude, I now understood the comment about Christians. I reached out and put my hand over hers. "Look, I'm not an expert about this kind of thing, but I do know God will help you through it."

She pulled her hand away. "Well He sure didn't take very good care of my husband. If this is the best He can do, I'll take care of myself, thank you."

The words were said quickly, but they were heavy with pain. My previous dislike for the woman turned to compassion. "People make choices," I said gently. "Sometimes they're not God's will at all. He's not a giant puppet master pulling our strings, you know."

She used her napkin to wipe her face. "I thought God controlled everything," she sniffed. "Everything that happens is His will."

I smiled. "Now that really doesn't make sense, does it? If that were true no one would ever go to hell. No one would suffer. Didn't Jesus pray that God's will would be done on the earth as it is in heaven?"

She stared at me for a moment. "I—I guess so."

"You've read what heaven is like, right?"

Looking more composed, she put her napkin back in her lap and glanced around to see if anyone had noticed her outburst. Even if they had, Harmony residents were too kind to let her know it. No one appeared to be paying any attention. "To be quite honest, Gracie, I don't know much about the Bible. Our minister says it's just a nice guide, but it doesn't mean much today."

Wow. One of those. I prayed quickly and quietly for help. "I don't believe that, Susan. The Bible is God's Word to us. His love letter, if you will. His Word is spirit and life. Not just words on a page."

"So you believe in heaven?"

"Yes, with all my heart. And just like it says in

the Bible, it's a wonderful place without pain, sadness, death, or sickness."

She sighed so deeply, she sounded like a big balloon losing all its air. "So you're saying that this world isn't like heaven because people make poor decisions?"

I nodded. "That started a long time ago when a man and woman named Adam and Eve made some really bad choices. God gave them the right to do it though, because He wants us to be His children, not His robots."

She stared down at the table for a moment while she made circles with her finger on the surface. "So it's really not God's fault that my husband made the choice he did."

"No, Susan. It's your husband's fault. God loves you so much. He'll comfort and support you through this if you'll let Him. And if your marriage can be saved, He'll help you with that, too."

"You—you seem to really know God," she said, another tear rolling down her cheek. She picked up her napkin once again and dabbed at it.

"Well, not as much as I want to, but I'm working on it. What about you?"

Her grief-filled eyes locked onto mine. "The way He's presented in my church, He feels so far away. Like someone I know *about* but not someone I really *know*. Does that make any sense?"

I nodded. Here I thought I came to meet with this woman so we could talk about Hannah and her parents, and now it looked like I was going to lead her to the Lord. Life is weird. I couldn't help but wonder what would have happened if I hadn't listened to that voice telling me to keep my rear end stuck in this booth. I took a deep breath and began to tell her about the great exchange. The life that Jesus died to give us—one free of sin and full of forgiveness. I explained that knowing who Jesus is isn't enough. We must know why He came and what He did for us. Then we must accept the exchange of our sinful life for His righteous one. I also told her that God has a plan for each of us. A wonderful plan that He formed before we were born. Not only can we find forgiveness and acceptance but we can also discover His personally crafted path made just for us.

"I want that new life, Gracie," Susan said, her voice breaking. "I need forgiveness, and I want to find out what kind of life God has for me. I'm tired and unhappy. My way isn't working at all. I want His way."

Right then and there we bowed our heads and prayed together. Susan asked Jesus to forgive her and promised to live every day of her life for Him if He would come into her life. By the time we finished, we were both crying. And Leah, who waited until we were finished, had tears in her eyes as well when she returned to our table. She put our plates in front of us and then leaned over and gave Susan a big hug. I tried to hold my breath, afraid of making this odd hiccup noise that happens when I get too emotional. Unfortunately, although I tried my hardest not to let it out, it showed up anyway. This of course, sent Susan and Leah into gales of uncontrolled giggles. I could feel my face get hot, and I looked around the now-crowded restaurant to find the other customers staring at us. But instead of looking at us like we'd lost our minds, they were smiling. I guess most of them realized what had just happened. All I could do was shake my head. Being a Christian is certainly not boring.

"What was that noise?" Susan finally asked when she could breathe again and Leah had left the table.

"I'm not really sure. I've had it ever since I was a kid. Unfortunately."

She chuckled. "It's so funny."

"Yeah, thanks."

"Oh Gracie, if I can get saved in a diner, in front of all these people, you can certainly get over making a weird noise."

She had a point. "Okay, I guess that's fair." After praying over our food, I dug into my fruit salad. It was delicious. Flavorful chunks of apples, oranges, blueberries, and bananas mixed with strawberry slices and walnuts. And to go with it, the best banana bread I'd ever tasted. It was still warm from the oven. Hector was an artist in the kitchen, and Harmony was blessed to have him. Although I was certain seeing Susan ushered into the family of God had helped to make everything, including my salad, seem much sweeter.

Susan took a bite of her chicken. Her eyes widened with surprise. "Oh my goodness," she said after swallowing. "This is the best fried chicken I've ever had. Even better than my grandmother's."

"Not bad for a greasy spoon, huh?" I said with a wink.

She smiled. "Sorry about that. I've been so upset all day. When I got to Harmony, I was looking for someone to unload on. Then I saw the way the people dressed, and for some reason it made me even angrier. I don't know why." She stared past me for a few moments. "I—I guess I was mad at God, and seeing these people. . .well, I decided to take it out on them."

"But then you met Abel and Emily."

"But then I met Abel and Emily," she repeated softly. "The love of God just flowed out of them, and I knew I didn't feel what they felt. My relationship with God wasn't like theirs. It confused me." She studied me closely. "I really do want to talk to you about this situation with Hannah, but to be honest, I think I searched you out because I knew I needed help. I couldn't talk to the Muellers since I'm investigating them. But they said so many wonderful things about you, as did several other people I spoke to, I just knew somehow you were the person I could reach out to."

I put my fork down. "Well, I'm not sure why anyone would be saying nice things about me. I'm the one who took Hannah to Wichita. That trip seemed to set this whole thing off."

She shook her head. "I don't think so. I spoke with the Vogler boy. . .Jonathan? He said Hannah was on her way to see him when she disappeared."

My mouth dropped open. "Wait a minute. Do you mean she was only going to meet with Jonathan? She wasn't running away?"

Susan shook her head. "No. According to Jonathan, she wanted to show him her new outfit, and they were going to try to figure out what she should do next. But she never said anything to him about leaving home before school was over."

My heart dropped to my feet. "Sheriff Taylor talked to Jonathan, but the boy didn't tell him that Hannah was going to meet him that night."

"I know. Jonathan said he was afraid of the sheriff so he kept that to himself. But when I talked to him myself, he came clean because he's so worried about her."

"Oh Susan. I've been trying to tell Pat that she didn't run away, but he wouldn't believe me. You know about the woman in Topeka who was found dead?"

Susan nodded and took a bite of her mashed potatoes. "Wow, delicious." She pointed her fork at me. "Yes, the story's all over the news. Why? Do you think Hannah's disappearance is related?"

"I don't know, but I think it's possible."

Susan seemed to mull over this information. "It sounds like Hannah's case should be carefully investigated."

I agreed with her, even more convinced that Hannah could be in serious trouble. We ate quietly for a while until I broke the silence.

"Susan, I'd like to ask you a question."

She nodded.

"It's about the reason you came to Harmony."

"Well, we almost always follow up complaints filed by someone in the community."

"Can you tell me who called you about Hannah?"

She shook her head. "Sorry, that's confidential. I will tell you that it's someone who claims to know the family."

I frowned at her. "I'll bet anything it was Esther

Crenshaw. Just so you know, Esther's a busybody who's always causing trouble."

She didn't confirm my suspicions, but a quick look of recognition at Esther's name told me everything I needed to know.

"Don't worry about it," she said. "I intend to report that there's no evidence of any kind of abuse. Right now, I'm more concerned about this serial killer thing."

"Me, too. Is there anything you can do to get someone to take Hannah's disappearance more seriously?"

She chewed and swallowed another bite of chicken. "I think so. We work with the KBI frequently. Let me see if I can get someone to look into it."

I reached across the table and squeezed her arm. "Oh thank you, Susan. I'm so grateful."

She shrugged. "You save my soul, I ask someone to take a closer look into a missing child case. Seems fair."

"*I* didn't actually save your soul, but at this point, I'll take any help I can get."

We both laughed. I focused on my food, and Susan did the same. Between bites, she told me how she'd gotten involved with helping children. Her own childhood had been anything but ideal. Even as a little girl, she'd dreamed of helping other children escape the pain she'd endured. I knew that many abused children have a hard time trusting a God who calls Himself a Father if their earthly father was cruel. Susan's road wasn't going to be easy, but I truly believed she would be okay. Now that she and God were walking together, He could bring real healing and restoration into her life. Beauty for ashes. I purposed in my heart to keep her in my daily prayers. Sometimes healing can be painful. Facing our fears isn't always easy.

After scooping up my last juicy bite of apple, I asked, "So what will you do about your husband and your friend?"

She rested her chin on her hand and stared at me. "I have no idea, but I think I'll take some time off work and get away by myself for a while. God and I need to spend some quality time together. If I immerse myself in His presence, and in His Word, maybe I'll know what to do next."

"Do you mind if I ask you how you found out your husband was cheating?"

"No, I don't mind." She looked down at her plate. I got the feeling she was trying to screw up her courage. "My supposed friend came to me and told me about it. She insisted I give Brad up. She tried to convince me that it was God's will. That they're supposed to be together, and that our marriage is a mistake they're trying to correct."

"Susan, God doesn't work that way. He doesn't condone adultery, and He hates divorce."

She frowned at me. "So if I decide to leave my husband, God will hate me?"

Her question hurt me down deep inside. "Absolutely not. God will never, ever hate you. Never. It's not possible. He loves you, and He'll love you every single day of your life. No matter what you do."

"But does He want me to stay with Brad?"

"I can't answer that. I'm sure God will heal your

marriage if that's what you both want. But God doesn't expect you to stay in an adulterous relationship. If you want to stay, I guess it's going to be up to Brad."

Susan was quiet, and I felt I should also be silent and allow her to think things through. As Sam had pointed out, I'm not Holy Spirit junior.

Leah came to pick up our plates. "How about dessert?"

Susan started to say no, but I told her about Hector's cobbler. We sent Leah to the kitchen to bring us back some cobbler, along with a pot of coffee.

"I'll have to diet for a week to make up for this dinner," Susan said as we waited.

"Keeping my weight under control is a constant battle in Harmony. My only hope is working out in the orchards with my fiancé. It's a better workout than what I used to get in the gym."

Susan asked some questions about my life, so I told her about my upcoming wedding and shared a little about the kinds of freelance jobs I was doing. My description of trying to send work over a dial-up Internet line made her laugh. She had a few questions about the conservative Mennonites who live in Harmony, and I explained their way of life to her the best I could. She seemed to understand. I noticed that she carefully steered our conversation away from her personal life during the rest of our time together. That was okay with me. She'd already shared a lot with someone who was really a stranger. We finished up our visit pleasantly, and when we parted company outside the restaurant, she vowed to see what she could do on her end to get more KBI interest in the search for Hannah. She also gave me her card and made me promise to keep in touch with her.

I stood outside by my car as she drove away, heading back to Topeka. Thankfully, a nice breeze made the heat almost bearable. I'd just started to open the door when I noticed a red truck parked on the other side of the street. A sticker was attached to the back bumper. I closed the door and ran across the street to get a closer look. Even though it was getting dark, a nearby street lamp made the image clear. I stepped back into the shadows as someone came out of one of the stores and got into the truck. Rufus Ludwig started the engine and drove away. I stared at his bumper sticker as he passed by me.

I could clearly see the image on the sticker as I watched him disappear down Main Street. A big, black bear.

FOURTEEN

I woke up Wednesday morning after a night full of bad dreams. My worst nightmare was easy to interpret. Hannah in the back of a red truck, calling for help. A bear chasing after her and gaining ground. I woke up from the first round of dreams, my body drenched in sweat.

Sleeping on the floor in the living room certainly wasn't as comfortable as my bed. I pretended it was just fine, though, because I knew my father would feel badly if he thought I hadn't rested well.

I'd called Sam when I got home and told him about Rufus's truck. He sounded interested but not alarmed. Then I called Pat and gave him the lowdown on Rufus and repeated what Susan told me about Jonathan. Pat was more than a little angry that the boy hadn't been honest with him about meeting Hannah, but my hope that this information might convince him that Hannah had been abducted was dashed.

"This still doesn't prove she didn't take off on her own, Gracie," he said gruffly.

I sighed with frustration. "But you have to admit that she obviously wasn't planning to run away when she left home. She didn't tell Jonathan about it. And what about the fact that none of her clothes were missing?"

"I considered the clothing. But if she was leaving her Mennonite roots behind, I figure she wouldn't take any of those long dresses anyway."

"Look, Pat. There's no reason to believe she was planning to leave Harmony that night. Please, just keep an open mind, okay?"

"I believe I am. I think I proved that when I talked to the KBI about Hannah. You need to give them time to do their jobs."

"Okay, okay. What about Rufus's truck?"

"I'll look into it. I doubt seriously that Rufus is the man we're looking for, but the last thing I need you to do right now is to make him suspicious. Stay away from him," he warned. "Do you understand me, Gracie?"

After giving him my promise more than once to mind my own business, I hung up the phone. I tried to focus instead on my plans for the day, but it wasn't easy. I prayed Rufus wouldn't get apprehensive and try to run. I also prayed that Pat would move quickly. We couldn't take a chance on losing the only suspect we had.

After a hearty breakfast, we all planned to go to Sam's. Dad and Sam intended to tour the orchards and get to know each other better, a proposal Sam found slightly terrifying, while Mom and I went over wedding plans with Sweetie. I'd told Pat where I'd be so he could keep me posted on Rufus. Hannah had been gone two days now, although it seemed much longer.

I cooked a big breakfast of scrambled eggs, bacon, and toast, and then Mom and I cleaned up the kitchen.

"Dad and Papa took baths last night," Mom said as she put the last of the clean dishes away. "Do I have time to take a quick bath myself?"

"We're not due at Sweetie's until two," I said. "There's plenty of time." I looked up at the clock on the kitchen wall. "I think I'll drive over to Abel and Emily's and see how they're doing. Do you think Dad can keep an eye on Papa?"

My mother laughed. "Asking your father to watch over any member of his family is like asking a mother hen to guard her eggs. It's part of his nature. Just let him know you're going."

I hung up the dish towel on the rack and went off to find Dad. He and Papa were on the front porch. Papa rocked in the rocking chair while my father sat on the top step drinking his coffee. I knew he felt nostalgic here, remembering his boyhood. For a moment it struck me as rather odd that thirty years after leaving Harmony, he and Mom were finally back. But now his daughter lived in the house he'd grown up in, and he was a man, taking care of the father who'd once taken care of him. I stood in the doorway and watched them for a while before I said anything, touched by an odd feeling of enchantment I couldn't explain. I just knew I didn't want it to pass me by too quickly.

"Think I'll run into town," I finally said, keeping

my voice soft so as not to frighten Papa.

Dad cranked his head around and smiled at me. "Sounds good. Have you asked Ida if she'd like to come with us today?"

Man, I'd been thinking so much about Hannah and her situation, I'd almost forgotten about Ida. "You know, I haven't. I'll go call her right now. She'd probably enjoy being part of the wedding plans."

Papa grunted. "Weddings were simple affairs in our day. The bride wore a blue dress. The groom wore a black suit. Then after the ceremony there was a banquet with singing and storytelling. The first night, the couple stayed with the bride's parents. And after that, they visited the homes of other relatives and friends who attended the wedding. There were no wedding rings and few if any flowers."

I pushed the screen door open and came out on the porch. "You weren't at Mom and Dad's wedding, were you?"

Papa took my hand, and I sat down on the porch rail next to him. "No," he said shaking his head. "We wanted them to get out of town and away from Harmony. You know, we should have followed them. It's one of the greatest regrets of my life—and of Essie's, too. But we were conflicted back then. Even though we believed Daniel and Beverly belonged together and we encouraged them to leave, we also felt we couldn't just up and go with them. We thought being submissive to our bishop was being submissive to God. We were wrong. Our bishop was the one who wasn't submissive to God. It took several years for us to see it."

"But you encouraged us to go, Papa," Dad said. "And gave us enough money to get started. You have nothing to feel badly about. You and Mama were wonderful parents. Always."

Papa didn't say anything, just kept rocking in the warm July morning air, holding my hand.

"So what did Mom wear when you got married?" I asked my father. "She told me once it was just a plain dress because it was all she had."

"She wore my mother's dress," Dad said with a smile. "Dark-blue linen that brought out the color in her eyes." He sighed. "She was the most beautiful thing I'd ever seen. We were married in the home of a Mennonite pastor and his wife, friends of my parents who left Harmony before we did. We stayed the night with them, and they treated us like their own children."

"Owen and Darlene Papke," Papa said. "Two of the finest people I ever knew."

"They live in Florida now," Dad said. "We still exchange Christmas cards and call each other at least twice a year. They mean the world to your mother and me."

"What dress will you wear at your wedding?" Papa asked.

"I bought one while I was in Wichita. It's lovely. White, with embroidered flowers around the neckline."

"Look, Gracie," my father said slowly, "maybe I should warn you. Your mother actually brought the blue dress with her—just in case you wanted to wear it. But she fully understands that you may have something totally different in mind. So be prepared when she brings it up, but don't feel pressured. You know your mother. She's the most sentimental person I've ever known, but she also loves you more than her own life. The blue dress is only here in case you want it. You're under no obligation whatsoever to wear it."

I was a little stunned. An old blue linen dress? For my wedding? "Thanks for the heads-up, Dad. I'll just tell her I already have a dress. I'm sure she'll understand."

"Of course she will, Snicklefritz. Don't worry about it."

I let go of Papa's hand, got up, and kissed him on the cheek. "I'll get you both some more coffee. Then I'm going to call Ida and head over to the Muellers for a visit. I'll be back in plenty of time to go to Sam's."

I took their cups and got them both fresh, hot coffee, and then I called Ida. She was thrilled to be included in the wedding plans. I thought about calling Abel and Emily, but I was afraid they wouldn't let me come, and I was determined to see them, even if Emily was still angry with me. To get to their house, I had to drive through the middle of town, right past Ludwig's Meats. I realized why I hadn't noticed the bumper sticker on Rufus's truck sooner. He always backed his truck up to the store so he could unload new purchases of meat from local ranchers. Unless I walked down the sidewalk in front of his business, I couldn't possibly see the back of his truck.

I drove past the church, but Abel and Emily's car wasn't there. During the week, Abel could usually be found in his church office, but since Hannah left, he and Emily spent most of their time at home in case she showed up. Sure enough, I found their car sitting in its usual place at their house. Gathering up my courage, I parked behind it and walked to the front door. I waited awhile before knocking, butterflies beating their wings furiously inside my stomach. A few moments later the door opened. Abel smiled when he saw me.

"Oh Gracie," he said. "How nice of you to come by." He hesitated and glanced away from the door. After a moment he turned back to me. "Please, come in."

"I don't want to upset Emily," I said quietly. "Is— is it okay?"

He put his big, meaty hand on my shoulder. "Of course. She'll be glad to see you."

I wasn't so sure about that, but I walked into the house anyway. "Have you heard anything, Abel?"

The big pastor shut the door behind me. "Nothing. Not a word." He pointed toward the interior of the house. "Emily and Jonathan Vogler are on the back porch.

"Jonathan? I hear Hannah was on her way to meet him when she disappeared."

Abel nodded. "Yes, we just found that out recently. Jonathan's parents sent him here to explain what happened. We've just started talking to him. Why don't you join us? Maybe you can add some insight to our conversation."

I followed him, but I wasn't certain I'd be able to help much. When we entered the lovely enclosed back porch, Emily's favorite room, I was shocked by her gaunt appearance. Her haunted eyes locked on mine. I winced at the pain I saw there and waited for her to rebuke me for coming. But she didn't. Instead she rose and put her arms out.

"I'm so sorry I blamed you for causing Hannah to leave us," she said. "You've been a wonderful friend. I've just been so frightened." She raised her face from my shoulder. "I—I can't sleep at night. I don't know where she is or what's happening to her, Gracie." A shudder racked her frail body. "I don't know how much more of this I can take."

I wanted to comfort her. I wanted to tell her everything would be all right—that all we could do is trust God to take care of Hannah. It was the truth, but for some reason I felt she would take it as a rebuke. I didn't want to sound judgmental or sanctimonious. As I held her I sought heaven. What could I do to help? Again, just like at the restaurant, a voice spoke to me sweetly and softly. When Emily released me, I led her back to the chair where she'd been sitting.

"Abel," I said, "I wonder if you'd read the ninety-first Psalm to us? It's so comforting, and I think it would help now."

"That's a wonderful idea, Gracie," he said in his deep, reassuring voice. I knew his emotions were as raw as Emily's, but as the man of the house, he was working hard to maintain a calm exterior for his distraught wife.

Abel took his Bible from the table next to him, flipped it open, and began to read the comforting scriptures to us. I glanced at Jonathan. His eyes were wide with fear. Perhaps his concern was for Hannah, or perhaps it was for his role in her disappearance. But whatever he was feeling, I watched as he visibly relaxed. Emily's face changed as hope began to ignite a spark inside of her. The wonderful words became life in that room. They encouraged us to trust God, to make Him our refuge. Emily took a deep breath as Abel read that God has given His angels charge over us—to keep us in all our ways. And as Abel finished the psalm, the promise that God will be with us in trouble and deliver us when we call on Him, filled the atmosphere around us as if God Himself had just made us a personal promise. I could tell I wasn't the only one who felt it.

Abel closed the Bible and gazed lovingly at his wife. "Emily, I know that Hannah will return to us. I believe it with all my heart. God has spoken to us today."

For the first time since I'd come into the room, Emily smiled. She wiped her wet eyes with the tissue in her hand. "I feel it, too," she said in her quiet voice. "No, it's more than just a feeling. I believe it in my heart." She looked at me. "Thank you, Gracie. God has used you to bring us comfort. Hannah will be all right."

I believed it, too, but I also felt an urgency in my spirit. Time was of the essence. I silently asked God to show me whatever I needed to know. Whatever

I needed to see in my efforts to help bring Hannah home.

"We were just talking to Jonathan about the night Hannah went missing," Abel said. He turned his attention to the young boy. "Would you please start over, Jonathan? I'd like Gracie to hear everything."

Jonathan was dressed in jeans and a plain, blue shirt. I noticed that his shirt had no buttons but instead was closed with hooks and eyes. This was an Old Order style that not many Mennonites wore anymore. His long chestnut hair hung longer than most boys his age, and his large dark eyes were fastened on Abel. He was a handsome boy, and I could see why Hannah was attracted to him.

He cleared his throat, obviously nervous. "L–like I said, sir, she told me during the day, after church, that she wanted to see me that night." He hung his head. "We'd met a few times at night before she left town. We shouldn't have done it. I know it was wrong. I–I'm so sorry. Maybe if I'd said no. . ."

"Never mind, son," Abel said gently. "I'm tired of hearing how everyone blames themselves for what happened. The truth is that Hannah chose to sneak out of our house. Her decision put her in danger. I know you would never have done anything to hurt my daughter."

The boy's eyes filled with tears. "It's true, sir. Hannah means a great deal to me. If I can do anything to help. . ."

"You should have told the sheriff about this when he questioned you," I said, not bothering to keep the edge of anger I felt out of my voice.

"I—I know. I was just so scared when he showed up. I'm trying to make up for that."

"Just finish your story," I said. "And this time, please don't keep anything back. Maybe you'll tell us something that will help us to find her."

He nodded and swiped at his eyes. "Hannah told me to meet her at our special place." He looked at me shamefacedly. "We used to meet in a clearing behind your house. You know, where they found that body."

My mouth dropped open. "Why would you want to get together there?" I remembered that my mother and father used to meet at the same spot when they were young. What was so special about that clearing?

"It's so beautiful," the boy said. "There's a place where you can sit and see the lake, but no one can see you. The trees hide you. And besides, it's halfway between our houses. It only takes us about twenty minutes to walk to it."

I looked over at Emily who had gone pale. This was the same spot where she used to sit and gaze out at the lake before she was raped by the man who was later buried there. The memory of that pain must be assailing her now, at a time she didn't need to be thinking about it. She met my eyes, smiled bravely, and visibly gathered herself together.

"Go on, Jonathan," she said. "How often did you meet there?"

He shrugged. "Several times before she left for Wichita. Maybe five or six times. We would just sit and talk." He hung his head. "I could talk to Hannah about anything. She understands how I feel about. . . well, everything."

"So that night, the night she disappeared, you went to this same spot?" I asked.

At my question, his eyes grew large. "No. That's just it. My father and I worked hard in the fields that day. It was so hot, and I was so tired, I couldn't stay awake. I didn't wake up until the next morning." He stared at Abel. "If only I'd gone, I could have saved her."

I thought about the place I'd found the bracelet. It was about a mile away from my house, but it was on the road to Jonathan's.

"Would Hannah have tried to walk to your house if you didn't show up?" I asked the upset young man.

He thought about it for a moment. "I—I don't know. I don't think so. We'd told each other that if something should happen, if our parents weren't sound asleep when we were supposed to leave, we should just forget it. If one of us didn't show up, the other one was supposed to go home."

This information sure didn't explain how Hannah's bracelet got to where I'd found it. "Did she say what she wanted to talk to you about?"

He nodded. "She said she had something to show me. Some new clothes she got in Wichita."

"Anything else?"

"Yes. She had a gift for me. Something someone gave to her that she wanted me to have."

I picked up my purse and dug around in it until I found what I wanted. "Is this what she planned to give you?" I held up the bracelet I'd found on the road.

He shrugged. "I don't know. She didn't tell me. She did say it was something I couldn't wear in public. That I'd have to keep it a secret."

"It has to be this bracelet," I said to Abel. "She didn't bring anything else back that I know of." I showed him the spacers that declared *Love, Friend,* and *Forever.* "I think she meant this as a way to tell Jonathan how she felt about him."

Abel took the bracelet from my hand. "But how did you get it?"

I took a deep breath and told him about finding it on the road and how I was certain it was a message from Hannah to let us know she was taken against her will. I knew the knowledge wouldn't comfort her parents, but I believed they needed to know the truth. About everything. When I finished telling them about the bracelet, I made a quick decision to spill my guts about the rest of it.

When I finished, Abel was silent. "The sheriff told us about the girl who was murdered, but he assured us that it had nothing at all to do with Hannah."

"He might be right, but I think we need to consider it. The most important thing is that we realize she's in trouble. Finding the bracelet where I did, and the fact that it was closed, is an indication that Hannah was trying to send us a message."

"Someone told me that the girl in Topeka was kept alive for several days before she was killed," Abel said, his voice trembling. "So if this is true, and if Hannah was abducted by this man, she might still be alive?"

"Yes. That's why it's so necessary for us to find her as quickly as possible."

"But why did Sheriff Taylor tell us Hannah wasn't abducted?" Emily said, her hands clasped together so tightly her knuckles were white. "He keeps assuring us that she's just run away and that he'll find her."

"Because he really believes that," I said. "I tried to tell him that he might be wrong, but he hasn't listened to me. The good news is that he's finally contacted the KBI about Hannah. And Susan Murphy is also going to get in touch with them."

"Mrs. Murphy? The social worker?" Abel looked puzzled. "Why would she help us? She seems committed to taking Hannah away from us when she comes home."

"She's not going to do anything like that," I reassured them. "She and I had a long talk, and she thinks you're great parents. She's trying to help us find Hannah, too."

The Muellers were silent. I knew I wasn't supposed to tell them about the serial killer theory, but I couldn't help it. I felt time was of the essence.

"I don't like being kept in the dark about my daughter's disappearance," Abel said. "Sheriff Taylor should be giving us this information, not you, Gracie. I think we need to ask him to come over here and speak to us. If there's anything else. . ."

"There is," I said. I felt like someone had opened the floodgates. A part of me tried to hold back, but I couldn't seem to control myself. I told them about the red truck and the bumper sticker. Then I told them about Rufus.

Abel jumped to his feet. "You're telling me that this man may have my little girl?" His face was red with anger. "Why hasn't the sheriff looked into this? You told him this last night?"

"Yes, and he's probably checking it out now," I said, flustered by his reaction. "It's important that we let him do his job. If we tip Rufus off too soon, we might not find Hannah."

I stood up and tried to grab Abel's arm. He shook me off. "Nonsense," he growled. "I'm going over there now and get my daughter." He pointed at Emily. "You stay here. I'll call you as soon as I can." With that, he stormed out of the house.

I jumped up and ran to the phone in the hallway, fear squeezing my chest. I called the sheriff's department in Council Grove. Pat wasn't in the office, but they patched me through to the radio in his car.

Thankfully, he picked up right away. I quickly explained the situation. After bawling me out profusely, he hung up. He'd just left Harmony but promised to turn around and hightail it to Rufus's shop. After a quick word to Emily and Jonathan, I ran out to my car and took off after Abel. His car wasn't even in sight. By the time I got to downtown Harmony and parked in front of Ludwig's Meats, Abel was already inside the shop. I jumped out of my car and pushed open the front door. As I did, I saw Pat's patrol car speeding up the street. He almost ran into a horse and buggy that had pulled out from the curb. He squealed his brakes and swerved to avoid a collision. Then he slid up next to my car, jumping out and pointing at me. I figured he was trying to tell me to stay out of the store, but I couldn't let something bad happen because I'd shot my mouth off before I should have. I pushed the front door open and ran into the main shop area. Abel was there all right, and he had Rufus in a head-lock. The frightened man was trying to say something, but no words came out of his mouth. Probably because Abel was cutting off his air supply.

The door swung open behind me and Pat rushed past. "Abel, let him go!" he yelled.

"He has Hannah," Abel cried. "He has my little girl!"

Pat grabbed Abel's arms and pulled. "No, he doesn't," he shouted. "Abel, Rufus had nothing to do with Hannah's disappearance. He wasn't even in town the night she went missing."

Abel didn't seem to hear Pat. He just held on to Rufus who was beginning to gasp frantically for air.

"Abel! Listen to me," Pat said loudly, putting himself only inches from the enraged father's face. "Rufus doesn't have Hannah. He doesn't. You've got the wrong man."

Finally, Abel's grip seemed to loosen a bit. I heard Rufus take a deep breath. Then he began to struggle, trying to get out of Abel's arms.

Pat pulled hard and finally forced Abel to loosen his grip. The meat store owner dropped to the floor and then half-crawled and half-scurried to the other side of the room. Pat held on to Abel for dear life. Then he pushed him up against the counter, pinning his arms behind him.

"Abel, I checked Rufus out right after Gracie told me about the truck. He told me he spent the night with his sister in Topeka and then picked up a new freezer Monday morning before driving back to Harmony. I checked out his story first thing this morning. It's all true. He wasn't even in town the night Hannah disappeared. He didn't get back until the next morning." He turned and glared at me. "And it might interest you to know that the other murders associated with the serial killer you're so interested in couldn't have been committed by Rufus because he was in the army—and in Iraq during the last two. Before that, he lived all the way across the country from where the other killings occurred. And his bumper sticker is about the Chicago Bears, the football team? Rufus is from Illinois. Gracie, I asked you to keep quiet about this. Do you see what your interference has caused? What if Abel had seriously hurt this man?"

My lips couldn't form a response. He was right. It was my fault. I'd jumped the gun and had almost caused a tragedy. I turned around and fled the building. Then I drove home as quickly as I could, determined to keep my nose out of anything further having to do with Hannah Mueller. I almost ran off the road several times because I couldn't see through the tears that flooded my eyes.

FIFTEEN

Although I didn't want to explain to my family what I'd done, it was obvious I was upset when I came in the door. Mom and Dad took me into the kitchen and sat me down at the table so Papa couldn't hear us. After I spilled out the whole story, my mother scooted her chair over next to mine and held out her arms. I fell into them.

"Honey," she said in a soothing voice, "you were trying to help. Your zeal to find Hannah overcame your sense of discretion. It happens. Especially to someone like you who cares so much. Pat will understand, and so will Abel. You need to forgive yourself." She held my tear-stained face in her hands and looked deeply into my eyes. "Your concern for others is one of the qualities that makes you so special. You meant no harm, you just wanted to rescue Hannah if there was any way possible."

I nodded but couldn't stop crying. "I really did. But Mom, you should have seen Abel. I didn't know he could get so angry. I thought Mennonites were supposed to be peaceful."

My father chuckled. "Snicklefritz, I don't care who

Abel is, he's a father. He saw the chance to save his daughter, and he went for it." Dad reached over and stroked my arm. "He did the same thing you did. He reacted out of his emotion. Trust me, he's just as sorry as you are. Maybe even more so. He's not blaming you right now. He's blaming himself."

"Re–really?" Somehow knowing that Abel had messed up, too, made me feel a little better.

As my parents tried to comfort me, the phone rang. My dad left the kitchen and went into the living room to answer it. A few minutes later, he returned. By then, my mother had fixed me a meat loaf sandwich and a tall glass of milk. Comfort food, but it helped. Somehow I couldn't be too upset munching on a meat loaf sandwich. The ketchup on top combined in a weird way with the mayo my mother had slathered on the thick pieces of white bread. It was delicious.

"That was Pat," Dad said when he came back into the kitchen. "He said to tell you everything is all right. Abel apologized to Rufus who took it pretty well considering. Pat's on his way here."

"No!" I exclaimed, spitting out a good chunk of meat loaf onto the kitchen table. "I don't want to talk to him." Listening to him yell at me was the last thing I wanted to endure right now.

"Gracie, he just wants to make sure you're okay. He's not mad. In fact, he said to tell you he understands."

That sure didn't sound like something Pat would say. But I couldn't see my father joining forces with Pat against me. Maybe it was his job to hold me down while Pat took out his revolver and ended my trail of terror. "Whatever," I said finally. "But I've had all the conflict I can take for one day."

"Speaking of today, what time are we leaving for Sam's?" Dad asked.

"We're supposed to be there by two." Then something struck me. "What about Papa? Will he be able to come?"

"He's still pretty sore," Mom said. "I'm staying here with him. You and Sweetie go over the wedding plans by yourselves. You can tell me all about it when you get home, and then we'll all get together again in a few days. This will give us time to talk about everything and see if you want any changes."

"Wait a minute," I said, shaking my head. "You're the mother. Your part in the planning is crucial. Maybe I could..."

"Stay here?" she said with a smile. "Sorry. I think the bride needs to be present." She came over and hugged me. "It's okay, sweetie. Really. Dad wants to get to know Sam a little better, and you need to hear what Sweetie's come up with so far. I'm really not necessary this time around. Besides, I love spending time with Papa. Once you make the big decisions, I'll help with the details."

I chewed and swallowed the last bite of my sandwich, not certain my mother was really happy to be stuck at home. But I had little choice. Since my father was determined to talk to Sam today, she seemed to be the only person available to watch Papa.

"Okay, I guess," I said slowly. "But I still think

you should be going."

"Why don't you see if Sweetie can come over here Friday for lunch?" Mom said. "I'll fix us all something and that way no one will have to stay home alone with Papa. And I'm sure he'd love to see Sweetie again."

"That sounds good." A loud knock on the door made me jump. Pat. I was extremely embarrassed by my actions and had no idea how I could face him. If Rufus really had been involved in Hannah's situation, I could have scared him away. I'd spoken out of turn and did so after Pat had trusted me with information I should have kept confidential. From now on, I was pretty sure he'd never tell me anything he didn't want the whole world to know. And how was I ever going to face Rufus? I might never be able to set foot in downtown Harmony again.

My father started to get up.

"You stay off that leg, Dad. I'll get it." Reluctantly I went to open the front door, but before I had the chance, Pat pushed it open and came in. I didn't say anything, just stood there, waiting for the inevitable.

"That was quite a scene," Pat said, his expression solemn. "I guess I don't really need to say anything about what happened, do I?"

"No. I'm sorry. I just got so. . .so. . ."

"Enthusiastic?" he finished for me.

"I was going to say manic, but enthusiastic sounds better."

"Pat, have a seat," my dad said pointing to the rocking chair. Papa was on the couch, sound asleep, so I stood next to my father who sat in a chair across from Pat.

"Just wanted you to know that the situation is under control," Pat said. "Rufus survived, and Abel has calmed down. He's thoroughly appalled by his actions."

"Mennonites are taught to live at peace with everyone," my father said. "He must be extremely upset about the way he treated Rufus."

Pat shrugged. "Most of the cases I'm called out on have to do with families who can't get along. For all his religion, seems Pastor Mueller didn't do much better than anyone else."

I looked over at my dad who frowned at Pat. Were we going to get into a debate on religion? I'd been praying for Pat for months, but I wanted the Holy Spirit to prepare the ground of his heart before I tried to sow seed. Right now, his heart seemed too hard to receive the love of God. My father must have sensed the same thing because he stayed quiet. Not the way my volatile father usually did things. I was very well aware of where my "enthusiasm" came from.

"So now what?" I asked. "Maybe Rufus isn't the killer. But someone has Hannah. We've got to find her before it's too late."

Pat raised one eyebrow and stared at me. "Well, with your friend Susan Murphy bugging the KBI, we may end up with too much attention focused on Hannah. I'd rather have avoided that."

"What are you talking about?" I asked with fervor. "We need all the attention we can get. Time is running out!"

Pat shook his head. "If Hannah has been taken by

a stranger, and I'm emphasizing the word *if*, the more activity you stir up, the more likely he is to take off or kill her. But I don't suppose you thought of that, did you, Miss Marple?"

I stared at him with my mouth open. "Why did you call me that? Sam is the only one..." I pointed at him. "You got that from Sam, didn't you?"

"I plead the fifth." He stood to his feet. "Now you listen to me, Gracie Temple," he said, his eyebrows knit together so tightly they looked like a unibrow. "Under no circumstances whatsoever are you to put your pretty little nose into this investigation again. And I'm as serious as I can be about this. Believe it or not, I actually know what I'm doing. I realize you don't believe it, but it's true nonetheless." Pat looked at my father. "Can I enlist your help to keep her concentration focused on her upcoming wedding instead of my case?"

"Your case?" I sputtered. "You said there wasn't any case. You said Hannah ran away. You said..."

"What I *said* was that I'd take care of it," Pat said sternly. "I've been listening to you. If you can remember just a couple of hours ago, during the ruckus you caused at the meat store, I told you I'd followed up on your information about Rufus, remember?"

I thought about it for a moment. "I—I guess you did."

"Yes, I guess I did. And if you have any more great ideas, I want you to share them with me. But I want you to let *me* take care of checking them out. Am I making myself clear?"

I nodded. "Got it. I'm not looking to cause any more violent confrontations for a while." I studied his face for a few seconds. "Wait a minute, just *when* did Sam tell you about the Miss Marple thing? He certainly didn't do it while I was around."

Pat headed toward the door. He put his hand on the knob and smiled at me. "Well, maybe he told me this morning when we had breakfast."

"You and Sam had breakfast? Are you serious? Does this mean. . ."

"It means that we may be making some progress." He glared at me. "And I think it will continue unless I have to lock up his fiancée for impeding the course of an investigation."

"I am *not* impeding anything! I've been trying to. . ." The look on his face brought a quick halt to the rest of my protest.

"Grace Marie. . ." my father warned.

"Okay, okay," I snapped. "If I have any more bright ideas, I'll contact you first before I do anything about them."

"You promise?" Pat said.

I held my right hand up. "I swear. But please, please, Pat. Do everything you can to find Hannah. I believe she's alive, but we need to locate her soon."

Pat took his hand off the doorknob and his eyes sought mine. "And why are you so sure she's still alive?"

"Because God told us she is."

"God told who, Gracie?" he asked slowly.

"The Muellers and me."

Pat didn't respond, but the look on his face spoke volumes.

"Look, you don't believe in God, but we do. And I'm telling you that God told us she's alive and that she's coming home."

"Then why do you need me?"

I shrugged. "Maybe God wants to show you that He really does exist and that He has a plan for you. Maybe saving Hannah is part of that plan."

Pat shook his head and stared at me like I'd just escaped from a loony bin. I could take his anger, but I really hated to be on the other end of his pity. "Gotta go," he said finally. "Work on your wedding. Stay away from anyone else you think looks like a good suspect."

"I said I would." I could hear the petulance in my voice, but I was tired and disgusted. Mostly with myself.

Pat was halfway out the door when he stopped again. Now what?

"Hey, one other thing. Something that's been bothering me. I need you to tell me who told you about the color of the truck and the odd bumper sticker."

I hadn't wanted to reveal the source of the information, but I no longer cared about protecting secrets. I just wanted Hannah to come home. I told Pat about Bill, carefully going over the conversation I'd had with him at the restaurant. "Why did you want to know?" I asked when I'd finished. "Is it important?"

"No, not really. It's just odd, that's all," Pat said. "No one was supposed to know about it."

"Bill's nephew works for the paper, and he has a friend on the police department." I watched his expression change. Doubt was clearly written on his face. "Do you have some reason to think Bill wasn't telling the truth?"

"Not really. I guess that makes sense, but the police swear no one leaked that information. Just seems weird, that's all." He said good-bye to my dad and told me once more to mind my own business—for good measure, I guess. Then he left.

I started to ask my father if he'd thought Pat's manner was a little odd, when Papa suddenly moaned from the couch. Dad got up and went over to him.

"You okay, Papa?" Dad asked.

"Yes, fine," he answered. "But I need to take a trip to the bathroom, and I'm a little unsteady on my feet. Would you give me a hand, son?"

My father helped Papa up and guided him toward the bathroom. I checked the clock. A little after one. Less than an hour until we were due at Sam's. I sat down at my kitchen table and thought about Pat's interest in the source of my information. Surely he couldn't suspect Bill of anything. He was one of the nicest men in Harmony. Then I remembered Bill's red truck. What if he didn't really have a nephew on the Topeka paper?

My conversation with Pat echoed over and over in my mind. Suddenly I realized how ridiculous my suspicion sounded. Bill Eberly wouldn't hurt a fly. And why in the world was I so focused on men in Harmony anyway? It didn't really make much sense. Pat said the murderer had committed crimes in other states. As far as I knew, Bill had lived here all his life.

Jumbled thoughts collided with each other inside me, and I could almost feel my blood pressure rise. Pat was right, I was out of control. Bill Eberly was not and never could be a murderer.

I thought back to the strong sensation back at the Muellers' when Abel read the ninety-first Psalm. I was certain God had reassured us that everything would turn out okay, but I still felt this nervous fear rolling around inside me. A sermon I heard in church popped into my head. It was about God's wisdom being peaceful. Well, I sure didn't feel peaceful. Either I would have to have faith that God was watching over Hannah, or I'd have to follow fear. I chose faith. It took an effort to push the voice of panic away from me, but I made the decision to do it.

"You okay, Snicklefritz?"

My dad's voice startled me. He was helping Papa back onto the couch. "I'm fine, Dad, thanks. How are you feeling, Papa?"

"With my fingers, Gracie," Papa said. He lowered himself gingerly to the couch and my father covered him up with the quilt.

"Can I get you anything?"

"A cup of hot chocolate would be very nice." Papa smiled. "Essie used to make me hot chocolate when I was sick, and it always made me feel better."

"She did the same thing for me," I said. "Right now a cup of cocoa sounds like the perfect prescription for both of us."

My mother came into the room from the basement where she'd been washing clothes. "What's the perfect prescription?" she asked.

"Hot chocolate."

She laughed. "It's almost one hundred degrees outside, and you people want hot chocolate?"

"Hey, sounds good to me," my father said. "It's great anytime and in any weather."

"Well, Gracie Marie," Mom said with a smile, "I think the womenfolk should retire to the kitchen and whip up some cups of hot chocolate. What do you think?"

"I completely agree."

We started toward the kitchen, but I stopped when Papa called out my name. "Hey, Gracie," he said with a grin. "What do you call a cow with no legs?"

My parents joined in and we all said together, "I don't know, Papa. What do you call a cow with no legs?"

We laughed when he exclaimed, "Ground beef!"

My mother and I worked together to prepare the hot cocoa. Then my family and I spent the next thirty minutes talking and enjoying each other until it was time to pick up Ida and go to Sam's. For just a little while, the world felt normal, and everything seemed to be the way it should be. But there was someone missing. Until Hannah was home, nothing would really be the way it was supposed to be again.

Sixteen

When we got to Sam's, he was waiting on the front porch. He'd changed his regular work clothes for clean jeans and a light-blue shirt that brought out his blue-gray eyes. I could tell he was nervous, but I had no doubt Sam would win my father over completely. Sam was everything a father could ever want in a son-in-law. He was certainly everything I'd ever dreamed of in a husband. Sam and my dad took off toward the orchard while Ida and I followed Sweetie into the kitchen.

"Been workin' on these plans for a long time," she said when we sat down.

She poured us both a glass of iced tea and put a plate of cookies on the table. Sweetie's coconut pecan cookies. They were out of this world, but I only took two. My wedding dress was tight enough. If I ate too many, I'd never get into it.

"Sorry to dump so much of this on you," I said. "I really appreciate everything you're doing to help me."

"Oh, pshaw," she retorted. "Ain't much work at all. I did expand things a bit, though, since you decided everyone who wanted to come was welcome."

"Expand things, how?" I asked, not sure I wanted to hear the answer.

"Well, I asked Pastor Jensen if we could move the ceremony from the small chapel to the main sanctuary. He said that weren't no problem. 'Course this means we'll need more decorations, but the women's Bible study has taken over all that. They're gonna put big white-ribbon bows on the ends of the pews with purple silk irises in the middle. And you'll carry a bouquet with red carnations, yellow dandelions, and purple irises."

Ida's eyebrows shot up. "What an unusual bouquet, Gracie. Why those flowers?"

I smiled at her. "The red carnations are a symbol of love, the dandelions remind me of the wildflowers that grow in Harmony, and purple irises are my favorite flower. They were my grandmother's also."

Ida reached over and put her hand on mine. "What a beautiful sentiment. This will be an extraordinary bouquet."

"I hope so. I saw one like it on an online wedding site a while back, and I fell in love with it."

"There will be a large bunch of the same flowers in a vase on the stage where you say your vows and another bouquet on the table at the reception," Sweetie continued. "Ruth has a long red floor runner we'll use for you to walk on up to the front of the church." She squinted at me. "How's all this sound so far? Is this what you wanted?"

"It's perfect," I said. "What's going on with the food?"

Sweetie shuffled through her notes and pulled out a handwritten piece of paper. "Hector has suggested three different menus. He said you should look them over and see what sounds good to you." She chuckled. "And he said to tell you if you don't like these ideas, toss 'em out and tell him what you want. Whatever it is, he'll find a way to do it."

Ida glanced at the list Sweetie put on the table. "Ach, this is so much fancier than what I had at my wedding."

"What food was served at your reception?" I asked.

"It was very simple. Much too simple for young people today, I imagine." Ida wrinkled her nose as she sought to remember. "We had the most delicious roast chicken with stuffing, along with mashed potatoes and gravy. I believe my mother made creamed celery and coleslaw. Of course, there was homemade applesauce." She covered her mouth with her fingers and giggled. "It was very good, but it was not as good as yours, Sweetie. My mother would not be pleased to hear me say this." She lowered her hand and screwed up her face again. "I remember delicious cherry pie and tapioca pudding with bread. There were warm biscuits fresh from the oven served with butter and jelly." She closed her eyes and sighed. "It was quite a feast."

"My father said Mom wore a blue dress for her wedding," I said. "What did you wear?"

Ida nodded. "Ach, yes. A blue dress. Plain without additional adornment. And a black prayer covering to show I was now a married woman." She smiled at me. "I know this sounds unattractive to you, liebling, but Herman whispered into my ear that I was the most beautiful bride he ever laid eyes on." She sighed. "And I believed him. Herman always made me feel he was blessed to be my husband. No woman could ask for more, ja?"

I nodded my agreement.

"I guess all this wedding folderol seems foolish to you," Sweetie said to Ida.

"Not at all," she responded. "A wedding is about the bride and groom and their commitment to God. I know Gracie and Sam will put Him first in their lives. I have no doubt of their love or their ability to pursue the life God has for them." She reached over and patted my shoulder. "The traditions we follow at a wedding shouldn't be our main focus, child. It is what is in our hearts that matters, and how we live after our vows."

"Wise advice," Sweetie said.

I sighed. "Yes, it is, but all these details sure seem important right now." I frowned at Ida. "My mother brought her blue dress for me to wear."

"Tradition used to be that the wedding dress was only worn once and then kept as a remembrance because it is so meaningful," Ida said. "It is very touching that she has offered it to you."

"I'm sure it is," I said, shaking my head. "But I bought a beautiful white wedding dress in Wichita, and I planned to wear it."

"Then wear it," she said emphatically.

"I don't know. I've been thinking. . ."

"Wait a minute, Gracie girl," Sweetie said. "This is your wedding. You wear what you want. I know your mama feels the same way. Just 'cause she brought that dress with her, it don't mean she expects you to wear it."

"Sweetie is right," Ida chimed in. "I know your mother wants your wedding to be everything you desire. Why are you thinking about this?"

I let out a deep breath. "I don't know. It's just been on my mind. She never got the wedding she wanted. If it would make her happy. . ."

"It is *your* day," Ida said. "One day when we are allowed to be a little selfish. You let your heart lead you, liebling."

"Okay." I smiled at the two women who were so important to me. "It was just a thought. Let's move on." But it was more than just a thought. The idea had been rolling around in my mind ever since my father told me about the dress. The idea of being married in Harmony—in the same dress my mother had worn at her wedding tugged at my heart. It gave me a sense of being a part of something really special. A connection to the past. "Ida, tell me more about your own wedding," I said, pushing the menu from Hector out of the way.

Ida described a day that began at four o'clock in the morning. All the chores were done first, and then the wedding helpers arrived around seven. Weddings were usually held in the bride's home unless it wasn't large enough. First the ushers, dressed in black suits with bow ties, took their places near the front door. Their wives stood with them. When the guests arrived, they were seated on long wooden benches that had been brought in just for the ceremony. The wedding actually started at eight thirty in the morning and lasted about three hours.

"Three hours," Sweetie exclaimed. "My goodness, after gettin' up so early folks would be plumb tuckered out by the time the couple finally says 'I do.'"

Ida laughed. "Believe it or not, no one seemed the least bit tired. It was such a wonderful day, I suppose the excitement kept us going."

"Did you go on a honeymoon?" I asked.

"Well, it was not the kind of honeymoon that brides and grooms go on today. We spent our first night in my parents' home, and then the rest of the winter we visited many of the other relatives and friends who attended the wedding and stayed at least one night with them."

"Yikes," I said. "That's not my idea of a honeymoon."

Sweetie snorted. "And just where are you and Sam going after the wedding?"

"Well, with the harvest and everything. . ."

Sweetie winked at Ida. "They ain't goin' nowhere. They're stayin' here to finish pickin' fruit."

"Yes, but that's because there's nowhere else we want to be," I said quietly. "Being in Harmony as Sam's wife, and living in this beautiful house. . . Well, there's no honeymoon spot on this planet that appeals to me more."

"Ach, liebling," Ida said. "This is why Sam is the most blessed man in the world, and you are the most blessed woman. You have found God's will for your lives. In His will is more joy and peace than any place or possession the world could ever offer."

We spent the rest of the afternoon going over other details of the wedding. As we double-checked the guest list, I thought of C. J. Bradley.

"I wonder if C.J. would like to come to the ceremony," I said. "I don't know him very well, but since the whole town is turning out anyway, it might be a good chance for him to connect with some of the town's people. Might help us round up some additional help for him, too."

"I think he'd like that," Sweetie said. "But why don't you just ask him? I don't think we need to send out another invitation, do you?"

"No problem. I'll run by there and invite him."

"I am so glad C.J. is home and caring for Abigail," Ida said. "It puts my mind to rest."

"Me, too," I said. "Oh, and remember the story you told me about C.J. and the girl he loved when he was young?"

She nodded.

"Well, they're together again after all these years. Isn't that wonderful?"

Ida looked surprised. "I am glad to hear that. Maybelline Parker told me she thought Melanie had passed away. I am so pleased to know that she is alive and well." She frowned. "I wonder if Abigail knows about Melanie. She would not be happy."

Sweetie made a clucking noise with her tongue. "That woman is just plain cantankerous. I'm glad to see her plan to break those two kids up didn't succeed after all. It mighta taken awhile, but the good Lord put back together what Abigail tried to destroy. Good for Him."

"Yes," Ida agreed. "I will pray that this time C.J. finds happiness with the woman he loves."

"I'll pray for him, too," I said.

Ida laughed softly. "Ach, I just remembered what his initials stand for."

I raised my eyebrows. "Must be good. What is it?"

"He was born during Abigail's involvement in some kind of odd religion. His mother named him Cosmic Journey."

Sweetie burst out laughing. "Are you kiddin' me? That poor man."

"Oh my." I covered my mouth with my hand. "I'd rather be called Snicklefritz than something like that."

Ida nodded. "A name left over from the sixties, I believe. Maybe C.J. has had it changed. Anyway, I hope so."

"And I thought being saddled with Myrtle was bad," Sweetie said, giggling.

I didn't mention that most people wouldn't want to be called *Sweetie*, but she loved her nickname. Ida cast a quick glance my way, and I grinned at her. She was probably thinking the same thing I was.

We moved on to looking over Hector's choices for the reception dinner. I finally decided on a menu, and we set a time for the wedding rehearsal.

"The rehearsal dinner will be here," Sweetie said. "I may not be cookin' for the reception, but I sure as tootin' can handle dinner for the families and Pastor Jensen."

We'd just started talking about that menu when the front door opened and my father's voice boomed out. "Anyone here?"

"We're in the kitchen," I hollered.

Sam was a few seconds behind my dad, and as soon as I saw his face I knew something was wrong.

"You about ready to go, Snicklefritz?" Dad said. He ignored Ida and Sweetie, which wasn't like him.

"I—I guess so." I looked at Sweetie. "Why don't you finish the menu for the rehearsal dinner on your own? I trust your instincts."

She nodded but didn't say anything. I could tell she'd picked up on the tension in the air. Part of me wanted to throw my hands up in the air and say, "What now?" Surely there was enough drama going on around me without my father and my fiancé having problems.

"Dad, why don't you and Ida go on out to the car? I want to talk to Sam a minute."

My father hesitated for a second or two, but finally he helped Ida up and silently guided her down the hall and out the door.

"Okay, what in the world is going on?" I asked Sam after we heard the front door close.

He slumped down in a nearby chair. "Wow. I really don't know what happened." He shook his head. "Everything was going just fine, and then all of a sudden your dad went off on me."

"What do you mean he went *off on you*?" I couldn't keep the exasperation I was feeling out of my voice.

Sam rubbed the side of his face. "We were talking about the farm. You know, why Sweetie and I chose peaches and apples. Then he started asking about our berry crop. Suddenly, he started going on and on about weather and crop failure. What would happen if we had a couple of bad seasons? I tried to explain how we operate, that we have savings in reserve in case we have a poor crop, but he wouldn't listen to me. Your father seems to think I can't take care of you properly."

"I have a job, too," I said. "It's not like we're completely dependent on the farm to—"

Sam slapped the table with his hand. "I don't need your money. I can take care of us just fine."

Stunned, I couldn't form a response fast enough. "I—I..."

He stood up, his face flushed and angry. "I don't need you or anyone to support me, thank you. If you don't believe I can provide for you..."

"All right, that's enough, you two," Sweetie bellowed. "I won't have you goin' at each other like this." She jabbed a finger into Sam's chest. "Sit down, young man. And I mean now!"

Sam slid back into his chair like a whipped puppy.

"And you..." she said, narrowing her eyes at me. "You watch the way you talk to this man. He don't want no woman supportin' him. It ain't respectful to talk to a husband like that."

I wanted to ask just what she knew about husbands seeing that she'd never been married, but I wisely kept my mouth shut. Sweetie was on a rampage, and it was best to stay out of the way when she let loose.

"Now the way I see it, you're both wrong. . .and you're both right." She pointed at Sam again, but this time kept her finger out of his midsection. "Gracie has a talent, boy. And she not only wants to use it to help support the family you're gettin' ready to make, she has a responsibility to use the talents the good Lord gave her. You don't need to sound like some old-school, he-man type who's gonna take care of his little woman. This here marriage is gonna be a partnership, buddy. And you better get used to it." She swung her gaze over to me, her irritation making her look like she'd been "suckin' on a pail full of lemons." Another one of Sweetie's favorite expressions. "You gotta understand that Sam is gonna be the head of your house, young lady. You gotta treat him like you respect him, even when you don't." She shook her head. "I may not be married, but I done watched some folks down through the years. It's the marriages where both people treat each other with respect that make it through the storms of life. I seen some women pick, pick, pick at their husbands until they turn into almost nothin'. Man's gotta feel like his wife looks up to him." She moved her face a little bit closer to mine. "And if you want your husband to change, you go talk to God about it. Don't nag him yourself. Only God can change the inside of a human bein'. I seen folks turn into different people when their spouse quits harpin' at 'em, and they put the situation at the Lord's feet." She glanced at Sam. "This is for both of you. You both gotta love the good stuff and turn the other over to God. It's the only way it'll work. I'm as sure of that as I'm sure Gracie's daddy is gonna come around."

"And how could you possibly know that?" I asked.

Sweetie nodded and looked off into the distance. It was obvious she was thinking about her answer. After a moment she said, "That man is dealin' with the past. He ain't mad at you, son. He's mad at himself. You two gotta give him time to work it out. He'll be okay. I guarantee it."

My father, who was supposedly "gonna come around" honked his car horn as a sign he was getting impatient.

"Sweetie, I hope you're right," I said. I got up, went over to Sam, and wrapped my arms around his neck. "I'm sorry. I'm sure everything will be okay. Give me time to find out why my dad's upset." I smiled over at Sweetie. "Correction. Give me time to pray for my dad. Sweetie's right, we've got to give God a chance to work this out."

"And if He doesn't?" Sam asked glumly.

I slapped him playfully on the head. "How about we just believe, and leave the rest of it up to Him? My mother told me once that faith doesn't have a Plan B. There's no option for failure. I say we stick to Plan A."

Sam was quiet for a few seconds before he chuckled softly. "I have no chance against two women of faith, do I?" He reached up and grabbed my arms, pulling me down to him. Then he kissed me. "Okay, okay. Plan A all the way."

My father's car horn blared again, longer this time.

I kissed Sam once more, ran over and threw my arms around Sweetie, hugged her, and then hurried out the front door. I opened the car door and slid into the backseat. Ida sat silently in the front passenger seat. The air was thick with tension, and I got the feeling that Ida and my father had been talking before I came out of the house. Must not have gone well. Dad drove Ida home and started to get out of the car so he could assist her to her door, but I jumped out quickly and announced that I would help her instead. I had Ida's door open before my dad could protest. Holding on to my arm, she got out of the car and we walked slowly toward her porch.

"Your father is dealing with some painful feelings," she said quietly as we stepped up on her stairs. "You must be patient, liebling. God is speaking to his heart." She smiled up at me. "Everything will work out the way it is supposed to. I believe it in my heart of hearts."

When we reached the top of the stairs I hugged her. "Sweetie said the same thing. I think you're both right, although I can't figure out what he's so upset about. I know he's felt bad about Uncle Benjamin, but I thought he was just about over that."

Ida glanced back at the car where my father sat waiting. "Sometimes we make choices, Gracie. At the time, they may seem right in our minds, but in our hearts they may not set as well. We might ignore the voice of the heart; we may even cover it up with other things. But one day we will face it again, and then we must decide. Was the choice wrong or right? And if it was wrong, what can we do about it now?" She shook her head. "We make a mistake if we torment ourselves about the past since it does not really exist anymore. It is nothing more than a memory without weight or substance. The key is to leave the ghosts of yesterday behind and move forward with new choices. It is never too late with God." She reached over and kissed me on the cheek. "Now your father faces a past choice—and a new one. I am afraid Sam only represents the choice he made long ago— one he may now regret. When Daniel realizes that today he can choose again, and that's it's not too late to get back what he lost, he will drop his misplaced anger toward Sam. I promise this." She stroked my cheek. "You trust God, liebling, ja?"

I wrapped my arms around her. "Ja," I whispered. "Ja." I waited until Ida's front door closed behind her before I went back to the car. I glanced at my father when I got into the front seat, but his expression didn't invite conversation. We pulled out onto Faith Road and had almost reached my house when I noticed something strange on the road ahead. A black buggy was stopped on the side of the road, not moving. No one seemed to be near it.

"Dad, I want to check out that buggy. It looks like Gabe and Sarah's."

He drove past the house and parked on the side of the road. I got out and walked up to the side of the black buggy. Sarah Ketterling lay slumped over in her seat. I jumped up next to her and called out her name. Then I tried to rouse her, but she didn't appear to be breathing.

SEVENTEEN

My father helped me lift Sarah out of the buggy and onto the ground. He winced more than once from supporting her weight on his leg, even though she felt light as a feather to me. After checking her breathing, he yelled at me to go home and call John while he did CPR. I got in his car and quickly drove the short distance back to my house. I pulled the car up near the house, jumped out, and ran inside to the phone. Thankfully, John answered right away. My breath came in fast spurts as I told him about Sarah.

"I'm on my way, Gracie," he said. "Try to get her cool and continue CPR until I get there."

I hung up the phone and ran to the kitchen to get a pail of cool water and a towel while trying to explain what was going on to my mother. She promised to pray for Sarah as I hurried to the car.

When I got back to my father, I told him what John had said.

"She's breathing," he said, "but it's shallow." He frowned. "Help me get her out of these clothes."

"Oh Dad. I don't think. . ."

He stared into my face, his jaw tight. "Gracie, do

you care more about this girl's modesty or her life?"

I reached down and unfastened Sarah's cap. Then with Dad's help I rolled her onto her side and untied her apron.

"Foolish to wear all these clothes in hot July weather," Dad said, his face flushed with frustration. "She probably has heatstroke."

"Maybe that's why John wanted us to cool her down." I unpinned the back of her dress and pulled it down. From a situation last winter when Sarah had been found in the snow, I knew she wore a kind of sleeveless undergarment with an attached slip under her dress. She was still covered but now would feel much cooler. I moved the heavy clothes to the side and put her head on my lap. Then I began to wipe her face with cool water. My father bent over to check her breathing.

"We need to watch her carefully in case we need to start CPR again." He tried to find a comfortable position kneeling next to the unconscious girl, but the pain on his face was evident.

"Dad, I know CPR. If she needs it, I can do it."

"We may both need to assist her."

"No. I can take care of it myself." I gently pushed him away. "You get off that leg. I don't need to take care of both of you."

He started to argue with me, but his face suddenly went white from pain. He struggled to stand up. I left Sarah and helped him to his feet, guiding him over to the buggy where he sat down on the back axle. Once I knew he was comfortable, I returned to Sarah and continued to keep her face, chest, and arms damp. Finally, I heard a small noise, and her eyes fluttered open.

"Sarah, can you hear me?"

She seemed confused at first, but then she stared up at me. "Oh my," she whispered. "What happened?"

"You fainted."

She started to sit up, but I gently pushed her back down. "We don't know why you passed out, Sarah. I need you to stay still until John gets here. You're probably just overheated, but we need to make sure."

Although I'd been concentrating on making sure she was breathing, I was stunned by how thin she was. Her breastbone and ribs were visible beneath her damp undershirt.

"John?" she said, her voice thin and high pitched. "John's coming here?"

I wiped her face with the wet rag. "Yes, of course. He's a doctor."

Sarah's hands flew to her chest and she felt the thin material of her undershirt. "Oh Gracie! I can't have him see me like this. Please. . .please. . ."

"Young lady," my father said in a gruff tone, "wearing all that heavy clothing on a day like today is ridiculous. No wonder you fainted."

Sarah's dark eyes were huge in her pale face. "Gracie. . ."

The plaintive plea in her voice moved me to action. I pulled up the top part of her dress, covering her chest. "I will not put the rest of it on, Sarah," I said, trying to sound as firm as possible. "I just won't do it."

Her thin fingers encircled my wrist. "Thank you, thank you. This is enough." Once again, she struggled to sit up, and once again I resisted her efforts. It didn't take much. She was so weak.

"Stay still," I scolded. "You're not moving until John takes a look at you." The hot sun beat down on us. I could see how easy it would be to get heat exhaustion on a day like today. However, Sarah's condition seemed to be more than simple heatstroke. Her obvious weight loss and the blue tinge to her lips worried me.

The sound of a car's engine caused me to look up. John screeched to a halt a few yards from us. He jumped out of his SUV and ran toward us, a leather bag in his hand.

"She's breathing now and awake," I told him as I gently put Sarah's head on her folded cape and stepped back so he could get close to her. While he looked her over, I checked on my father. He still seemed to be in pain and sweat ran down his face. "Let's get you back in the car where there's air-conditioning." Surprisingly, he didn't argue.

"I'll just wait for you," he said, leaning on my shoulder and hobbling toward the car. My father's not the kind of person who likes to sit on the sidelines during an emergency. By the time I got him situated, my concern for him had grown.

"Gracie!" John was calling my name, so I made sure Dad was okay, and then I ran back to where John knelt in the road next to Sarah.

The look on his face alarmed me. He handed me

a card. "This is the number of Emergency Services in Sunrise. I need you to call them right away and ask them to send an ambulance as soon as possible."

"What's wrong, John?"

He spoke softly to Sarah and got to his feet, leading me a few feet from the silent young woman who lay prostrate in the road. "This isn't heatstroke. She's been having chest pains, and she's very weak." He glanced back at Sarah, his expression one of desperation. "I think it's her heart. It's serious, Gracie. Very serious."

I grabbed his arm. "John, she's going to be okay, isn't she?"

With fear-filled eyes he shook his head. "I don't know, Gracie. I really don't."

"I'll call this number and be right back." I raced toward the car without saying another word. When I got in my father could see I was frightened.

"What's going on?"

"Sarah's in trouble, Dad. I've got to call an ambulance." I pulled into my driveway and opened my door. "You stay here. Mom can get you inside while I call for help." I ran up the steps and into the house, yelling for my mother who hurried in from the kitchen. After a brief explanation, she went out to get my father. I dialed the number on John's card and gave our location to the dispatcher who answered the phone. He promised to have someone there within the next fifteen minutes. I hung up and jogged out to the porch, ignoring Papa who sat on the couch, watching all the turmoil.

"Let us know what happens, Gracie," my mother said as I raced past her and my father. Dad was going up the steps slowly, but at least he was home where Mom could look after him. One patient out of the way.

I backed out of my driveway, almost knocking over my mailbox. Then I gunned the motor and sped back to where Sarah and John waited. After assuring John I'd placed the call, I knelt next to Sarah whose frightened eyes sought mine.

"John says something might be wrong, Gracie." Her voice was so soft I could barely hear her. "I haven't felt good for a while, but I thought it would pass. We've been working so hard in the shop. . ."

"That's not it," John interrupted, his tone harsh. "You didn't do anything about it because you were afraid to come to my office. You've risked your health because of me."

Sarah's already pale face turned even whiter. "No, that's not true. Please. . .please don't say that. . ."

Without any warning, her eyes rolled back in her head and she fainted. John called her name several times, but she didn't respond. I cried out involuntarily because she looked dead. John pulled her dress down and began doing chest compressions, his face grim.

"Watch for the ambulance, Gracie," he said in a tone that shook me to my very core. "Make sure they don't miss us."

I ran out on the road so I could see any approaching vehicle. Within a few minutes, I spotted the ambulance barreling down the road, creating a storm of dust behind it. I waved my hands like a crazy person, making sure they saw us. They pulled up next to the buggy and two emergency workers jumped out, carrying equipment. John shouted instructions to them. One of the emergency workers inserted a needle in Sarah's arm, attached to a plastic bag of clear liquid. The other moved into the spot where John had been working and put his head on Sarah's chest. He took out something that looked like large scissors and cut down the length of the rest of her dress, throwing it aside. Then he opened the metal box he had with him and grabbed a couple of paddles. After adjusting some knobs on the instrument, he put the paddles on her chest and jolted Sarah. Her body jumped. He checked her, shook his head, and then repeated the procedure. Once again, he shook his head. In the meantime, the other worker gave her a shot and told the man with the paddles to try again. This time, he seemed satisfied with the results and ran over to his vehicle to get a gurney out of the back. All three men loaded Sarah up into the back of the ambulance. I heard the emergency technicians talking to John, but I couldn't distinguish what they were saying. It was like my heart was pounding in my ears, and all I could hear was the sound of it beating. I began to pray with all my might, not caring who heard me or if I sounded deranged. One of the men jumped up into the back of the vehicle with Sarah while the other ran to the front, jumped in, and sped off. John jogged back to me.

"They wouldn't let me go with them so I've got to follow in my car."

"John, please tell me she's going to be okay." My voice shook, and I felt tears course down my cheeks.

"I—I don't know, Gracie," John said. "I really don't." He grabbed my hands. "You say this God of yours is good—that He loves us. If that's true, He'll save Sarah." The anguish in his voice was palpable. "You've got to pray. . .please. Please pray that she lives."

I lowered my head and prayed with every ounce of faith in my heart. "Dear God, thank You for providing everything we need for life. We draw on Your goodness and Your mercy for our friend Sarah. We declare that she will live and not die, and that she will completely recover. Thank You for hearing our prayer." I started to say "amen," but surprisingly, John began to speak out loud.

"God, I know You don't know me, but I believe You're there. I've seen You in the lives and hearts of these people in Harmony. In the life and heart of Sarah Ketterling. Please God, I love her. Save her. Heal her. If You do, I'll serve You the rest of my life. I promise."

I waited a moment and then said, "Amen."

John hugged me and hurried toward his car.

"Call me!" I yelled after him. "Call me after you check on her!"

I had no idea if he heard me or not. He drove away so quickly that when the dust cleared, I couldn't see his SUV any longer. I got in my dad's car and drove home. After parking in my driveway, I put my head down and prayed again. This time, I prayed for two lives. One for continued life in this world, and the other for a life in eternity.

Eighteen

Friday morning dawned with cloudy skies and rain. It was most welcome. We desperately needed it to help cool down temperatures and aid thirsty crops. There was more good news. Sarah had been moved to a hospital in Topeka and had improved so much it looked as if she could come home by Monday. She'd been diagnosed with cardiomyopathy, a disease that attacks the heart muscle. Caught early, it can be treated successfully with medicine. Sarah had ignored her symptoms for a while, causing her to feel weak and finally lose consciousness. According to John, if her condition had been left untreated, she could have easily died. He called me several times from Topeka, but I hadn't actually seen him since Sarah's collapse. Except for running back and forth to Harmony for a few patients who couldn't wait, he stayed by her side constantly.

I'd promised Ida I'd drive her to Topeka to see Sarah that afternoon. The drive would take us around an hour and a half each way. I was happy to have some time to spend with Ida, and frankly, I needed a break from Papa. He seemed to be having more and more confused episodes. His insistence about finding a wedding present from Mama had grown stronger. It was all we could do to talk him out of it. My father finally told him we'd found it, and everything was all right. I didn't like lying to Papa, but Dad said it was the kindest thing to do. At first it seemed to calm him down, but last night, he woke up about three in the morning, worried once again about this imaginary gift. Although his delusion bothered me and losing sleep didn't thrill me, I was touched that he longed to give me something for my wedding. And though he was doing better physically after his fall, the decision was made to keep him downstairs so we wouldn't have a repeat of his previous accident. Besides the 3:00 a.m. episode, my concern for Hannah and Sarah kept me tossing and turning at night. Hannah had been gone five days now. After a visit with Jessie yesterday when I went to lunch with Sam, my concerns about Bill had returned. When I'd asked her about her mother's new relationship, her response reignited my suspicions.

"Mom seems happy," she'd said, "but I don't know. Bill makes me uncomfortable. I get the feeling he's hiding something."

That was enough to send me over the edge and hound Pat until he did some checking up on Bill. Although he did have a child who lived in the area where a couple of young women had been abducted and killed, he hadn't been there during the time it happened, and had never been to Arizona or New Mexico in his life. Ever. Turned out Jessie's "uncomfortable" feelings were nothing more than that, probably a leftover reaction to the abuse she suffered at the hand of her father. Pat reminded me after spending time following up another useless lead that Rufus still wasn't speaking to me—and might not for quite some time.

"For crying out loud, Gracie," he'd said in a tone that didn't invite further discussion, "just because this guy *might* have struck in Topeka, and we're still not sure of that, it doesn't mean he lives around here. You're imagining things, and it's causing me a lot of trouble."

"I never said he lived here," I'd answered hotly. "But Hannah is gone and whoever picked her up was in this area. It's entirely possible that he's been here before."

His answer, mumbled under his breath, wasn't something his mother would be proud of. I'd pointed that out to him, but it didn't do any good. He'd just hung up on me.

After everything that had been happening in Harmony, going to Topeka sounded like a vacation. And although it was almost impossible since there was an APB out on Hannah and no one had spotted her, in the back of my mind, the thought that I might find her on the road between here and Topeka was overwhelming, even if it was unlikely.

Every day that Hannah was gone gave Abel and Emily more opportunity for stress. But the supernatural assurance they'd received when we'd read the ninety-first Psalm seemed to hold them up.

I could see the battle to believe in their faces, but I also observed the peace of God sustaining them. They were determined to trust God with their daughter's safety, and my respect for them grew immensely. Faith is easy when the stakes are small, but to see them walk in assurance when the life of their beloved child was on the line showed their true devotion to their God.

A little before three o'clock I said good-bye to my parents and left to pick Ida up. She wanted to stop by and see Abigail before we left town, and I'd gladly agreed to take her. I'd been planning to ask C.J. to the wedding, and I looked forward to seeing the progress he'd made on his mother's house.

Ida was ready when I pulled up to her place. She sat on her porch with a basket in her lap. I got as close as I could so she wouldn't get too wet. Then I jumped out of the car to assist her.

"What have you got in the basket?" I asked when I reached her.

"I made us a nice supper," she said with a smile. "I thought perhaps we could stop along the road and eat."

"I'd planned to take you out to a restaurant. There are some great places to eat in Topeka."

"Oh my, Gracie," she said, getting to her feet while holding the basket in her hands. "That is not necessary even though I appreciate it very much. I have two roast beef sandwiches, and two tuna salad sandwiches, homemade pickles, apples from Sam's trees, and some of Mr. Menlo's baklava. We will not need to buy anything when we have such good food with us."

I reached out for the basket. "Sounds delicious, Ida. We'll put it in the backseat so it will stay cool. We might want to eat before the hospital so nothing will spoil."

Ida took my other arm, and I helped her down the steps. "I think that is a good idea. I am so excited about our trip. I can hardly wait to see Sarah. I have been praying for her." She leaned her head against my shoulder for just a moment. "Thank you so much for taking me today. It blesses me so."

We stepped carefully through the puddles on the ground while the rain fell steadily. "I'm looking forward to it, too," I said. "Sweetie is coming to my house today to talk wedding plans with my mother, and frankly, I need a break. I know it's my wedding, but I just want to walk down the aisle and say, 'I do.' I want to be Mrs. Sam Goodrich, and I wish I could do it without all the fuss."

Ida waited until I opened the car door. She carefully folded her long skirt beneath her and positioned herself into the passenger seat. I closed the door and went around to the other side of the car, placing the basket in the backseat before I got behind the wheel.

"I know it feels that way now, Gracie," she said when I got inside the car, "but someday you will cherish the memories of your wedding. Even though my ceremony was very simple by today's standards, it was very special to me, and I think of it often." Her voice grew soft, and she looked away from me and out the window. "Especially when I lost Herman. Then the memories came rushing back like a flood. Herman looking so young and handsome in his black suit. The look on his face when we were declared man and wife. The joy we shared with our friends and families. It was one of the best days of my life." She turned to look at me. "It will be this way for you, too. Please do not take it lightly, ja?"

I nodded. "I won't, Ida. Thank you. I think everything else that's going on is stressing me out. My mind is on Hannah and Sarah. And Papa has gotten worse the last few days. It's hard to concentrate on anything else."

Ida was silent for a moment. When she spoke, there was hesitancy in her voice. "Perhaps this will bring you some comfort, liebling. I had a dream last night about Hannah." She smoothed the thick material of her dress with her aged-spotted hands. "She was in a dark place, but there was an angel standing beside her, and the light from the angel began to drive away the blackness that surrounded her. And there was peace, Gracie. Great peace. The angel looked at me as if I stood in that place with them, and he said, 'Fear not. God is watching over Hannah and she will come home soon.'" The old woman looked at me with tears in her eyes. "Many people believe that God no longer speaks through dreams and visions, but this is not so. 'And it shall come to pass in the last days, saith God, I will pour out my Spirit upon all flesh: and your sons and your daughters shall prophesy, and your young men shall see visions, and your old men shall dream dreams.'" She touched my arm. "I believe this dream is inspired, Gracie. I believe our Hannah will come home."

Something rose up inside of me after hearing Ida's words and strengthened my faith. Her dream confirmed what the Muellers and I believed God had already told us. I'd learned to trust this elderly Mennonite woman who knew God in a way many people didn't. "Oh, Ida," I said. "I also believe God still speaks today, and I'm so glad you shared this with me. This is the second time He's sent reassurance of Hannah's return."

"Ja, ja," she said, "but this is not all."

"There's more? What is it?"

"The angel said one more thing. He said, 'Tell Grace she must have eyes to see and ears to hear.' And then I awoke."

I was so surprised, I swerved the car before gaining control and slowing down. Thankfully there was no other traffic on Faith Road. "Th–the angel mentioned me by name? What does that mean?"

"I believe it means God will use you to bring this precious girl back to us," she said simply. "You must remember what he said and make sure your eyes see and your ears hear."

"I have no idea what that means, Ida."

"Ach, Gracie. You must just pay attention. God will show you what He wants you to know. You must stay open to Him." She made a clucking sound with her tongue. "And do not let your mind fill up with worry and fear. I find it is harder to hear what God has to say when these two emotions crowd out my peace."

Ida and her *peace*. Her peace guided her constantly, and I'd begun to understand that her peace was the voice of the Holy Spirit living inside her. She'd taught me to look for *my* peace and follow it. And something inside told me her dream and the words she'd shared with me were very important. I turned them over in my mind until we pulled up into Abigail's driveway. The difference in the house in just the short time C.J. had been working on it was impressive. The yard was cleaned up, and the porch had been rebuilt. Other repairs had been made, and the house was being painted.

"Oh my," Ida said when she saw it. "This is so wonderful. So many people have tried to help Abigail, but her pride turned them away. I guess it took her son to accomplish what an entire town could not do. And just look at the wonderful results."

"Yes, he's done a marvelous job, hasn't he?"

She nodded. "I know we cannot stay long," Ida said, "but perhaps Abigail will at least see us for a few minutes."

As if on cue, the rain began to come down in torrents. "Wait here," I told her. "I have an umbrella in my trunk. I'll get it." I popped the trunk latch, got out of the car, and hurried to the back. Thankfully, the umbrella was still there. I'd been worried I'd taken it in the house when I'd cleaned out my car. I slopped around to Ida's door, opened it, and helped her out. We both tried to stay under the large umbrella Allison had given me on my last birthday. Clear plastic with colorful dots, I felt a little ludicrous holding it over

Ida's bonneted head. I'd always thought the umbrella was cute, but now it just seemed silly. Although it was slow going, we finally made it to the porch. With the rotting wood replaced, the floor felt sturdy and safe. I knocked on the new door that had been installed, and a few moments later, it swung open.

"Gracie!" C.J. said with a smile. "I'm so glad you stopped by. Come in, please."

I helped Ida inside first. There was a rug near the door and we both carefully wiped our wet feet. C.J. looked at Ida oddly and hesitated. Then recognition showed in his face. "Mrs. Turnbauer?" he said. "Is that you?"

Ida smiled. "C.J., it is so good to see you again. It has been a long time, ja?"

"Yes, yes it has." He held out his arm. "May I take your cape?"

"Ja, ja. It is very wet though. I do not want to make a mess."

"That's no problem. I'll hang it up on the coatrack. There's a rug underneath to catch the water."

"Thank you, young man," she said gratefully.

I quickly scanned the room. The furniture was old and worn, but the room itself was neat. A metal fan whirred from a corner. Since I knew Abigail had no electricity, I was surprised. C.J. noticed.

"It runs on batteries," he said. "It's been so hot working here without air-conditioning, I went to Council Grove and bought a couple of them. The other one is in my bedroom."

The rain outside had lowered the temperature

quite a bit, and with the fan running, the inside of Abigail's house was quite pleasant.

"Where is your mama?" Ida asked. "I don't want to bother her, I would just like to say hello. We are on our way to Topeka to visit a friend in the hospital, so I thought we would stop by for a minute or two."

"I'm glad you did," he said. "Mama is lying down, but if you'll wait, I'll be glad to tell her you're here."

"I do not wish to wake her," Ida said hesitantly. "Perhaps we should come back another time."

"No, she's not sleeping. Sometimes she gets uncomfortable in her wheelchair and likes to stretch out for a while. I'm sure she'll be thrilled to see you."

"C.J.," I said, "before you get your mother, I—I wanted to explain something. Why Papa Joe didn't recognize you. He—he's ill. It's Alzheimer's."

His face fell. "I'm so sorry, Gracie. I guess that explains it. I mean, it's not as if we were close when I was young, but I really thought he'd remember me. Joe wasn't too crazy about me back then, and I certainly don't blame him. I was rather rebellious, I'm ashamed to say."

"Well, I just wanted you to know. I didn't want you to be offended."

He shook his head. "I'm not offended, but I'm certainly sad to hear about his condition. Joe Temple is one of the finest men I've ever known."

"Thanks," I said sincerely.

He nodded. "I'll get Mama." He pointed toward an old couch that had seen better days. "Please have a seat. She'll be out in a minute."

Ida and I sat down gingerly on the faded piece of furniture. I brushed something that looked like cookie crumbs from one area, and we had to avoid a spring that had pushed its way through the material.

"I know you and Abigail believe in a simpler life," I whispered to Ida, "but does that mean you can't have decent furniture?"

She shook her head. "We try not to make material things too important, but perhaps Abigail needs furniture that will not cause injury to her or those who visit her." She leaned in closer to me. "Help has been extended to her, but she refuses it." She put her hand on mine. "Real humility isn't found in living a life of poverty, Gracie. Outside expressions do not reveal the heart. True humility comes from believing and obeying God above our own thoughts and feelings. I am afraid Abigail thinks that if she looks poor it is proof she is humble. I believe it is actually misplaced pride. She is too proud to let others bless her. I do not think this is pleasing to a God who wants to provide for His children through the love of His people. How can we fulfill His mandate to give when people like Abigail will not receive?"

She put her hand back on her lap, and I thought about what she'd said. There was a man in our little church back home in Fairbury who made a big show of being poor. Because he had so little in worldly goods, to him it signified that he was more spiritual than the other people in the church. One day when his car broke down and couldn't be repaired, my mother and father, who'd just purchased a new car, decided to give the man their old one, which was still in very good shape. My father took it to a mechanic and had him go over everything, spending almost three hundred dollars in repairs. When my parents gave the man their car, he seemed to accept it gratefully. But the next Sunday, when he pulled into the church parking lot, the once-beautiful vehicle was a complete mess. The windshield was cracked and the body was covered with dents and dings. My father was horrified, thinking the man had been in an accident. He rushed over to see what had happened, my mother and I following behind him.

"Were you in collision?" Dad asked. "Are you okay?"

"Oh no," the man said, his chest swelling with a sense of importance. "I took a sledgehammer to it so I wouldn't become proud of driving something that looked so nice." The man's wife and child stood behind him. The wife stared at the ground while the man's ten-year-old son just looked embarrassed.

My father was so angry he couldn't speak. He turned around, grabbed my mother's arm, and ushered us into the church building. That was the last time my parents ever tried to help him. Eventually his wife left him and took their son with her. I'd wondered for years what had happened to them, but ever since I continued to pray that they would discover who God really is and wouldn't be permanently scarred by this man's strange behavior. Eventually, the pastor confronted him about his confused ideas, but this so-called humble man didn't take kindly to the correction. He left the church after standing up in a service and railing against the "pride and arrogance" of the pastor and the other members. Then he left to find another church where he could play his game of false humility.

"You are very quiet, child," Ida said. "Have I offended you?"

"Not at all," I answered. "In fact, you've just explained a situation that I hadn't thought about for a long time." I quickly told her the story.

"Ja, ja," she said, nodding her head. "This is a very good example of what I mean. This poor man tried to build his own righteousness through his works, and we cannot do that. Our righteousness is of God only." She took a deep breath. "This is what I have tried to tell Abigail down through the years, but I am afraid I have been unsuccessful. As I have told you before, living the life I live is a choice. Not a judgment on others, and not a source of spiritual pride. But Abigail . . . Well, I do not think she believes the same way."

A noise from the other room stopped our conversation. C.J. pushed a wheelchair into the living room. I was somewhat surprised to see Abigail up close. She wasn't as old as I'd thought she'd be. She looked to be in her late fifties or early sixties although I knew she had to be almost seventy. Her hair was pulled back from her face, probably in a tight bun, and her head was covered with a black bonnet similar to Ida's. She was dressed in black from head to toe, except for the white plaster cast that peeked out from under her heavy skirt. Once again, I wondered how anyone could wear so many clothes in the summer.

"Oh Abigail," Ida said, getting up from the couch. I held her elbow as she struggled to her feet. "I am so sorry to find out about your leg. I should have checked on you sooner."

Abigail arched one eyebrow and stared at Ida without smiling. "Well, I hear you have been busy attending that liberal church in town. Perhaps they don't teach taking care of your neighbors there?"

Ida toddled up next to Abigail and kissed her on each cheek. "Now Abigail, the church is not liberal. They also live a simple life. You should visit. I believe you would enjoy it. The pastor is a man of great love and deep understanding."

"Humph," she uttered. "We had a wonderful church until you broke it up. I believe you've also convinced the Vogler family to abandon true doctrine."

Ida laughed gently. "No, Abigail. I do not convince anyone to do anything. God alone is able to lead His sheep. And you know that our number began to dwindle because our dear brother Benjamin died. And then Gabriel and Sarah decided to attend Bethel, as I did. The Voglers made their decision later without any help from me. And the Beckenbauer brothers are too ill to attend church at all. It might interest you to know that Abel and Emily Mueller visit them regularly and help to care for them. They have become very good friends."

"Oh, pshaw," the woman spat out. "The brothers are taking help because they have no other choice. I would help them if I could." Her voice took on a whiny tone. "But as you can see, I can't do much for anyone." She leaned over and rubbed her cast. "I've been in this chair for a month now. It doesn't get any better." She reached up and grabbed C.J.'s hand. "Thank God my son is here to take care of me."

C.J., who still stood in back of his mother's wheelchair, winked at us. "Now Mama, you know the doctor said your bones were healing nicely and that you should be able to start getting around with crutches before long."

Abigail quickly pulled her hand from her son's. "You just say that because you want to abandon me again." She put her hands up over her face. "I am so alone. There isn't anyone who cares about me."

"How did you break your leg, Abigail?" Ida asked, ignoring her friend's attempt to gain sympathy.

"I tripped on the stairs carrying my laundry to the basement," she said. "I lay on the floor for days because no one cared enough to check on me."

"But I believe Kenneth and Alene Ward bring you groceries almost every week, isn't that true?" Ida said.

Abigail turned her face away and wouldn't answer.

"That's who found her," C.J. said. "And it was only a couple of hours after she fell. Not days. They called an ambulance and stayed with her at the hospital. They also called me. Nice people."

"You have no idea how long I was on that hard cement floor!" Abigail cried angrily. "You were nowhere around and haven't been for years. You don't care anything about me."

"Now Abigail Bradley," Ida said emphatically, "you stop this right now. Your son left his job to come here and help you. This is not the right way to treat people. Especially your own flesh and blood."

Abigail's expression turned even more irate, but she clamped her thin lips shut.

C.J. sighed. "I'm sorry for my mother's behavior." He patted her on the shoulder. "She has been in quite a bit of pain. I'm sure it's not easy to stay cheerful when you hurt so much." He smiled at us. "May I get you ladies something to drink?"

Ida leaned over and hugged her friend, and then she walked back over to where I sat. "No thank you, C.J.," she said. "As we told you, we are on our way to see a friend in the hospital. I just wanted to check on Abigail. We should be on our way."

"Just like you to rush off," Abigail barked, abandoning her momentary attempt at silence. "You leave me alone for months, and then when you do come by, you only stay a few minutes. I guess you can check me off your list of things to do now."

"Mama!" C.J. said. "That's enough. I think it's time for you to go back to bed. Maybe a little sleep will help calm you down. And perhaps another pill?"

"No! You give me those pills to keep me quiet." She looked at us, her eyes wide. "He tries to keep me asleep so I won't complain."

I couldn't help thinking that if I were C.J., keeping his mother knocked out on medication would be a temptation I wasn't sure I could resist. However, it was obvious he was going out of his way to care for her.

"We must be going, Abigail," Ida said. I stood up and held out my arm so she could hold on to me. "I will check back with you soon. And C.J., please let me know if there is anything I can do to help you. Gracie, can you give him my telephone number? I can't ever remember it." She turned and smiled at him. "I know there is no phone here, but if you need to reach me, you can do so in town, from the restaurant."

I opened my purse and pulled out a small notepad. I wrote down Ida's number and then my own and handed the paper to C.J.

"Thank you, ladies. I truly appreciate it. So far we're doing fine, but if I do need something I'll certainly call you."

"I'd like to invite you to my wedding, C.J." I gave him the details while his mother glared at me. "I understand if you're too busy, but I'd love it if you could come."

"I'll certainly try. I appreciate the invitation." He took Ida's cape from the coatrack and helped her into it.

We made our way to the front door to the sounds of Abigail grumbling about being deserted by people who called themselves her friends. I couldn't wait to get out of there and away from that unpleasant woman. We said good-bye to C.J. and he closed the door behind us. The rain was still coming down so I popped open the umbrella and held it over us until we were inside the car.

"Man, that woman is something else," I said when we were both safe inside. "How can you be so kind? I just wanted to punch her."

Ida's nose wrinkled up as she giggled. "Oh, Gracie. I do not think you would ever strike a woman in a wheelchair. No matter how obnoxious she was."

"I wouldn't place a bet on that," I said under my breath. I started the car and began backing out of the dirt driveway we'd come in on. My concentration was on my rearview mirror, and I forgot about the big mud hole I'd driven around when we'd arrived. My back tires suddenly sank down into it, and it was clear after several attempts that I would need assistance to get free.

"We're stuck, Ida," I said. "I've got to go back to the house and get some help."

The old lady nodded. "I'm sure C.J. will give us the assistance we need."

I started to open my door, thinking what a mess I was going to be after wading through the mud hole in the rain, when my door flew open. C.J. stood there in a gray plastic rain covering, a hood over his head.

"Stay in the car," he said. "I'll get my truck and pull you out."

"Oh thank you so much," I responded with relief. "I'm sorry. I should have gone around it."

He smiled, water dripping from the edge of his hood and past his face. "No, I should have filled it before this happened. It's my fault." He pointed to the front of my car. "I'm going to put a chain around your bumper and attach it to the back of my truck. I don't think you're stuck too badly, so I don't believe it will cause any damage to your car."

I grinned at him. "That's fine. I'd rather mess up my bumper a little bit than sit in this hole until it dries up."

He laughed and shut the door. Ida and I waited a few minutes until C.J.'s truck came around the back of the house. Of course it was red, just like every other Tom, Dick, and Harry in the county. I almost laughed. I had no intention of falling for this again or leveling any further accusations toward anyone in Harmony.

C.J. pulled around in front of us and wrapped a couple of thick chains around my bumper. I'd turned off my wipers so it was hard to see him. He came back to my window. I rolled it open.

"Turn off your engine and put your car in neutral," he instructed.

"Okay." I rolled my window back up and turned off the engine. Then I shifted into neutral. It was almost impossible to see anything with the rain pouring down and hitting the windshield, but I heard C.J.'s motor rev up. Then slowly we began to move. Within a couple of minutes, we were out of the hole. C.J. got out of his truck, removed the chains, and waved us on. I lowered my window once again and yelled "Thank you!" to the now thoroughly drenched man. I started the car and turned on my windshield wipers. For the first time I got a good look at C.J.'s red truck.

And his bumper sticker with a big black bear emblazoned on it.

NINETEEN

I drove the rest of the way to Topeka without saying anything to Ida about C.J.'s truck. For crying out loud. Did everyone with a red truck have a compulsion to stick an image of a bear on his bumper? I'd made Pat investigate two men because they had red trucks. Only one had a bear bumper sticker. Besides, what if the witness who saw the truck in Topeka was wrong? What if the animal on the bumper sticker wasn't a bear at all but some other animal? Rufus's Chicago Bears bumper sticker wasn't the least bit odd seeing as how he'd moved here from Chicago. Maybe the image on C.J.'s sticker was something else entirely. With all the rain, I hadn't seen it clearly. I'd feel pretty stupid if the sticker was actually a shout-out for the *I Love Koalas Club*. I decided to stop back by Abigail's and get another look at that truck before I did anything stupid. I tried to put it out of my mind, but I couldn't help thinking if Hannah showed up in a day or two, sorry that she'd run away and thinking that she could just waltz back into town after causing all this trouble, the next person Pat might have to physically restrain would be his future daughter-in-law.

We were almost to Topeka when I spotted a park by the side of the road with covered shelters. The rain had slowed down to a light sprinkle. I pulled off the road and into the park. "Maybe we should eat here," I said to Ida. "What do you think?"

"Ach, it is just lovely, Gracie," she said with a smile. "Yes, let's stop here."

I parked as close as I could to the shelter, and we both got out. I carried the picnic basket to one of the covered tables. Surprisingly, it was clean and didn't need to be wiped down, a condition not always true when it came to eating outside. I surveyed the area. Very nice. Lots of trees and pleasant landscaping. I compared it to the park in Harmony, which was one of my favorite spots in town. One reason I loved it so was because it reminded me of a special place in Wichita where I'd spent many happy days.

O. J. Watson Park is the epitome of what a park should be. It contains a beautiful lake full of ducks, geese, and even a crane or two, with tall trees full of lush leaves and wildflowers that grow along the paths. And Watson Park has something else unique to Kansas—an actual yellow brick road that winds through it. It's still my favorite walking trail. I used to go there on the weekends just to walk the road, enjoy nature, and watch children laugh as they rode ponies, pushed paddleboats across the sparkling water, or caught a ride on a special train that chugs around most of the perimeter of the park. Over the years, the friendly park staff had grown to know me, and every time I went there, it was like visiting dear friends. My love for Watson Park had helped me to realize that this city girl longed for the beauty and silence of the country long before I was able to recognize it.

"Are you here with me, Gracie?" Ida said, chuckling. "You look so far away."

I laughed. "I guess I was. I was remembering a special place I used to visit in Wichita. This park made me think of it."

Ida breathed deeply. "Ja, this is lovely. I would rather eat outside any day than sit in my house or in a restaurant. Many days I take my lunch out on the front porch and eat it there."

I'd just started to open the picnic basket when I remembered we had nothing to drink. I mentioned my concern to Ida.

"Ach," she said with a smile, "I remembered. Open the basket."

I looked inside. There were two Mason jars with iced tea nestled between a thick towel so they wouldn't hit against each other and break. I removed the jars and the food, and we spent the next forty minutes enjoying our supper. The sandwiches were delicious, the pickles crisp and tart, and the baklava sweet and flaky. By the time we finished, I couldn't eat another bite.

We packed up, got back in the car, and drove to the hospital. I was using directions copied from the Internet, but I missed our turnoff the first time. The second time around I found the hospital without any problem. I parked, and Ida and I went inside. I had Sarah's room number, but I wasn't sure how to get there. A kind receptionist gave us directions. It was amusing to see all the odd looks aimed Ida's way.

In Harmony, conservative Mennonite clothing went unnoticed. Ida's was somewhat more severe than most, but no one ever paid any attention to her. Here, she stuck out like a sore thumb. I was certain she wasn't used to the stares since she hardly ever left Harmony, but she carried herself as if she had no idea she was garnering attention. Finally we found Sarah's room. The door was open, and as we entered we immediately saw Sarah sitting up in her bed. She looked so much better than she had when she collapsed, I was filled with joy.

"Gracie! Ida!" she called out when she saw us. Her face lit up in a smile. She wore a hospital gown, and her long black hair hung down past her shoulders. "I am so glad to see you both!"

I hurried over to her side and put my arms around her. "I'm thankful to see you looking so well, and I'm grateful to God for taking such good care of you."

She patted my back with her small hand. "God is good, isn't He? He brought just the right people to me when I needed help." She tightened her arms around me. "Thank you, Gracie. Thank you for all you did for me. And thank your father for me, too, won't you?" She let me go and lay back on her pillow. "The doctors say I can go home soon. Then I'll be able to offer my thanks to your father in person."

"He'll be happy to see you."

Ida, who'd gone around to the other side of the bed gave Sarah another big hug. "I prayed for you, dear, sweet Sarah," she said, her voice cracking with emotion. "I knew the God who heals would keep you safe."

"He has done exceedingly above and beyond, Ida," Sarah said solemnly. "The most recent tests are good. The doctors say I am responding very well to the medicine they've prescribed. I'm already feeling much better than I have in a very long time."

"That's wonderful," I said.

"Well, well. Look who's here." Gabe's deep voice rang out from behind us. I turned around to find him smiling at us. "Gracie and Ida. Two of my very favorite people. I'm so glad to see you."

He held out his arms, and I embraced him. Goodness, he really was turning into a great big teddy bear in Mennonite clothing. He also greeted Ida, and then helped her into a nearby chair.

Sarah asked about Hannah.

"Nothing new," I answered. "It's been five days now. I'm ready for her to come home."

"I feel badly for Abel and Emily," Gabe said. He walked over to Sarah's bed and took her small hand in his. "I know how it feels to wonder if you might lose the most important person in your life." His voice broke.

I reached over and put my hand on his shoulder. "I know you do. We're all so grateful nothing really awful happened."

Sarah gave me a beatific smile. "And that's not all God has done, Gracie. You'll never guess."

I frowned at her. "I give up. What else has He done?"

"Great and mighty things." I immediately recognized the voice that boomed from behind me. John came up next to the bed. I almost gasped at the change in his expression and the different look in his eyes. There was a light that hadn't been there before.

"Oh John," I said, overcome with emotion.

"Now, now, Gracie," he said, grabbing my hand. "No tears. I've spent the last two days being weepier than any man should be."

"Ach, my dearest John. You have met my friend Jesus, ja?"

He smiled. "Yes, Ida. I've met your friend. And it didn't happen just because He saved Sarah's life, although that started it. After we got to the hospital, while the doctors were working with her, I went to the chapel, got down on my knees, and asked God to reveal Himself to me. I'd heard the story of salvation many times and rejected it because I couldn't be sure it was true. I needed to *know* God. To know in my heart He was real. I couldn't believe just because people told me I should—or even because the message of the cross was so appealing. I needed to experience the presence of God for myself." He tried to blink away the tears in his eyes. "And I did. I can't really explain it. All I can tell you is that God visited that room. He visited this man, and I will never, ever be the same."

If we hadn't been standing in a hospital, I think I would have jumped up and down and shouted at the top of my lungs. Even the sedate and dignified Ida looked as if she had some Holy Ghost fire in her belly.

I threw my arms around John and hugged him as hard as I could. "I'm so happy, John. So very happy."

"Now you're more than my friend," he whispered into my ear. "You're my sister."

"And proud to be," I replied softly. I let go of him and smiled at everyone in the room. "Now if Hannah would just come home, everything would be perfect."

Sarah nodded. "We will all keep praying."

"I know the whole town of Harmony is praying as well," Gabe said.

His reminder about Harmony made me think about Sam. I rifled through my purse, only to realize I'd left my cell phone at home. Cell phones are so useless in Harmony, I tend to forget I have it. "Is it okay if I use your phone, Sarah? I'd like to call Sam and tell him we got here safely."

With Gabe's encouragement, I called Sam's house collect. He answered after the second ring. I waited while the operator confirmed that he would accept the charges.

"So you made it," he said after the operator left the line.

"Yes, we're here. I'm in Sarah's room, and she looks incredible."

"Did you have any problems with the rain? It poured buckets and buckets here."

I briefly told him about getting stuck at Abigail's, but I left out the part about the truck. I was determined to look at C.J.'s bumper once more before I said anything to anyone else, even Sam. And especially Pat.

"I'm just glad you're okay," Sam said. "I told you to get rid of that car. It's too small and lightweight for the country."

"Could we deal with this some other time?" I asked impatiently. "Is Sweetie over at my house?"

"Yep. She's been there for a couple of hours. Took some strawberry pie with her."

"Sweetie and her pie. For goodness' sake. And why didn't you go with her? I mean, this is your wedding, too. Maybe you should get more involved."

There was silence on the other end. Finally he said, "Look, Gracie. I'm putting on a monkey suit. That should be the only thing the man has to do. The rest of it belongs to the woman."

"You did not just say that," I retorted. "When I get back there..."

He burst out laughing. "I'm kidding."

"Laugh all you want, monkey suit boy. You're still in trouble."

"Hey, that Murphy lady called. She needs to talk to you. I told her you were going to Topeka. She wants you to call her. She says she has something important to tell you."

I thanked him, told him what time I thought we'd be home, and then hung up. Gabe, John, Ida, and Sarah were visiting and didn't seem to be paying any attention to me, but I didn't want to take the chance they might overhear my conversation with Susan. I stepped out into the hall and asked a nearby nurse if there was another phone I could use. She directed me to an empty room. I dug through my purse and found the business card Susan had given me. I dialed the number and after several rings, she answered.

"Susan, it's Gracie. Sam said you'd called?"

"Yes, Gracie." She lowered her voice a couple of notches. "I told you I'd check with the KBI about Hannah Mueller? Well, I did. As you suspected, until recently they were treating her disappearance as that of a runaway. Pat Taylor has already asked them to see if Hannah's situation could be tied to the murder in Topeka. I voiced my own concerns as well, and they promised to step up their efforts." She sighed. "I hope it helps. I pushed about as much as I dared."

"Thank you so much," I said, deciding not to mention that Pat had already told me about her involvement. "I'm glad Pat actually followed through, but I'm sure your input will push the investigation forward even more. I'm so relieved to know that the KBI is finally taking Hannah's case seriously." I cleared my throat and hesitated.

"Is there something else?"

I carefully explained my concerns about C.J. Bradley. "I don't want to overreact, Susan. It just seems odd. C.J. showing up now and his truck matching the description of a vehicle that might belong to a serial killer."

"You should probably contact Sheriff Taylor first," she said.

"I would, but so far, he's been less than enthusiastic about my suggestions."

She grunted. "I understand completely. He's got a hard head." She paused, and I could hear papers shuffling in the background. "Give me a few more details about this C.J. person."

I quickly told her everything I knew. "Let me see what I can do," she said. "Hopefully, they'll follow up on this lead now that they're headed in the right direction."

"Can you please keep my name out of it? There's

already one former suspect who won't talk to me. I don't want to make another enemy."

"I'll try. If I find out anything helpful on this end, I'll contact you. And keep me updated, okay? I'm still praying Hannah will just show up. She may be a little worse for wear, but she may also be much more thankful for her good home and her loving parents."

"I sure hope you're right." I thanked her again and hung up. I felt bad going over Pat's head again, but after the bawling out I got about Rufus, I had no intention of mentioning C.J. to Pat. Even if I did, I felt pretty sure he wouldn't take it seriously.

I headed back to Sarah's room, ready to apologize for interrupting our visit to talk on the phone. But when I entered her room, I saw something that made the words stick in my throat. John stood by Sarah's bedside, holding her hand. And Gabe, who was only a few feet away, was smiling. He must have noticed the dumbfounded look on my face because he laughed.

"Now don't get emotional," he said, "but the three of us are working things out." He slapped John on the back. "If things keep going well, there may be more than one wedding in Harmony this summer."

I felt so overwhelmed I grabbed a nearby chair and sat down. "I can hardly believe it," I said rather breathlessly. "Can this be true?"

Sarah giggled. "Why, Gracie Temple. You're the one who told me God could do anything—that I shouldn't give up hope. Now look at you."

"You're right. It's just that. . .well, Gabe. . ."

"I told you that Sarah couldn't be unequally yoked," Gabe said. "Now Sarah and John are one in the Spirit. John has made it clear that he respects Abel Mueller and our church and has no problem attending there."

"And I also told him that I'd wear sackcloth and ashes if it made him happy," John interjected. "What I wear is meaningless to me. What I feel on the inside means everything."

Gabe cleared his throat. "Which also helped me to realize that it isn't our traditions that make us who we are. It's our hearts. And John has one of the most honest, sincere hearts I've ever come across. I love him like a brother now. Loving him as a father won't be hard at all."

"And guess what else?" Sarah said. "Papa says I can wear prettier colors from now on. Like the other ladies in church."

Gabe nodded. "Abel has convinced me that dressing modestly doesn't mean we must look as if we're on our way to a funeral."

"I pointed out that if God painted all the flowers with color, why wouldn't He want His people to be clothed the same way?" Sarah's eyes twinkled, but I knew it wasn't because of the new dresses she would be wearing. It was because God had saved John and given them both the deepest desire of their hearts.

I sighed with happiness. So many wonderful things were happening in Harmony. Maybe it was a sign that Hannah's situation would soon be resolved as well.

We visited for about another twenty minutes, but it was clear Sarah was getting tired, so Ida and I excused ourselves and headed home. We were both so happy that we chatted nonstop all the way. I wondered if Ida would agree with Gabe's acceptance of John before he actually joined the church, but I needn't have worried. She was ecstatic, but not just because it looked as if Sarah and John would finally be together. The elderly Mennonite woman rejoiced more that John had finally found his way to God.

As we headed down the road to Harmony, I told her I needed to make one quick stop. "There's something at Abigail's house I need to check," I told her. "If you don't mind, I'd rather not explain. Would it bother you to sit in the car for a few minutes and wait for me?"

She frowned. "No, liebling. If it is something you must do, I will be glad to wait. But is there something that troubles you? Is there anything I can do to help?"

I assured her there wasn't and asked her to trust me. Then I turned down the road that led to Abigail's house, grateful that the rain had stopped so I wouldn't end up soaked by the time I finished my mission. Thankfully, there was a line of trees that hid a section of the road from the house. I left Ida in the car while I trudged down the road with a small flashlight I kept in my glove compartment. I left it off since there was still enough light left to see the way. However, it wouldn't last long. Any daylight peeking through the still cloudy skies overhead would soon disappear. The flashlight would help me to see C.J.'s bumper and would also guide me back to my car. The flashlight was my dad's idea. He had a strict list for my glove box. Registration, title, and flashlight. Check. I sent up a prayer of thanksgiving for my father as I approached the house. I felt fairly safe. Unless someone specifically looked out the windows on the west side of the house to see if some crazy girl was wandering through the field, I wouldn't be noticed. Even so, as I got closer, I tried to be as quiet as possible. Unfortunately, the rain had created a lot of mud. My sneakers weren't as sneaky as they should have been. A weird sucking sound occurred every time I took a step. It was noticeable to me, but I consoled myself with the knowledge that it wasn't something anyone inside the house could hear.

I made my way around to the back of the house and was surprised to find nothing. No truck. Had C.J. gone into town? Was ruining my best sneakers all for nothing? A quick glance through the yard revealed the large outbuilding I'd noticed during my first visit. The door on the front was unusually large. More like a garage door. Maybe the truck was inside. I crept up to the building. Although the structure appeared to be decrepit, it was actually much sturdier than I'd originally thought. I found a regular door in the back and pulled on the latch. The loud creak made my heart race. I peeked around the corner toward the house to see if anyone else had heard it, but no one stirred. I could see that the windows were open and the curtains were drawn back, probably to get some air circulating. The shimmering lights from inside came from oil lamps. Even though they usually have a glass hurricane cover to protect the flame, air can still get inside from the top and make the flames flicker. It gave the house an eerie look, creating shadows that appeared to be caught in some kind of macabre dance. A shiver ran down my spine, but I reminded myself that no one knew I was there.

I slipped inside the dark building. Sure enough, the truck was parked inside. Feeling my way around the side with my hand, I made my way to the back. Turning on the flashlight, I aimed it on the right bumper. There was a bear on the sticker all right, standing on top of a hill. I moved the beam of light along the bottom border. It read *CALIFORNIA REPUBLIC*, and over the bear, on the top left side, was a star. "It's a California flag," I whispered into the dark. Well, that didn't seem very ominous. How many people from California had them? I sat on the bumper for a moment, trying to decide what to do. Should I let this go? Or should I call Pat? The war in my mind waged against the feeling in my gut. Where was my peace? I knew that's what Ida would ask. At that moment, I had no idea. Ida. I needed to get back to her before she began to worry. I stood up and started toward the door when I heard a loud thumping noise. It frightened me so much a small scream escaped my lips. Was C.J. out there? Had I been discovered? I waited several seconds, but there was only silence. I crept closer to the door. There it was again! Two thumps this time. Was someone knocking on the wall outside the makeshift garage? I had two choices. I could step outside slowly and confront whoever was out there, or I could take off running like the devil was chasing me. After looking carefully around the corner and seeing no one, I chose the latter. Of course, with all the mud, the devil probably could have simply strolled next to me and not broken a sweat. But I moved as fast as I could, keeping the light from the flashlight in front of me. At this point, I didn't care who was watching. It was so dark outside, no one would be able to clearly see me.

"Look, Mama," C.J. might say. "There's a strange light bouncing through the field."

That was a lot better than, "Look, Mama, Gracie Temple is running around outside like an insane person. Wonder what she's up to?"

I finally made it back to the car, but my sneakers were so caked with mud I could barely lift my feet. I opened the car door, sat sideways, and pulled them off. A weird slurping sound accompanied my task. Now what? I felt a hand on my shoulder.

"Hand them to me, Gracie," Ida said. I swiveled around and saw that she'd removed a towel from the basket and had it on her lap. "I was certain you would need help with your shoes when you returned. Let me clean them for you while we. . .make our getaway? Is that the correct phrase?"

I started to protest, to tell her that my schlepping through a muddy field in the middle of the night had nothing to do with anything underhanded, but she wouldn't have believed me. And she would have been right. So I just handed her the shoes, closed the car door, backed up a bit, turned the car around, and headed back to the main road. I waited to flip on my headlights until I was certain my car couldn't be seen from the Bradley house. I kept looking in the rearview mirror to see if a red truck was on our tail, but no one followed us. When we turned onto Faith Road, I breathed a sigh of relief. Ida carefully wiped my shoes off the best she could, leaving globs of wet mud inside the towel, which she held on her lap. The entire time she didn't utter a word.

"Aren't you going to ask me what I was doing?" I said finally.

"No, liebling." Her voice was soft in the dark interior of the car. "You do not have to explain everything to me. If it is my business, you will tell me."

Odd how the fact that she *didn't* ask for an explanation made me want to give her one, but I decided not to. Lobbing false accusations against your neighbors was a big no-no in the Bible. However, in my mind *thinking* about it wasn't quite as bad. I needed some time to sort things out before adding C.J. to my list of bogus suspects.

"Thanks, Ida. I appreciate it. I'll tell you one of these days why I did this. But for now, if you don't mind, I'd rather not."

"I trust you, Gracie. In fact, I knew you were someone I could trust from the first moment I met you. Nothing has changed. Nothing ever will."

And that was it. I glanced over at the elderly Mennonite woman, dressed in her Old Order clothes, and was surprised to realize that Ida Turnbauer was one of the best friends I'd ever had. As much as I loved Sarah, I wasn't as close to her as I was to Ida. I started to get a little emotional, so I tried to turn my thoughts back to C.J. Bradley before I burst out into a chorus of "Wind Beneath My Wings." A song Ida had probably never heard in her entire life.

The fear of offending C.J. and the real possibility that my actions could cause Pat to consider using his gun to stop me from causing any more trouble played against my overwhelming desire to find Hannah. By the time we reached Ida's, I'd made my decision.

I helped Ida up the stairs with her basket. "If you'll give me that muddy towel, I'll wash it and return it," I said when we reached the porch.

"No, liebling," she said. "I am happy to wash the towel. It is no trouble at all."

I knew arguing with her would be useless so I didn't. "Thank you, Ida. I had a wonderful day. Spending time with you is a joy."

"Why, my precious girl," she said, patting my cheek with her hand. "That means more to me than you could possibly know. You are such a dear friend."

"As are you." I kissed her cheek and waited while she opened her front door. Then I set the wicker basket inside. "I'd be happy to carry this to the kitchen."

"Thank you, Gracie. But that is not necessary. It will be fine here until I am ready to clean it out."

I said good-bye and left, still basking in the glow of treasured friendship. On the way home, I looked at the clock on my dashboard. Nine o'clock. I had one last thing to do before bed. I had no plan to tell Pat I'd asked Susan to follow up on C.J. It would make more sense to hang myself now and get it over with. But if I voiced my suspicions about C.J. and he contacted the KBI himself, there was a chance he would never know about Susan's involvement. It was a chance I was willing to take. So when I got home I called Pat.

One more time.

TWENTY

Let's just say that the phone call didn't go well. At all. The first time, he just hung up on me. After letting the phone ring and ring the second time around, he finally picked up. I launched into a lengthy explanation as to *why* I felt he needed to follow this lead. Then I promised profusely that this would absolutely be the last time I bothered him with a possible suspect. That seemed to finally get his attention, although I had to listen to several minutes of ranting and raving, including the use of some words I'd actually have to look up to understand. I had the distinct feeling these pearls of "wordom" would not be found in my handy Funk and Wagnalls. When he finally calmed down a little, I tried again.

"Look," I said firmly, "we can't leave any stone unturned. If it makes you feel any better, I think this is the last red truck in Harmony you'll need to worry about. I've probably checked out all the rest. I just didn't see this particular truck until today."

"Well thank goodness for that," Pat replied, although it sounded more like, "Well. Thank. Goodness. For. That." I had no idea why his words were spoken with so much emphasis and definition. Perhaps getting them out coherently took extra effort.

"C.J. isn't from around here," I explained. "He's from California, and he probably lived there when some of those murders took place. And you said there were others in Arizona and New Mexico, right? Obviously, your killer lived somewhere in that part of the country. C.J. fits the bill."

The silence from the other end of the phone line wasn't very reassuring. Finally a long, drawn-out sigh came through the receiver. I wondered if he had any air left. "All right, Gracie. One last time. But I mean it. This is the end. My deputies are beginning to think I've lost my mind. Spending all this time on a runaway."

I bit my lip and didn't utter what had become my mantra the past few days. *Hannah is not a runaway.* I didn't have the nerve to say it again or to tell him that thanks to Susan, the KBI might get more involved in his case even without his help. I wasn't sorry I'd contacted Susan. I couldn't take the chance that Pat would drop the ball or refuse to follow up on C.J. At least now I had two people pushing for an investigation of C. J. Bradley. Hopefully, this plan wouldn't blow up in my face. After all, Pat was about to become my father-in-law. Holiday dinners could be tense.

"Changing the subject for a moment," he said. "Sam called and invited me to the wedding rehearsal. And the dinner."

"Oh Pat. That's great news." And I meant it.

"I'm assuming that means I'm also invited to the wedding?"

"You haven't gotten an invitation?"

"Not yet."

Mom told me the invitations were mailed out several days ago. Pat obviously hadn't gotten one because he wasn't on Sweetie's list. She'd handled most of the local invitations while my mother worked mainly on the relatives that lived out of state. I was determined Pat would get an invitation if I had to mail it myself. "I'll follow up on that," I said. "But you're definitely invited."

"Good. I think Sam and I are starting to make progress. For the first time I'm beginning to feel like a real father."

"Just remember that you're also a real father-in-law. No matter how much I irritate you."

He snorted. "I keep trying to remind myself of that. Frankly, it's getting harder and harder."

"Thanks." I heard Mom and Dad getting ready to head upstairs for bed. "Hey, gotta go. Will you let me know what you find out?"

"Yes, Gracie. *If* I find out anything."

I said good-bye and hung up the phone feeling a little better. Suddenly Ida's dream popped back into my mind. *Eyes to see and ears to hear.* Maybe noticing C.J.'s bumper was what I was supposed to *see.* Perhaps we were finally getting close to finding Hannah. After hearing about Ida's dream, I felt even more certain that Hannah wasn't dead. My hope was high, and I had no intention of backing off the search for her.

"We're going upstairs," Mom said. "Will you be okay down here?"

"I'm fine. Might raid the fridge though. I'm a little hungry."

"We gave Papa a pill about an hour ago," my father said. "I think he'll be quiet for a while. If he wakes up during the night again, don't hesitate to give him another one."

"Okay," I said. "By the way, how's your knee?"

"Dr. Keystone stopped by this morning on his way to Topeka," Mom said. "He looked at your father's leg and told him what I've been saying for months. He hasn't been allowing his injury to heal properly. John wrapped it up and handed Daniel his cane with a warning that if he doesn't start using it all the time, he'll put your father back in a cast."

"I just saw John in Topeka earlier today. When was he here?"

"About thirty minutes after you left," Mom said. "He had a couple of emergencies earlier today. Then he stopped by to see Daniel. He told us he was on his way back to Topeka. He must have passed you."

"He sure is putting miles on that SUV of his," I said. "With what people around here pay him, I hope he doesn't go broke."

"I think his mind is on love," Mom said smiling. "Not money."

I laughed. "I'm sure you're right about that."

After they went upstairs, I checked on Papa. Sure enough, he was sound asleep and snoring. Smelling something good coming from the kitchen,

I investigated and found that my mother had made peanut butter cookies. I grabbed several, made some hot chocolate, and went into the living room. It seemed silly to try to be quiet when talking to my parents hadn't roused Papa, but I tiptoed to the rocking chair, put my food on a nearby table, picked up the phone, and called Sam. I kept my voice as low as I could but loud enough so Sam could hear me while I gave him a rundown of my day. As I'd expected, he scolded me for going back to Abigail's.

"You might as well save your breath," I said. "I'm glad I did it. We have to know if C.J. *is* involved. There's no way I can simply ignore the situation. He's probably innocent, but if that's true, he has nothing to worry about."

"Well, here's something you might not have thought of, Grace," Sam said, his tone a couple of notches higher than normal. "What if C.J. *is* the serial killer, and he saw you sneaking onto his property and spying on him? What do you think he would do?"

His words brought me up short. "I—I hadn't thought of that." And I hadn't. I'd been so focused on Hannah that the whole idea of my own safety never occurred to me.

Sam exhaled loudly. First Pat and now Sam. I seemed to be making the men in my life breathless. "Did he see you?"

I shook my head before realizing Sam couldn't actually pick that up through the phone. "No, I'm sure he didn't. I was careful, and no one followed me when I left."

"Did you leave anything behind that might tell him you were snooping around?"

"No. Nothing." *Except big, muddy footprints all around the area where his truck was parked.* While Sam continued to reproach me, I tuned him out and thought about those footprints. But with relief I realized the ground had been really wet. It wouldn't take long for mud to ooze back into my tracks. There shouldn't be any sign of my visit by morning. I started to relax a bit.

"Did you hear me?" Sam said.

"Certainly. I agree completely." It was the only thing I could come up with. Hopefully it fit.

"Thank goodness. I thought I'd have to fight with you about it."

Uh-oh. "Um, could you just repeat that one more time for clarification?"

Silence. After a long pause, he said, "You weren't listening, were you?"

"I'm sorry, Sam. My mind drifted. It's been a long day. Tell me again?"

"Forget it. It wasn't important." His tone softened. "I know it's been rough. We'll talk more tomorrow. Any family plans?"

"Not yet. Problem is, Papa can't go anywhere right now. Unless you guys come over here, there's no way we can all get away together."

"Maybe it's better that way. I don't think your father wants much to do with me."

"I *am* going to talk to him, Sam. I just haven't had much time. Trust me, everything will be all right."

"And just how do you know that?"

"I know that because God put us together, and I'm fully confident He'll take care of this situation. Besides, my father is a just man. Something's bothering him, and it has nothing to do with you. Dad's pretty introspective so I know he's trying to figure out why he's so upset. As soon as he deals with whatever's on his mind, he'll make things right with you. I guarantee it."

"I hope you're right. We need to get this straightened out before the wedding."

I heard a noise behind me. Papa Joe was sitting up on the couch, staring at me. "Hey, Papa's awake. I gotta go. Don't worry, I mean it."

"I love you, Grace."

"I love you, too, Sam. Good night."

I put the phone down, quickly downed the last of my chocolate, and went over to check on Papa.

"Why, Gracie girl," he said when he saw me. "Has everyone else gone to bed?"

"Yes, Papa. It's after ten."

He swung his legs around and sat facing me. "All this sleeping during the day has made it hard to get any shut-eye at night. I've got to get on a better schedule."

His shifts from normalcy to confusion were emotionally draining. How long would he be with me before retreating into that other world again? Although the good times made me happy at first, I'd actually begun to hate them. It was like being teased. First you soar and then you crash.

"I think I missed dinner, Gracie. How about a meat loaf sandwich?" he said with a smile.

"Sounds great, Papa." I got up to go into the kitchen. Papa rose shakily to his feet, obviously intending to follow me.

"You wait here," I said. "I'll bring it to you."

"I've been rotting on this couch all day. If you don't mind, I'd love to sit in the kitchen with you for a while."

I offered him my arm, and we made our way slowly to the kitchen.

"Are you still sore?" I asked.

"Just a smidgen. But those goofy pills they give me take away most of the pain. I feel pretty good right now."

"I'm glad, Papa." I helped him into a chair, and he watched me while I got the meat loaf out of the refrigerator.

"Gracie, when was tennis mentioned in the Bible?"

I turned to stare at him, wondering if he was drifting away again. But his quick smile and the twinkle in his eye told me he was still there.

"I don't know, Papa. When was tennis mentioned in the Bible?"

He winked at me. "When Moses served in Pharaoh's court."

I laughed. "Oh Papa. That's awful."

"I know." He fell silent while I got out the mayonnaise and bread from the bread box.

"Gracie, it's time for us to get your wedding present."

The jar of mayonnaise almost slipped from my hand. "Oh Papa." I set it down on the counter. I couldn't stop my tears even though I knew I wasn't supposed to let Papa see my pain.

He got up slowly and came over to me. Taking my hand, he led me to a chair. "Gracie," he said, sitting across from me, "I know there's something wrong with me, but this isn't part of that. You need to trust me."

I couldn't speak, so I just looked at him.

"Your grandmother made a wedding present for you right after you were born. She loved you so much, and she wanted to create something special for the day you became a bride. When we left Harmony, it was left behind. It's my fault, I took the wrong trunk. Your uncle Benjamin was given the task of protecting it. He knew it was to be yours, and he swore to get it to you someday. Of course he died before he could honor his word. Your grandmother never forgot that gift, and before she died, she made me promise I would get it to you. That's the main reason I wanted to come with Daniel and Beverly. Of course, I wanted to see Harmony again, and more than anything else, my beloved granddaughter. But I also knew I had to fulfill that promise to Essie." He shook his head slowly. "Sometimes I forget exactly where it is or how to find it. But tonight, my mind is clear." He reached out and grabbed my hands. "We must retrieve it now, Gracie. I can't trust my mind past my next thought. Do you understand?"

I nodded, picked up a napkin from the table, and wiped my face. "Where is this gift, Papa?"

"Unless someone has moved it, it's in the basement." He waved his hand toward the meat loaf sitting on the counter. "Let's have our sandwiches after we find it. There is no time to waste."

"But you're not supposed to go down the stairs."

"I understand. But I can tell you where to look, and you can find it yourself."

Oh please, God. Don't let this be his imagination. "All right, Papa. Where is it?" I knew every inch of that basement. There couldn't be anything hidden down there that I hadn't seen. Fear made my chest tighten, and I tried to shake it off.

"Is there still an old trunk in the basement made out of wood with a metal latch on the top? Do you know the one I mean?"

I nodded. "Papa, I've been through that trunk. There were some pieces of silver, some old papers, and a couple of quilts that I put on the beds upstairs."

"Yes, that would be the right one."

I frowned. "One of those items is my wedding present?"

He shook his head. "Remove them from the trunk. You'll find a leather tab on one side of the piece of wood at the bottom of the trunk. It's a false bottom, Gracie. Pull the tab up. The gift is under there. Essie put it in the trunk to keep it safe from air and from moths."

"Okay, but you have to stay here, okay? Don't leave this chair."

"I promise, but please hurry." He looked at me strangely. "Sometimes the lonely place comes for me,

313

and I can't fight it off."

I nodded, not trusting my voice at that moment. I got up and opened the door that leads to the basement, being careful to shut it behind me. Fear that Papa would try to follow me made me hurry so quickly I caught my foot on one of the steps and almost tumbled the rest of the way down. Thankfully, I was able to grab the banister just in time. When I reached the bottom of the stairs, my heart pounded so hard it felt as if it might jump from my chest.

The basement was dark, so I switched on the light. The trunk Papa referred to was in the far corner, covered with drop cloths and supplies used when Sam and I painted the house. I quickly moved everything out of the way, praying that this wasn't some kind of wild goose chase. Papa had been talking about a "gift" from Mama ever since he'd arrived in Harmony. Had he been right all along? Had this been more than a result of the disease that ravaged his brain?

I unlocked the trunk, opened the lid, and carefully removed the items inside. Two old quilts in worn condition that I'd taken from upstairs; some pieces of family silver, simple in design but treasured by my grandparents; a pair of Mama's shoes wrapped in plastic, too precious for me to throw away; and an old album full of school papers belonging to my father and Uncle Benjamin. Once these had been removed, there was nothing left. No "tab" evident to my eyes, and the bottom of the trunk felt solid. I was just about to give up when I had an idea.

I jumped up and ran to a large closet full of old

tools that had once been used by my grandfather. Inside one of the tool chests I found a thin piece of metal shaped almost like a fingernail file. I hurried back to the chest and tried to insert it between the bottom of the trunk and the side, figuring this was probably an exercise in futility because there wasn't any space below the wood bottom. But surprisingly, the tool slid in several inches. I stopped and examined the outside. Sure enough, the bottom appeared to be higher than the edge of the trunk that sat on the floor. I tried to wiggle the tool out, but it was stuck. After several attempts, it finally released. The piece of metal slid out, but something was attached to it. I pulled it a little more and discovered a piece of leather. Could this be the tab Papa talked about?

I yanked on it. Nothing. I pulled again, and the bottom of the chest moved a bit. I kept tugging until the piece of wood was loose enough I could grab it with my fingers and remove it. After putting it on the floor next to me, I stared down at the trunk. There was definitely something there, covered with material. With trembling fingers, I peeled back the layers. Underneath, I found a quilt. I lifted it out, put it on the floor, and began to unfold it.

As the design started to emerge, I began to sob. It was the most beautiful quilt I'd ever laid eyes on. The middle was splashed with various hues of breathtaking purple irises. The gorgeous flowers were just as vibrant as the day Mama stitched them together with love. They were surrounded by reddish blocks, just like the bricks that encircle Mama's garden. The quilt's background was the color of a Harmony sky, and additional irises and colorful pinwheels added to the overall depth and beauty. A deep-purple border framed the entire quilt like a picture frame. I looked closer, and although it was difficult for me to see through my tears, I found the words *Faith*, *Hope*, *Wisdom*, and *Royalty* stitched into the corners of the incredible design. I could see the tiny pieces of thread around the purple border, and in my mind's eye, I could envision Mama sewing each small stitch. How could Mama Essie have known almost twenty-five years ago that irises would be my very favorite flower just as they were hers? I'd chosen purple irises as my wedding flower, and now, as if she'd known it long ago, she'd sent this gorgeous quilt just in time for my marriage to Sam. I felt her gentle strength and overwhelming love in that room with me. This truly was a wedding present from my grandmother. And my grandfather had delivered it, just as he'd promised. I wept for a while, wiping my eyes on the hem of my shirt. Then I remembered Papa. I folded the quilt and carried it upstairs. He still sat in the chair where I'd left him.

"I found it, Papa," I said, my voice shaky. "It was right where you said it would be."

He let out a deep breath. "I kept my promise," he said softly. "I kept my promise."

I sank down on the floor in front of him, holding the quilt next to me. "Yes Papa, you kept your promise. It's the most beautiful wedding present anyone could give me. Thank you."

I laid my head against his legs, and he reached down and stroked my hair. After a few minutes he said, "Gracie, why don't cannibals eat clowns?"

"I don't know, Papa. Why don't cannibals eat clowns?"

He didn't say anything for a moment. Then softly he said, "Because they taste funny."

"Oh Papa," I said laughing through my tears. "Now that joke is the best one yet."

"Always end with your best material," he said. "I'm tired, Gracie girl. I really need to lie down."

"What about your meat loaf sandwich?"

"Not tonight. Maybe tomorrow."

"That sounds good, Papa." I got up, carefully put the folded quilt over a nearby chair, and helped Papa to his feet. He leaned into me as we walked back toward the living room. When we reached the couch, I quickly straightened his pillow and pulled back the covers. He sat down slowly.

"Thank you, Snicklefritz," he said. "This was one of the best evenings of my life." He sighed deeply and sank down on the couch. I pulled his covers up. "Sorry I didn't get to tell Daniel and Beverly good night." He reached out and grabbed my fingers. "If I'm asleep in the morning when they get up, will you tell them I love them?"

I patted his hand. "Of course Papa. But you can tell them yourself."

He nodded. "That's right."

Suddenly he blinked several times. "Gracie, one other thing. You must stay away from. . .from. . ." He shook his head. "He's evil. You know who I mean, right?"

"Yes, Papa. I know who you mean. I promise to stay away from him." Papa's revulsion of Jacob Glick had survived the years in fine shape. I thought about reminding him once again that Glick had been dead for thirty years, but I knew it didn't really matter. Papa would only forget. Hearing him drift away once again made my heart ache, but I was grateful for the time we'd been given tonight. It meant more to me than I could say.

"That's fine, Gracie. Think I'll nod off for a while." He brought my hand to his lips and lightly kissed my fingers. "I love you, you know." Suddenly he sat up. "Why Essie, there you are. It's about time." He smiled at an empty corner of the room. "Gracie knows you love her, Essie." He looked at me. "Isn't that right, Snicklefritz? You know your grandmother loves you?"

"I know, Papa. I know."

I got up and fetched the quilt from the kitchen. Then I pulled my rocking chair near the couch and watched Papa as he fell asleep, Mama Essie's beautiful quilt on my lap. I woke up a couple of hours later when someone kissed me on the head. Startled, I turned around to see if Mom had come downstairs, but no one was there. I was alone.

I sat there for a while, running my hands over the beautiful quilt, remembering how Mama Essie used to wake me when I'd fallen asleep as a child—with a kiss on the head. I thought about the times we'd spent as a family—Papa telling his silly jokes and singing

"I've Been Working on the Railroad" while he swung me around with his strong arms. The way he used to tease Mama, and the funny way she wrinkled up her nose when she laughed, making her look like a little girl even when her hair was gray and the spring had left her step. Mama and Papa had built a strong family through faith in God, the love they had for each other, and the determination to always believe that with God, anything was possible. Like Papa fighting against the shadows that tried to overtake him because he'd made a promise to the woman he loved.

And like Mama Essie kissing me on the head to let me know everything was all right.

After a few more minutes, I gathered my courage and got up to check on Papa Joe, confirming what I already knew in my heart.

Papa and Mama were finally together again, and the darkness that had tried to defeat my grandfather had been conquered once and for all.

TWENTY-ONE

I think we should postpone the wedding."

Dad shook his head. "Papa would be horrified by that idea, and you know it. He wouldn't want to be the cause of disrupting your special day."

"But it feels too soon. How can we celebrate my wedding so quickly after Papa's funeral?"

My mother was making sandwiches while Dad and I sat at the table in my kitchen. We'd arranged for a funeral home in Sunrise to make the arrangements for Papa's service. Papa had always made it clear that he only wanted a graveside service. "I don't want people sitting around telling long-winded stories about me," he'd say. "Just plant my body in the ground. As long as the good Lord knows where it is, that's all I care about."

"You're sure about burying Papa here?" I asked. "I thought he'd want to be next to Mama."

My father cleared his throat and stared at the tabletop for a moment before answering. "Actually, we're probably going to have Mama moved here, too."

His statement took me by surprise. "Wow. I—I don't understand. Didn't Papa and Mama buy a double plot in Nebraska? Isn't that where they wanted to be buried?"

Mom stopped her lunch preparations and gazed at my father, a strange expression on her face. "I think you need to tell her, Daniel."

I looked back and forth between them. "Tell me? Tell me what?"

"Your mother and I had a long talk on the way up and back from the funeral home," Dad said. "It was clear we needed to face some feelings we've both been having. Papa's death brought everything out into the open."

I was tired and although the sadness I felt over losing Papa was overshadowed with the knowledge that he and Mama were finally together, I wasn't in the mood for riddles. "I guess you need to explain what you mean. I'm not getting it."

My father cleared his voice again. "Haven't you noticed that your mother and I have been behaving a little. . .oddly since we've been in Harmony?"

I smiled for the first time since Papa died. "As opposed to?"

My father's eyes narrowed. "Okay. Let's say our behavior is a little stranger than normal, will that do?"

I nodded. "I can accept that."

"Gee, thanks." He shook his head, but I saw the corners of his mouth turn up.

Mom came up behind me, carrying our plates. She'd made us sandwiches with potato salad. "Your father has been concerned about my impromptu buying spree. Of course there's nothing wrong with buying whatever I want, but you know me, Gracie. I'm usually. . ."

"Cheap?" my father interjected.

She frowned at him. "I was going to say *thrifty*, thank you."

"I have to admit I was curious about all the purchases you made in town," I said. "You could almost open your own store. So what was that all about?"

She got three glasses down from the cabinet. "Well, the explanation happens to be the same reason your father took a dislike to Sam."

"Okay, now I'm confused. What do those two things have to do with each other?"

My father sighed. "Well your mother was trying her best to buy Harmony, and I've been jealous of Sam even before I met him. And it's because. . ."

"You miss Harmony." The light had finally come on, and I was surprised by the revelation. "I thought you two were thrilled to get away from here. What gives?"

My mother got a pitcher of tea out of the refrigerator. "We weren't thrilled to go, Gracie. We hated leaving. We loved Harmony. But Bishop Angstadt's hold over our church stood in the way of God's will in our lives. In the end, we had no choice."

As she filled our glasses, Dad picked up where she left off. "When we moved away, I think we tried to put Harmony out of our minds. It got easier when Papa and Mama followed us to Nebraska. And when Benjamin cut himself off from the rest of the family, the only thing that made sense was to turn our back on

Harmony for good." He shook his head. "But the truth is, we never really forgot this place. It's always been home." He reached over and took my hand. "When I met Sam, I disliked him because he had what I'd lost—a home in Harmony. It sounds so selfish, but in my defense, I didn't realize why I reacted so strongly to him...until Papa died."

"But what does Papa's death have to do with anything?"

Mom brought us our drinks and sat down beside me. "Because when we thought about sending Papa's body back to Nebraska, we both felt the same way. That we didn't want his grave that far away from us."

I frowned at her. "But he wouldn't be far away from you. He'd be..." I stopped and stared at them, my mouth hanging open. "You're moving back to Harmony, aren't you?"

My mother leaned over and put her arm around me. "Only if it's okay with you, Gracie. We realize you've made a life here, and we don't want to butt in—"

"Are you serious?" I exclaimed, cutting off the rest of her sentence. "I would *love* to have you here!"

Dad grinned. "Then it's settled. We'll start looking for a house right away."

"You don't need to do that. You can live here."

Mom squeezed my shoulder. "But this is your house, Gracie. We don't want to..."

"Now how many houses do you think I can live in at one time, Mother? It's perfect. After the wedding, I'll move into Sam's, and this house will be yours."

"We'll buy it from you, Gracie," Dad said.

"Don't be ridiculous. I don't want to sell it to you. This house should have been yours in the first place. If Uncle Benjamin hadn't been so confused about things, it would have gone to you anyway. I know he'd want you to have it, Dad. And you know it, too."

My parents stared at each other for a moment. Then my mother broke out in a smile. "Okay Gracie, if you're sure. After the wedding, we'll go home and put the house in Nebraska up for sale. Then we'll come back here for good."

"And we'll bring Mama back, too," Dad said. "Our family still owns several plots in the Harmony cemetery. Mama and Papa will be right next to each other. The way they should be."

I picked up my glass of iced tea and took a big gulp. Then I put it down and smiled at my parents. "Papa's last gift wasn't the quilt from Mama. It was bringing his family back together."

My father grabbed my mother's hand. His voice broke as he said, "I believe that's exactly right, Gracie. He brought us all home. And with the quilt, even Mama is here with us."

For some reason, I didn't tell him about Mama's kiss. My pragmatic father might not believe me, and for now, it was between Mama, Papa, and me. And I wanted to keep it that way.

We spent the rest of the day together. It felt right, sharing memories of Papa while planning his funeral. Sweetie brought over enough food to feed us for a week; Ida hitched up Zeb and drove over to comfort us. She added her own tales of Papa and Mama, and it helped all of us to be reminded of how many lives they'd touched. Abel came by to see if he could help us. He looked tired, and when he offered to do the graveside service, at first my father refused, not wanting him to think about us until Hannah was found. But when Abel convinced him that he needed to concentrate on something besides his missing daughter, my parents gratefully accepted. Pastor Jensen stopped by while Abel was there, and they both went outside on the front porch for a while. I think it was just what Abel needed. Pastors minister so much to others, sometimes they don't get much ministry themselves. They were out there a long time. When I checked on them after an hour or so, they were praying together.

By the time supper rolled around, we were all exhausted from answering the phone and receiving people who stopped by to drop off food or offer their condolences. Finally, around seven o'clock, the only people left were Sam and Sweetie.

"You folks sit still," Sweetie told my parents. "I'll heat up some of this food for you, and then Sam and me will get outta your way."

"I wish you'd stay," Dad said. "And Sam, I'd like to talk to you for a few minutes, if you don't mind."

I hadn't had a chance to tell Sam about my dad's recent revelation. I smiled reassuringly at him, but the look on his face made it clear he was apprehensive about what my father planned to say. Dad led him out on the porch, and they took up the same spots Marcus and Abel had shared earlier in the day. While Sweetie fixed dinner, Mom and I shared the good news that they were moving back. Sweetie was so happy, she got weepy. Something she doesn't do often.

"It's been me and Sam for so long," she said, sniffling. "Then our darling Gracie came along, and now you two. It's startin' to feel like a real family. I ain't had one since I was a small girl. I'm feelin' really happy about it right now."

I laughed. "I'm feelin' real happy about it, too."

Right before dinner was served, Sam and Dad came back into the house. Sam looked relieved, and Dad looked more relaxed than I'd seen him since he'd come to Harmony. I knew he missed Papa but even though no one said it, we all felt that Papa's burden had been lifted. Watching him disintegrate from Alzheimer's was much worse than knowing he was rejoicing with Jesus and dancing on streets of gold with Mama. Alzheimer's is a thief, and what it had tried to rob from Papa had been restored by God. I'd prayed for a healing on earth, but Papa had been healed in heaven instead.

After dinner I showed Sam and Sweetie the quilt Mama had made for me.

"Why, land's sake if that ain't one of the most beautiful things I ever seen," Sweetie said. She ran her fingers lightly over the top. "But it looks almost brand new." She scrunched up her face. "You say it had some kinda material around it?"

"Yes. It was in a wooden compartment below the main part of the trunk."

"Mind if I take a look?"

I told her to go ahead, and she went down in the

basement for a while. When she came back up, she had a smile on her face. "You're real blessed that the quilt lasted the way it did. Your grandma was one smart lady. The wood was varnished and she wrapped the quilt in unbleached muslin. Best way in the world to keep a quilt in good shape. She knowed just what she was doin'."

Sam loved the quilt and didn't even complain about the flowers. We agreed it would be hung on the wall somewhere in the house. Sweetie had already informed us that the beautiful purple room would belong to us. I had a feeling the quilt would end up there.

After Sam and Sweetie left, my parents headed to bed. We were all wiped out from the day's events. We'd decided to have the funeral on Tuesday, and keep the wedding on Saturday. Since the invitations had already been sent, it seemed the easiest solution. For just a moment, I felt badly that Papa wouldn't be able to see me get married, but I had a witness in my heart that he and Mama would be watching.

Sam drove Sweetie home and then came back. We sat on the front porch, holding hands, and rocking next to each other until way after the sun went down.

"One more week, and we'll never have to say good-bye at the end of the day again," Sam said as stars began to light up the heavens.

"I know, I know," I whispered. "Just good night."

The next day we all went to church and after the service had lunch at Mary's. People kept stopping by the table to offer their condolences. Carmen, Hector's wife, informed us that they had finally decided to change the name of the restaurant from Mary's Kitchen to The Harmony House.

"Hector thought about changing it to Hector's House, but he felt it would be better to honor the town instead of drawing attention to one person."

Connie overheard her sister and came up to the table. "He also think about calling this place Ramirez Restaurant," she said with a heavier accent than her sister, "but he afraid everyone believe we only serve Mexican food." She laughed and took off to greet Harold Price and Kay Curless. Harold, a widower who had made the restaurant his second home, beamed. And Kay, a beautiful woman who had also been a widow for many years, looked as happy as she could possibly be. It was apparent that these two wonderful people would no longer be alone.

We were getting ready to leave when Pat walked in the front door looking upset. "Good afternoon, folks," he said when he reached our table. "Sorry to disturb you, but I wonder if I could talk to Gracie for a moment."

Sam shook his head. "Why is it that every time you say that, I get a bad feeling?"

Pat grunted. "Probably past experience."

Sam nodded. "You've got that right."

I put my napkin down and excused myself. "Please don't let anyone take my plate. I'm not finished."

"Well, that's what happens when you get hauled off by the police before you finish eating," Dad said.

"I'm not being hauled off by the police," I

protested. Unfortunately I spoke a little too loudly. People at several nearby tables looked at us with interest. I followed Pat over to a table across the room where we wouldn't be overheard.

"What now?" I asked once we were seated. "Is there any news about Hannah?"

He shook his head. "Nothing about Hannah. But your friends at the KBI have certainly been busy."

I offered him my most innocent look. "What are you talking about?"

He glowered at me. "I think you know exactly what I mean." My continued silence seemed to exasperate him. "It might interest you to know that pulling your social worker friend into things may have backfired on you. Big-time."

"What are you talking about?"

"The KBI looked into Hannah's disappearance all right. And the first thing they did was stop by and question C. J. Bradley."

"Oh no." I felt the blood drain from my face. "They weren't supposed to. . ."

"I thought so," Pat said with a note of triumph.

I just stared at him. "Does C.J. know?"

"Does he know what? That you're the one who contacted the KBI about him?"

I swallowed hard. "Yes."

"I'm not sure. I wasn't there so I have no idea what was said to him. I just know they had quite a long visit."

I thought for a moment. "If he's the person they're looking for, they've just tipped him off. What if he runs?"

Pat folded his arms across his chest and leaned back in his chair. "I don't think he'll be doing anything like that."

"How in the world can you know that?" When several customers turned to stare at us again, I realized I needed to calm down. I lowered my voice. "There's no way to tell what he might do next."

"I'm pretty sure he's not going to take off because he's not the serial killer we've been looking for. If he leaves, it will probably be because someone called the KBI on him."

I sighed with exasperation. "You're not making sense. What are you trying to tell me?"

"I'm trying to tell you that authorities in Kansas City caught the guy."

I was stunned. "What do you mean they 'caught the guy'?"

"How much clearer do I have to make it? A couple of hours after the boys in black interrogated your friend C.J., the police cornered the killer they've been looking for in an apartment in Kansas City. C.J. had nothing to do with the murder in Topeka." He held up his hand. "And before you ask me if they're sure they've got the right man, the answer is yes. Without a doubt. The DNA matches, and to top it off, he confessed. Seems he's pretty proud of himself and wants everyone to know what he's done. A real nut job."

The reality of what Pat told me hit me like a ton of bricks. "But that means. . ."

"That Hannah is a runaway, just like I said. This

guy was singing like a noisy canary. He was asked about Hannah, along with a couple of other runaways. He didn't know anything about them. He killed the girl in Topeka all right, but he had nothing whatsoever to do with Hannah's disappearance."

"Then where is she, Pat? What's happened to her?"

"I can't answer that question, Gracie. I'm still in touch with your friends from Wichita. No one's seen her." Connie came up to the table to see if Pat wanted anything, but he waved her away. "I know you're worried, but I just don't believe she was taken against her will. As far as that bracelet, she just lost it, and that's all there is to it." He leaned forward, his forearms on the table. "Look, I'm going to keep searching for her. You need to concentrate on burying your grandfather and getting married. Let me take this on for you, okay? Let it go. . .just for a while."

His attempt at kindness touched me. "I won't let it go until Hannah is home, but I'll try to ease off a bit. If you promise to do everything you can to find her."

"I really have been doing my best, but I'll go over it all again. If there's any way to bring her back, I'll do it. You have my word."

"What about C.J.? Does he know the killer's been caught?"

Pat nodded. "I went over there myself and told him. Apologized for bothering him. He was very gracious about it, but he wasn't thrilled about being suspected of serial murders. He talked about going back to California."

Guilt washed over me. "But his mother needs

him." I put my head in my hands. "This is all my fault."

Pat reached over and pulled my face up. "You were trying to save your friend, Gracie. Sorry I came on so strong. Don't beat yourself up because of me. There's no harm done. The KBI halted their investigation of C.J., and he won't be contacted again."

"They were actually investigating him? How far did they go?"

"Well, they started a background check. And of course they questioned him and were checking out his whereabouts around the time of the murders."

"Would C.J. have any way to know about the background check?"

"No, I don't think so."

I took a deep breath. "Well at least that's something."

"So now what are you going to do?" Pat asked.

"About what?" I was pretty sure what he meant, but I hoped I was wrong. I wasn't.

"About C.J. Don't you think you should talk to him? Explain? Apologize? Something? You might be able to talk him into staying if you tell him why you suspected him of taking Hannah."

I stared at Pat, trying to come up with a reason that I *shouldn't* confess to C.J. and beg his forgiveness. Problem was, no sensible reason sprang to mind. "All right," I said finally. "I'll do it. Even if he hates me forever, maybe he'll stay and finish the work he started on his mom's house."

"Good girl." Pat stood up. "I'll see if I can dig up any new leads on Hannah, and you spend time with your family. Is that a deal?"

"Hey, one last question?"

Pat raised an eyebrow. "What?"

"This serial killer. Did he have a red truck and a bumper sticker with a bear on it?"

He grinned. "He was driving a purple truck, and the only bumper sticker he had said GIVE A SQUIRREL A HOME. PLANT A TREE."

"No bear?"

He shook his head. "Nope. Just a squirrel."

"So he doesn't mind killing human beings, but he's worried about squirrels?"

Pat shrugged. "Gracie, the guy's insane. I don't think I'd take his bumper sticker too literally."

"I guess," I said glumly. "Boy, this has been a rough couple of days."

He smiled at me and held out his hand. I took it, and he pulled me to my feet. "Everything's going to be fine. I promise."

I nodded but didn't respond. Nothing would be "fine" until Hannah was safely home.

I went back to the table. Thankfully my food was still there, and Connie had refilled our bowls of mashed potatoes, creamed corn, gravy, and coleslaw. A new platter of fried chicken had also appeared. Before I had a chance to finish what I'd started to eat before my discussion with Pat, Connie whisked my old plate away and put a new one in its place.

"Cold food no good for you," she said. "You eat nice hot food now, sí?"

"Thank you, Connie," I said, grateful for her

kindness. "Hot food is always better."

She bobbed her head in agreement and left the table with a big smile on her face.

I ate Hector's delicious dishes until I felt like the buttons on my lightweight summer dress might pop off and cause injury to some of the other diners.

After we left the restaurant, we drove to the Harmony cemetery where my father pointed out the other gravesites that belonged to our family. As I stood there, seeing where Papa and Mama would be laid to rest, the thought crossed my mind that someday, Sam and I might also be buried here. The idea gave me the shivers. Good thing the real me would be in heaven, not caring one little bit about the shell that had contained me on this earth. The cemetery was actually situated in a gorgeous location. It sat about a mile out of town and was surrounded by tall trees that shaded almost the entire area. Large monuments of carved angels or other figures decorated the grounds, and carefully tended flowers offered color and graceful beauty. After the initial creepy feeling that came from possibly standing on my own grave, I had to admit that this was the most beautiful cemetery I'd ever seen.

We went home and everyone took a nap, including me. Not something I usually do, but with all the stress of losing Papa, I was physically and mentally exhausted. At first I tossed and turned on my bed, but when I did finally fall asleep, I dreamed that Hannah was calling my name, pleading with me to save her. She kept saying the same thing over and over. "Help me, Gracie. Use your eyes and ears. Please use your eyes and ears."

After a couple of hours, I woke up, drenched with sweat. By the time I got up, took a quick shower, and changed clothes, it was almost dinnertime.

"Can you guys heat some of this food up?" I asked my parents after my shower. "I have a quick errand to run."

"We're still stuffed from lunch," my mother said. "If your father gets hungry, I'll make him something. I'm not the least bit interested in eating."

"Thanks. I shouldn't be too long."

"Where are you going?" Dad asked. "Or are you too old to account for your whereabouts?"

I grinned at him. "I get the distinct impression I'll never be old enough for that in your eyes."

"You've got that right," he said, peering over the top of his reading glasses. My father reads the paper religiously every Sunday. He doesn't care about the newspaper during the week, but Sunday never passes without him sticking his nose into newsprint and only coming up for air when absolutely necessary. My dad's copy of the Topeka paper could only have come from the restaurant. Since the paper isn't delivered to Harmony, Hector faithfully drives to Sunrise every Sunday morning and buys twenty or thirty copies for residents who want to read it. Dad must have gotten to the restaurant very early to snag one of the prized copies.

I grabbed my purse and my keys. "If you must know, I'm going to apologize to someone. Since I don't do it very often, I might be a little while."

My mother smiled at me. "If you're apologizing to Sam, take your time. It's not good to have tension between you two right before the wedding."

I started to tell her my mea culpa had nothing to do with Sam, but trying to explain the whole story of my transgression against C.J. Bradley seemed like too much effort. Besides, I was still extremely embarrassed about it. I nodded, said good-bye, and left.

My drive to the Bradley place seemed to take longer than normal. Probably because I wasn't anxious to get there. As I pulled into the driveway, I didn't see C.J. anywhere. I thought about knocking on the door, but if he'd followed through on his threat to leave town, I was pretty certain his mother wasn't going to be glad to see me. I got out of my car and checked the back of the house, hoping I'd find him working. Nothing. Then I looked in the garage to see if his truck was still there. I swung the door open. No truck.

I stepped inside the large, empty building, allowing the door to close behind me. I needed to think. Maybe he'd just gone to town. It didn't make sense for him to take off so quickly. I noticed tools lying around on the ground, as if someone had left in the middle of a project. Surely he would have taken the time to put them away if he was leaving Harmony for good. I was headed toward the door when my foot caught on something, and I almost fell.

"What the heck?" I said out loud. As I leaned down to see what it was, a strange thumping noise startled me. It was the same sound I'd heard when I was there the last time. This time, instead of running out, I decided to find out what it was. There it was again. It sounded as if it was coming from beneath the floor. I reached down to see what I'd stumbled over. There was a large metal ring lying on the ground. When I tried to pick it up, I realized it was attached to the floor. Another *thump*.

I could have sworn I heard someone whisper, *"Tell Grace she must have eyes to see and ears to hear,"* and I felt a presence in that garage. It was almost overpowering. Sweat broke out on my forehead that had nothing to do with how hot it was. I got down on my knees and pushed the dirt away from the ring. I tugged on it as hard as I could, but it didn't budge. I realized there was a latch secured with a lock several inches from the ring that kept the trapdoor from opening. Spotting a pair of metal cutters mounted on the wall along with several other tools, I got up, removed them, and went back to the latch. It took me a couple of minutes to finally cut the lock open. Sweat poured down my face. Even before I pushed the trapdoor open, I knew exactly what I would see below the floor of the Bradley's garage.

And I was right.

Hannah Mueller stared up at me.

TWENTY-TWO

"Gracie, is it really you?" Hannah's voice was weak, and she blinked as if the light hurt her eyes.

"Yes, it's me," I said softly. "We've got to get you out of there, Hannah. I don't know where C.J. is."

"There aren't any steps down here. Can you find a ladder?" She began to sob. "Hurry, Gracie. He's crazy. He'll be back soon."

I spotted a stepladder against the wall and ran to get it. I'd just started to lower it to Hannah when I heard a noise. I whirled around and found C. J. Bradley standing near the garage door.

"What do you think you're doing?" he demanded. "You're trespassing on private property."

"Trespassing? Are you serious?" My fear of C.J. began to turn into rage. "Have you had Hannah here this entire time? Do you know how worried her parents have been?" Other questions exploded in my mind that I was afraid to ask. But right at that moment I was only thinking about the fact that Hannah was alive. He took a step closer, and I bent down and grabbed the pitchfork that lay at my feet.

"I don't know what you're talking about. There's

no one named Hannah here. Just Melanie. I came back to Harmony, and there she was, just walking along the road. She waited for me all these years." His tone took on a kind of singsong quality, and he looked at me the way someone might look at a child. He shook his head and gave me an odd smile. As the setting sun peeked in through a window beside me and lit up his features, I realized I was looking into the face of madness. Hannah was right. C.J. Bradley was definitely crazy.

I attempted to control my anger and think clearly. I had to save Hannah. "C.J., Melanie isn't happy down there." I tried to push the emotion out of my voice and sound as soothing as possible. Keeping him calm might help us get out of the spot we were in. "I know you love her and don't want to see her unhappy. Why don't you let her go? Then you can really be together."

He cocked his head to the side as if listening to a voice I couldn't hear. Then he shook his head slowly. "No, I can't do that. Melanie tried to run away from me. I can't let that happen." He shrugged. "Wedding jitters, I guess. It will pass."

I could feel my heart pound as if it would burst through my chest. "But don't you think she'd relax more if she could walk around some? She doesn't look comfortable."

He looked at me like a chicken might study a bug before pouncing upon it. "Yes, you're right. It's time for her to come out. She won't run away again. Melanie loves me. She told me she does. I'm taking her back to California. We'll get married there. Maybe on the beach." He stared at me. "You're not going to interfere, you know. I won't have it. My mother ruined my life once. I won't let it happen again." He took a large hunting knife from his pocket and pointed it at me. "Get back so I can help her up the ladder. Then we're leaving. You can stay down there until someone finds you. I'm—I'm not a killer, Gracie, but this is my last chance to get it right. No one will stop me this time. Not even your grandfather."

"What are you talking about?"

He snorted. "He caught me once when I was a kid. You know, with a girl. I let her go. No one got hurt. But he told me to stay away from all the girls in the town. And he told my mother what I did. She talked to Melanie's parents. They said I couldn't see her anymore. Then they left town and took Melanie away from me." His voice got soft. "Mama tried to beat the devil out of me. She promised Joe Temple I would never do that again so he wouldn't tell anyone else." He shook his head. "But the devil came back. He always comes back, you know."

My poor grandfather had recognized C.J., but hadn't been able to communicate the truth about him to us. Instead, he'd just exploded, warning us about evil. I'd thought he was talking about Jacob Glick. If only I'd realized. . .

C.J. brandished his knife and took another step toward me. "Now get out of the way, Gracie. Right now."

"There's no way I'm letting you take Hannah from here. No way in this world." I stepped between him and the hole in the ground where Hannah cowered, holding the pitchfork up between us.

"Then whatever happens is your fault," he said, raising the knife up over his head. But before he could get any closer, the door to the shed opened slowly and Pat Taylor came inside, his gun drawn.

"Put the knife down right now, C.J.," he growled, "or I'll blow a hole so big in you I'll be able to walk right though you instead of goin' around you. You got it?"

C.J. hesitated for a moment, and then after what seemed like an hour, let go of the knife. Pat immediately moved in, kicked it away, pushed C.J. to the ground, and handcuffed him. While he called for backup, I lowered the ladder down to Hannah and she climbed up. She was dirty and disheveled, but I'd never seen anything so beautiful in my entire life. She collapsed to the ground, and I got down beside her, holding her as she wept.

"I'm gonna lock this piece of pond scum in the back of my car so you all don't have to look at him anymore," Pat said, pulling C.J. to his feet. He looked completely disoriented—almost as if he didn't know where he was. "Are you both okay?"

"We're going to be fine," I said. "This is the second time you've saved my life, you know."

"Yes, I realize that. And it's gettin' old. Let's put a stop to it."

I stroked Hannah's matted hair. "And just why are you here, Pat? I didn't tell anyone where I was going."

"I'm aware of that. From here on out I'd like your

daily itinerary if you don't mind. It will make rescuing you much easier." He pushed C.J. toward the door. "That background check the KBI started on this guy turned up some interesting information. He's a sex offender registered in California, and they suspect him of two attempted kidnappings in the past six months. Both of them girls about Hannah's age and description. I put two and two together—and then I figured you could only be right where you shouldn't be. And surprise. Here you are."

I smiled. "Thanks. Again."

He nodded and pushed C.J. out of the garage.

I put my hand under Hannah's chin and asked the question I didn't want to. "Hannah, did he. . . hurt you?"

She shook her head. "No, Gracie. I'm fine. He— he acted like we knew each other. Like we'd been engaged for a long time or something. He kept calling me Melanie. At first I tried to tell him I didn't know him. And I begged him to let me go." A sob tore from deep inside her. "But it made him mad. Really mad. I was afraid he was going to kill me. So I started acting like I really was this Melanie person, hoping he'd let me out. But he didn't. It's so dirty down there, and sometimes he forgot to feed me. I haven't eaten for a couple of days."

I smiled at her. "We can certainly take care of that. This is Harmony. Everyone and their cousin will be bringing you food."

She laughed through her tears. Then she grabbed my hand. "Thank you, Gracie. Somehow I knew it would be you who would find me. I prayed so hard that you would."

"Well God heard you. And so did Ida Turnbauer."

"What do you mean?"

"I'll tell you about it later. I expect there are a couple of people who would love to see you as soon as possible." I put my arm around her. "Can you walk?"

She nodded. "Let's get out of here."

I pulled her up, and she leaned against me. "Yes, let's." We walked over to the door, I swung it open, and Hannah and I stepped out into the light.

TWENTY-THREE

Sweetie's dining room was full for the rehearsal dinner. Not only had she put all the leaves in her dining room table, but she'd had to put up two other card tables to accommodate everyone. In her usual capable way, the room looked beautiful and the meal delicious. Prime rib, new potatoes with fresh green beans, Waldorf salad, homemade rolls with apple jam, and a chocolate mousse cheesecake that was so good it rivaled any dessert I'd ever tasted.

The atmosphere was light and happy, but there were questions about the strange events over the past two weeks.

"So no one knew how disturbed C.J. Bradley really was?" Pastor Jensen asked as we enjoyed cheesecake and coffee.

"Papa Joe knew," I replied. "And I should have. The clues were all there. Papa's reaction every time he saw C.J. His story about getting back together with Melanie. Although I'd forgotten, Ida told me Melanie had blond hair and blue eyes like Hannah. C.J. had a twisted view of life—and particularly of women. I saw that when he reacted badly to Jessie, but I dismissed it. His mother brought him up in her own deformed brand of religion. The world she created was void of love but full of judgment. And her anger toward men after her husband left caused her to pass some perverted ideas about relationships to her son. C.J. began acting out with local girls when he was a boy. When my grandfather caught him and informed his mother, she only made it worse by trying to 'beat the devil out of him,' as C.J. said. Then he lost Melanie because of his destructive behavior. I think he built Melanie up in his mind as the only way to save himself. If Melanie could forgive him and love him, he'd be free of the demons that had haunted him for so long. Add that to Abigail's religious views that stripped real love out of the equation, and C.J.'s life became a breeding ground for mental illness. If Abigail hadn't distanced herself and her son from almost everyone in Harmony, someone might have recognized how much trouble the boy was in. Perhaps he would have gotten the help he so desperately needed."

"But then he left to go to college," Mom said. "You'd think he'd be able to figure it out for himself once he got around normal people."

"It was too late for him by then," Susan said. Although she wasn't actually part of the wedding party, I'd invited her to dinner. Abel and Emily were so grateful for her help in getting the KBI to dig up the information that led to C.J.'s arrest, they'd wanted to thank her personally. Their profuse expressions of appreciation obviously embarrassed the social worker, but I could tell she was pleased to have helped bring their daughter home.

"What about them other women he assaulted?"

Sweetie asked. "I mean, thank God he didn't hurt Hannah. . .physically anyway. But sounds like he treated her differently from the rest."

Susan shrugged. "I don't have any details about the other cases, but my guess is he's been trying to replace the love he lost for a long time. He sees Melanie as the perfect woman. Something about the women he hurt made him angry. He probably discovered they were flawed, and he couldn't accept it. Hannah never did anything to ruin that perception." She shook her head. "This may sound crazy, but it's possible that hiding Hannah in that cellar saved her life. If he'd spent more time around her and discovered she was just as human as everyone else, he might have harmed her."

"Not long ago, he found out Melanie had passed away," Pat said. "Is that what pushed him over the edge?"

Susan nodded. "I'm certain he couldn't accept knowing that he'd lost her forever. Lost his opportunity for some kind of redemption. So he decided he had to get her back. The night he saw Hannah walking down that dirt road, his warped mind turned her into Melanie. Hannah was his last chance for happiness."

"And he kept her hidden because he didn't want his mother to see her?" Dad asked.

Susan nodded. "Or anyone else. Maybe old Abigail was the world's worst mother, but her son's fear of her helped to protect Hannah. Also, people kept showing up at the house to help with repairs even though he tried to keep them away. Obviously he didn't want anyone to uncover his secret. It's possible that all the attention kept him from leaving town sooner with Hannah. If he had, she might not have been found in time." She smiled. "Please understand that as far as C.J.'s mental condition, I'm just guessing. I'm not a trained psychologist, but I've seen a lot of abuse."

"Well, it rings true to me," Pat said. "That man definitely has a screw loose somewhere."

Sam nodded his agreement. He and Pat were on their way to building the kind of relationship I'd been praying for. Pat had saved my life twice, and Sam's appreciation was helping to bridge the gap between them. Even Sweetie seemed to be accepting Pat. She certainly hadn't thrown her arms around him and welcomed him to the family, but she wasn't shooting him dirty looks anymore either. So progress had been made.

"How is Hannah?" my mom asked the Muellers.

"Much better," Emily said. "She wanted to come tonight, but I think she needs some time alone to sort out her feelings."

"Did she explain why in the world she got into C.J.'s truck in the first place?" Pastor Jensen asked.

"Yes, she did," Abel said. "She was walking over to Jonathan's house when C.J. pulled up next to her. He introduced himself as Abigail's son and told her Emily and I were looking for her. Hannah believed him. But after she got into the truck, she realized he wasn't taking her home. That's when she knew something was wrong. The only thing she could think to do was to toss her bracelet out the window when he wasn't looking."

"Thank God she did," I said. "If I hadn't found that bracelet, I might have accepted the idea that she'd run away."

Hannah's views of Harmony and her Mennonite lifestyle had changed—for now. Her "modern" clothes had been taken by detectives for evidence, but she wasn't the least bit sorry to see them go. She'd run back to her simple dresses and her prayer covering almost as if they were a special kind of protection against evil in the world. Sadly, I knew that wasn't true, but her desire to stay home and out of trouble was the best thing she could do for the time being. I had no idea if she would one day leave Harmony and go to Wichita— or some other large city—but at least she was safe and would have plenty of time to heal from the scars C. J. Bradley had caused through his own brokenness.

"Will C.J. go to jail?" Ida asked.

"Hard to say," Pat answered. "For now he's locked away. He's being evaluated to see if he's competent to stand trial. I suspect he's not."

Ida smiled at me. "I am so grateful you had 'eyes to see and ears to hear,' liebling. God used you to bring our Hannah back to us."

I sighed. "But I was way off. I thought Hannah had gotten mixed up with a serial killer, and here she was in Harmony all the time, right under our noses. I can't help but wonder whether we would have found her sooner if we hadn't gotten distracted by the man who killed that woman in Topeka."

Pat grunted. "I didn't get distracted by the girl in Topeka, and I missed it completely. You kept telling me Hannah had been abducted, but I wouldn't listen.

If anyone's at fault for not finding her sooner, it's me. Not you. Thanks to you and your snoopiness, Hannah Mueller is home safe. No one could have done better than you did."

"You're giving me way too much credit, Pat. You're forgetting that I accidentally stumbled on her. You're the one who followed the leads and saved us both."

"That's true," Abel said, smiling. "But only after you wouldn't let it go, Gracie. Pat got those leads because you kept pushing."

Pat grunted. "Yeah, and I have a feeling I'm in for a lotta years of being pushed around."

I grinned at him. "You can count on that."

"Well, all I know is that my daughter is home, safe and sound," Emily said, her bottom lip quivering. "And I'm grateful to everyone who had anything to do with it. Thank you from the depths of our hearts."

"Amen," Abel said.

"Well," my father said, standing to his feet, "why don't we move on to the reason we've gathered together tonight? To celebrate an upcoming wedding." He frowned. "Now just who is it that's getting married? I can't quite remember."

"Very funny," I said, laughing.

"Oh yes. I remember now. I think my beautiful daughter Gracie and her handsome fiancé Sam plan to say their vows two days from now." He smiled at me. "Gracie Marie Temple, you have been our treasure from God from the day you were born. We are thankful every day that He chose us to be your parents." His voice caught, and he paused a moment before continuing. "You know, it's not easy to give away something that's precious to you. When I first arrived in Harmony, I wasn't sure about this strapping, blond farm boy you'd fallen in love with. That is until I realized there wasn't anything wrong with him at all. In fact, Sam Goodrich is everything I ever wanted to be—but wasn't. Stupidly, I took it out on him. I'm grateful to God that He helped me to realize what I was doing before I caused damage I couldn't fix." He rested his gaze on Sam. "I know you've forgiven me, son, but I want to say publicly that I'm sorry for ever making you feel uncomfortable." He reached over and took my mother's hand, pulling her to her feet. "Beverly and I want to welcome you to our family with open arms. We both want you to know that if we'd been asked to create the perfect man for our Gracie, we couldn't have designed anyone better than you."

"Now Daniel and I want to share something with you and Gracie," my mother said, smiling. "I hope it's advice that will guide you throughout your years together the way it has helped us. Our marriage has lasted for thirty years because we've tried our best to walk in the love of God, and fulfill His calling for us. So many Christians spend their lives searching for 'their ministry,' yet they miss the most important ministry God will ever give them. Gracie, if you will wake up every morning knowing that your first ministry is to Sam, and Sam, if you will wake up every morning knowing your most important ministry is toward Gracie, you will both see miracles in your lives. When God can trust you in this important calling, He'll lead you into other exciting areas because He knows your priorities are right. If you will remember to put each other first in every situation, you will forge a relationship that adversity can't destroy and the devil can't steal. Please understand that there will be storms. I wish I could say they won't come, but they will. But please trust us when we tell you that if you will build your house on the Rock, you will stand." She leaned against my father and gazed into his eyes. "Daniel and I have had our share of trouble, but thanks to God, we have had victory through each and every situation." She reached over and picked up her glass of iced tea. "Sam, I want you to know that in our eyes we don't see you as our son-in-law. The law of love is even stronger than the law of man. You are our son from this day forward. We will support you no matter what happens. We will always believe the best about you. Our words, our actions, and our hearts will always express the confidence and love we have for you."

My dad picked up his glass. "Gracie, you will always have an important place in our hearts—one that no one else will ever fill. But your mother and I want you to know that we are stepping back to take second place in your life. Behind your husband. We are here to love you both, to support you both, and to help you in any way we can. But we won't get in your way. Your mother and I release you to your husband. And now," my father said, "will you all stand and raise your glasses to Sam and Gracie."

Everyone at the table stood to their feet.

"May their lives be full of God's grace, and may their home always be overflowing with His love."

Dad smiled at me, tears glinting in his eyes. I felt Sam grab my hand. "To Sam and Gracie."

"To Sam and Gracie," everyone repeated.

I couldn't speak, and Sam blinked back tears. "Thank you," he said to my parents. "I feel so blessed to be part of this family. And blessed to finally have my father in my life." He paused in an attempt to rein in his emotions. "But if no one minds, I'd like to take this opportunity to thank the one person who's always been there for me." He turned toward his aunt. "Sweetie, you stepped into my life when there wasn't anyone else. You gave me a home and all the love anyone could possibly need. I will be eternally grateful to you. I love you more than I can say and so does Gracie. If it wasn't for you, I wouldn't be standing here now, and I wouldn't have the wonderful life you've made possible." He held up his glass of iced tea. "I know tonight is supposed to be for Gracie and me, but I'd like to ask everyone to raise their glasses to Sweetie, who took a chance on a skinny, frightened, messed-up boy, and in doing so, brought us all together."

Sweetie's face crumpled as everyone in the room toasted to her. She tried to say something but couldn't get the words out. The love in the room was palpable, and I was overwhelmed by it. In this special moment, I felt an odd sense that my whole life had been rushing toward this place and these extraordinary people. Even more, to the heart of this incredible man who would soon be my husband.

"If you don't mind," Abel said smiling, "I'd also like to offer a toast to Harmony, a special place that God has blessed with protection and love. We've had our challenges, but He has been faithful. Emily and I have seen His hand many times down through the years. And now, in bringing our Hannah home to us." He looked at Ida who stood next to him. "And I want to honor Ida Turnbauer and the other women of Harmony who prayed over this place so long ago. God has answered that prayer in a mighty way. We've been faced with evil, but the Spirit of God has always prevailed." He held out his glass and said, "To the praying women of Harmony."

Every person in the room echoed his words.

"Is there anyone else we should toast?" my father said jokingly.

Pat cleared his throat. "If it's okay," he said softly. "I didn't plan to say anything, and I don't want to take attention away from Gracie and Sam."

"Of course it's all right," Dad said. "I think this is a night for saying what's in our hearts."

Pat nodded and turned toward Sam. "If I'd known about you sooner, son, I would have been there for you. It's important to me that you know that. I also want to tell you how much I regret my casual actions toward your mother. All I can say is that I was young and irresponsible. But I will never, ever regret the result of our relationship. You've turned out to be the kind of son any father would be proud of. And you're marrying one of the best women I've ever met." He paused for a moment, his jaw working. When he continued, his voice shook. "I'm not a churchgoing man, but I can't dispute the feeling that there is a divine hand in all of this. I look around this room, and I have to believe that there is a loving God who has a plan for all of us. Even though it's hard to believe that I could be a part of His grand design, tonight I feel it so strongly I can barely express my gratitude." He took a deep breath and held it a moment before letting it out. "Sam, thank you for allowing me into your family. And my thanks to all of you for opening your arms to me. I intend to spend the rest of my life making you glad you did." He held out his glass. "To family."

Once again, everyone repeated the toast. I looked at Sam who had tears streaming down his face. This was a night neither one of us would ever forget. A look around the table didn't reveal anyone else who felt the need to speak—or who wasn't so moved they couldn't even if they'd wanted to. When we sat down, almost everyone was in tears. After a few moments of silence, conversation began to break out once again. I gazed around the table and felt such deep gratitude to God for my good fortune. In Harmony, I'd found more than just a simple town full of loving people. I'd found my life, and I'd grown to know my heavenly Father more intimately.

Earlier in the day I'd experienced a tinge of melancholy knowing that Mama and Papa wouldn't be sitting in the church on Saturday when I walked down the aisle. But I had a strong sense that somehow they were with me and it helped. Somehow I knew they would be watching when I said my vows to the man of my dreams.

It was another hour before guests began heading home. Sam and I stood at the front door to say good-bye and thank them for coming. The Muellers and Ida were the last to leave except for Pat and my parents.

"Oh Gracie, thank you from the bottom of my heart for everything you've done for us," Emily said as she came up to me. She put her arms around me and hugged me tightly. "God brought you to this town—and to me. I love you, and I will always be your friend."

Emily's sweet comments touched my heart. "And you'll always be mine," I whispered back. "Tell Hannah everyone is praying for her, will you?"

She let me go but kept her hand on my arm. "She knows that, and she wanted me to tell you that she will be at the wedding." She looked at her husband. "Abel, will you go out to the car and get Hannah's wedding present to Gracie?"

Abel nodded and went out the front door.

"I know wedding gifts are usually given after the ceremony, but Hannah asked that we give this to you tonight," Emily said.

Ida, who had been waiting next to Emily, stepped up to me and opened her arms. "Oh, liebling," she said softly, "I am so happy. The joy of the Lord wells up like rivers of living water in my spirit."

I wrapped my arms around her and she stroked my hair. "God has used you in great ways in my life," I told her. "I wish I had the words to tell you what you mean to me."

Ida released me and chuckled softly. "Ach, Gracie. We do not need words. I understand because I feel the same way about you."

She gazed up into Sam's face and took his hands. "I know you will take good care of my Gracie, and she will take good care of you. I pray that you will know the kind of love my Herman and I shared. The same kind of love that Gracie's grandparents had for each other. And the kind of devotion her parents feel for each other. If you will put God first and follow the words they spoke to you tonight, you will live with joy unspeakable and full of glory. Putting others first is the love of God, is it not? He gave everything for us. Now we follow His example and give our lives to each other."

"Thank you, Ida," Sam said, leaning down and kissing the old woman's cheek. "And if I ever forget, even for a minute, I expect you to remind me."

She laughed. "Ach, you can count on it, liebling." She reached out and took Emily's arm. "And now I must go back to my little house and rest. I must confess that the excitement of the last few days has made me very weary."

Just then Abel came back into the house with a large wrapped gift in his hand.

"I'm going to help Ida to the car while you deliver Hannah's present," Emily told her husband.

He held the door open for the two women who made their way outside to the porch and down the stairs. I turned my attention back to Abel who handed me the large square-shaped package.

I grinned at him. "I know what this is. Why don't we go into the living room where I have more room to open it?"

Sam and Abel followed me down the hall. Pat, Mom, and Sweetie were busy clearing dishes from the dining room. I put the package down on the living room table and started tearing off the paper, handing it to Sam. As I suspected, a large wood frame and canvas were revealed. After unwrapping it completely, I turned it over to reveal a beautiful painting.

"Oh my," I said, tears once again filling my eyes. I'd need massive amounts of water to replace all I'd lost that night. I even felt a little dehydrated. "Sam, look."

In the painting, a man and woman stood in the middle of an orchard. Although you couldn't see their faces, it was clear the couple was Sam and me. We were surrounded by beautiful trees, full of ripened fruit. A golden light from above bathed us in a soft radiance. My head was on Sam's shoulder, and his strong arm circled my waist. Even the ground beneath us glowed. It reminded me of Adam and Eve in the Garden of Eden. Written at the bottom of the canvas were these words: *And God Almighty bless thee, and make thee fruitful.*

"It's—it's incredible," I said, my voice catching from the emotion that overtook me. "Abel, tell her this picture will be have an honored place in our home forever."

"I will." The big pastor smiled. "I thought you'd like it. We gave Hannah permission to paint again, and this is what she chose to do. Her mother and I have agreed that she has been given a gift from God that must be used for His kingdom. When you're ready, we'd like you to start Hannah's lessons again."

Sam stuck his hand out to Abel who grabbed it. "It's an awesome gift," he said after clearing his throat. "Please tell Hannah how precious she is to us."

Abel shook Sam's hand with vigor. "Why, Sam.

She already knows that." He smiled at both of us and left the room. Sam and I remained, staring at the painting. The style made me think of Thomas Kinkade. The scene absolutely glowed with almost unearthly light. It took everything I had to tear my gaze away.

"We've got to find a wonderful place for this," I said to Sam. He started to answer me when Sweetie's voice interrupted.

"Gracie? Sam? Where are you two?"

Sam put the painting on the coffee table. "We're in the living room, Sweetie," he called loudly.

"Well, get into the kitchen. Pat has something to talk to us about."

Sam and I looked at each other. "Wonder what this is about?" he said.

"One way to find out." I grabbed his hand and pulled him toward the hallway.

When we reached the kitchen, we found everyone gathered around the table except for Sweetie who was rinsing dishes at the sink.

"Please, sit down," Pat said in a solemn tone. The expression on his face was one I'd seen before, and every time it had preceded bad news. But that couldn't happen tonight. Hannah was home, C.J. was locked up. What could he possibly say that could make a dent in this perfect evening?

"Sweetie, I need you to sit down, too."

Sweetie started to argue with him, but she was trying hard to turn over a new leaf with Pat, so she put her dish towel down and came over to the table. She plopped down next to my mother. Sweetie was quiet, but her frown expressed her irritation. She couldn't abide a dirty kitchen.

All eyes were fixed on Pat, who cleared his throat and rubbed his hands together before finally speaking. "Right before dinner, I got a call from a detective friend in Colorado." He hesitated again.

"Well for cryin' out loud, Pat, spit it out!" Sweetie declared. "Ain't nothin' you can't say. We're family now, remember?"

He nodded. "Yes, I know. And this is family business. That's why I waited until everyone else left."

"What is it, Pat?" I asked. "Is something wrong?"

He shook his head. "No. I mean, I don't believe anyone will feel that way. Anyway, I hope not."

Sweetie glared at him. If he didn't get to the point soon, that family feeling she had could be in serious jeopardy.

"Terry called to tell me that he's located Bernie."

A small bomb exploding in the middle of Sweetie's kitchen table couldn't have produced more shocked expressions.

"Bernie who?" Dad asked.

"Bernice Goodrich," I said quickly. "Sam's mother."

"Oh my," Mom said breathlessly.

I grabbed Sam's arm. His face had gone white.

"Where is she?" Sweetie asked.

"She's in a hospital in Wyoming. She's been there over a month," Pat said.

"Is—is she all right?" Sam choked out.

Pat shook his head. "No, not really. She's pretty sick. Hepatitis." He gazed into his son's eyes. "But she's clean. I wish I could tell you more about her condition, unfortunately I just don't know. I called the hospital, but they wouldn't tell me anything since I'm not family."

"Well, I'm sure as shootin' family," Sweetie barked, standing to her feet. "You give me the number of this place, Pat. I'll call them right now."

He reached for his wallet, pulled it out of his pocket, and opened it. Then he removed a folded piece of paper and handed it to Sweetie. "That's it. Sure would appreciate it if you'd let me know how she is."

Sweetie took the paper from his hand and stared at it for a moment. Then she came around the table to where Pat sat. She put her hand on his shoulder. "I'll make sure you know all about how Bernie's doin', Pat. Thank you for bringin' her back to me. I'll never forget it. Never." She patted his shoulder then left the room. Sam sat silently. He looked stunned.

"How do you feel about this, Sam?" my father asked.

"I—I don't know," he said softly. "To be honest, I never thought I'd hear from my mother again."

Pat stood up. "I should have given you this before," he said to Sam. "Just wasn't sure you'd want it. But now I think you should have it." He reached into his shirt pocket and pulled something out. "It's Bernie's letter. The one she sent me when she told me about you." He held it out toward Sam who only stared at it. "She writes about you, son. About how much she loves you and how she only left you because she was afraid of ruining your life. Maybe she made the wrong choice, but she made it out of love. I think if you'll read this, you might understand her a little better."

Sam's gaze seemed locked on the letter, but he still didn't reach for it. I was about to grab it for him, when he suddenly took the folded paper from Pat's hand. "I can't promise I'll read it right away, but I will when I'm ready." His own eyes sought his father's. "Guess I'm learning that forgiveness and understanding brings peace. Holding a grudge only causes pain." Sam and Pat stared at each other for several seconds. Then Sam said, "Thanks. . .Dad."

Pat hung his head, nodded quickly, and mumbled something about having to get home. For just a second I thought about following him, but then I realized the tough lawman needed to be alone. Sam and I heard the front door close.

"Good for you," I said.

"You know what?" Sam said, sliding the letter into the pocket of his slacks. "It *is* good for me. I've wanted to call someone 'dad' my whole life. It feels absolutely fantastic." His smile lit up his face.

"I think Pat feels just about as good as you do."

"I hope so." Sam yawned and stretched his arms behind his head. "I could use some coffee. How about you?"

"Sounds good."

Mom and Dad begged off, deciding to go home. Dad's leg was bothering him and they were both tired. I kissed them good-bye and promised to let them know about Bernie. It was hard to watch them leave without me. Frankly, I was exhausted and wanted nothing more than to go home and fall into bed. But even more than I wanted sleep, I needed to know what Sweetie found out about her sister. We'd just poured our coffee when Sweetie came into the kitchen.

"I called the hospital and told 'em who I was. They're gonna check with Bernie before they'll tell me anything."

"Will she let them speak to you?" I asked.

Sweetie sighed deeply. "Land sakes, I hope so. Wish I could predict what Bernie will do, but I just can't. All we can do is sit and wait."

Sam got up and poured Sweetie a cup of coffee. We all sat at the table until the phone finally rang. Sweetie jumped up and answered it. She was silent for quite some time, listening to whoever was on the other end. Finally she said, "Tell her I said not to worry. I'll take care of it. I'll call her back tomorrow. You tell her that, hear me?" Seemingly satisfied with the answer, she said good-bye and hung up. Sam and I stared at her expectantly as she came back to the table and sat down.

"Well, she's sick, but there's hope. She's gonna need a liver transplant. She's on a list, and her chances look okay. Nothing for certain, but if she can last long enough for a liver to become available, she might actually pull through."

Sam let out a deep breath. "Can we talk to her?"

His aunt stared at him for a moment, her expression unreadable. Then she smiled at both of us. "She'll certainly be talkin' to me, son. I'm goin' up there to be with her until she's well."

Sam's mouth dropped open. "What do you mean? You can't leave."

Sweetie reached over and took his hand. Then she grasped mine. "You two have each other now. Bernie has no one." Her eyes filled with tears. "Lord knows I love you both so much it hurts, but you don't need me no more."

Sam started to say something, but she hushed him.

"When you was a little boy, you needed me real bad," Sweetie said gently. "And I loved bringing you up. I loved every single moment of it. But now you got Gracie." She moved our hands together and took hers away. "You gotta be able to see this as clearly as I do. My sister is all alone, and you both could use some time together without someone else hangin' around. It's the perfect solution." She chuckled. "Don't be thinkin' you're gettin' rid of me though, Sam Goodrich. You have my word. If Bernie gets better, I'll bring us both back here." She rubbed her eyes. "And if she don't, well I'll come back alone. But either way, I'll come home one of these days."

"I can't imagine living here without you," Sam said in a choked voice.

"I know," his aunt said softly. "But this is my choice, son. And I need you to support me."

Sam didn't speak, but he nodded slowly. At Sweetie's suggestion, we all went outside and sat on the porch, rocking quietly until the sun went down and the air cooled. No one said it, but we all realized it would be the last time the three of us would be alone together for a long, long time.

TWENTY-FOUR

Saturday was the most wonderful day of my life, but it rushed past me like a mighty wind that sweeps in and out so quickly you're not sure it was ever really there. A few memories will always stay burned into my memory, though. Sam, standing at the front of the church in his black suit. As I walked down the aisle, I was certain he was the most handsome man I'd ever seen in my entire life. My mother told me once that in her eyes, my father outshone every man she'd ever met. As the years went by, she never changed her opinion. At the time, I couldn't understand why she didn't seem to notice his wrinkles, the extra skin under his chin, or the way his stomach got a little larger every year. But on Saturday, I understood it completely. I knew that the rest of my life, I would see Sam standing there, his sun-bleached hair combed neatly into place, his incredible gray eyes looking at me beneath dark lashes, his expression one I will always remember. He told me after the ceremony that he was so overcome by my beauty he could barely breathe.

And I will always recall my mother's face when she saw me wearing her blue dress, a white-lace shawl around my shoulders, and a bouquet of red carnations, yellow dandelions, and purple irises in my arms. My white dress was packed away in a trunk, waiting for the day my daughter would decide between it. . .or a plain blue dress that carried more meaning than beauty.

A sea of faces passed before us that day. My mother and father, Pat, Ida, Gabe, Sarah and John, Sweetie, Emily and Abel. Each face precious to me. Every person part of a large, extended family. And of course, Hannah. Although we didn't get much time to speak, she hugged me tightly and whispered "Thank you," into my ear.

There was great food, courtesy of Hector and Carmen, and wonderful gifts given by all the people who love us. Our reception overflowed with laughter and the joy of the Lord. But little by little, people drifted away. Bill Eberly drove Sweetie to the airport after the reception. It was hard to see her go, but Sam and I both knew she had made the right choice.

As quickly as the whirlwind of excitement that weddings bring reached its peak, it was over. My mother and father went home to the house that had sheltered the Temple family for over fifty years. Sam and I drove home to the big red house, our truck stuffed full of gifts we'd find places for later. Although everything we'd been given blessed us, my grandmother's quilt and Hannah's painting would stay at the top of the list.

We changed clothes and went out to sit on the porch. We were finally alone. Buddy curled up at my feet, and Snickle lay down on Sam's lap. The third rocking chair sat empty, and Sweetie's absence was deeply felt. We pulled our rocking chairs together and held hands until the sun went down.

Finally Sam said, "I think it's time to go inside, Mrs. Goodrich."

"I agree." I turned to look into the stormy gray eyes of the man I would spend the rest of my life with. "Hey Sam, why don't cannibals eat clowns?"

He chuckled softly. "I have no idea. Why don't cannibals eat clowns?"

"Because they taste funny."

Sam's warm laughter drifted into the night air. "Is this what I can look forward to for the next fifty years?"

I squeezed his hand. "You got it, bub."

He leaned over and kissed me gently, and then he stood up. "I can hardly wait."

I let go of his hand. "Hey, give me just a minute alone, okay?"

He smiled. "Just don't take too long."

"I won't."

He called Buddy and Snickle, ushering them both into the house. When the door shut behind him, I looked up into a sky full of glittering stars. A verse from the eighth Psalm popped into my mind. *When I consider your heavens, the work of your fingers, the moon and the stars, which you have set in place, what is mankind that you are mindful of them, human beings that you care for them?* Tearfully, I whispered a prayer of thanks to the One who had led me to Harmony,

Kansas, so He could reveal His plan for me—a plan far beyond anything I could have ever dreamed. I rocked for a while in the soft, summer air, wrapped in His love. Then I got up and opened the front door of the house I'd loved from the first moment I'd seen it, and went inside, ready to begin a brand-new, wonderful adventure.

ABOUT THE AUTHOR

NANCY MEHL lives in Wichita, Kansas, with her husband, Norman, and her rambunctious puggle, Watson. She's authored eleven books and is currently at work on her newest series. All of Nancy's novels have an added touch—something for your spirit as well as your soul.